We are God

Jordan Mund

ALL THINGS
THAT MATTER
PRESS

ISBN: 9781733444842

Library of Congress Control Number: 2019953706

Author Photo by Rebecca Mund

Cover Design by All Things that Matter Press

Cover photo from Unsplash

Published in 2019 by All Things that Matter Press

For Rebecca

Chapter 1 ~ The Eternal Era

I will be dead soon; everyone must know that by now. I don't know when exactly, it could be weeks or years, but it will be soon. So, I've decided to spend my remaining time writing this story. I suppose, then, I should begin with this confession: I've never been much of a writer. Not to say that I've never written anything; it's just everything I've written I did so very long ago. So long ago that it no longer feels like it was me who did it. Some other version of me, perhaps. But, really, I don't know of anyone who writes anymore. Nothing happens now that's worth writing about anyway.

Of course, that's not to say I never imagined myself writing something like this. I always thought I should give it a try, and I always thought I had ample material from which to draw, but what I always lacked was direction. I could never decide to what purpose I should take aim or to what end. No one wants to hear a story with no ending, after all. I write now because very soon I won't be alive to write anything at all. But of course, that's not the only reason. In fact, a reason far more meaningful has drawn me to tell this story, for you see, I've come up with an ending.

I'm sure everyone, if anyone, reading this probably already knows a great deal of my story. It appears I've become quite the sensation. As I'm writing this from the upstairs study of my aging home, three men, clad in black, armed with guns and truncheons, are sitting around my kitchen table playing cards and smoking cigarettes to pass the time. They are tasked with preventing me from escaping before my trial but the whole situation is a farce. In my current state I can barely walk down a flight of stairs yet the powers that be think three armed guards are necessary to keep me from planning and executing a daring escape. They also seem to care little for the fact that in my state I probably only have a couple years left to live. I've done my homework, you see, and the average life expectancy of a Mortal, immediately before their extinction, was somewhere round ninety-years-old. People lived longer than that of course and many much shorter but that was a good average. Well, I've calculated that my current physical state is, in fact, about equivalent to that of a ninety-year-old Mortal. I'm sure everyone reading this will have seen pictures in history books of what Mortals looked like when they lived to be that age, so you can imagine what I look like now. They call me the Old Man now, or so I've heard. A term that used to refer to millions of people at any given time now refers only to me. But there will be more.

Many will want to know why I did what I did. I must admit that at first it was simply because I wanted that one thing I couldn't have, a natural death, a fitting end to my story. But time changes people and their motivations. I have every intention of explaining myself in these pages but to do so properly I must cover a lot of ground. So bear with me. I don't have much time, but I do have much to say.

So, let's begin. There are countless reasons for my aberrant or, as I'm sure the historians will record, heretical research. It was about eight decades ago, around but not exactly the year 450. I began my unconventional quest while ostensibly researching new technologies that would never exist—at least not for quite some time. The number of scientific breakthroughs had slowed to such an indefinite cessation that it was very easy for me to work long hours with no results without raising any suspicion. It was the lack of new discoveries over the last two centuries that led me to consider my role in this life. According to our history books, the advancements made by our Parents before the Eternal Era were, quite literally, astronomical compared to now. The 3rd century BEE was defined by things like the splitting of the atom, the first space shuttle launched into space, the first visit to our moon, the internet. Our only real discoveries of late have been simple improvements to our near ancient body shaping and facial restructuring technologies and all that nonsense we value so much just so we never have to get bored of the face we see in the mirror. But why not? What else is there? There are no more frontiers, no more adventures.

I should note that I was born during the first century EE, so I was there when the excitement of immortality was still fresh, much more exciting than what it's become. I knew a great many of our Parents during that time, many of whom had great influence in the creation of the immortal code and the establishment of the Overman Project. I truly wish they had the opportunity to be made immortal. How unfair. Just imagine discovering such an extraordinary miracle only for it to be denied you. It is no one's fault though. At the time the procedure required an unfertilized ovum; one was either born this way or not.

But that's not why I'm writing. I have a specific goal in mind, but I seem to be having trouble maintaining focus. My mind is like a prison search light scanning a pitch-black expanse for a meandering escapee. When I get him in my shining beam, I can describe him in every detail. But he is elusive.

I was born in the Health Sciences Center in Winnipeg, Manitoba on 26 May, 88. Those formative years, happened so long ago. Only by supplementing my memories with history books, my own journals, and photographs can I attempt to paint a picture that might resemble something like the truth. In the beginning, when the first Immortal was born, much controversy arose over whether or not it was ethical to grant someone eternal life without them having a chance to say if they wanted it, especially in a world where they would go on living while their family and friends would all eventually grow old and die around them. It was a fair question I suppose, one that never received an answer. It was easy to sidestep the dilemma and proceed with the project since most people at the time agreed that death was a most unpleasant experience, even though no one who said so had yet experienced it. And besides, they argued, Mortals didn't get a say in their existence either.

By the time I was born, the Overman Project was already well established with a fairly large immortal population, so the general public had more or less come to terms with the idea of a small group of people living forever. Still, there were many groups who protested the project, especially religious groups who held onto the idea of life after death. They saw death as simply the next step of their existence. I wonder if they were right. I wonder if the next life is just an eternal, ethereal party with drinks that never run dry. I wonder if they can see us from whatever heaven they stumbled into and are laughing at our miserable state as we mope and moan and drag our feet round the surface of this decaying Earth. Or maybe death really is the end and they are all lost to oblivion as I will soon be. Or maybe they are still here, as spirits or reincarnated as our animal friends and food. All I can do now is wonder and wonder still if I'll ever know.

But where was I? I was born 88 years after the Immortal Code had been written so there were plenty of Immortals already alive and working in the OP. I spent my formative years in schools which included both Mortals and Immortals. It was there that I met Nate. But I'll come back to him. I want to try and keep this in chronological order. Nate comes later.

Chapter 2 ~ Hauntings: An Origin Story

For the better part of my existence I've lived every moment, awake and dreaming, haunted by memories of things I have done. To remember a time before the haunting is impossible but even to imagine it in its infancy would be to remember a time that is so far from the present that it has faded into dreamlike remembrances, more fantasy than reality. I want to forget like other memories are inevitably forgotten, to have those memories grow dim and eventually vanish but I reanimate them, reignite them, and keep them alive like a nurse at the bedside of a patient or, perhaps more accurately, like Dr. Frankenstein, for my imagination has certainly fused fantasy with reality to create horrifying memories that only barely resemble the truth. But the fact remains that the memories, what I call the Haunting, cannot die as I cannot die so it stays with me, looking over my shoulder, peering at me from shadowy corners and through cracks in the wall. My Haunting has grown since it was first conceived. It started out as a small insignificant thing born from a small and insignificant moment, but it quickly grew as new regretful moments were added to it. It is the nature of hauntings to begin small, growing in one's periphery, only to be realized after it is far too late to stop it. Our Parents had to live with their hauntings, too, but they had an end in sight. Gravestones were traditionally engraved with the epitaph "rest in peace" implying that wherever they had gone after they died their hauntings wouldn't follow.

It all began with a minor theft and a white lie when I was probably somewhere between five and ten years old. It's very likely that this was not my first offense but, if I did behave immorally beforehand, I was too young to remember. I was raised in a family of five—three boys and two girls—in an Overman community in Winnipeg. At the time it was one of the only Overman homes in Manitoba; most others were in Ontario, Quebec or British Columbia. Our caretakers were Mortals, a man and a woman. This was very common at the time. You see, in the early years the Project was designed so that Immortals were raised in a very similar fashion to Mortals. Even though we shared no biological relation to our caregivers, we grew up with a deep fondness for them and they at least appeared to reciprocate. We slept in two rooms, one for the boys and one for the girls. A boy, whose name I can no longer recall but for this story I will refer to him as Jack, slept in the bed next to mine. It was he that would be my victim, my first of many.

Jack always had a small bag of candy that he kept in his nightstand. It bothered me because he would take out only one piece at a time and nibble on it, biting off one tiny morsel before putting it back. I was never able to exhibit such will power, instead devouring any piece of candy I could get my hands on and swallowing them before my tongue could know the flavor. Because of this, at any given moment, Jack would always have candy in his possession while I would possess the sweet stuff only for the few seconds it took to send it tumbling down my gullet. By now it is probably easy to guess my crime; I stole Jack's candy one night after dinner while he was still at the kitchen table slowly nibbling away at his mashed potatoes. I took it and, although I intended to hide it, found myself shoving as many pieces as I could into my mouth before anyone could find me.

The second part of my inaugural delinquency is possibly just as easy to predict. Jack, having discovered my theft not long after dinner, made a general accusation to me and the other boy who roomed with us, hoping for either a confession or a pointing finger. I obliged by pointing my finger with such unflinching certainty that the other boy was punished, being forced to go a full week with no candy at all.

Such was the small beginning of my haunting. I have no intention of documenting every sin I've committed. I have neither the time nor the memory for such a colossal undertaking. I'm sure enough will be known about a great many of my sins before I have a chance to tell it myself. I only include the anecdote above to give an example of how hauntings are formed. Amongst the multitude of events that add to my haunting—like pebbles of sand made into bricks made into a fortress – there are a few which stand immense. It is on those that I will try and maintain my focus. However, to fully appreciate the gravity of the things I have done one must know the backstory. It is here that I will begin the story of my dearest friend Nate.

Chapter 3 ~ Nathanial Karski

His name was Nathaniel Karski but neither I nor anyone I knew called him that. We all shortened it to Nate. It seemed to suit him better—I don't know why. We met at Tates Elementary School in Winnipeg which included both Mortals and Immortals in the classroom— this was early enough in the Eternal Era that schools were still mixed. We were nearly the same age, he was only older than me by four months and eight days, but for reasons none other than the vicissitudes of life, he was born to a mortal family while I was born into the Overman Project. At that age, mortality and immortality hardly meant a thing to us. We were informed even then that I was an Immortal and he was not, but neither of us knew what that was or what it meant or even which one of us was better off. The only things to which we compared ourselves were childish things like his curly black hair to my straight blonde hair, which caused both of us to be greatly envious of the others' hair.

It's not an easy task to write about him. Not only because it's difficult to remember so long ago but because I miss the man terribly and it hurts, physically, to think of him. Somewhere in this cluttered house I have photographs and videos, many of which I have committed to memory so I can, at any time, close my eyes and see him. Even now as I sit here and tap at this keyboard I can close my eyes and immediately begin watching him celebrate the day of his wedding—comically big cigar in one hand and a glass of red wine in the other—or recall in perfect detail a still image of him standing on the steps of his house watching me with a confused expression, possibly as to why I am snapping his photo. Why did I take that photograph? Maybe his eventual, inevitable absence was causing me to become sentimental and so I acted on that sentimentality spontaneously. But that's just a guess. I really have no idea.

Nate was a strong person. Not physically strong; he was quite short and proportionately slight, but he had a fire in him that could shake the Earth. For example, one time in school, I cannot recall our exact age, I found myself the target of three boys armed with eraser bits and slingshots. One of the boys, an Immortal, lives not far from here. The other two must have been Mortals. They chased me down the hall firing their weapons without remorse. Somehow Nate got wind of the abuse and came to my rescue. He managed to trip one of the bullies and commandeer his slingshot. A fight erupted and promptly ended with

Nate chasing all three of them out the school doors firing only occasionally to keep them moving.

The only other person Nate was so vigilante towards was his younger brother Jonny. His full name was Jonathon but like Nate we shortened it. Nate was fiercely protective of him which caused me to be fiercely jealous of him. Fiercely may not be the correct word because I managed to keep my feelings hidden under a calm veneer, but they were always simmering under the surface, like an active inferno under a still lake. To my knowledge I never acted upon my jealousy. I may have though. The thing about memories is that it's hard enough to recall events that happened so long ago when you want to remember them but when you don't ....

After graduating high school, Nate and I both attended the University of Manitoba. At the time, Immortals were expected to acquire a degree at a regular University before being given a position in the Overman Project. I only attended the U of M because I was familiar with the city and because Nate insisted we continue our education together. Although we were not roommates, we didn't even live in the same dormitory, we still saw much of each other.

I wonder if we had gone to different universities if we would have maintained our friendship. I wonder a lot about Nate and the what ifs. What if we were both immortal? What if we were both mortal? What if I was mortal and he was immortal? So many memories that could have been so different if there were only slight changes.

I've heard it said before that we are shaped by our memories. Our entire being is made up of what we remember, like a sculpture formed of memories rather than clay. Without our memories we'd be nothing, empty husks. The decisions we make, the way we respond to things, these are all features that grew out of our experiences, our memories. Our memories are us. They're what we are made of. The trouble with this idea is the unreliability of memories. I have countless memories of Nate stored away but I can never be sure they are accurate. The only memories I have that I know are certainly true are the ones which I can compare to videos of him. Photographs also work but only for the microsecond in which he was captured. But often I will find myself remembering a specific event before referencing a video or photo and will be shocked at how inaccurate my memory was. Something is almost always different. Sometimes it's only a small detail that doesn't have much effect on the essence of the memory but other times I remember completely different people being involved and in a completely different setting. So, if we are the product of our memories, and I admit that I am quite warm to the idea, then our entire being is an amalgam of probable falsehoods.

We are God

I seem to have gotten off course again. Where was I?

Chapter 4 ~ World Travel

Nate was always fascinated with other countries and cultures. Having hardly left the province save for the occasional family camping trip and having never left the country, adolescent Nate allowed his developing imagination take him to all the places he wanted to see. When he was finally an adult with the means to physically visit the places, he had already explored in his dreams he jumped at the chance and kept on jumping with no end in sight. For him there was never a last country or a final trip. He wanted to explore every corner of the planet and then explore them again.

The first country we visited together was America. I had been there many times before on field trips with the Overman Project while Nate had never crossed a border that wasn't provincial. It was still quite a new experience for me, though, since my previous visits had been orchestrated rather stringently and usually only consisted of cities. Nate and I travelled wherever we wanted. And because we were driving a car, we were able to make up our itinerary as we went along.

After this first trip, we made a habit of travelling together as much as possible throughout our university career and well after. Although I can't remember the order in which these trips occurred, except of course that our first trip was through America, I do remember many of the places we visited.

In Iceland we bathed in the blue lagoon, watched whales jump out of the ocean and a geyser jump out of the earth. We ate hakarl, rotten shark meat, and drank Brennivin, a type of schnapps native to that frozen part of the world which was much more pleasing to the pallet than the hakarl. Although he always wanted to return to that part of the world to explore ice caves Nate never managed to go back. I have since visited more times than I can remember.

That will be a common theme you'll find in these pages: "more than I can remember." For the truth is I cannot remember much. I can't, for example remember how many times I visited China. But the first time was with Nate. We did everything a couple of tourists are supposed to do. We walked on the Great Wall and through the Forbidden City, we saw the Terracotta Warriors, and rode bicycles along the old city wall in Xi'an. Our favorite place, or perhaps it was just my favorite, was Yangshuo, a village surrounded by tall karst peaks often shrouded in mist. We explored caves outside the village, rode on bamboo rafts down the Yulong River, and drank cheap Chinese beer.

Nate and I tried to learn a bit of Mandarin to assist us in our travels but neither of us got anywhere close to proficient and ended up relying far more on ridiculous hand gestures to communicate. Remember, this was during a time when myriad languages were still used all over the world so knowing more than one had a practical value. Although Mandarin was the official language, China still fostered hundreds of distinct languages and dialects so that two people from neighboring provinces might not be able to understand one another. Although so many ways of communicating were cause for much confusion it also added such vibrant color to the world. We lost so much with the Mortals. So much we may never get back. I once argued with Nate that so many languages are debilitating at best and divisive at worst. He replied simply that one language really isn't enough to express all varieties of thought in the human mind. I believe he was right.

It may have been somewhere in China that Nate and I had a particularly significant conversation in which he told me he wanted to "settle down" with someone someday. Yes, I believe it was on one of those bamboo rafts I mentioned earlier. Our boatman was an old man who spoke not a word of English and wore a perpetual jovial grin. Other rafts would approach us selling souvenirs and drinks. I can't remember if we bought any trinkets, but we certainly armed ourselves with plenty of beer. In lieu of a bottle opener our obsequious boatman would tear the tin caps off with his teeth.

With the foaming copper restorative in our hands, sun above us and water below, Nate told me about his plans for the future.

"Settle down?" I asked. "With someone?"

"Well, yes. That's what the term means. If I didn't intend to settle down with someone the term wouldn't really have any meaning, would it."

"Sure it would," I replied, leaning my head back so the sun hit my face directly. "You can settle down with or without someone. Who says you can't be settled alone?" I closed my eyes as if intending to drift off to sleep.

"But there'd be no reason to be settled if you were alone. If you're alone, you can pack up and unsettle at a moment's notice. That's not really settled, is it?"

"Just because you aren't permanently settled doesn't mean you aren't settled. One can settle and then unsettle."

"Yes, but the term generally refers to a permanent arrangement."

"Whatever, okay, so you want to settle down *with* someone? That's what you're saying?"

I heard him gulp some beer. "That's what I said, yeah."

"So, who is this woman?"

"What woman?"

I opened an eye and glanced over at him. "*The* woman. You said you wanted to settle down with someone. Who is this person?"

"I don't know yet." He took another gulp. "I'm just saying that eventually I think I will, you know, settle down with someone."

I could write forever little moments like this between Nate and me. Perhaps if I had more time, I'd write a thousand pages just of conversations with Nate as the main character.

"But you have no one in mind? Are you taking applications? Interviews?"

"Well, not at the moment. I don't have a career lined up either, but I plan on getting one and I have an idea of what I want to do."

"I suppose. But everyone *needs* a career," I said lazily and followed with a yawn.

"I don't suppose you're capable of understanding, then."

I opened my eyes and turned to him. He was relaxed with his face to the sun and eyes closed. "What's that supposed to mean?" I said, feigning offense.

"It's not your fault. Some people just don't possess the capacity to settle down. Some people don't possess the capacity to appreciate good literature or fine wine." A facetious smile crept on his face. "You're content with your boxed wine and a trashy novel while I prefer—"

"Boxed wine?" I sat up and turned directly to him.

"There's no shame in having poor taste."

"I don't read trashy novels. And I've seen you drink boxed wine before. Many times, in fact. Besides, I thought we were talking about settling down."

"Aren't we? I don't suppose you're capable of understanding my metaphor, then. All those trashy novels have turned your brain to mush."

This was the first he had told me about this. I must have assumed he would want something like that since it was enormously common amongst Mortals, but I honestly hoped that he'd eschew this particular tradition. Settling down meant that he would have a partner with whom he would share his life. They'd live together, go to social events together, travel together. It should be no surprise then that I was hoping for a different future for Nate since all such time spent with a partner would obviously mean less time spent with me. I was undeniably selfish in this regard but by this time I was already starting to understand the great, dreadful, and fast-approaching end that was the fate of all Mortals. Time was speeding up as it was moving forward, it seemed. I figured that Nate probably only had between fifty to seventy years left, and I had already been well exposed to the effect time had on the Mortal body. Even if he managed to avoid every disease that could shorten his life, age alone would act on his body like a disease, slow and malicious and terminal. The effects of that disease called age begin to manifest decades before its whimpering finale. Our time was already frustratingly limited. Why split that time among more people? At least, this is what I thought at the time.

Like he wanted, Nate did eventually meet someone and settle down. But I'll get back to that later. More on travel.

We visited Morocco, I remember, where we ate couscous and rode camels through the Sahara Desert. Morocco was beautiful then. In Casablanca we visited mosques and watched the faithful pray. I loved watching them. There is something I still find alluring about religion. Even as an Immortal who had no need for an afterlife, I always thought it incredibly moving. There are so many fascinating features that accompanied religious belief—discipline and devotion combined with culture, art, and poetry.

In Rome we, of course, did everything a tourist is expected to do with one addition: we attended a speech by the philosopher Fredrick Mesnick in Saint Peter's square. He stood on a small stage and spoke to, what seemed like, a million-strong crowd crammed shoulder to shoulder, all captivated by his words. In his speech I remember he said that by achieving immortality "we can now say that we have replaced God with our own transcendent qualities achieved through our own genius. In the Bible," he continued in his familiar baritone, "in Ephesians chapter two verse ten, it is written that we are God's 'workmanship.' That may have been true then, but *now* we are no longer his at all. *Now* he can no longer claim ownership of us for *now* we are, as one body of countless parts, God incarnate." He paused and for a moment all was silent. "God incarnate," he repeated as his icy stare swept over the crowd and everyone present felt as though they each had direct eye contact with him. "*Now*, he has been replaced by us." What started as a cheer from one person erupted into a roar from the crowd. Professor Mesnick held up his hand and we all quieted. He then said further, "For what we have achieved and what we have become, we have no one to thank but ourselves. I say again: we are one. We are perfection. We are God." I burnt those words into my memory, reciting them to myself before bed for decades as if they were part of some sacred scripture. I remember the crowd that day, yelling, screaming, clapping their hands. It was deafening but it was contagious; I too was yelling and clapping and cheering. In the fervor I lost myself and forgot I was with Nate, someone who wasn't going to live forever as "one, perfection, and/or God." Talking to him later he didn't seem as impressed with Professor Mesnick's speech as I was, and it was possibly then, after Rome, that I began to understand the great divide that existed between Nate and myself. Between Mortals and Immortals.

I still wonder if Professor Mesnick were an Immortal if he would still give such speeches. Probably not. I don't think anyone now can be bothered to cheer like they did then. I wonder what he would say if he were able to give a speech now.

***

I suppose I should make another confession: this work is full of lies. I've already told many and I'm going to tell many more. They are not complete lies, though. Within them there is much truth. But the thing is, there is not much I can remember beyond a few decades ago. So, I must lie if I want to even attempt to tell this story. So, like I promised, I will tell a story about Nate, but I won't promise it will be true.

Chapter 5 ~ A Real Fake Story

This story takes place a few years after Nate met his wife but before they were married. Her name was Marie. She had chin-length black hair which she kept intentionally disheveled. Her features were small and sharp, and she often adorned herself with various accessories. On this evening she wore a collection of necklaces of varying length and her left arm was decorated with three thin bracelets which appeared to be made of bamboo. The three of us had gone out for dinner like we often did. We were eating Hong Kong style noodles at a little hole-in-the-wall restaurant somewhere in downtown Winnipeg. The place only had one table made of chipped particle board surrounded by four small wobbly stools. We all three ordered the spiciest item on the menu. Spicy food was one of the only things on which all three of us found common ground. Although Nate and I had many things in common, Marie and I shared few interests except, of course, our mutual love of Nate. It seemed to me that on everything which Nate and I agreed Marie disagreed, and on everything which Nate and I disagreed, Marie agreed. Despite our differences, however, we all agreed that even the best dish could be improved with a little bit of spice.

I'm not sure how we came upon the topic but sometime between our slurps and sniffs we began to talk about Shelley's poem, *England in 1819*. I remember Marie especially had a fondness for poetry and so it was likely she who brought up the topic. However it came up, we couldn't seem to get past that first verse, "An old, mad, blind, despised, and dying King," because Nate couldn't keep himself from wondering what effect immortality would have had on that particular work if the king in question was in fact "old, mad, blind, despised, and *undying*."

"Nothing would ever change, would it," he said, sniffed, and sipped his ice water. "Things progress because one generation dies and the next chooses to do something a little differently. They learn from their predecessors and build on it. Then they get old and are unable or unwilling to change, but then they die and are replaced by others who learn from them and improve and so on and so forth. But if there was no death, or more specifically, no new life, there would be no change at all." He tossed his chopsticks into his bowl and leaned back in his chair to give his burning mouth a break. He wiped beads of sweat from his forehead and breathed deeply through a wide, gaping mouth. "Without the old generation dying off to make room for new, younger ideas that mad King would rule forever," he said, and I noticed a wet curl stuck to his forehead which he brushed away with his sleeve. "There would be no hope for change ... ever. No hope for progress. It would be stagnation." He leaned forwards to have another go at his noodles. "Entropy."

"I don't know about that," I said, always eager to defend my kind. "The longer we live the more chances we have to change. That mad King might eventually learn the error of his ways and decide to be a better person."

"It is possible," Marie joined in. "I like to think I'm wiser now than I have ever been and fifty years from now I'll hopefully be wiser still. It's possible that given enough time, even the most foolish person will learn to improve." Marie sat with her legs tightly crossed and her arms pulled close to her body, looking like a half-folded lawn chair. As she talked, she'd periodically pause to stir her noodles until a few were wrapped well around the end of her chopsticks as a tight, bite-sized ball. "But there is no reason to believe that *everyone* gets wiser when they get older. Time allows for whatever is fertilized to grow. After a couple centuries of neither seeing, nor feeling, nor knowing, one should not expect a sudden change of heart." She popped the ball of noodles into her mouth.

"However," Nate continued. "People usually reflect their environment at least to some degree. Some of the vilest criminals became so because of traumatic childhoods, because their environment was destructive, but many have been reformed because they were put into an environment in which their innate goodness, because I do believe that humanity is innately good, could be cultivated. Environment has a lot to do with how people think and behave towards others."

"So, do you think the king would change or not change?" I said.

"Depends on his environment but considering that he's already quite old, I'd say his environment has not made him any better yet and probably won't. However, if his environment were made up of folks who were prone to change, they could have a positive effect on him just by transforming his surroundings. Of course, this would require everyone else to be up for change which in my opinion is unlikely. It's more likely that everyone who made up the King's environment would also stagnate which would allow the King to continue his own stagnation. So ...," he paused for dramatic effect and held out his hands as if he were about to reveal a hidden playing card, "I say he would not change. This, however, is not to say that immortality as it exists today is going to lead to maniacs eternally ruling the world. The Overman Project, I believe, and my darling fiancé will likely disagree with me, has noble intentions while the subject of Shelley's poem did not." He then smiled in such a way that let me know he was about to say something he thought amusing. "Whatever the case, if you and your lot do fuck everything up, you're the ones who will have to deal with it forever." He would never laugh when he said stuff like this but smile just enough to let his audience know his intent.

After a moment of nothing but loud slurps, sniffs, and the clinking of ice in our glasses, Nate tapped his chopsticks on the edge of his bowl and said, "How does that poem end? Something about graves."

Marie, having memorized a library's worth of poetry, provided Nate with the necessary information. "'… graves from which a glorious phantom may / Burst, to illumine our tempestuous day.'"

"Right," Nate said, "From graves a phantom might burst to illumine …" he paused and turned to Marie who mouthed, "… our tempestuous day," for him. "Right, 'our tempestuous day.'" Then he flashed that same smile. "Sounds like Shelley agrees with me."

After slurping our last noodle and drinking our bodyweight in ice water, we stacked the ceramic bowls and began to make our way to a nearby pub. The pace was set by Nate and Marie who always seemed to have enough time in their day to waste on slow walks. I, for the most part, preferred a quicker pace but conceded to their preference on this occasion. While we crept along, we talked about unimportant things that made us laugh. I'd often jump and slap street signs as if they were imaginary hoops through which I would toss imaginary basketballs. I used to do stuff like that. Once at the pub of choice, Nate held open the door and Marie and I walked in. We found a round table in a dim corner. The place was mostly empty but there was a musician playing soft, acoustic folk songs at the opposite side of the room on a guitar covered in stickers with political slogans and pictures. One of them was a drawing of the American Statue of Liberty fused with a famous depiction of the ideal Overman that was popular at the time and eventually used in OP propaganda. Underneath it read in bold black letters, Libertè, Egalitè, Fuckery!

Soon after sitting down Nate held up his mobile phone. "Jonny just shot me a message. He's at a club down the street and is going to pop in here for a bit." He plopped the phone on the table and stood up. "Gin?" Nate pointed a finger at me. I nodded "Red?" His finger was now aimed at Marie. She nodded. "And whisky," he said sticking his thumb to his chest. He hopped to the bar and placed the order. When he returned, he was holding three drinks in two hands and placed them on the table carefully.

We took a break from talking to each other to enjoy the drinks, the atmosphere, and the music. The man playing was very good. Although his songs were very soft and melodic, the lyrics were the kind one would expect from a man with a guitar covered in political stickers. He sang about the Overman being an overlord and even suggested that the secret ingredient in the philosopher's stone was dead Mortal children. "That's a bit dramatic, isn't it?" Marie noted.

In between songs, and likely because of their content, Nate asked my opinion on the growing number of Immortals that had begun to fill seats in political positions. This was a problem that was foreseen decades previously but was only now becoming an issue of concern for the Mortal population. The thing managed to become quite a dilemma, for them at least, because even though they were warned about it, it happened at such a slow and gradual pace that very few found it alarming until the whole situation had passed the point of no return. How it worked was this: Immortals were beginning to surpass in years even the oldest Mortals so that those who had the most political experience, and were therefore most qualified, were Immortals. Because of this, whenever a Mortal in a position of power died or stepped down, often due to poor health, the most qualified candidate to replace them was an Immortal, and we didn't have things like death or disease to force us to step down. This caused for a slow increase of Immortals until we had suddenly filled the majority of positions in public offices, not only in Canada but in countries all over the world. Once that happened, the rate at which Mortals were being replaced with Immortals began to increase dramatically and it soon became apparent that governments would one day soon be made up entirely of Immortals.

"Well, it's a tricky situation," I said. "I guess one side could argue that those jobs should be given to whomever is most qualified. If more Immortals are qualified, then more Immortals should be given those jobs."

"Yes but—" Nate began.

"Yes but," I held up a finger and exaggerated an expression of condescending poise. "There are others who could argue that to represent the population equally, there should be proportional representation. If seventy-five percent of the population is Mortal, then seventy-five percent of those representing the population should be Mortal."

"And which one of those opinions do you favor?" Marie asked, and then sipped her wine as if to show that she was finished speaking and a figurative spotlight was now shining my way.

"Well that depends on whether I am having drinks with Mortals or Immortals," I said, and took a sip of my own.

It was at this time that Jonny burst through the pub doors, for bursting was how he usually entered rooms, and jogged, literally a slow run, to our table. The room was suddenly filled with a steady stream of laughter, backslaps, handshakes, hugs all to the sound of, "Hey."

"Look who it is!"

"Jon Jon the leprechaun."

"How's it going?"

"Where you been?"

"You look pissed."

"Get another chair."

"Have a seat."

"Waiter!"

"A beer for my brother," all said in the few seconds it took to approach our table and have a seat.

"What have you three been up to tonight?" an obviously intoxicated Jonny asked while his brother patted his shoulder and messed his hair.

"I can't remember," I said, honestly finding it difficult to recall our conversation just thirty seconds ago.

"Proportional representation or—" Marie started, always the most sober and least excitable of the group.

"Right!" Nate interrupted and then realized he had done so. "Sorry, dear. You were saying."

"Proportional representation?" Jonny jumped in with disgust.

"As in, should the percentage of Immortals in political positions—"

"I know what it means," Jonny laughed. "It just doesn't matter though. None of that matters. We're all fucked regardless of what we do."

"And why is that?" I asked, amused at Jonny's ability to stumble into a conversation and commandeer it.

"You were born of a woman, right? One of those surrogates your lot hires." He was leaning comfortably back in his chair with his beer resting on his lap. Jonny looked a lot like his brother but was taller and lankier and objectively more handsome with a square jaw. Despite these noticeable differences there was never a question that they were brothers.

"Was I born of a woman?" I repeated the question, grinning incredulously. "How else would I have been born?"

"I'll take that as a yes," Jonny said, took a drink from his bottle and released a loud belch. "This is the problem, you see. Women don't have big enough birth canals."

"Oh my God," Marie exclaimed and shook her head.

"What are you saying, you maniac?" Nate shouted with a laugh.

"It's true," Jonny continued ignoring the reactions of everyone at the table. "They are simply too small." He finished off the bottle and in the same movement leaned forward and slammed it on the table. "Our prefrontal cortex," he motioned to his forehead as if he were going to pull out his brain to show us, "is made to fit through a woman's birth canal. That is the part of the brain responsible for problem solving, abstract thinking, that sort of thing. We make irrational decisions, like electing an entire cabinet of Immortals, because this part of our brain is too small. And it's too small because if it were bigger it wouldn't fit through a small hooha."

An incredulous Marie mumbled, "Fascinating."

"And it's not the woman's fault. It is our fault. You and you and me," he said, singling out the males. "Sometime in prehistory we said to the woman, we like you better when you are tighter. Because we were insecure about our small knobs. Big hoohahs made us feel inadequate so we decided, collectively as a gender, that it was *your* duty to make *us* feel secure with the size of our knobs. It was stupid but it was the small prefrontal cortex talking. You see, we were too illogical to realize what we were doing. The women said it's our small cocks that are the real problem. But we men," Jonny thumped his chest mockingly, "who at this time wouldn't take advice from any woman—again, this was because of the small brain—wouldn't listen to what they said." Jonny raised his empty bottle in the air and shook it at the bartender who nodded and disappeared to fetch another.

"I have never heard this story before," Nate said shaking his head.

"But it's true. We're stupid because we demanded small cooters. But we demanded small cooters because we are stupid."

"What a tragic cycle," Marie said, still shaking her head in disbelief.

"So, we didn't need immortality," Nate confirmed, "What we really need are bigger knobs and bigger cooters!"

"Now you see," Jonny said and then turned his attention directly to me. "So, whoever ends up running the country, it doesn't matter. Mortal, immortal. They all still came out of the same small birth canals we do you and so will always have the same dumb, primate brain that we have. You're only as smart as the size of the—"

"We get it, Jon," Marie said, holding up a hand.

"Well, lesson learned," I said.

"Just living forever isn't enough." Jonny apparently wasn't finished. "Tell the Overmen," he pointed a finger at me, "that progress depends on bigger cooters."

"First chance I get," I assured.

The evening turned to night and then to early morning before it came to an end.

I wish that were a real story. I could write about these moments forever. It's easy to get lost in them. There's nowhere else I'd rather be.

We had countless nights like this, yet I can't remember a single one in much detail. All I have is a million little fragments, like puzzle pieces that can be arranged in any order. The pieces are all true but the picture they create may not be. In this way everything I write on these pages will be both true and a lie. I'm afraid that is the best I can do.

Chapter 6 ~ Marie

Nate and Marie met while we were all in University. By our third year, Nate and I had a well-established group of friends. One of those friends was Rueben, someone who would go on to inhabit my most despised memories. But this was before all that. I can't remember how Marie and Rueben met, perhaps I never knew, but he was the one who introduced her to our clique. She quickly became a regular fixture in the group before the rest of us noticed that her relationship with Nate was becoming slightly more significant than her relationship with the rest of us. It also became apparent that Nate was eager to reciprocate. Only a few months after meeting each other they were seldom seen walking hand out of hand.

My relationship with Marie was rather complicated. Although I quite enjoyed her company at first, after she commandeered the attention of my dearest friend like a soulless pirate, that was my opinion at the time, I had trouble maintaining any degree of affection towards her. After she took charge of his life, Nate couldn't travel like he used to, he couldn't drink Brennivin like he used to, and he couldn't spend time with me like he used to. Things never returned to the way they were before she showed up.

I remember thinking how unusual a thing like romantic relationships were. The idea of giving yourself over to one person forever lacks obvious pragmatism for us. But for them, there was no forever. For Marie and Nate, for example, it was a way of sharing moments in their lives, a way to comfort each other in the constant face of impending death, or at least that's what I imagine. Mortals would promise each other at their wedding ceremonies to remain committed to one another until they died—*till death do us part*. It was a contract of sorts. It was a way of saying that each will try to make the other's life as comfortable and happy as possible, to comfort each other, like agreeing to watch the end of the world together, hand in hand. Such a commitment was impossible to compete with.

As I mentioned earlier, Marie and I had little in common. In fact, our mutual love for Nate was just about all we had in common. But that love was also the very thing that caused such enmity between us. He was simultaneously our glue and our repellent.

I'm making it out worse than it was. I believe she bore no ill feelings towards me, at least none that she displayed. I sometimes describe our relationship as if we both equally disliked each other but the truth is that she treated me, for the most part, with perfect grace and hospitality.

It was I who made our relationship so disagreeable. Not directly, but I think it's likely that my feelings manifested themselves in some ways.

Marie was studying philosophy when she first appeared in our lives, philosophy of science to be precise. Although she did eventually earn her MA, she ultimately abandoned her original plan in order to pursue a career in journalism, a decision that confused most of us at the time. Her reasons behind such an unusual, and rather unpredictable, veering off the intended path, she said, was rooted in her gradual incredulity to and disgust with the events that were shaping our world. The events that eventually led to the world we live in today. She was very political even as a teenager and this interest grew alongside her love of the sciences. And while it was always a close race, eventually, shortly after earning her MA, her intense interest in politics managed to eke into first place.

I wonder what she would have accomplished as a philosopher. I wonder, if there was a way to reach into the past to see what she would have done would we all experience a collective feeling of remorse for forcing her to choose a different path, a path that, considering the fate of the Mortal population, did little to prevent its demise. After all, instead of spending her life contemplating things that we still contemplate today, she spent her life fighting for a group of people that no longer exist.

She began her new career as a researcher for the Canadian Broadcasting Corporation but didn't stay there long. After less than a year she was offered a job writing for a political magazine called *The Future*, and her reputation as a scrupulous journalist began to grow.

Chapter 7 ~ Nate the Novelist

At University, Nate studied history and English literature with the sole aim to become a novelist when he finished. After he graduated, he went straight to work writing a few short stories, which he managed to get published, and then a few years later his first novel was published, although it was his third attempt. It was a wonderful story about a man whose wife and five children are all killed in a terrible train collision. I realize now after writing that sentence that it doesn't sound "wonderful," but there's more to it than that. I have a copy of the manuscript somewhere in the mountains of clutter in my house. I've read it many times. The man in the story is overcome with grief but continues to live his life alone from day to day. Meanwhile, his wife and children are all reincarnated as various animals. That's when it starts to get *wonderful*. The mother is a sparrow, one of the sons is a rabbit, a daughter is a white-tailed deer, etc. All the animals are able to reunite and try to help the man get through his sorrow in clever, often hilarious, and sometimes heartbreaking ways.

For example, at one point the badger, who was the man's eldest son in his previous life, becomes concerned that his father is going to attempt suicide. So, the badger goes about hiding anything he thinks his father might be able to use to kill himself. The thing is, the father doesn't actually intend to kill himself, but many of the things the badger hides are things the father needs such as rope for repairing his hammock or knives for cutting vegetables. In the end, the father becomes quite frustrated and starts to think he may be losing his mind. It's quite funny. I'm not doing it justice by my pathetic description. Nate had a gift. He was able to write in such a way that his stories could be sad and funny at the same time. Like the story I so insufficiently summarized, he could write about the prospect of suicide after the death of a man's entire family and still make the reader laugh.

That first success made him financially fit enough to write full time and live a very comfortable life. Unsurprising to many, including myself, the financial success of this book also eliminated the last good argument against marriage, which was the cost of a wedding, and he soon announced to me that he was going to ask Marie to marry him. The conversation took place in a coffee shop over two Americanos with a splash of milk each. He seemed nervous because I think he knew that I disapproved of marriage on a fundamental level.

"What do you think about it?" he asked, as if, for just a moment, he was speaking not to a friend but a sure-to-be disapproving father.

I hesitated then said, "I think you two are fantastic together."

"You do?"

"I ... do."

"Really?"

"Really."

I sipped my coffee while avoiding eye contact.

"Really?"

"I said really, didn't I?"

"You did but ... I heard what you said but your face seems to be saying something different."

"My face?"

"That's right."

"Don't listen to my face. My face doesn't know what it's talking about."

"So, I should believe your unconvincing voice?"

"That's right."

"Why?" he said suddenly exasperated. "What's wrong with her?"

"I never said anything was wrong with her."

"But you clearly don't approve."

"I didn't say that. Remember, my face is an unreliable source of information. Ignore what my face is doing, even now. In fact, it might be best if you faced the other way for the rest of this conversation." I tried hiding behind my coffee cup. "Could you turn around please?"

"I'm not turning around."

"No worries. Know what, I can just as easily turn around myself. I'll do it." I spun around in my chair. "Better? Can you still hear me? Because you'll still want to hear my voice. My voice is the source you can trust."

"Don't be a dick," I heard him say. "I really want your honest opinion."

"I'd rather not," I said with my back still to him.

"So you don't want me to marry her."

"I didn't say that."

"You either don't want me to marry her or don't want me to get married at all."

Although both allegations were correct, I couldn't admit to either. "I also didn't say that."

"You don't like Marie." His voice sounded like he had just made a discovery.

"Don't put words in my mouth."

"It wasn't your mouth that said it."

"Don't put words on my face."

"Could you please turn around, for Christ's sake?"

I turned around sheepishly, worried I had caused irrevocable offense.

"Why don't you like her?"

"It's not that I don't like her. I really do think she's lovely and you two are wonderful."

"Then what is it?"

"Well, you're both quite young. I mean, are you sure you want to commit to the person you've been with since you were twenty years old? Don't you want to see what else is out there?"

"I'm fine thanks." He flashed a smile which showed me he wasn't completely annoyed with me. "I love Marie."

"But it could have not been Marie. What if you hadn't met her then? There is a very good chance that you would have met someone else by now and it's entirely possible that you could have been here asking me what I think of you marrying Tina or Wendy or some other name. The only difference would be that in that time you would have also met several other women on whom you would have passed and been all the more certain that Tina was meant for you. But since you have not been in a relationship with anyone besides Marie for the last ten years, you have no one to compare her to and so cannot, in my opinion, be all that certain that she is the one you want. Tina might be the one. You need to consider Tina."

"Who the fuck's Tina?"

"The one! Possibly. The point is, the sample size is too small to formulate any reasonable opinion."

Nate laughed, thank God, and then his dark eyes shot to the side as he contemplated a response. Finally, he said, "Being in love is like having children, I think. Before a—"

"You don't have any children," I quickly clarified.

"Well yes, obviously."

"Neither do I."

"Most obvious," he said, subtly dipping his head to the side. "But—"

"What are you going on about then?"

"I'm trying to explain my love for Marie in a way you might understand."

"By talking about children?"

"Okay, a dog then. You had a pet dog growing up."

"I hated the mongrel."

"Well, what do you have that you love?"

"Lots of things."

"Something specific. Imagine one of those things. The thing you love the most."

At the time I had refurbished an antique gramophone on which I used to listen to big band records. "I love my gramophone."

"That you do. Don't know if that will work for this but I'll give it a shot. So, before you had that gramophone you didn't miss anything."

"Well, before I had my gramophone, I wanted *a* gramophone. I had all those big band records, after all."

"Right, but you were still happy to go about your life without one. You knew your life would be better with a gramophone, but you didn't think you couldn't live without a gramophone. Then you got it, put all that work into it, and suddenly can't imagine your life without it. If your gramophone were to have a sudden and tragic accident you couldn't simply replace it with another. Nothing could."

"I suppose I did put a lot of effort into fixing it up," I said contemplatively.

"You could eventually bring yourself to buy a new gramophone that you might possibly learn to love, but that new gramophone would never be able to replace the one that was tragically taken from you."

"So being in love is like having an antique gramophone and having an antique gramophone is like being in love. Is that right?"

"I think we're starting to get somewhere. Not far, mind you, but we may have taken a step."

"Are you planning on getting a gramophone?" I asked, pretending not to understand.

"No!" His laughter began to punctuate his speech again so that his words seemed to bounce. "I mean … it's like something you love."

"Yeah, I get it. I was just being facetious."

"It's like this with love. Could I love someone else besides Marie? Of course."

"I get it," I said.

"Just to make sure you do. I am in love with *Marie*."

"I'm perfectly aware now. Your gramophone analogy was tailor made for my comprehension."

"I can't replace her with someone else."

"That message has been sent and received." I lifted my coffee cup and smiled sarcastically.

"Without her now there would be something missing, something irreplaceable."

"Yes, that idea has been cemented."

"Before I met her—"

"No need to finish. Nothing could be understood more. No one understands anything better than I do, you now. It is clear as crystal."

"Do I have your blessing though?"

"My blessing? I'm not a fucking rabbi."

"Whatever, do you approve?"

"If my approval will put a quick and complete stop to this … whatever this has become, then you have my approval, blessing and anything else you might require."

"Great." His face suddenly brightened so much I felt I should squint. "You'll be my best man?"

"I will be your best man and quietly stand by doing nothing as you permanently tether yourself to that … interloper. Even though it will be akin to watching you willfully tie yourself to a cinder block and hop off a perfectly afloat cruise ship with a fully stocked bar."

"I'm glad you are able to see things clearly now."

"Yes. Perfectly clear."

They were married about a year later.

Although they always talked about having children, they decided to put it off for a few years since Marie's burgeoning career had left little time for a proper family. This turned out to be a decision they grew to regret deeply for reasons I will soon explain.

Chapter 8 ~ Jonny and Kara

Much to everyone's surprise, Nate's younger brother Jonny also eventually married. No one really thought he was the "settling down" type and it's entirely likely that he never would if he hadn't met Kara who everyone agreed was probably the only woman in the world with whom settling down was possible for him. You see, Jonny was always wild and so we assumed such a demeanor could never be tamed. And we were right. Kara was so compatible with him because she had no intention of taming him while maintaining the most tamed demeanor any of us had ever encountered. She was always calm, collected, sober, even seemingly a bit detached at times. And it was this extreme opposite to her husband that we figured was what made them so perfectly matched. Nate and I surmised that they both loved the other for their traits because they were so foreign to each other—almost exotic. And because of this mutual admiration neither ever dreamt of trying to change the other.

Kara became pregnant almost immediately after they were married to which Jonny joked, "Putting a wedding ring on forever means putting a condom on never." Roughly nine months later they had a baby boy and named him James. Since this was after the laws limiting procreation were passed, they were forced to have the boy secretly and quite illegally. They gave birth to James in their apartment in Winnipeg with the help of a young midwife and raised him with the help of some generous friends who were willing to risk a great deal for the young lad. At first, we were all confused as to why Jonny and Kara decided to take such a risk. They didn't intend to get pregnant, but they made a conscious decision to keep the baby. Part of me still thinks the reason for this was not necessarily because Jonny and Kara wanted a child but because neither would stand to let someone else tell them what to do. In this way James was a protest, something that probably had a significant effect on the shaping of his life.

About a month after James was born Kara and Jonny held a party to celebrate. I remember seeing James for the first time, laying in a white wicker bassinette on his back with his arms and legs spread lazily, his head turned to the side, eyes closed, breathing heavily. He wore a white and yellow patterned onesie. His head was already mostly covered in wispy black hair, which would eventually turn light brown as a toddler before returning to black again as a teenager. His nose was a small button, his lips were a rose bud. When he was awake and his eyes were open, I remember they were blue, but would eventually turn dark brown, almost black, like his father and uncle's. Most of all I remember him sleeping perfectly, without a stir, in that bassinette.

Jonny was entertaining guests in the dining room and Nate, Marie, Kara and I were standing round the bassinette conversing in whispers over the sleeping infant.

"He's adorable," Marie said, leaning over him with a soft smile.

"You don't think he looks weird?" Kara asked, also leaning but with an unsure grin.

"All babies look a little strange. Especially at first. Oh, I wish he were awake so I could hold him."

"I'm afraid he's likely out for the night."

"You're lucky. My cousin's baby slept all day and was awake all night. I think I can see you in him," Marie said to Nate who was making sarcastic faces at me and didn't hear what she had said.

"What was that?"

"Look," Marie reached down and rubbed little James' earlobes. "His ears, you and Jonny have identical ears and James has them, too."

"I can see it," Kara smiled and examined the sleeping infant's ears herself.

"I'm never good at these kinds of things," Nate said. "All babies just look like babies to me. People always say, he looks like his mum or he looks like his uncle, but I can only see a baby. You know what I mean?" He said to me.

"I guess," I responded and joined the rest in examining James' ears. "But I don't know, ears seem to be rather specific in their shape and those ears right look exactly like yours. And yours look exactly like Jonny's."

"You can't tell," Nate scoffed.

For Mortals the likeness between them and their children was a way to, in a way, extend their life. Sure, most Mortals didn't live longer than a century but if they had children and those children had children then their DNA, their "blood" would live on. It was as close to immortality as they could get.

"How was the labor?" Marie asked, tilting her head and widening her eyes as if to ask, was it horrible?

"Well, I never want to do it again. So, there's that." Kara took a sip from her soda and lime with a far-off look as if she were remembering some sort of trauma. "I guess it wasn't even that bad but the horror of having something grow inside you before being forcefully ejected—"

"Hold the phone," Nate said suddenly. "I'm going to go see how Jonny's doing. You coming?" he said to me.

"No, I'll stay for a bit." I found the whole thing fascinating. I still do.

Nate gave me a solid pat on the back before leaving.

Knowing I could never have a child myself made me extremely curious about them. I suppose I was aware even then that if the day ever came when Mortals ceased to exist then so would children. I listened intently as Kara described the horrifying ordeal. She said she began to feel contractions at around 7:00 in the evening but ignored them, believing them to be false labor pains. Finally, she said, around 11:00 she had Jonny call the midwife for the pains were beginning to feel like true labor. The midwife arrived and the pushing and grunting began. The whole process was long, painful, and, it still seems to me, impossible. The pain and discomfort first led her to want to stand and then lay down on her back. They soon discovered that baby James was in the posterior position: he was facing up instead of down. This caused an assortment of complications including a great deal of pain, that is, a great deal more pain than if there were no complications at all. It was also concerning because sometimes such a complication requires a caesarian and since they were delivering the child at home and since the child was illegal, they couldn't go to a hospital to have the procedure performed. But, fortunately, a switch to a squatting position allowed Kara to deliver the child without such extreme medical intervention.

"That's incredible," Marie said, her mouth agape. I noticed her breathing had increased as if she were watching a particularly suspenseful film. "How is everything … you know, down there?"

Having a child often caused a great deal of damage to the woman's body.

"It'll never be the same," Kara said stolidly followed by a sigh which seemed to display a demeanor of acceptance.

"Really?" Marie said, and her mouth dropped more.

"I have some exercises that the midwife got me on and as long as I keep it up, I shouldn't be in any great risk of a prolapse."

Marie put a hand to her heart.

"A pro …?" I began sheepishly but too interested to not ask.

"… *lapse*, as in my innards dropping out my …" she tilted her head while ascertaining whether I could handle what she was about to say, "… my vagina. Sorry," she said, showing concern for my fragile male sensibilities.

"So, are you going to have another one? I know you said you don't *want* to do it again, but *would* you do it again?" Marie asked. After hearing about what an ordeal it all was, I was expecting an immediate and resounding no.

"Well, we'd like to but …" Kara looked down at her sleeping son lovingly. "It's going to be hard enough having one child we have to keep hidden from the world, you know. So probably not."

Marie nodded sympathetically.

"Luckily we have a good group of people who'll help us out with this one. But another would be … it just wouldn't be a good idea."

"How about you?" Kara whispered even quieter than we already were. "Do you think you and Nate would ever …?"

Marie shook her head so slightly it was difficult to catch. "I'm afraid it's just not in the cards for us. At least not now. And the way things are going it probably won't be for a very long time."

We all three then looked down at little James and a melancholy seemed to fill the room.

"I understand," Kara whispered.

The silence was abruptly broken when Jonny marched into the room and, trying to whisper but failing, said, "What do ya think of my son?"

"Shhhhhhhh." Kara put a finger to her lips and scolded him with her eyes.

Jonny instinctively put a finger to his own lips seemingly without realizing it and said with drunken sincerity, "Sorry." He then turned to me and said in a proper whisper, "Do you think he looks like a Karski?"

"His ears do."

"His ears?" Jonny tilted his head and looked down at his son. "Who cares about ears?"

"Okay," Kara said and moved towards him. "Get out. You're going to wake him up." She grabbed him by the shoulders, spun him round, and began pushing him towards the door. "You're drunk."

"Well, yes," Jonny laughed, trying not to spill his drink as he was forced closer to the door.

"This is the nursery. No drunks allowed."

James would be the last Karski.

Chapter 9 ~ My Life Then

During this time when my friends' lives were changing, mine remained relatively the same. After university I, like all Immortals at that time, was immediately put to work in the Overman Project. Even though I had obtained a PhD by this time, the job the OP assigned me had nothing to do with my credentials. My job was essentially that of a lobbyist but instead of lobbying for a product, I *was* the product. Canada and the US as well as much of Western Europe were already well on their way to a full embrace and adoption of Immortality as the eventual first world standard. Other countries, however, were moving much slower towards the Overman's goals for reasons far too complex and varied to get into in these pages. I was recruited to convince these slow-moving countries why immortality was exactly the jump-start they needed.

My sales pitch was essentially this: the primary source of many of the problems that plague these nations, socially, economically, et cetera, stems from the incompatible differences between people groups. One religious group fights with another because they cannot agree on which ancient book or interpretation of an ancient book is true, or truest, so they fight each other. One ethnic group fights with another ethnic group because they don't like the color of their skin or remember a history in which they were persecuted by said ethnic group. Higher classes don't get along with lower classes and chopstick users don't get along with fork enthusiasts, so they attack one another based on their preferences. So many differences among so many groups of people will always inevitably lead to conflict. As long as these differences exist, people will continue to fight amongst themselves. Every war, skirmish and fisticuff, could have been prevented if the playing field had been levelled. Immortality, I told them, makes everyone the same ethnicity, religion, culture, and class. Everyone is of equal social standing and equal enlightenment. It is the panacea, the answer to every problem, the final never-ending chapter of human existence.

My pitch now makes me feel rather sick to my stomach, from both embarrassment and shame. I can't remember exactly but I'm sure it did then as well. Maybe not to the degree it does at this late stage of my life. But I'm sure I never truly believed such nonsense. Not completely, anyway. Yes, in many ways one Immortal is indistinguishable from the next; we all have essentially the same origins, are members of the same class—the only class. We can alter our appearance so easily and so drastically now that no one thinks of discriminating anyone else for how they choose to look since we've all looked a hundred different ways by now. But we are not clones. Each of our brains functions uniquely. No one thinks exactly the way I do. I doubt we'll ever get to a place in which we are all the same. It terrifies me to think of such a ghastly future of interchangeable automatons. But if, perchance, in the future it becomes achievable to create a society of completely identical clones, we'll suddenly find ourselves with a charge of obsolescence and be forced to go the way of the Mortal.

The work I did as an ambassador may have been the first moment in which I started to question the magnanimity of the Overman Project, although as you'll see, it took a lot longer before I rejected it. I realized that those who sent me to country after country knew that I was being sent to lie, just as I knew. I kept lying, though, and they kept sending me. I suppose we all thought the lies were necessary to reach our goal of universal immortality and we all assumed such a goal was worth the price of a few principles.

My work as ambassador was mostly part-time since my primary focus was my work at the university. My study of choice was biochemistry and molecular biology. I told people, and probably myself, that my interest in these fields was rooted in my fascination with immortality and a desire to understand it better. But the truth, which I never admitted, was that I was more fascinated with mortality and wanted to understand *it* better. This curiosity obviously led to my current state. It's entirely possible that I always knew, somehow, that by pursuing those disciplines for the reasons I did, I'd end up where I am today.

Although my scientific work allowed me to explore my passion and work as an ambassador allowed me to see many exotic locales, I still say that my life ultimately changed little because, unlike my Mortal friends, I was making progress only vocationally. Between my scientific investigations and my ambassadorial duties, I hardly had time to maintain the relationships I already had and no time at all to cultivate new ones. Although I'm sure it bothered me at the time I, like most, accepted it as a natural corollary to preparation for eternal life. I think we all agreed that the relationships we would develop now would be ones built ever so slowly and they would therefore be much stronger than the short-lived friendships Mortals could offer. We tended to see everything in that light or thought we ought to. Things that take a long time to achieve are better since the longer something takes the better it will be. Friendships with Mortals, we assumed, would never be as strong as those with Immortals because Mortals simply didn't have the time. Just wait, we were told, when you're 500 years old you won't even remember those friendships you had with Mortals, but your fellow Immortals will be closer than family.

I didn't really accept their rationale, but I was also a member and I knew even then that too much questioning might jeopardize my membership. Yet at the same time, I was also aware that the more time I spent catering to the OP's demands, the less time I had to spend with Nate and the rest. My story is not unique. For all Immortals at that time, there were no other paths to take. We were preparing to live forever and so it was commonly thought that such preparation would and should take a lot of time and effort. This meant that no Immortal had any time to think about relationships, something I'm now convinced was an intentional side effect. This further increased the already obvious dichotomy between Immortal and Mortal by forcing one to keep their distance from the other. Even if it wasn't foreseen by the Overman Project, I believe that once they realized it was there, they enthusiastically encouraged it. In fact, I believe that even during this early period of the Eternal Era, only a little over 100 years after the birth of the first Immortal, they had already begun to entertain the possibility of a world without Mortals and wanted to make sure that Immortals would be fully capable of doing what needed to be done should the goal of a Mortal-free society ever be pursued. And of course, they must've already considered the possibility that such a pursuit might require more compromise of more principles. They knew that fraternization between Mortals and Immortals would become a problem if Immortals ever became attached to Mortals in some way, so they gave a few nudges in the right direction to prevent as much as possible Mortal and Immortal relationships.

Whether or not their attempts were successful depends on the person. I don't think they were as successful as they hoped considering the force with which the Mortal Revolution hit us. I had my own role in that conflict which I will get into soon. But the fact remains that many Immortals today probably remember many Mortals who were not only good people but great friends.

Chapter 10 ~ A Friendly Gathering

Despite the many obstacles, we all still managed to maintain a relatively close relationship. Not just Nate, Marie, and myself, but others as well. Nate's brother Jonny and his wife Kara, for example, were regular fixtures as was their rapidly growing son James, although at this time he was still much too young to be anything like a conversationalist. And then there was Reuben who would often make appearances at our gatherings. I haven't written much about him yet, have I? What is there to say? I guess I'll start with the basics.

Reuben was a bright-faced Immortal with bright yellow hair that was always combed back with plenty of grease. It was always so perfectly sculpted and solid that it was impossible to be certain it wasn't in fact some sort of clay helmet formed and painted to resemble hair. His face was always dragging around an unwilling smile which showed off teeth that matched the brightness of the rest of his blinding façade. He knew Nate since kindergarten but didn't become a regular fixture in our group until university, where he introduced Nate to Marie. He was around often enough that his presence at our gatherings was never a surprise even if it was rarely expected and, at least in my opinion, never hoped for. He was like a lingering character that would never let someone forget he existed no matter how hard one might try. Am I being too hard on the man? If you think so then you never knew Reuben.

But this isn't about Reuben, the little toad. Although he was at the party I'm about to describe, his presence was merely known in the same way a lamp in the corner was known. He had little effect on the room yet could be found if one so desired. Although I don't know who in their right mind would ever have that desire.

We had all congregated in Nate and Marie's apartment. Although it wasn't terribly large, the main room, which included their kitchen, dining room, and living room, was big enough to host parties. One entered the place from the south and to the east one would see the only other doors in the place which led to the only other rooms. These were, from north to south, the washroom, which also contained a washer and dryer, a small closet, and the bedroom. In order to utilize the space as best as possible, Nate and Marie would rearrange the furniture whenever they were having a get-together to maximize space.

The guests at these frequent gatherings included people of all stripes: writers, journalists, artists, teachers, students, professors, politicians, philosophers, trade workers, and business professionals.

Every conversation one began with a stranger started with, "And what do you do?" followed by "And how do you know Nate and Marie?" After the initial introductions, conversations could go in any direction depending on who was involved. It was like a mixture of random chemicals floating about the room which, when combined with another, create unpredictable reactions. The conversations were often heated but never boring.

In the middle of the room was a cluster of furniture on which one could often find Marie surrounded by an assortment of characters.

"I read your article." An immortal man, with whom I had worked in the past and had unwisely invited to the party, yelled over the music.

"Which one?" Marie turned her head and leaned towards him. She was sitting in an armchair while the clearly drunk man had crept up just behind the right side of her.

The man's voice rose and fell as he spoke as if he were speaking while sitting on a mechanical bull. "The one which claimed that the incr*easing* influence of the Im*mortals* may have, rather, if I may say, un*believable* repercussions on the *fabric* of *society* if they are not *reined in*."

"I think I said the repercussions would be on the rights of Mortals, not society as a whole."

"I can't *say* I see *much* of a difference. Do you *really* think the Immortals are planning to e*liminate* every last *Mortal* on the *pl*a*net*?"

"Again, I don't believe I made that claim." By this time the small group sitting around her had stopped what they were doing and had turned their attention to her and her interlocutor.

"But you *seem* to believe that they have some rather ne*farious* plans for *Mortals*."

By this time Marie couldn't supress a bit of a laugh. "I don't believe they have a specific plan. No. It's not a grand conspiracy. It's just that whenever one group of people manages to gain unchecked power over another, they tend to use it for their own ends despite the effect it may have on everyone else. It's human nature really."

"Well, as an Im*mortal* myself I have to disa*gree* with you. *I* for *one* simply do *not* have *anything* against *Mortals*."

"Again, I didn't say—"

"But I *do* have to *say*, I don't think *any* Immortal has *anything* against *Mortals*."

"Possibly but—"

"I'm *not* finished." It had become clear to Marie, and everyone else present, that the man speaking was already two sheets to the wind and well on his way to three. "To *make* such a claim is pr*eposterous*. Im*mortals*, such as my*self*, are no more ass*ailants* than you are *victims*, which is to *say* not at *all*. Im*mortals* like my*self*," he placed a hand on his chest and lifted his chin, "have ob*tained* the positions of *power* we *have* by *merit* a*lone*. We *work* hard and are *simply* the *most* qua*lif*ied. The *problem*, you see dear, is *not* that we have *tak*en power from *you*, but that *you* have re*fus*ed to *keep* the power for your*selves. Some*one had to *fill* these positions of *power* and those most *qual*ified should *nat*urally be the ones to *do* so."

"I'm not sure I can say anything that might clear things up or change your mind, can I?" Marie asked, smiling.

"I *highly* doubt it."

"Well, I'll give it a go anyway."

Jonny had noticed the inebriated man from across the room and immediately abandoned his conversation to see if he could join his. He made his way to the crowd and stood next to the man and slightly behind. As he continued to speak Jonny began to imitate his swaying in an exaggerated manner.

"Because you know," Marie, who had by this time turned so far in her chair to face the inebriated man that her right leg was draped over the chair's right arm, couldn't help but keep the conversation going. She never gave up a chance to try to change someone's mind no matter how futile a task it might appear. "A quick look at the statistics of the last couple of years shows that Mortal schools have become severely underfunded while Immortal schools have found themselves with a steady increase in their budget. Don't you think that may have something to do with the fact that the Manitoba Board of Education is made up almost entirely of Immortals?"

"Of *course* not. The Im*mortal* schools are *new*er are they *not*?"

"Of course."

"So, they re*quire* more *money* just to get *start*ed. *Your* schools have been around for *ages*. It simply costs a *great* deal *more* to open *new* schools than to main*tain old* ones."

"But that still leaves the question, why must Immortals have their own schools. Would it really be so bad for Immortals to go to school with Mortals?"

"*This* old argument again. *May*be *some*day, when the world has *finally* accepted Im*mortals* then the two worlds can be *in*tegrated. But until *then*, Mortals and *I*mmortals simply would *not* get a*long*."

"I went to school with Mortals," I stepped in after listening for too long. "In fact, I went to school with her husband." I motioned to Marie with my drink.

"*Well*, then *you* of *all* people should under*stand* ex*actly* what I am *saying*." His swaying was getting more precarious leading someone to suggest a sit-down. "I'm *fine*, I as*sure* you," he said as he gracefully tilted a little to the left, then a bit back, then a tad forward before finally completely to the right where he met the floor with a thud. The noise was accompanied by many gasps from the many observers and before he was aware that he was no longer standing, Jonny had dropped to the floor next to him and was helping him up. How or why he did not manage to prevent the poor man's fall, considering his proximity to him, was unclear but I believe he simply couldn't bring himself to prevent such a satisfying finale to the discussion.

The barely conscious man was gently placed in a comfortable armchair in which his head dropped back, and he immediately began to snore.

"That was exciting," Marie joked from behind a glass of pinot grigio. "Where did he come from anyway?"

"I believe he may have come with me," I had to confess. I often brought random people from the Overman Project to these gatherings. It gave me a chance to form relationships with people who were either powerful or would someday be and it also gave them a chance to formulate relationships with Mortals. I think that was my reasoning anyway. "I brought a few of them with me. I suppose I should learn to discriminate."

"What do you mean?" Jonny piped up while attempting to use the man's snoring to give flight to a tissue. "He was hilarious." He looked up and smiled deviously. "He still is if I'm honest."

"Let him sleep, Jon," Marie said.

"He's sleeping perfectly well. If he's able to entertain while taking forty winks, then all's the better. I think I need something lighter."

"Rip it into smaller pieces," Nate said hopping over to his brother. "Like this."

Chapter 11 ~ The Party Continues

The events of these parties would sometimes take a dark turn. This was the beginning of a tumultuous period in our history, after all, and often that impending tumult was glimpsed at, especially after a few cocktails to knock down some inhibitions.

Some moments after everyone had become bored with the unconscious man's snoring a booming voice was heard above the music and chatter. "Go fuck yourself then!" the voice said carrying through the flat and drawing everyone's attention.

"What that?" Nate muttered and joined everyone in witnessing the new development. What everyone saw was a young pregnant woman being berated by a middle-aged man and Kara between them holding her arms out like she was trying to prevent two pillars from collapsing.

Jonny, fearing his wife might need assistance, ran towards the commotion and joined his wife between the two. The rest of us swiftly followed.

"What's going on?" Marie asked when she arrived.

"This bitch ish carrying one of their babiesh," the middle-aged man barked with somewhat slurred speech. "She's a traitor!"

"Who cares?" someone yelled. I noticed the pregnant woman had tears streaming down her face. She didn't move but I couldn't decide if she was afraid to leave or determined to stay.

"She'sh a traitor to her shpeciess." The man had a permanent scowl and kept looking the woman up and down as if sizing up an opponent.

"You know there are a lot of Immortals here tonight," Kara said, still standing between them, although by now she had turned to face the man directly ascertaining he was more of a threat than the frightened pregnant woman. "If you don't like Immortals then you can leave."

"I haf no problem with Immortals ash long as they find their own way to make their own babiesh. But to sssssell yourself like thish whore—"

"That's enough of that," Kara managed to say before giving the man a sharp slap across the mouth. Everyone in the crowd first gasped and then swarmed the man before he could return the blow even though he gave no indication that that was his intention. Instead, the only reaction he exhibited was somehow enlarging his eyes three times their size before he was promptly hauled off to a corner to cool down.

The woman's name was Olivia we learnt after sitting her down. The man's accusation was correct; she was a Mortal carrying an Immortal fetus.

"I just needed the money," she said without being prompted but it was clear she felt she needed to explain herself.

"You don't have to justify yourself to anyone," Marie informed. "Forget about people like that idiot."

"I don't know why I said anything. He seemed fine one moment and then something I said must have tipped him off. I don't know. We were just talking and then …" she blew her nose into a tissue handed to her by Jonny.

"Don't worry about anything. I'm sure he'll have some regrets about this in the morning."

The practice of Mortal women carrying Immortal children was, as I believe I've just shown, a very contentious issue. As the dichotomy between Mortal and Immortal continued to grow people, like the cantankerous middle-aged man I described, began to see the world as made up of two incompatible groups. Although we were still years from the revolution, battle lines were already beginning to be drawn.

"How far along are you?" Kara asked. "If you don't mind me asking."

"Eight months," Olivia said and gave an uncertain frown.

"How do you feel?"

"Physically I'm fine. Everything looks great in there. But it is hard to think that once he's out I may never see him again." Tears began to fill her eyes again, but a sniff and a wipe cleared them up. She cleared her throat before continuing. "When I signed up for this I did it just for the money of course and didn't consider the attachment, you know." She rubbed her belly again. "But, on the bright side, I was told that doing stuff like this makes it easier to get a birth permit. So, when I'm ready to have one of my own I should be able to do it legally, ya know."

I could see Kara's face twinge when she said, "legally." I wondered what Nate and Marie were thinking then, too.

Once everything seemed settled again and the partygoers had resumed what they came there to do, I wandered round the room until I found Nate by the bar which was just a foldable table with a brown sheet over it covered in bottles of spirits.

"It's been an exciting evening so far hasn't it," I said while fixing a drink.

"That it has. And the night's still young."

"That it is." I glanced at the clock and a dread filled my stomach. "Well, not that young."

"No? You have somewhere to be?"

"Unfortunately, yes. But not yet." Having completed mixing the concoction in my tumbler I held it up for Nate to clink his against.

We turned around to survey the party only to see the stomach-churning face of Reuben who had been standing directly behind us, presumably waiting for access to the bar. We both jumped at the sight of him.

"Jesus!" I said, clutching at my heart.

"Sorry about that. Didn't mean to startle you."

Nate and I both took a step to the side so Reuben could walk between us and mix his drink.

"Great party, Nate," Rueben said, hunched over the bar like a creature from a children's campfire horror story. He finished mixing whatever poison he drank and turned to face Nate while I stupidly stood behind him.

"Thank you. How're things?" Nate always treated him with dignity and respect because for some unfathomable reason Nate liked the man.

The two of them talked for a moment before Reuben slithered away to bother someone else. After he was gone, I rejoined Nate and couldn't help but question his loyalty to such a slug.

"I don't see why you have such a problem with him," Nate laughed after I had made my opinion known. "He's an old friend and he's never done anything to me or anyone else I know. In fact, he introduced me to my wife. He's never done anything to you has he?"

"There's something about him. He doesn't have to do something to prove he's a horrible bastard. He's a horrible bastard with or without an example. He's made completely of evil. Just because he hasn't done anything to prove it yet doesn't negate the fact that that is what he is. Like a gun that hasn't been fired yet."

"I get it," Nate said laughing. "Now shut up."

The night wore on. With drinks in hand, Nate and I first sauntered over to what appeared to be a heated debate. Two men were involved and were standing facing each other with fingers wagging. The first had evidently said something the second disagreed with and so the second was trying his best to develop a rebuttal but the first wouldn't let him finish a sentence. A third person, who must have seen the commotion from afar, ran to the second's aid by offering his own counter. The first was now sparring with the two of them and barely holding his head above water. Luckily for him a fourth entered the ring to pick up some of the slack and wasted no time dealing two sharp jabs, one to the second's ego and another to the third's style of dress but none to their actual arguments. The second would have none of that and returned the fourth's stinging jabs with an expertly landed haymaker aimed at the fourth's idiosyncratic way of speaking rendering him speechless. It was at this moment that Nate and I, having seen enough of the fruitless match, continued our wandering.

We next ventured towards the snack bar, another foldable table with a maroon sheet over it covered in bowls and plates of every imaginable bite sized food item, where another group seemed to be in another passionate conversation. But instead of outrage, they appeared to be discussing a mutual love or obsession. Although it wasn't clear when we first arrived, after the mention of Dostoevsky elicited one member of the conversation to put a hand over her heart, throw her head back and release an emotional, "Ohhhhhhhhhh my god," we realized they were gushing over their most beloved authors. This conversation was kept to a much lower volume; in fact, loud outbursts were reserved only to demonstrate the level of awe with which one can be struck by a piece of literature. Tolstoy elicited a simultaneous outburst by all involved making me believe this was a conversation about Russian literature specifically, but next came a mention of Dickens and I then deduced it was about literature from the Victorian period. I was again proven wrong, however, when a mention of Sophocles brought still more moans of pleasure with a few apparently competing for longest and loudest as if such a competition would merit them the title of supreme admirer. It was then that Nate and I realized the specifics of the topic weren't important; the point was not to talk about literature but for each bibliophile to display their passion for it. When the moans had quieted three more people opened their mouths at once naming three more authors and another cacophony of exaltation erupted.

It was then that I was forced to acknowledge the time and I told Nate that I must leave.

"The night's still young," he insisted. "Are you not having a good time?"

"Oh, I'm having a marvelous time. But I have to catch a flight tomorrow morning to Montreal for a conference and then I'm off to Taipei. You know … the Overman Project."

"It's fine, of course." We began walking to the bedroom where the bed held all the guests' coats. "We're adults now," he laughed, "and have to behave like adults once in a while."

"I'd rather not. You know I'm never one to want to leave a party that's still raging. I'd rather be the last to leave." I grabbed my coat and slung it over my arm. We began making our way back through the crowd of lively partygoers and towards the dreadfully quiet and boring looking door.

"I know," Nate said. "It's too bad though that we don't get to see each other like we used to. And when we do it seems our time is always cut short."

"It's a busy time of our lives, I suppose." We arrived at the front door. I looked round the room. The group that had been yelling about politics were now laughing. The man who screamed at poor pregnant Olivia was sitting on a foldable chair sipping water. Kara and Jonny were dancing energetically to the music. Marie was engaged with another woman in conversation and kept leaning either backwards or forwards in laughter. "If things were different ..." I began.

"I know." Nate hugged me and I was suddenly filled with a terrible feeling, like I was being split in two.

"Say goodbye to everyone for me," I said. "I'll call when I get back."

I entered the hallway and Nate closed the door after me. Down the empty hall I could see the staircase which would take me outside, and then far away from here. The hum of the party behind the closed door swelled and shrunk rhythmically like waves on a beach. As I walked towards those lonely stairs and then down, that hum diminished until it could only be heard as a memory repeating itself in my head.

Chapter 12 ~ The World Changes

The Immortal population continued to grow and with it the dichotomy between them and Mortals. With the growing population and ever-expanding resources, the Overman Project's efforts eventually led to the creation of "Immortal neighbourhoods." This meant that many younger Immortals were never raised in the company of Mortals. They never had a chance to have a single Mortal friend. This naturally led to an even greater wedge that continued to force its way between the two groups of people. In addition, the strong presence Immortals were gaining in governmental positions meant that the Mortals, despite still being the majority of the population, were finding themselves having to fight for proper representation.

Rights of Mortals began to be infringed, at first, in rather inconspicuous ways before becoming excessively obvious. The biggest infringement on the rights of Mortals came quite early in the struggle with the aforementioned laws regarding mandatory contraceptives and birth permits, the very same that forced James to be raised in secret. The reasons made sense to us at the time at least. With fewer and fewer deaths, the population was growing at an unnatural rate. This population crisis led to hunger crises in many countries around the world, civil and international conflicts, and the emergence of violent hate groups along with issues that rise when living conditions plummet. These issues that had little to no effect on the Immortal population as the tens of millions of Immortals alive at that time were mostly in affluent communities in developed countries. Despite the fact that most Immortals were in positions in which the world's growing problems could be easily ignored, the threat of overpopulation eventually posed enough of a threat to cause us to take action.

There were many Immortals who protested on behalf of the Mortals, great thinkers and activists who formed groups whose sole purpose was to try to persuade governments of various nations to consider their actions on moral grounds. The problem was that these governments were far too infected with Immortals, or rather Overmen. This meant that those civil rights groups, even ones headed primarily by Immortals, went mostly unheard and unacknowledged. There were also many Immortals and Mortals in government positions who were sympathetic to the Mortal cause but by this time they were too small of a minority to make much difference. Trying to inhibit the growth of the Mortal population was something politicians just accepted as nonnegotiable. They did what they could by speaking up for the rights of Mortals when they could, but they could only do so much. Surprisingly, there were also countless Mortal politicians who enthusiastically sided with the Immortals on these issues. It was odd, in a way, but I think their reasoning was simply they still had to live their life to the end and since Immortals were the future, aligning themselves with them guaranteed a solid future of political power. While they were mostly puppets of the Overmen, they sought financial comfort while they were alive. I don't blame them. We all know the result now so it may have been better for some to live their life siding with the enemy than to fight for a dying cause.

After the laws requiring prospective parents to obtain a birth permit were passed, my friends started to become politically active. Marie was always quite political since her job was to investigate injustice and report on it, but Nate was never overtly expressive about his political opinions. The "anti-child" laws, as some had begun to call them, had a devastating effect on my friends who always intended to have children but had put it off in order to focus on their careers. Although they continued to apply for permits, they were never accepted, even with my influence. I was too naïve then, honestly. I should've known they'd never be accepted. Few Mortals were. It soon became apparent that most of the pregnant women walking round were surrogates for the Overman Project, carrying fetuses that were assembled in a laboratory. See, the point of these laws was not to keep the population at a manageable level; it was meant to slowly rid the world of undesirables, a term that had become synonymous with Mortals in some elite circles.

I guess there's no reason for me not to admit that I voted for these bills to be passed. I'm ashamed of it, even though my having voted against them wouldn't have changed anything. I still feel a strong sense of regret at having betrayed my friends. But really, this was just one more addition to my already sizable haunting of which you already know much about. That's all I have to say about my role in it. I would prefer not to remember more if I don't have to.

The continued anti-Mortal actions of world leaders eventually led to many protests. I believe the largest world-wide protest in human history took place at this time. There had never been one like it before or since. I took part in some of these with Nate, Marie, Jonny, and Kara. I remember the protest in Rome in which four million people showed up to declare fair and equal rights for Mortals. We were situated in Saint Peter's Square standing almost in the same place we were when we heard Professor Mesnick speak about the wonders of immortality all those years ago. This time, however, we and millions of others were the ones who were demanding our voices heard. It felt empowering, like I was a part of something bigger than anything I had been a part of before. It was bigger than the Overman Project; I felt a part of the human race.

This may seem hypocritical since just two paragraphs ago I admitted to having voted for the exact thing I was protesting. And there is no other word that would properly describe it; it was entirely hypocritical. I can't, to this day, justify it. The way I understood it at the time was that I had two priorities: one with the Overman Project and another with my friends. As long as I fulfilled my duties to both, I thought I was morally in the clear regardless of how contradictory those duties were. I know now, and I absolutely knew then despite refusing to admit it, that that kind of reasoning is cowardly and amoral. Loyalties are not chosen for us. We choose to whom we are loyal. And even after we establish our loyalties, we must still employ reason when deciding how our loyalty will manifest itself. The Overman Project essentially gave me life which was reason enough for some degree of loyalty.

But they didn't demand just some. They demanded complete loyalty, and complete submission. Ever since we were born, we were under the thumb of the Overman Project, even at the very beginning when it was run by our Mortal Parents. We were expected to do what they said without question. We were expected to eat, sleep, think, and dream the Overman Project. And we all did for centuries because we felt we owed them an unpayable debt. But we didn't. No more than the Mortals were expected to spend their entire lives serving their parents. Eventually they left the nest. This analogy doesn't really fit though because Mortals depended on their parents to survive, at least for those first years. I know this will sound like blasphemy to many, but we didn't depend on the Overman Project. If anything, they depended on us to survive. They needed a reason to continue to exist, so they kept making us until there was no more room for anything but us.

Chapter 13 ~ First Steps to Betrayal

Forgive me if it seems as though I have been wasting a great deal of time writing about the early years of the Eternal Era. I'm sure all you care about, my dear reader(s), are the why's of my actions. But if I am to properly explain why I did what I did, then I must make clear the history that set the stage for my actions. I know a great many of us likely have no memory of a mortal friend or family member and so might not have a clear understanding of what happened during that time or what Mortal men and women were like. If I am to make you understand anything, then I must first make you understand Mortals.

While in Rome for the protest in Saint Peter's Square, Jonny and I would often spend late nights in Nate and Marie's hotel room. We would stay sometimes until an eastern glow appeared in the sky, talking about equal rights for Mortals and the best strategies to make our voices loudest. We would talk about historic protests and revolutions and pondered the historic significance of the activism in which we were currently involved. Basically, every conversation, every moment of our waking lives, was consumed with efforts to resist the Overmen, despite my continued affiliations with them.

The following account is from a typical night. Nate was sitting cross-legged on his hotel bed with a drink in his hand, probably a whisky of sorts. Marie was lying on her side next to him sipping a drink of her own, nodding and interjecting at times. Jonny was sitting on the chesterfield and I was reclining slightly in the computer chair with my feet crossed and resting on the corner of the bed.

"After Rome, what next?" Nate asked. "Obviously we all can't stay in Rome waiting until our every demand is met. And, although the world is watching, all the weight of the resistance cannot be put on the shoulders of those here. That would make it too easy for the Overmen. Nate was always careful to never say Immortal in this context. He wanted to differentiate between the Overman Project and Immortals. "If they can somehow squelch what is happening here, then that could be the end of it. We need to get protests like this happening all around the world with the same ferocity as this one."

"I agree," said Jonny. "In Canada there are similar protests in Ottawa, Toronto, Halifax, Vancouver, I think. All over the place. But none are quite as big as Rome. And I feel like they are all somewhat dependent on Rome, like they feel Rome is the focus and the rest are just peripheral, so if this fails, they all will probably fail."

"That's exactly right," Nate said. "That's why we have to put more effort into organizing around the world. Any contacts we have we should use."

Although I can't remember what we said or what actions actually came of these conversations, I do remember feeling like we were connected to the entire world in such a way that we four, in that tiny hotel room, could really mobilize enough people to change the course of history. It was an incredible feeling of power. Not the kind that one person or group has over many, or that we had over the Mortals, but the kind of power that can only be experienced in a community.

Later, the same hotel room was filled shoulder to shoulder with activists Nate had collected from the square. Nate stood on a chair holding everyone's attention. "The most powerful person in the world is still dependent on the people over which he rules. The kind of action we are talking about here," he pointed his index finger forcefully to the floor, "is to recognize that their power is only possible because of us, it only exists within us, and can be taken away by us." Nate liked to give speeches like this. "The people have power to make their rulers bend the knee," he sometimes had a flare for the dramatic, "to make the richest beg, the strongest collapse. When we organize, nothing can stop us because all power comes either from the people's actions or their submission. If we act, we are the most powerful force on the planet. If we submit, we give that power away. We must never submit, comrades!"

Nate would often manage to rile people up. He'd give speeches like this on stages in front of thousands of people. They'd roar and hold up clenched fists. I'd roar also and extend my fist. Although he already had a great number of fans who enjoyed his novels, his reputation as an orator and leader of people began to grow with these speeches. It was exciting to see his passion explode from his slight frame, looking even smaller on a stage surrounded by thousands, and infect everyone whose ears were functioning. Even in his hotel room, we'd show up for our nightly visit often exhausted from the day only to be given a second burst of vigor as if his words were some incantation for a restoration spell.

Although I love to imagine these memories, for imagining them is the closest I will ever get to remembering them, they're all still tainted from my split allegiance. In fact, even while in Rome, while I was planning with my friends the next step to defy the enemy, I was also openly divulging all these plans to their enemy. You see, I had been recruited to betray my friends. It sounds more dramatic than it was; all I did was go out for lunch with a friend of mine from the OP, Larson, and we'd talk about my friends amongst many other things. I say it was all I did but the Devil, as they say, is in the details. The structure of these conversations was deliberate; it diminished the seriousness of the thing, made it more palatable. If they were to get me to write a report and place it under a park bench to be picked up by a man in a long, dark trench coat, I'd have felt like my actions were far more nefarious than I did. Instead, it felt to me, even though I knew exactly what I was doing, that I was just having a casual conversation with an old friend.

I'm still not entirely sure the exact reasons I did what I did. It was an amalgamation of many different things; fear, sense of duty, but I don't know if there was any one thing I can point to as the main starter. Doesn't matter now I suppose. No one can properly explain the real reasons any of us did what we did. But maybe cowardice doesn't need an explanation. Heroism does, which is likely why there are far fewer heroes than cowards in the world.

But fear was a major factor and something I want to take a moment to address because everyone was afraid back then. You must understand, at the time, it was quite terrifying for all of us. And this fear was cultivated by those who knew how to exploit it. Although, as I have already mentioned, the food shortages and multitudinous wars did not really affect us directly—they mostly occurred in countries whose names many couldn't pronounce—we were made to feel like they could spill over any moment if we didn't act soon. The fear was palpable. The Overman Project did an incredible job at propagating the idea that Immortals and well-off Mortals were at constant risk of being directly affected by the problems of poorer countries. We were led to believe that if we did nothing, we'd certainly fall victim to the troubles of the world and the Eternal Era would be the shortest, and most ironically titled, of any before it. So, if I did betray my friends for my own sake then it can be understood, I hope, that my fear, although we now know was not justified, was made to look as though it was justified.

I don't know if there were any other Immortals who behaved so duplicitously as I did. Maybe there are others like me who have been haunted by memories, wondering if everlasting life is worth it if it is accompanied with everlasting remorse. Am I the first person to think these things or just the first to act on them? What will happen after I'm gone? Will more people follow in my footsteps? Will the Mortal Revolution be reborn centuries after it had been so thoroughly suppressed?

I knew a few of us who held some deep sympathies for the Mortals. Many abandoned the Overman Project all together in order to show their support for the Mortal cause. There were ways you could tell if someone was secretly rooting for the other side, usually in their expression. Sympathizers would have a much different expression when they talked about them, one of concern, like they were thinking about a loved one who was unusually late coming home. The biggest give away was how they reacted when others were talking about them. Most Immortals who were fully backing the Overman Project would listen to a story about Mortals like they were hearing a story about a rodent infestation. They had an immediate air of superiority about them, their noses all aimed a little higher, the corners of their mouths dipped down as if fishhooks with weights attached to them were pulling on either side. It was so apparent that I was never sure if they were intentionally trying to make their faces look like that, to show their solidarity with other Mortal-haters, or if their disdain was so entrenched that it was an involuntary reaction. Sympathizers were much different, though. Even if they were trying to hide the fact that they were in support of Mortal rights, you could still tell by the way they listened so intently to their stories. They would laugh at the funny bits, ask follow-up questions, and remember their names. They would basically treat them the same way they would treat Immortals.

Chapter 14 ~ Whispers of Revolution

Nate's work became increasingly political. It's odd since he never had a natural interest in politics. Growing up, if I were to ever ask him about politics, I'm sure he'd have shrugged and asked for a proper definition of the word. It's not that he didn't care, he always had strong opinions about certain issues, but he was more interested in bigger ideas. "Politics are regional, cultural, they don't encompass any universal truths about the world. I want to write about things that are important now but also things that have been important in the past and will be in the future. I want to write about things that transcend cultures, creeds, politics. Something that's relatable to all humanity. The Human Spirit, you might say." He said the reason he became political wasn't because he found a previously dormant interest in the topic but that he gradually became so angry that he simply couldn't help himself. "Anger is a fabulous motivator," he'd say. He never enjoyed politics, admitting it put him in increasingly bad moods, but he felt trying to ignore it would put him in worse moods. He started to write essays in political magazines, something I never would've dreamt of him doing before, and his novels were becoming more and more blatantly political. His last few books were never published due to censorship. One depicted an alternative history in which, instead of immortality, everyone was granted longevity. Instead of some living to ninety-years-old while others live forever, everyone's average lifespan was about 200-300 years. A sort of compromise. In this world everyone was equal, and no group had to be subjugated to obtain equality. One character in the book says "Equality is not worth it if the only path to it is through unprecedented inequality. World peace cannot come from world war, love cannot come from hate."

During this period there were multiple intervals in which my luncheons with Larson would cease and I could support my friend's without feeling like a liar or double agent. But these moments were always fleeting. Eventually Larson would return, and I would be forced to resume my weekly betrayals.

Larson had a calm yet disinterested demeanor. He usually seemed as though he was lazily drifting through our encounters with his mind, not on something else, but not immediately present, either. It was as though he didn't want to be having these luncheons but didn't have anything else to do either. His indifference made it easier to talk to him as I often felt that whatever I told him would be forgotten before he had a chance to report it to his superiors. His appearance reflected his demeanor. His hair was sandy, curly, and styled just enough for him to be able to make credible a claim of effort. He had also a long, red goatee which I believe he grew only so he would have less face to shave.

"How are things?" he asked in his warm, casual way.

"Fine. For the most part. Of course, I've been busy but aren't we all these days."

"It's true, very true. Not enough hours in a day and not enough days in a week and all that."

And then, after our food arrived, we'd talk in between bites.

"Have you been watching any good movies lately, anything interesting?" The words drifted out of his mouth as if he were speaking in sighs.

"I have," I'd say with a mouthful and then nod rhythmically until I had swallowed as if my nodding reassured him that I had more to say. "I've been watching a lot of old film noir, black and white films from the dark ages."

"Really?" was all he would say followed by a forkful of scrambled eggs.

"Yeah, it started when I watched Casablanca with some friends," it would have been Nate and Marie, but I never talked about them to Larson except when I had to, "and loved Humphrey Bogart."

Swallow. "What a name, eh." Another forkful.

I had my own forkful of gradually cooling eggs hovering between my mouth and the plate, but his incessant questions kept them from reaching their final destination. "Yeah, it was a different time I guess—different time, different names." The eggs began their ascent ...

"You were saying, though?"

...and then returned to the plate. "Yeah, so I watched Casablanca and really liked it."

"Great film." Another bite.

"You've seen it?"

"I've been told."

"Anyway, from there I started to watch other Bogart films which eventually led to other film noir."

"Is Casablanca considered film noir?"

I dropped my fork to my plate, "You know, I'm not sure."

"How does one define film noir?" he lay his cutlery on his empty plate and pushed it away from himself.

"I'm just realizing how little I know about the topic."

This would continue until I had managed, somehow, to finish my meal, although it was only achieved through a series of perfectly sized bites intermixed with perfectly timed questions and responses. We'd have a cup of tea or coffee and talk more of asinine things. But right before we were done, after we had received the bill, he'd ask how my friends were. We both knew what this meant.

The way he would do it was this: he'd keep his eyes on the bill in his hand, trying to calculate the tip. I knew what he was about to ask me. I knew exactly what he wanted me to say. And I knew exactly what I'd say. But I don't think I ever volunteered the information. I always made him ask.

"So how are Nate and Marie?" He would ask just like that as if they were old friends of his he hadn't seen in a while. But also, with such nonchalance that it often felt as though he wasn't even listening. He'd always seem too distracted by the bill in his hand or the people walking past the window or the perpetually swinging kitchen door that creaked whenever a waiter hurried through. But I knew he was listening. And I would tell him everything.

"They've organized a protest this Saturday at the Parliament building ..." or something like that. I can't remember what I used to tell him. It doesn't matter.

Nate's reputation as a political activist and dissident continued to grow which meant the threat of repercussions grew as well. Many people started to get arrested for their activism, often on dubious charges. This is about the time that the first rumor of the now infamous internment camps began to surface. At first, no one was sure they were real. Many had heard from a friend whose distant relative knew someone in the military who told them that they were being built. Many dismissed the stories as just rumor, but the rumor persisted until they were heard from a friend whose distant cousin's friend was sent to a camp, and then a friend whose wife's friend was sent to a camp, and then from a friend whose brother was sent to a camp until finally everyone knew someone, or at the very least someone who knew someone, who had been arrested unexpectedly and whose whereabouts were completely unknown.

When the rumor of the camps started to become substantiated by actual evidence, often by the work of journalists who were swiftly sent to the very camps they worked to expose, the word revolution began to appear on everyone's lips. Our hotel rooms were suddenly cramped with more people and our talks were suddenly more heated. People had myriad views on how, when, and what form the revolution should take. Many talked of violence, which as we all know became a common tool, many others talked of more peaceful sit-ins, protests, and other forms of civil disobedience.

"A violent response would be to play right into their hands. They want more excuses to put us in those camps," Nate said having to yell above a raucous gathering who somehow managed to squeeze themselves into the room. The door was open, and people spilled out into the hallway. "If we attack them, they can paint us as violent extremists or terrorists and it would be very difficult to argue against that charge. Right now we have almost every human rights group in the world on our side. We have to keep them on our—"

"Those groups don't give a shit about us," said an angry young man who managed to raise his high-pitched voice over everyone else's. "We all know that."

"Of course they do," a woman's voice soared above the noise. "That is their only job, to care about us."

"We're getting off track," Nate yelled with his hands in the air, trying to quiet the room. "The point is violence—"

"Violence is the only thing their afraid of," yelled another. "They will live forever as long as something doesn't kill them."

People started shouting louder but it was impossible to know if they were agreeing or disagreeing.

Another stood on the bed suddenly as if he were about to yell eureka. "He's got a point. All they have to differentiate themselves from us is the length of their lives. If we shorten them, they'll be just like us."

A collective "Yeah," shook the walls of the hotel.

"We're not killing anyone," someone, possibly Nate, yelled. "That's not an option."

"No. We won't kill them. But if we can convince them that we will start killing if we don't get what we want …" It was impossible to know who was speaking at any given moment now.

A few more shouted, "Yeah."

"If we beat the piss out of a few of them, make them fear for their lives—"

"How many would you have to threaten like that to make them change? Thousands. But you'll never get to that many because just one violent action on our part could be enough to—" He was cut off again. The shouting erupted in multiple corners of the room making it impossible for any conversation to be heard. No strategy was agreed upon that night.

***

A few weeks, later Nate was taken away from his hotel room in Berlin. It all started when I heard a commotion from Nate and Marie's room which was next door to mine. I quickly jumped out of bed and popped my head into the hall where I saw a group of policemen standing at their open door. I could hear Nate's and Marie's voices yelling from inside their room and ascertained there were more police inside. Soon, Jonny's door, which was adjacent to mine, flew open and he was standing in the hallway with a red face and clenched fists and teeth.

"The fuck is all this?"

Kara soon appeared behind him in the doorway bouncing a crying James in her arms and rubbing her tired eyes. "Jon? What's going on?"

Our regular group of shouting, arm-waving protesters were away shouting and waving their arms in some other city. We had only come to Berlin to attend an art exhibit, the theme of which was civil disobedience, although no actual civil disobedience was planned. Nate was scheduled to speak but Jonny, Kara, Marie and I were the only others who followed him. This is why the police were able to arrest Nate without having to fight through a hallway crowded with angry and possibly violent men and women. They must have planned it that way. Any other night and they wouldn't even have made it to their hotel room door.

"Please get back into your room," an officer said, with two thumbs tucked into his utility belt.

"Don't tell me what to do. That's my fucking brother and that's my sister-in-law," Jonny shouted. The officer stuck out the palm of his hand as if he was stopping traffic. "Nate. Nate." Jonny began to yell. There were four police officers between the brothers, so Jonny stretched to see over them. Nate turned his head towards his brother's shouting and held out a hand to calm him down. Despite his attempts to remain calm himself he couldn't keep his fear from showing itself in his features. "Nate," Jonny continued. "We'll figure this shit out. Don't worry, they can't do this. We'll figure this out." It was odd hearing Jonny try to reassure his older brother after years of Nate doing that for him.

"Could you just tell us what's going on?" I asked trying to keep my voice from betraying a burning fury that had suddenly began to bubble up inside me. He assured me that they were just taking him in for questioning. I knew I wouldn't get any more information from them so I retreated to my room where I rang Larson, my *lunch-mate*, the only contact in the OP I could think of at the moment.

"Why are they taking him," I shouted into the phone.

"I don't know what you're talking about. Where are you right now?"

"You always know where I am. What do you mean where am I?"

"You're in the hotel with them now?"

"Yeah, of course."

"I'll see if there is anything I can do."

There was nothing he could do and any efforts he made were futile. All he could do was tell me he'd try which is all I could do for Nate. He knew this and I knew this already. I don't know why I bothered to call. I guess I still wanted to believe the Overmen wouldn't just arrest a man for voicing his opinion.

I hung up the phone and returned to the hallway. Jonny had taken James from Kara and Kara was trying to comfort a sobbing Marie who watched her handcuffed husband being taken away in a sea of uniformed police officers.

Chapter 15 ~ Quite the Reaction

What everyone feared most was that Nate was taken to a camp, never to be heard from again. What I feared most was that I was at least partly to blame.

The response to Nate's arrest was immediate and loud. Protests were organized all throughout Berlin which began to spread to other major cities throughout the world. His following suddenly grew exponentially. People all over the world were talking about the novelist who was arrested for his activism. His book sales were up, his portrait was seen on magazine covers and painted on the side of walls, and his name was suddenly familiar to everyone who was involved in the cause. Protesters would chant, "Where is Nat Karski? Where is Nat Karski?" For some reason they decided to drop the e from his nickname. It never took amongst his friends who held up signs with his face in all manner of colors and artistic styles. His face became a symbol and his name a slogan.

One portrait of him became particularly popular. It was designed by some famous graffiti artist who used a photo of Nate with a despondent expression on his face for inspiration. In the photo Nate is looking directly at the camera with sad eyes, incredulous, hopeless. It can still be easily found with just a quick internet search. The thing about the picture is I can't remember Nate ever making an expression like that, at least not regularly enough for it to be captured in such a perfectly framed photograph. I've never been able to find any expression or mention of such an expression in any of my photos, journals, or videos of him, at least not any in which he was being at all serious. Nate was, more than anyone I knew then or have known since, unwaveringly optimistic. He was often angered and sympathetic, even sad, but he was never hopeless. My theory as to the origin of the photo is that he was probably messing about with Marie. I've seen them do it. I have many photos which were the result of these moments. They would make faces at each other and snap photos. They would sometimes manipulate the photos to look distorted or they would add features like moustaches, wild hair, etc. I believe the photo used for this piece of recruitment propaganda was not an actual photograph of Nate looking hopeless but of Nate *pretending* to look hopeless. I'm sure after taking the photo, Marie immediately added a top hat and monocle or something of the sort. How that artist managed to obtain it is beyond me. It was useful though, I think, for recruiting more people to the cause. Symbols are powerful things; the origin of the symbols rarely matters.

About a month after Nate's disappearance I was back in Winnipeg and received a call from Larson. I asked him immediately where Nate was, but he said we would talk about it over lunch. I thought it was strange that he asked me to meet at a different restaurant than we normally did and at a different time. The place at which we agreed to meet was far from where I lived but I decided to walk to clear my head. I happened to pass by a large protest on my way and noticed many of the protesters were holding signs with Nate's face on them.

Larson wanted a more low-key meeting place, so he picked one in a less ostentatious part of the city to put it mildly. The street was full of potholes, the sidewalks were strewn with litter. I saw several plastic grocery bags that would dance spasmodically through the air every time a car sped past.

When I arrived at the spot, I could see Larson through the window from the sidewalk. He had already ordered a coffee and a plate of multigrain toast which appeared untouched. He caught sight of me through the glass door before I entered and stood. He looked agitated. When I sat down, he began talking to me immediately about Nate. There was no asking about my week, or what films I had recently watched. He looked concerned. But he also looked like he trusted me.

"I need ideas from you," he said quickly, and I could see that his knee was bouncing so much it caused his voice to bounce as well. I also noticed his hair was more dishevelled than usual as if the little amount of effort he normally put into it was time he couldn't waste.

"First, where's Nate?" I said, trying to remember that Larson was the enemy and forced myself to speak harshly like I was a cop in an interrogation.

"I don't know where, but I know he's fine. He's looked after." For some reason I believed him.

"A couple things. First, you may not know this, but you have a good reputation with the agency." *The agency* was shorthand for the Public Protection Agency, the intelligence branch of the Overman Project in Canada. "I'm just a messenger, a middleman. There's nothing I can do to help Nate, but you can. The Director will listen to you. However, you'll probably have to do something for him in exchange."

"What are you talking about? If Nate's not guilty of a crime, then he should be released regardless of what I do."

"In their eyes he is guilty. He's guilty of inciting violence, anti-immortal sentiments—"

"Anti-immortal sentiments? Violence?"

"I'm not saying these things, they are. I'm just letting you know what those who are holding him are thinking. And if they really do believe he's guilty then it's going to take some effort on your part to get him released."

I was being used. What I realized after the fact, but not at the time, was that Nate would have been released regardless of what I'd done. The enormity of the reaction to Nate's arrest was something the OP did not anticipate and would do anything to put a stop to. They had tried to silence someone but had instead made a martyr of the man. They knew that they had no choice but to release him, they were just trying to figure out how to go about it. And more importantly, they were trying to figure out what they could gain from his release. What they got was me. Or more of me.

I reluctantly agreed to help in any way I could.

"Very good." Larson, leaned back in his chair, seemingly satisfied, although still somewhat agitated. "What I need you to do is give me more information."

"About Nate? But you have him."

"Not Nate. Marie."

"Why her?"

"Why do you think? She's a journalist. Her entire job is to snoop. We need to know what information she's been collecting and what she plans on doing with that information."

"How do I go about that?"

"I don't care. Just collect it and give it to me."

"Okay." I nodded my head sheepishly and found myself unable to look Larson in the eyes. "And if I do this Nate will be released?"

"If you do this, we'll do what we can. But if you do this, and report only to me, the rest of your friends will be much safer. Do *not* report any of this to anyone else. Understand?" He said this last bit slowly and deliberately. A few days later I began to understand why for that's when the Tall Man showed up in my life.

The Tall Man visited me at home, the loathsome brute. He showed up in the afternoon without warning. He knocked and when I answered he curtly introduced himself as an agent without ever showing me identification. He never even told me his name. He was tall, hence my unimaginative nick name for him, slim, clean shaven, and wore an expensive looking suit. He wore a brown, brimmed hat, which he never bothered to remove, but I could tell he was completely bald underneath. He invited himself in and sat in my armchair as if he was relaxing at home and *I* was the intrusive guest.

"What did Larson tell you?" he asked, staring intently at me and sitting with perfect posture.

"You're from … the Public Protection Agency?"

"Yes," he said, looking annoyed at having to explain any more about his identity. He then laid his black and gold badge on the coffee table for me to see and left it there for the duration of our conversation as if it, too, was listening to my every word.

"Well." I removed my coat and hung it in the closet. "He told me to collect information about some people."

"Good. Do that."

I began cautiously walking towards the couch where he was sitting. "Do that?" I said confused. "Of course, I'll do that." I suddenly felt more confident than I should have. "That happens to be exactly what I had already planned on doing." I sat in an armchair across from him. "So, I guess you're wasting your time, aren't you," I said, trying to return his stare with the same intensity but was not successful.

He smiled in a way that made me want to squirm in my seat, like the very sight of him was enough to catch some sort of parasitic worm. "After you report everything to Mr. Larson," he went on, ignoring my pathetic attempts at intimidation, "you will then meet me right here in your living room where I will debrief you."

"Why?"

"You can't possibly expect an answer to that question." He stood up, picking up the badge and sliding it into his jacket pocket. "I'll be waiting here after every meeting." He walked to the door. "I'm sure I don't need to say this, but Larson cannot know about our meetings. Clear?"

"Of course."

He put a hand on the doorknob before turning to me once more. "I spoke to your friend Mr. Karski the other day. Your actions can have either a positive or negative effect on his circumstances. Don't be stupid."

I nodded sheepishly, conceding his power over me.

I did exactly what the Tall Man asked. I knew what was going on. Larson was likely a sympathizer, like me, and was now under investigation; this made us quite the odd couple then, I thought. After every meeting I'd walk back to my apartment with knots in my stomach hoping that just this once the Tall Man wouldn't be there but every time he was, standing next to my door, standing so straight that his left side seemed to perfectly mirror his right, like a photo altered to appear unnaturally symmetrical. There was never a hand in a pocket or one foot in front of the other, just this unnerving posture.

Most meetings I had with Larson resulted in little to report. Most things regarding articles Marie was writing meant little since those articles would be published the next day or two for all to see anyway. But after a month or two I reported to him a paper that Marie was writing, in which she mentions a "source" that had given her an alarming amount of information detailing an internment camp located somewhere in Northern Africa. I didn't tell him anything more than that, but it caused his eyes to widen and, while maintaining his usual phlegmatic air, asked me to tell him more, something I simply couldn't do.

"I'm sorry, old boy," he said appearing genuinely sympathetic, "but I'm afraid I'm going to have to ask you to get more information on that." He spoke so jovially that I found myself thinking of him as an old friend. "This could be a serious breach in security. If this source has already leaked information then, he or she will likely leak more, and if that happens, we could all find ourselves in somewhat of an awkward position."

"So, the internment camps are real?" I asked which seemed to catch him quite off guard.

"Listen," I could tell by the sound of his voice that he was uncharacteristically flustered. "Just find out as much as you can. And please, for the sake of the Overmen, for the sake of your friends, be discrete."

"Of course."

The Tall Man, that dead-eyed automaton, was waiting for me when I returned to the apartment. Sitting down in my living room he asked what he always did.

"I told Mr. Larson that Marie was busy writing a column on the possible existence of an internment camp in Northern Africa."

"Which camp would that be?" he asked robotically.

I was about to answer truthfully but my conscience suddenly appeared and stopped me, like a friend pushing me out of the way of incoming traffic. I can't explain why my conscience decided to appear then and there except that my increasingly favorable opinion of Larson was so juxtaposed to my increasingly low opinion of the Tall Man that one finally beat the other in the battle of loyalty. "No idea," I said and felt an immediate jolt of panic. But I managed to keep it down. "I don't think she knows either. I heard her talking and it seems as though her information is based solely on rumor."

"Rumors?"

"That's right." I felt my face grow red and found myself struggling to maintain eye contact.

"Is she prone to reporting rumors in her articles?"

"I think her argument will be, ah," I swallowed to buy time to think, "that these rumors have become much more frequent and so might merit at least a mention if not an investigation."

"Does she have any contacts in Africa?"

"Not that I know of."

"Find out."

"Of course."

"Anything else?"

"No."

"And Mr. Larson?"

"Nothing unusual. He asked a few more questions about the article, but ... um, nothing really more than what you just asked."

He nodded, stood up, and made his way out the door without saying another word.

I decided to trust Larson over the Tall Man. It was a huge risk but something about Larson's demeanor made me *want* to trust him and, more importantly, believing he was on my side gave me courage to face the Tall Man. I found out as much as I could about Marie's contact in Africa and passed that information only to Larson. The contact, it turned out, was originally a low-ranking member of a security unit in the American branch of the Overman Project. After proving herself supremely competent, she was offered a high-ranking position at the camp which was located near a military outpost in Egypt. Although the position was more prestigious and came with a much more impressive paycheck, she quickly became disillusioned first with the isolation—apparently, she was quite the socialite back in America—and then with the treatment of the prisoners. She admitted that her empathy for the prisoners developed only after her antipathy towards her superiors reached its zenith but once it made an appearance, it became her primary motivator. She reportedly confessed in a correspondence with her publisher, "If I had never grown to hate *them*, the Overmen, I probably never would have felt so much for *them*—the prisoners."

"Have you told anyone else about this?" Larson's face was strained with worry, an unnerving sight considering his usual demeanor.

"Of course not."

"Does Marie know you have this information?"

"Yes, of course. She told this all to me."

"Why would she do that?"

"Because she trusts me."

Larson didn't respond to that statement, but his expression told me he found my actions at that moment reprehensible.

Marie's contact, as far as I know, was never found out. Who she was is anyone's guess, but I was right to trust Larson and distrust the Tall Man. Unfortunately, my constant meetings with the Tall Man did not cease. But that's enough about him for now.

Chapter 16 ~ Homecoming

Nate was unceremoniously released a short time later. One early morning he was simply dropped off at his apartment. Marie was inside still sleeping when he knocked on the door. She answered cautiously, possibly thinking that someone had come to take her away.

I received a phone call from Marie later that day telling me Nate was back. Like her I had trouble believing it and asked to talk to him.

"He's sleeping now. He's …" I heard a tremor in her voice. "… a bit shaken up. Why don't you come over in an hour?"

I couldn't wait an hour, so I left my apartment with the intention of killing the hour with a walk. My legs, however, insisted on accelerating as if they weren't my legs but a jittery horse I couldn't rein in and before I knew it, I was nearly sprinting and felt incapable of slowing down. When I was too tired to run any longer, I'd slow to a walk but as soon as my body had recovered my legs began charging forwards on their own accord. I arrived after only half an hour. The thought of waiting for the other half to pass before I knocked on their door seemed an impossible task and so I hardly considered it. As soon as I saw their door I had to see if Nate was on the other side. I knocked loudly, louder than I should have but my body was exhausted from running and had lost all capacity for subtle movements.

When the door opened Nate was standing in front of me, having just woken from his nap. He had a blanket wrapped around him. His face was gaunt and pale, but he smiled warmly when he saw me.

"It *is* you," I said, still standing in the doorway as if I honestly thought the news of his release were a cruel prank.

"Come in," Nate motioned with his arm for me to come inside. "And close the door behind you."

We hugged for a long time. I was so glad to see him again. I didn't cry but I wanted to.

"What happened?" I said.

"Not a lot really." He talked as we walked into his living room and sat down, me on the couch and him on a large and comfortable looking computer chair. I could see Marie in the kitchen making some tea and sandwiches. "They kept me in a cell. It wasn't uncomfortable. They interrogated me a few times, asking if I had any connections to terrorist activities, bombings, propaganda, stuff like that."

"They never took you to a camp?"

"No. I was in Berlin the entire time. I think they began to second guess their decision moments after they made it."

"I thought you were gone."

"So did I to be honest. I was terrified. Absolutely terrified. I still can't believe I'm back in my living room. I was only away for a couple months but all this already felt like a distant memory." He ran his fingers along the arm of his chair. "Like this was all out of reach. Like, I could never be me again. My whole identity from now on was going to be a prisoner. I thought it was over. Everything." He waved a hand through the air and gave a subtle frown.

It was obvious he was dealing with a varied mix of emotions. I'm sure he was simultaneously feeling ecstatic, angry, relieved, anxious, and who knows what else. But the emotion that manifested most prominently in his features was melancholy.

I thought I'd try to cheer him up. "The reaction though," I said, shaking my head as if I still didn't believe it, "wow. I think it forced them to reconsider. I've never seen anything like it. You have a lot of dedicated fans. Probably a lot more now." He didn't seem cheered. But he didn't seem annoyed either, so I kept talking. "And now that you've been released people are celebrating in the streets."

"I don't know about that."

"The Prime Minister gave a speech welcoming you home"

"No, he didn't." Nate finally cracked a smile.

"Perhaps not." I smiled facetiously. "But people are counting this as a victory. And I must agree with them. This is a major victory, a possible game changer. We basically forced them to admit they made a mistake."

Nate's smile vanished. "They won't see it that way. They'll spin it some other way. They'll say that they were only holding me for questioning and had no intention of sending me anywhere. Or if they do admit to making a mistake, they will use this as an example of how willing they are to admit when they are wrong so all the times they don't admit they are wrong is because they simply aren't. This isn't a victory. Or if it is it's an insignificant one."

"But we showed what the people would do if they worked together, if they organize. We showed them, like you're always saying, that their power depends on us."

Marie entered the room and laid a tray of sandwiches on the table then disappeared back into the kitchen to retrieve the tea.

"We did. But we showed them we would only organize if they take away someone with a high profile. The Overmen have been abusing people for years and they didn't organize for them. Are they going to continue to organize and protest now that I've been released? Thinking that this is a victory is just going to give us an opportunity to pat ourselves on the back and go home. We shouldn't think of this as a victory but as one barely significant step towards a victory. We have miles to go." It was strange seeing Nate so cynical.

Marie returned with the tea. "But darling," she began while laying the tray next to the sandwiches and sitting beside her husband, "sometimes it doesn't matter why people make a fuss, just as long as a fuss is made. Because of you, thousands of people organized one of the biggest fusses in recent memory."

"Yes, and I appreciate that. And I hope that their efforts continue, and we experience more successes. But I can't shake the feeling that the Overmen have learnt a lot more from this than we did."

"I hear what you're saying. We don't have to talk about this now," I said sensing he was finding the conversation distressing. "I'm just glad you're home now. Now that you're back, we have loads of time to figure out how to make that next step."

"That's how we're all feeling right now," Marie said. "We're just happy he's back." She looked at me in a way that seemed to ask me to keep the conversation light. "I think we should have a party to celebrate though, eh?"

I nodded. "Yes, that would definitely be in order," I tried to sound jovial, but I couldn't carry on the act when I saw the despondent, distant look on Nate's face. I noticed Marie watching him, too, and when she looked at me for a moment, we both wordlessly shared with each other our concern.

"Would you like that, darling?" Marie asked to break Nate from his deep abstraction.

"Hmmm?" he said, as he turned to her realizing he had been momentarily lost in his thoughts.

"A party. We were thinking we should have a party to celebrate. Would you like that?"

"Yes, of course," he said seeming to have returned to the here and now. "That'd be lovely."

For weeks after his release Marie and I tried to produce some hope in Nate that the worst of this was over. We showed him news reports and brought him to dinners at which he was an honored guest, but nothing could shake him from the belief that there was something unspeakable about to happen. His experience as a detainee seemed to have convinced him that far from winning a major victory we were all, in fact, standing on the precipice of some great horror which only he had glimpsed and we were too oblivious to believe him when he admonished us to tread lightly.

Chapter 17 ~ A Mild Aftermath

Despite the camps remaining operational, the Overman Project did back off a bit and for a while it seemed that people stopped disappearing entirely. There were stories of people even reappearing, although I never encountered any of them. The Overmen were still, after all, denying the camps' existence … or at least avoiding the topic. The Overman Project also began opening avenues of communication between themselves and Mortal communities as a way to "explain themselves" in such a way that would make their point of view intelligible while simultaneously "making strides to repair relations with the Mortal community."

Although many saw this sudden and unexpected turnaround on the part of the Overmen as some sort of proverbial handshake, anyone with a bit of skepticism was able to see through it. The Overmen did not actually care about repairing relations with the Mortal community, something that is so obvious now when we look back it is difficult to understand how anyone fell for the ploy. All they were doing was letting things cool down before it all exploded in their faces. The reactions were varied. Many of our closest friends continued to protest with us, refusing to accept anything than a formal admission to the existence and complete shutdown of the camps, equal rights for Mortals, and proper representation in government positions. Others broke off into different groups deciding that our tactics weren't sufficient. But most chose to believe the Overmen or at the very least tried their hardest to believe them.

What they were really doing was hoping beyond all reason that the horror that had been slowly creeping out of their nightmares and into their reality was finally over. They were simply too scared. They believed taking Nate was wrong and, of course, they believed taking anyone and putting them in a prison camp was wrong, but they were terrified that what was being said was true. They believed that if the world's governments allowed unchecked procreation to continue, they'd all starve or be killed by people trying to escape starvation. This fear was often disguised as pragmatism, but it only fooled those willing to be fooled. They weren't bad people, though, just scared people. I guess that's why it was so easy to believe that the Overmen were willing to make amends; some people wanted the horror to end so badly that they were willing to believe anything if it provided some alleviation.

Reuben, I believe, was truly afraid. He was stupid but he was not a hateful person, despite my dislike for the man. I believe he really loved his Mortal friends, just not as much as he loved himself. He knew Nate since kindergarten and would be devastated if anything happened to him. But I don't think he was able to reconcile his fear with his love.

***

We held a party at Nate and Marie's to welcome Nate home not long after his release. It was a packed house, full of friends of ours from university, fellow protesters, and many other random people such as the gentleman who ran Nate's favorite shawarma shop. Reuben was also there. I remember his reaction at seeing Nate alive and well. He looked so relieved one might have thought it was he who escaped internment. He shook Nate's hand and hugged him tightly and I believe he may have even cried. But later, after the party had been in full swing for some time, I saw another look on his face, just as intense but much different. He looked as though he was hanging off the gunwales of a sinking ship and wasn't sure if he should let go or hang on. It was a look of terror which he tried futilely to hide beneath a calm, content façade.

I spoke to him briefly during the night. He was standing by himself, watching everyone like a security guard monitoring a potential shoplifter. I only talked to him because our eyes happened to meet while I was standing too close to him to escape.

"How're things?" he said, forcing me to walk closer to him and commit to a conversation.

"Good. Very good. Now that's he's back." I motioned to Nate who I could see was sitting on the couch surrounded by a large crowd.

"Yeah," Reuben said, bobbing his head up and down and then when he couldn't think of anything to say began taking long, drawn out sips from his tumbler.

"Well," I began and was about to follow with, "I'm going to grab a drink," and politely walk away. But before I could finish my sentence Reuben thought of something to say and blurted out, "Do you think anything's going to change? I mean, after all this fuss over him?"

I sighed and accepted the fact that I was going to have to suffer through a chit-chat with this pathetic little man. "Do I think anything's going to change?" I repeated his words to give me time to consider. "Ah, I doubt it, if I'm honest. It's great that Nate's been released but I don't think the OP is now going to pursue an agenda of equality. They're just pumping the breaks a bit until everyone is convinced they're going to change. And then things will return to how they were."

"That's what I think, too." I was hoping that would be enough but then he asked, "And what about the food shortages. They say that they're so bad across Africa and the Middle East they're starting to creep into Europe. They say they're getting so bad that if nothing's done, we're going to see a flood of desperate refugees appearing on our shores. And if that happens, we'll see those same food shortages here. Won't we?"

I was getting the feeling that he didn't want me to give him my opinion but was hoping I would say something that might calm his nerves. "I don't know, man. It's a complicated issue. I think there's a lot that can be done, a lot better and probably more effective things than what the OP is alleged to be doing."

"Like what?"

"Well, the problem of course isn't actually food quantity but food distribution." As I talked, I began to feel something growing inside my chest, restricting my breathing. I realized like an infectious disease I might be contracting Reuben's anxiety. "There's more than enough food in the world, it just isn't getting to the people who need it." The longer I stood next to him, engaging with him, the more the feeling grew. I kept talking, displaying all my knowledge on the subject but even my own arguments were unable to dispel the feeling that I might be wrong and if I were wrong the Overmen were right. "That's why we organize," I continued but my voice didn't sound like me anymore. It began to shake, and the pitch rose, and I hated the sound of it because it sounded to me like Reuben's trembling contralto. "I think it's likely that the OP is using the fear and uncertainty to their advantage. They want to prevent Mortals like Nate from having children. This whole business of overpopulation and famine and floods of immigrants is just to keep people scared enough to allow them to do what they want." When I finished speaking, I felt my entire body was trembling.

"But you still work for the Overmen, don't you?"

"Well, we have to don't we."

"We don't have to. There's no law saying we must."

"It's complicated, I suppose. There are many different sides to the Overman Project. I like to think I work with the less malignant sides." Talking to him, every word that passed over my tongue tasted disgusting to me. "Look, I should go over there and see how Nate's doing."

"Sure," Reuben looked even more terrified now than he did when I started talking to him and I knew exactly what he was thinking. I knew because he was thinking the same thing I was. He was thinking my explanation didn't matter; he was thinking the facts didn't matter and he would do anything to quell the horrible fear.

As I made my way over to Nate something struck me as odd. The party, although filled with many of the same faces that normally appeared at these gatherings, was quieter, like everyone was speaking in hushed tones. Like they were afraid someone might hear them. Everyone seemed to be infected with the same thing Reuben, and now I, was.

I spent the rest of the night sitting with Nate, Marie, Jonny and Kara. We sat on several chairs and couches which had been arranged haphazardly around a coffee table upon which was a mess of glasses, bottles, all of which had varying degrees of liquid in them, and small plates with varying amounts of bite-sized food. Nate wasn't very talkative. He sat surrounded by admirers and friends all of whom wanted a moment to talk to him, but his mind was elsewhere. Possibly still in that jail cell, still unable to compute the events of the last few months.

"I'm just glad you're here now," said a man who had fully saturated himself in Nate's melancholy. "We thought we'd lost you there." He slapped Nate's knee. Nate responded with a forced smile and an acknowledging nod.

"Me, too, man," said another. "I don't know what we would have done without you."

Nate gave him the same response.

"Shall we have a toast?" someone else suggested but abandoned the idea when no one seemed up for it.

"What are your plans now?" another asked.

"Um, the same," Nate answered before immediately returning to what was going on in his head.

This was the way of things for the entire evening. People tried to engage him but Nate, being unable to engage, only gave short vague answers. Finally, after a couple hours of this, Nate unexpectedly let out a groan and stood up stiff and slowly like he was already a frail old man.

"Everything all right?" someone asked. "If you need anything just ask.

"Yeah, I just need a walk. Some fresh air, ya know. Marie, would you like to ..." he motioned with his head to the door. "Of course, darling." The feeling of disappointment from everyone else not asked to join him was palpable. Jonny must have noticed this, too, because he looked at me and grinned uncomfortably.

After Nate and Marie had left the apartment and Kara had excused herself to check up on a sleeping James, Jonny leapt from his seat to the empty one next to me and whispered, still grinning, "That was all very uncomfortable, eh?"

"Well, he needs more time," I whispered back and smiled at the few who remained seated. "Everyone's so happy to have him back and they all want to talk to him, but he's too easily overwhelmed now."

"Of course," Jonny said, continuing to whisper and smile and nod at anyone who looked our way. "I think he's happy to *be* back. But I also think he's *not* enjoying his newfound celebrity status. He's sitting here with an expression on his face like he just found out his parents were siblings."

"He was already a celebrity."

"But I mean, he's starting to realize that these people care more about him than they do the person sitting next to them. Isn't that the opposite of what he wanted?" He shook his head and sipped from his beer bottle. "But he's all right my brother. He just needs time. Time to think. Time to process. Mostly though he needs time to breathe. These fuckers love him; they're all here just to see him. But until he gets his mind sorted and put in order, they're all going to have to accept the fact that he's not Nathaniel Karski the writer and socialite, he's Nathaniel Karski the mind-fucked ex-prisoner."

Nate and Marie stayed away for almost the entire party, returning only when most of the guests had already left. He didn't say much after he arrived and didn't stay up long much to the disappointment of everyone who had waited for his return, myself included. He went to bed and, according to Marie, didn't leave it until the next evening.

This didn't last forever. That famous writer and socialite slowly began to return to replace the ex-prisoner, although it took nearly half a year before that transition became obvious. But he did eventually begin to resemble his old self again. Slowly his eyes began to twinkle and his smile, I mean his genuine smile, began to take as little effort as it once did. And when he had fully recovered, or at least as much as he ever was going to, he wasted no time.

Chapter 18 ~ Activists, Rioters, Bombers, and Militants

The Overman Project, as predicted, never repealed its laws against procreation leading many Mortals, like Jonny and Kara, to have children illegally. Other promises such as their assertion that there would be reforms in the police force and the other branches of government either never came to fruition or, if they did, the reforms were counterbalanced by empowering other areas of government towards the same end. For example, the capacity of the police forces was in fact reduced, but at the same time the Public Protection Agency was granted far more power. And, of course, eventually the RCMP was absorbed by the Agency.

Over the years we met and cultivated relationships with many activists and dissidents from all over the world. Initially, we all seemed to have a similar goal, although many varied ideas were tossed round, which was, like many social movements before, based around the pursuit of equality through peaceful, non-violent means. These involved protests, art, and simply pleading with influential people. But after a while we'd run into someone whom we had not seen and would be shocked at how far they had removed themselves from those initial ideals. Some had begun to embrace violent protests which meant that instead of marching with signs or conducting a sit-in in a government office or chaining oneself to some piece of machinery or fence surrounding a property, they'd riot, throw bricks, and smash windows, and light cars on fire. This type of behavior was often met with a wall of police and clouds of tear gas. The rioters justified their behavior by claiming, somewhat accurately if I'm honest, that peaceful protests didn't seem to be working.

Others began forming underground groups in which they'd bomb empty buildings or assault influential people. They were much more organized than their rioting counterparts as one can expect from a group that consciously chooses to handle highly explosive substances. These bombers were met with international investigations and a poor public image. They justified their behavior by repeating the words of the rioters while adding that rioting alone, although often able to make headlines, was too easily passed off as the product of raging miscreants who should not be taken seriously. The bombers would be taken seriously because they were handling bombs which caused serious damage. The last class of resistor, the one that was arguably more serious than the bombers, were the militants. These groups were also the last to form and didn't do so until the revolution was already well on its way. They'd blow things up like the bombers and break stuff like the rioters and even hold protests like the protestors, but they'd also go on to form armed militias which would attack and kill Overmen and Overmen sympathizers. They justified their actions by claiming that bombing unoccupied buildings was not enough. The lives of the Overmen had to be threatened with death because anyone who values their life will find immediate motivation to listen to a persecuted people if not doing so might lead to their death. They had a much larger presence in countries that were less developed during that time but, as I'll explain, eventually became active across the world including Canada.

Reports would often appear detailing fighting in the Middle East or south-east Asia or Africa, usually between these groups and local governments. The first reports were not clear that these were Mortal militants. Many thought religious or other ideological groups were up to their old tricks and attacking anyone who didn't agree with their dogma but soon credence began to be added to the stories, like how the rumor of the internment camps began to grow into fact. There were many different factions and although they all insisted that their only prerogative was to fight for all Mortals everywhere, they somehow still disagreed vehemently with one another, enough that coalitions between the various groups were rare.

The Militants had a tremendously negative effect on activists everywhere. Their actions did little to stem the tide of Immortal influence and instead gave the Overmen a plenitude of excuses to brush our efforts to the side. After all, anyone who did not actively follow the events that led to these uprisings, including most Mortals, were unable to differentiate between the terrorists, the bombers, the rioters, and the activists. They were all lumped together so when an American embassy was attacked in Manila, those conducting a sit-in in London were included in the blame.

The Overmen used tailored propaganda to lump all resistors into one group, to make them all look like radical extremists and it worked incredibly well. By highlighting the activity of the most violent resistors they justified their own atrocities as necessary to combat those who "violently oppose the civilized society that we are so close to achieving." After the reaction that occurred with the construction of the internment camps and after Nate's disappearance, they realized that they couldn't act quite so aggressively as long as most people still saw the Mortal activists in a sympathetic light. I wrote above that anyone who was paying attention understood perfectly well that the Overmen had not abandoned their pursuit of reducing Mortal rights, they were just waiting for the right moment, the right excuse. And so they pushed, pulled, and prodded, refusing to give in to their demands, trying to sneakily pass legislature that would restrict more Mortal rights, and conducting intrusive investigations until the Mortals reacted in such a way that gave them the excuse they needed to deem anyone and everyone who was against them a threat to security. Suddenly, laws were being proposed all over the world that made everyone who was associated with or ever had been associated with the Mortal revolution a potential terrorist. Although it was still a while until any country passed such laws, the prospect alone was enough to escalate tensions.

Chapter 19 ~ Larson

With the introduction of the radical militias, life became extremely difficult for the rest of us. Nate and Marie were able to avoid being imprisoned because of their continued high profile, but we had many of our activist friends disappear quite suddenly. I wanted to protect my friends as best as I could but that meant having to betray them. Larson and the Tall Man continued to ensure their protection as long as I continued to give them what they wanted. With Larson this wasn't a problem since I was, by this time, convinced that he was a sympathizer. The Tall Man frightened me. He had no empathy for Mortals. I even became convinced that he lacked empathy altogether, not that he would have shown me any if he *were* capable. He didn't appear exactly thrilled that I, a product of the Overmen, bourgeoning scientist, and former international ambassador had publicly sided with the Mortals and their cause. He saw me as just another cockroach wearing the skin of an Immortal. To him I, in fact, *was* a Mortal, a non-human.

It was sometime in the middle of all this chaos that Reuben managed to creep out from my life's periphery to reveal to me and the world what I already suspected: that he was a slithering, cowardly little snake. I never trusted Reuben, I think I made that clear enough, and I was correct not to. Why anyone else did trust the ghastly serpent is beyond me but they did, and they paid for their lack of discernment. I know it was him. Some people still don't believe that it was him, but I know—I saw him.

I found out he was meeting with Larson after I saw the two of them eating dinner together at a table at the very back of a poorly lit, dingy gastropub in an equally dingy and poorly lit part of the city. It was a completely random thing to have seen them since this was an area which neither I nor anyone I knew visited on the regular. My own reason for stepping foot in that part of town and in that particular gastropub was to inquire as to the location of a particular street on which a fellow activist lived and with whom I was to meet for drinks in an attempt to convince him to use his connections to … but that doesn't actually matter. I was there for unrelated reasons and I saw Larson and Reuben having dinner together. They didn't see because of the lighting which was either dark red or dark blue or dark purple depending on where in the pub one was looking. I myself had to creep and squint to verify that it was indeed the people I thought it was.

I brought it up to Larson at our next meeting. I had wanted to let him know for some time that I suspected his split allegiance and thought Reuben's case might act as a perfect segue. We were sitting as usual—the same setting as the thousand times before. We were talking about the lack of rain for this time of year or something just as inane. I was nervous; I don't quite know why. Perhaps I wasn't as convinced of his sympathies as I thought.

"I saw you the other night," I said only after I had managed to find the nerve at the exact same time a lag appeared in the conversation.

"Oh yeah?" he said with a cautious tone.

"In the North End. You were with Reuben Paul."

He leaned back in his chair and looked as though he were about to scold me like a child. But he didn't say anything, so I kept talking out of nervousness.

"I was there to ask directions to a … it doesn't matter. I was there and I saw you two at the very back of that restaurant. You looked like you were having a conversation like this one."

He still didn't respond.

"How long has that been going on?" I thought a question might force a response out of him.

"What I do when I'm not here with you is none of your concern. It's *my* concern and the Overman Project's concern. Because of that, you don't need to know any more than to pretend you didn't see anything. Not because anything that you saw was inappropriate but because it's in your best interest to always pretend that I only exist at these meetings with you."

"I see," I said adopting the role of a scolded child.

"So, what did you see the other night in the North End?"

"Nothing," I said.

"Well I'm sure you saw something."

I was beginning to feel confused. "I saw you—"

"No, you didn't."

"I saw someone."

"I'm sure you did. I'm sure you saw lots of people."

"I saw a couple of people having dinner."

"Sure you did."

"But I didn't know them or recognize them."

"Fascinating story," he said with an ironic air and with that the stern father morphed back into the breezy Larson. But then I said, "I see lots of people, I guess, all over the place. For example, as soon as we're done here, I will go back to my apartment where I will see a tall, well-dressed man who always has lots of questions for me about that brief time in which you exist."

Larson tried but was unable to hide the look of consternation that consumed his features for a moment. He began to breathe deliberately, deeply. Then he removed a pen and began to write on his serviette while talking with a casual air, "What are you talking about? Is this man one of your activist friends? If he is, I should like to hear a lot more about him." He quickly tossed the serviette on top of my half-eaten omelette. It read: *You were joking. There is no man waiting for you. Behind Westminster United. 2:00 am.* "Well?" he continued maintaining the casual air but adding a bit of an accusatory tone for effect. "Who is this tall man of yours? Does he work with Nate?"

"That was a joke." I forced a laugh that I knew sounded exactly as fake as it was. "You were making me a little nervous. I joke when I'm nervous."

"You joke when you're nervous?" He was much better at this than me. I almost forgot that he was playing the same game I was.

"I guess I do."

"Well don't. I'm here to collect information from you, not jokes."

"I'm sorry. It was stupid."

"Yes, it was." I got the feeling he wasn't playing when he said this.

Westminster United Church, which shared the name of the street on which it sat, was a large grey building designed in a Gothic Revival style. At 2:00 am, when I approached the old church, the large grey stones were slick and shiny from a persistent light rain. I walked cautiously around to the back where a dark figure was standing with his back to the wall. The shadows made it difficult to see his face but his voice, although carrying an uncharacteristic yet subtle quaver, was familiar to me. Although he appeared little more than a silhouette, I could still ascertain that he was wearing athletic attire: shorts, hooded sweatshirt, runners. He wasted no time on formalities.

"How much do you know about me?" was the first thing he said.

"I *know* nothing really. But I *suspect* the secrets I've been spilling to you are safer with you than with that cold, dead-eyed fish whom I always find lingering outside my door. I also *suspect* you are under some sort of investigation and should start watching your back. Am I right?"

"What does this cold fish look like?" He didn't seem to be in the question answering mood.

"He's tall. Slim. Non-descript, really. No facial hair or *any* hair or any distinguishing marks that I'm aware of."

"Just tall and slim."

"Face a bit like a mannequin really."

"I see."

"And quite the cold fish."

"So you've said. What kinds of questions does he ask?"

"He asks me to tell him what I've already told you."

"Do you?"

"No."

"What do you tell him?"

"I make up stuff."

"Like?"

"It's not easy to explain. It's kind of on a case by case basis. I tell him … or try to tell him just enough to keep him from knowing how much I'm keeping hidden."

"Give me an example."

"Well, I told him the other day that Nate and Marie had started writing a pamphlet together which they intended to distribute."

"I remember you told me that, too."

"No, I told you that they had already written a pamphlet and were in the process of distributing it. My idea was that he would think he had more time to intervene when really, he was already too late. But it would, hopefully, still look as though I had tried to give him some valuable information."

"I'm starting to suspect that he doesn't give a shit about you at the moment." Larson's silhouette began to pace. His voice quavered more.

"What do you mean?"

"I mean he doesn't want to know what your friends are doing. He wants to know what you've been telling *me*. They are comparing what you tell them with what I put in my reports."

I felt a sudden sinking feeling in my stomach, like Dr. Frankenstein's abhorrence at seeing his monstrous creation for the first time. "So, I fucked you, then. I told them something different."

"No, you probably didn't. It wouldn't have mattered because I didn't write what you told me." I felt a slight relief thinking that my stupidity was irrelevant.

"What did you write?"

"Same idea as you, actually." He laughed nervously. "Who knows, our stories may have even resembled each other." I allowed a smile to momentarily appear on my face at the thought, but it didn't stay long. Larson kept laughing. "We really should have corroborated, eh, old boy?"

"Yes, we should have."

"Goddamn. Why didn't I think of that?"

"I'm so sorry, Larson."

"I suppose neither of us thought we could trust each other." The laughing stopped and I could feel his shadowed eyes had turned their focus on me. "Why did you tell me the things you did? Those are your friends, after all."

I was taken aback by the sudden question and its accusatory tone. "I don't know why," I said with hands raised in front of me. "I was scared. And I guess I didn't think I was telling you anything that was really damning."

"But you did. You told me a lot of things that you shouldn't have."

"I don't know," was all I could say.

"You realize that if I had reported what you said in some of those meetings your friends would probably be in far direr straights than they are."

"I don't know ... I don't know why I did it."

"You can't tell this nosy maggot anything like what you've told me. Keep lying to him. Keep dodging."

"Of course."

He seemed to scoff at my assurances. But he continued, nonetheless. "He might not bother you now because he's got me. But if he does, and he very well might, or if someone else is sent in my place ... well, I'm sure you know what you should and shouldn't do. You need to protect your friends."

"Yes, I will."

"Don't ever assume the next bastard they send you will have the same sympathies as me."

"Of course."

I was glad the darkness was hiding his features from me for I was sure his expression of disdain would have been too much for me to look upon.

"I don't think they were listening to our conversations," he said finally in a surprisingly comforting tone.

"I'm sorry?"

"At lunch today. That whole message-on-a-serviette thing was probably a bit superfluous, but I thought I best be cautious."

"Yeah, of course."

"It would be best that you practice the same level of caution."

"I will."

"I wasn't being paranoid, although if I would have had time to think about it, I should have figured that they wouldn't have bothered to go through the trouble of bugging our lunch-table in addition to questioning you. But the fact remains that if they feel the trouble is worth it, they have the means to bug a lunch-table." I suddenly realized that he was giving me advice on how to protect myself in the future, like he was preparing me for his imminent absence.

"I believe you."

"Nate and Marie, and Jonny and Kara, and all your friends ... they're better than the Overmen."

"I know."

"I really hope you do." He pulled his hood over his head and said, "I don't know if I'll see you again." Then he jogged off. He didn't wait for a response or even an indication that I had heard and understood. He just spoke quickly and disappeared into the darkness.

Larson disappeared, not only from my life after that night, but from the world and didn't reappear until centuries later, long after those dark days were over. We became reacquainted and are now close friends, I'm happy to say. In fact, he is my dearest friend and probably my only friend now. He has filled me in with the missing chapters that occurred after that wet and miserable night. He told me he tried to run, tried to flee the country. He intended to hide somewhere in South America or maybe an island in the Caribbean. He couldn't decide. But it didn't matter because he never made it out of Canada. He was arrested at a friend's lakeside cottage where he had sought, and ostensibly received, refuge until the arrangements for his entry into permanent hiding were ready. The friend of his, as it turned out, was the sort who chose to behave quite unfriend-like. He turned Larson in and that was that.

Larson told me he was eventually sent to a re-education camp. It was like a school, he said, in which the curriculum contained the same rubbish about Immortals being the "new-improved human models" that everyone was being taught those days but the method for instilling said information was drastically different than the average classroom. "There was little room for class discussion when the only options a student had were to either agree with everything being taught or endure having water forcibly poured down one's throat and nostrils," he said smiling, somehow managing to find some humor in the thing. "I told them everything they wanted to hear so they'd stop what they were doing, but I never told them an ounce of truth."

Chapter 20 ~ The Fear of the World

After Larson disappeared, and after a brief interview about his possible whereabouts, the Tall Man stopped showing up at my door, for which I was immensely grateful, but Larson was replaced by someone else, about which I was rather annoyed. This new interrogator certainly didn't have the bedside manner that Larson had. His manner was, instead, quite boring for lack of a better description. Our meetings were devoid of casual small talk or much talk at all for that matter, although we still followed the same basic format laid out by Larson. But instead of talking about ancient, classic films featuring long-dead screen legends, we ate in awkward silence. At the end of the meal, instead of nonchalantly asking for the report on my friends, this colorless dullard would ask directly while maintaining unnatural eye contact. "What do you have to tell me about the Karskis today? Are they planning anything we should know about? What stories is Marie currently working on? Anything that might concern us?"

I came to realize after a couple of meetings that his quiet, yet direct manner seemed to be the result of his own lack of social competence. He seemed the type that would be happier filing reports in a poorly lit basement office than slog through a vis-à-vis with another human. Our first few meetings, I admit, managed to intimidate me, not knowing how to respond first to the silence then to the death-like stare. But after a few weeks of this I began to realize that the silence was because he found it impossible to function in any social setting and the stare was simply overcompensation.

He was quite young, quite new at the game. He was shorter than Larson, well-built, and somewhere between not bad and not good looking.

Benedict was his name and he'd not stand for anything less than the full three syllables. I once attempted a Bennie, but its effect was to elicit from him an unconvincing stink-eye, like he was a poor actor playing a villain. This silly behavior made it easy to lie to the man, much easier than it was with Larson. And much, much easier than the Tall Man.

Months after I began meeting with Benedict, the Overman Project ramped up their campaign to convince the world that immediate action was needed in order to prevent the devastating effects of overpopulation. Remember, this was also during the time when the climate was already suffering greatly from centuries of unmitigated pollution. This real threat to the future of the human species, Mortal and

Immortal, allowed the Overman Project to add some credence to their fear-mongering tactic.

One day, after my meeting with Benedict, I arrived home to find someone waiting for me. The Tall Man being such a recent and unpleasant memory I instinctively thought the lone figure standing impatiently by my door was he. I approached cautiously, heart thumping, sweat beading—the usual nervous fare. Thankfully, it wasn't the Tall Man. But if the Tall Man held the title of my least favorite person, the one I met that day was a close contender.

"Reuben?"

"Sorry to bother you like this," he had the same look on his face he had been consistently sporting for the last year or so: abject fear poorly hidden behind geniality. "I was in the neighborhood and thought I'd pop in. When I realized you weren't at home, I thought I'd wait just a bit. I was actually just about to give up and head home."

If only I'd walked a little slower, I thought. Then said, "Glad you waited. Come in." And I held the door open for him.

"Tea? Coffee?" I asked when we were inside.

"Coffee would be lovely. Thanks."

I prepared two coffees while he stood next to me in a trembling silence. We then sat ourselves down in the living room, me on the armchair, he tucked in the corner of the chesterfield like he was cowering from some unseen predator possibly hidden behind the curtains.

"So, what's up?" I said, after growing tired of waiting for him to speak.

"I just need someone to talk to. Someone who understands."

"I don't know if I'm the right person," I said. Why was he here? And why did he think that I'd understand? Why did he think I would even want to listen to him? Although we frequented the same parties and maintained mutual friendships, he wasn't someone I tried to interact with. On the contrary, he was someone I made an effort to avoid.

"You're the only person." He spoke as if the matter was settled unequivocally.

"Well, I'll do what I can."

"I know," he said with the same emphatic tone as if I had been his lifelong confidante and this was just like old times.

"Which is?"

"It's a funny thing, fear," he began like he was reciting a rehearsed speech. "I have wonderful friends ... you know, they're your friends, too."

"Yes, I know."

"But I can't help this feeling now that they're going to be the end of us ... of all of us."

"Don't tell me you're buying into the horseshit about—"

"I'm not buying it. I know the facts. I know the OP is making far more out of it than the facts can support. But knowing these things isn't enough. Not for me. Because all the facts in the world still leave so much room for doubt. There is so much doubt in me and when I think of the consequences of us being wrong ... what if we're wrong? What if we overpopulate the planet to such a degree that every country on every continent is stripped of its resources? What if we're forced to welcome millions ... billions even? What if our love for our friends leads to the end of all of us?"

"It won't. That's insane. The Mortal population is actually in natural decline and has been for—"

"I know. But the Immortal population is rising."

"Yes, but that's for obvious reasons and the answer to that problem is not to infringe on the rights of Mortals. And it's not even a problem yet. It's become an excuse while real problems are left unaddressed."

"Yes, but there are many other factors and the fact that we can sit here and debate, no matter how strong one side might be, means there's always room for doubt. Always a chance we're wrong."

"That chance is so small—"

"Yes." He supplemented his interruption with a wave of his hand. "I know all of this. Like I said, the problem for me isn't the facts; the problem is the fear—the fear that we're wrong. Fear has an incredible effect on things, on the world. Facts lose their significance, their power. Fear will make us accept that truth is a lie, that the world is irrational and so we must be so, too. Fear becomes an obsession and we forget ourselves, thinking only of the fear, of how to stop it, of how to find one moment of reprieve. We even stop thinking about the source of our fear and instead focus on the fear itself. When it gets to this point, we'll do anything to stop it. We'll listen to anyone who will tell us how to stop it and we'll do whatever they say as long as what they say comes with the promise that the fear will go away. It's not just me, though. The world has become afraid, too—so very afraid—which means, of course, that the world is becoming irrational. They are ... we are all looking for a remedy and will grasp for anything that promises to be such a remedy. If the rest of the world has become irrational does it make sense for us to behave rationally?"

"What are you saying, exactly?"

My question seemed to break him away from his soliloquy and he seemed almost surprised to find me present. After a moment to collect his thoughts, he said, "On the way here I saw one of those billboards.

You know, the animated ones that show the world turning into a desert?"

"And the people wearing rags and eating dirt pies or whatever those things are supposed to be, yeah I've seen them? That's just a propaganda campaign. There are loads of those things. There's the one with the dying baby that was meant as a defence of birth permits. You *know* what they are. How they are meant to influence people."

"But what if there's even an ounce of truth in them? What if the future they depict is an actual possibility? You've seen what's been happening in other parts of the world. Look at what's happening in Spain—a monstrous drought."

"That's a different story. There are other factors involved."

"Maybe there are, but it's enough to convince me that there might be reasons to be afraid. And I am. I'm terrified"

"I've gathered that much. It seems as though you're saying that you're afraid of the fear that has engulfed the world. Nothing to fear but fear itself, that kind of thing."

"It's true, I guess. It's a snowball effect. People become afraid because of the threat of overpopulation, something that can be argued for or against; something that has some foundation regardless of how shaky. Then their fear begins to abandon that foundation in favor of a remedy, a remedy that has the potential for catastrophic consequences. Those consequences themselves then become a source of fear and the whole thing continues to erupt until the world has gone completely mad."

"Did you come here to tell me you're afraid? Because everyone is a little bit afraid, some more than others, obviously. It's not exactly news, is it?"

"I came here because I think we are one and the same. Kindred spirits, if you will." I wouldn't, I thought. "We both love our friends but are threatened by them. I came here because I need someone—like you, someone who is like me—to help me. I don't want the fear to consume me. I don't want it to control me."

"Why are you so convinced that we're the same?" I said, disgusted at the thought.

"Come on," was all he said, and I saw a glimpse of an ironic smile. What did he mean by that? Did he know about my secret luncheons with Larson or Benedict?

"What do you want me to do, council you?"

He shook his head. "No. Nothing like that. In fact, I don't want you to do anything. I just want you to know that I'm afraid. I hoped telling someone would help."

"Do you feel like it has?"

"No. No I don't. Maybe it'll take a while, like a slow acting medicine. Maybe by the time I see you again I'll feel right as rain."

"Maybe."

"Maybe. Well, that's that then. I'll leave you be." He stood up, leaving his untouched coffee cooling on my end-table. "Don't worry. I'm not going to start showing up at your door every other day. This was a one-time thing."

"No worries," I said, feeling a bit relieved.

"Goodbye then."

"Yeah. Bye."

He walked out the door leaving me sitting in my armchair while my own coffee remained untouched and cooling next to his. I sat for quite some time, hardly moving, frozen, petrified. I was very much aware of my own fear in that moment. Fear of the future. Fear that I resembled Reuben much more than I was comfortable with. Fear that we shared the same debilitating fears.

Chapter 21 ~ A Botched Attempt at a Warning

My conversation with Reuben didn't sit well with me, especially knowing he had been meeting with Larson. I assumed that after Larson disappeared Reuben would, like me, begin meeting with Benedict or someone else, possibly someone worse, possibly the Tall Man. I decided to follow him, remembering the day of the week I saw him with Larson and surmised that Benedict's schedule would remain the same as it was. So, on a Thursday afternoon I followed Reuben to a café in the exchange district.

I hung round the entrance of the café Reuben had entered to give him ample time to get seated, hoping by the time I walked in he'd be too preoccupied to notice me. When I entered I did so cautiously, trying to keep to the darker areas of the establishment. The café wasn't busy, which would make it difficult to keep from being noticed. Luckily, like most of the preferred places for meetings like this, it was darkly lit. The sound of a piano playing soft jazz poured from some mounted speakers and filled the room, allowing for conversations to maintain privacy, making this a perfect place for the type of meeting I was expecting Reuben to be having. And sure enough, there in a back-corner Benedict sat at a table trying very hard to appear intimidating. Reuben sat across from him trying very hard to appear calm, cool, and collected. I can assure you both men were failing at their respective attempts. Neither noticed me since one was busy trying very hard to maintain a rigid frown while the other was trying to keep his fear ridden body from trembling. I managed to sit at a table which provided me a view without putting me too close. I was unable to hear what they were saying but at one point I witnessed Reuben pull out from the inside pocket of his leather satchel a large square envelope. He handed it to Benedict who opened it and pulled out several typed pages. I had to know what was in there.

Slowly, I sat up from my seat, keeping my eyes on their eyes, and began making my way around the edge of the restaurant to avoid entering their line of vision. Keeping them in my peripheral, I crept to a spot four booths down from them so I was behind Benedict but in front of Reuben. Here I was forced to halt my encroachment as going any further would make me impossible to miss. I sat, not knowing what I might do next since further movement would surely have given away my game. Luckily, Reuben appeared unable to sit for longer than ten minutes without excusing himself to the washroom, what I assumed was his body's way of preparing for a fight or a flight in which carrying extra fluid might prove to be a handicap. So, the next time Reuben stumbled out of the booth and scurried towards his quick relief, I furtively slipped out of the fourth booth down and into the one directly behind Benedict. I sat with my head down and hands folded in front of me on the table. A waitress approached and, disguising my voice with a low rasp and some indistinct accent, I blurted the words, "Coffee. Black." She placed my order without saying anything that might force me to use that voice again whose falsity I was sure would become apparent if more than two words were required. I waited, received my coffee, waited some more. Before my coffee was cool enough to sip, I heard the washroom door open. I lowered my head further until I could feel the steam from my cup on my face. I heard the squeak of faux leather and the soft sigh of compressed foam as Reuben maneuvered his body back into the booth. I continued to wait. Listening for a reference, a description, anything that might provide me with some idea as to what was in that envelope. Larson wouldn't have mentioned it again, I thought. Larson was a professional. Luckily, they weren't. Luckily, I was spying on two fools who were so distracted by their respective, made-up roles they neglected completely the importance of discretion.

After a few minutes of anything that seemed particularly important to me, the anxious one inquired, "You're sure there is no way that will be traced back to me?"

The artificial one responded stoically, "No, I can't promise that. No one can, can they."

"What do you mean?" sputtered the anxious one.

"I mean," the artificial one began with unconvincing harshness, "that no one will deliberately rat you out, but things happen, don't they? I'm not here to rub your back and reassure you, am I?"

"Don't suppose I can take it back?"

"I'm afraid you're committed now. I can't just give it back to you now that you're having second thoughts, can I?"

"Well ... I just don't feel good about this?"

"Did you feel good before you gave it to me?"

"No, I didn't. I don't feel good about anything anymore."

I heard a sympathetic sigh coming from the artificial one as if his artificiality had momentarily slipped to reveal a human underneath. "I understand," he said, his voice softened a bit. "I have friends like yours, too. Or had, rather. But this," I heard what sounded like him patting his briefcase, "this is important for the cause. For the future. You did a good thing giving this to me. I know you care about her and her husband, you've known them for a long time. But what you're doing is more important. What you're doing, reporting stuff like this, is to protect us from them."

"From them?" the words erupted from the nervous one's mouth.

"Not them specifically. We all know people like them. But what they are. You know, what they're a part of. By themselves they're wonderful. But, together, that's what we need to protect ourselves from. And this article you gave me, it's not a reflection on Mary—"

"Marie."

"Marie. It's a reflection of the greater whole of which she happens to be a member."

That was enough for me. If I wasn't afraid of being found out I would have jumped from my seat and sprinted out of the café towards Nate and Marie's as quickly as my legs would take me. Instead, I was forced to stay slumped over my coffee until they had finished. Although they spoke more about Marie and her articles, nothing more was said to add to the initial revelation, only to reaffirm it. As I sat there, waiting in terrible anxiety for my chance to report my findings to my dear friends, I pictured in my mind how this happened. Marie often worked on an old computer with no internet access in order to keep from having her work hacked. Reuben, being a close friend of theirs, managed to get printed copies of her work directly off her computer. What I witnessed at the restaurant, I was sure despite lack of evidence, was just one of many times the slimy bastard had stolen her work and handed it over to the OP.

I didn't waste much time. Once I was able, I left the restaurant and proceeded immediately to Nate and Marie's.

"Everything all right?" Marie asked as I stumbled into their apartment in a frenzy.

"No. No, no, no. You're being monitored," I blurted out as I struggled to remove myself from my coat and kick off my boots.

"Why don't we get you situated in the living room and you can tell us what's going on. Nate," she yelled, and I heard Nate's muffled voice shouting, "Just a moment," from the kitchen. Marie sat me down with a glass of water which I sipped while waiting for Nate to appear.

"What's all this?" he asked, wiping his hands on a tea towel that was flung over his left shoulder.

"I'm sorry to barge in on you like this."

"No worries. Of course. What's the matter?"

"You two ... well, you for sure," I pointed to Marie," but I'm assuming both of you are being watched, monitored."

"What do you mean?"

I wanted to say, Rueben is telling stuffy agents from the OP all about your writing and research and organizing, everything. There are spies amongst your closest friends. In fact, I'm one of them. I've spilt your secrets to the same stuffy agents. But I'm … it's complicated for me. I told them some secrets because I was afraid. That's not an excuse, I know. I'm forced to meet with them. I must meet with them and tell them stuff. I try to lie, to tell them things I know won't hurt you, but I must admit that I have said things that I shouldn't have. But it's all right because the person I told those secrets to, Larson, he didn't pass them along. So even those times I did betray you two it had no effect. Your secrets were safe with Larson. And me … most of the time with me. But Reuben! Reuben is betraying you two, I'm sure of it. And what he's giving them could put you both in harm's way. You aren't safe anymore, not even amongst us, not even amongst your friends.

But I didn't say that much. I said, "I have reason to believe someone close to you is betraying you. Someone, I'm sure of this, is collecting your secrets and handing them over to Overmen agents."

"A friend of ours? Who?" Marie said, searching my eyes for any hint of an answer but I had to look away.

"I can't say."

"You don't know?"

"Listen, it could be anyone. The fact is that you could both be in a great deal of trouble. I don't know what information specifically this person has tossed their way, but they *are* monitoring you two. They are watching."

"What happened?" Nate said. "How did you find this out?"

"I have contacts; you know that. I'm still a member of the Overman Project."

"But who? Or how?"

"It doesn't matter," I said, and avoided Nate's eyes, too.

"Of course it does." He moved so he was standing directly in front of me, as if he was daring me to look at him. "What can we do if we don't know who to keep an eye on? We obviously need more information."

"Don't trust anyone," was the only response I could conjure.

"No one? Even you?" That hurt a bit and I let it show on my face. Nate noticed. "So, we *can* trust you?" he asked.

I didn't respond but Nate seemed to take my silence as a yes.

"If we can trust you, then who else can we trust?" Marie interjected. "My job depends on me trusting people. I have sources that I have no choice but to trust and who trust me in return."

"I said I can't tell you who … but … keep your work locked away."

"My work?" Marie folded her arms across her chest, looking like my adoptive mum scolding me for misbehaving. "No one has access to my work."

"Some people do." I raised my voice, losing a bit of patience. "People are coming and going all the time here. Don't leave it lying about. Lock it in a safe. All your research, your trusted contacts … don't let anyone near them."

"No one goes near them," Nate said defending his wife.

"I do," I shouted. "Your study is right there. Every time I'm here I have at least half a dozen opportunities to wander into the study and grab whatever's on the desk. It's right there."

"You do, yes," Nate continued. "Jonny also has free reign of the place. Should we start locking the door when you two pop in for a visit? Should I lock it now?" His tone had become sarcastic and a smile broke across his face, a mischievous smile, ironic and jovial. A smile that had become rare after his prison experience, a smile that I often yearned to see again and here it was, just a glimmer, but it was here, at a time when he should be lamenting the betrayal from his closest friends. He knelt to my eye level. "It's me. It's us. We don't want to become paranoid, shutting out everyone we know. But we need to know who's doing this. And we trust you, so tell us."

I wanted to tell him, but I didn't, or I couldn't. As much as I despised Reuben, he was an Overman, like me.

I shook my head. "Just don't trust anyone. Not even me."

I didn't see or speak to Nate or Marie until weeks later. It was at another one of their parties; I was almost surprised when I received an invite. I showed up, bottle of wine in hand, unsure of how I'd be received. I purposely showed up a little late so I wouldn't be the first one there. I didn't want to be left alone with them—forcing them to make small talk with me.

"You came." It was Jonny who answered the door. I looked passed him and was relieved to see many others already mingling in the background, drinks in hand. "I heard you exchanged a few words with my brother a few nights ago," he said casually and then grabbed the bottle of wine I brought and inspected the label.

"Yeah, I'd rather not talk about that to be honest," I said following him into the apartment.

"Of course," he said still reading the wine label as he walked. "It's not my business. And I don't care much either way. You guys have exchanged words before." He turned to me smiling and holding the bottle at eye level as if to show me what I brought. "May I?"

"Yeah," I laughed. His casual joviality managed to calm my nerves. I removed my coat and, seeing that all the hangers in the closet were already used up, tossed it across a nearby armchair on which three other coats had already been similarly tossed. Jonny disappeared to the kitchen presumably to find a bottle opener.

I walked in slowly, greeting people as I entered, scanning for Nate and/or Marie. I saw Marie first exiting the kitchen holding a bottle of beer in each hand. She saw me, smiled, kissed my cheek and wrapped her arms warmly around me. When her hands met behind me, I heard the beer bottles clink loudly together.

"Oh god," she said and broke from our embrace and examined the bottles. "Could you imagine if I smashed these just now? I must deliver these. I'll catch up with you in a bit."

"Yeah, sounds great."

"Grab a drink," she demanded affably and scurried away.

I continued my slow, what felt like, infiltration of the party. Just about every face was familiar; every eye I met came with a smile, a raised glass, a nod. I was welcome. But why did I still feel like I was intruding?

I met Nate. He was standing next to their unlit fireplace criticizing or praising some famous author while another man nodded in agreement. When he saw me, he greeted me like he always did—likely a smile, a hug, maybe a slap on the back, definitely a joke, or an anecdote. He, like Marie, like Jonny, welcomed me warmly as if there was never a reason for doubt. But I still had to force a smile.

I joined in the conversation as best I could, but I didn't feel like my old self. Like the ability for conversation had suddenly been lost. Like I was someone else altogether. An outsider who doesn't belong. An imposter. To be honest, I felt like Reuben, who was conspicuously absent for some unknown reason. As we talked, I kept looking round the room, but for what? For Reuben? Maybe hoping that his visage would bring me back to my old self. Or maybe it was something else, something that would re-establish my connection with my friends. I didn't find that, though. All I found was the study door, closed tight. Later in the evening I tried the door knob out of curiosity. Locked.

For most of the evening I kept to the sidelines, like a background character, an extra in a film. I hardly spoke to anyone, but I smiled a lot, nodded a lot, clinked my glass against others a lot, all the while feeling not like me but like a talentless actor trying to play me.

When the evening grew late, I didn't stay and chit chat with the Karski's. Instead, I shook hands, hugged, kissed, and said goodbye well before the night was coming to an end. I excused my behavior by apologizing and claiming I had too much on my plate the next morning and must have an early night. I doubt they bought it, in fact, I can say with almost certainty that they didn't. But they accepted it graciously and let me leave.

Reuben was never seen again. That is not to say that I didn't try to find him. I scoured the city for any sign of him. I went to the location of his regularly scheduled meetings with Benedict but found neither Reuben nor old Bennie. I went to his home, thought I'd pop in like he did to me at mine, but he either refused to answer or was not home. He simply vanished like a ghost, an apparition whose sole purpose is to antagonize and leave. Even to this day, over 400 years later, I still have neither seen nor heard from the man.

Then Marie disappeared. It happened while she was riding her bicycle home from work, sometime between 7:00 and 8:00 in the evening. It was in the middle of winter, in Winnipeg, and the Sun had already set for at least a couple of hours.

I can still picture it all in my mind: the air that night is windless, so the big, heavy flakes of snow fall gently, swirling only when disturbed by the movement of traffic. Out of the ether, a black van with faded white letters on the side, the name of an out-of-business extermination company, cuts in front of her forcing her to steer her bicycle into a snowbank. Men wearing black, their faces hidden behind balaclavas, jump out and grab her and her bicycle. A scream begins but is swiftly muffled by a mitted hand over the mouth. She and her bicycle are pulled violently into the vehicle. The door slides shut. The van returns to the ether. And that's it. She's gone, as if the snowbank into which she had fallen had consumed her completely.

Of course, none of us actually saw how it happened so the shock of losing her was more gradual. Nate called me that night to tell me she hadn't come home yet and wasn't answering her phone. He was still calm at this point, but the panic was starting to bubble beneath the surface. We weren't yet sure that her reason for being late wasn't because of something else entirely. We called her friends and coworkers who told us what time she had left the office. Then we left the apartment and walked the route she took to and from work every day. This trip took over an hour to complete. Neither of us noticed the snow that had been trampled from the struggle; it had already begun to disappear as the falling snow erased all evidence as if nature was in cahoots with the Overmen. On our way back to his apartment, Nate expressed hope that she'd be there waiting for him and he'd walk through the door and they'd laugh about it. She would tell him that she had got a flat tire and had to walk her bike to the nearest hardware store and her phone was dead, so she was unable to call. But that didn't happen. When we walked through the door the silence in the apartment was unlike anything I had ever experienced. The absence of sound was vociferous, more arresting than any noise could ever be.

I immediately began making phone calls. I remember thinking how badly I wished Larson was still around. I called Benedict, amongst others, who had better connections to the OP than me, but none could help. I kept calling and asking those I called to call others. I spent the entire evening with a phone to my ear and my eyes scanning contact lists for more people to harass. Nate sat quietly on the couch seemingly as if in a fugue state until an idea suddenly came to him.

"What if we do a press release?" he shouted, turning 180 degrees to face me so he was kneeling on the couch with his elbows resting on its back.

"Yes," I shouted back while covering the receiver with a hand. "Start thinking of what you'll say." I then returned my attention to whomever I was speaking.

"What should it say?" Nate said after turning back around to face the coffee table and opening his computer. But he couldn't think of anything to write. He was too lost in scattered, panicked thoughts about Marie. He typed a couple lines then stopped and resumed that blank stare.

When I had run out of people to call, I joined him in the living room. "Let's get started on that press release," I said, snapping him back to the here-and-now.

"Yes, of course. I'm having trouble getting my thoughts in order."

"That's why I'm here. Let's think. We need to make the world demand her release. Like what we managed when you were taken."

"We're not yet sure she has even been taken, though, are we?"

"It's rather likely don't you think?" I said.

He contemplated this for a moment. "If she's been taken, what are the odds of getting her back?" He looked at me and I saw all hope drain from him. His eyes lost focus and his whole face seemed to lose expression. I could see what was happening behind those eyes. He had just realized that he was likely never to see his wife again. He realized that they wouldn't have taken her unless they had good reason to do so, not after the fiasco that erupted when they grabbed him. After all that, they were aware of what kind of response taking her could produce. But they took her anyway. Nate also realized that such a dramatic response as the one that followed his disappearance was unlikely considering the fragmented state of the opposition. Activists were unlikely to organize with rioters for fear of what an association with them might do to their safety which was the same reason that rioters were unlikely to organize with bombers. And even if the dangers of association were not an issue, each one of those groups had split into many smaller factions with their own incompatible creeds and doctrines, at this point it was almost impossible to get one activist to agree with another. Also, the OP's propaganda campaign, aside from playing a major role in the fragmentation of the opposition groups, had successfully turned a large portion of the population against them which, we understood, would greatly reduce the support that was needed to recreate the sort of campaign that might lead to Marie's release. All this Nate realized in a single moment and I was witness to it.

"It's impossible to say now," I said hurriedly, trying to pull his mind away from defeatist thoughts. "We don't know anything yet. Let's work on that press release for now, old friend. No use getting ahead of ourselves."

We contacted several of Marie's colleagues at The Future, Marie's magazine, that very night to let them know what we suspected happened to Marie. They began writing their own articles and calling their own contacts and by the morning—Nate and I never slept that night—we had a good section of their next issue dedicated to Marie's disappearance and an official press release scheduled at a local news station. Nate and I agreed to both make a statement in order to get people to sympathize with him while my status as an Immortal and member of the Overman Project added validity to his plight. In addition, we had a number of supporters and sympathizers, most of whom knew Marie personally or were fans of Nate's, gather round the studio and protest a number of government offices.

I remember what we said. I have the recording in my collection. I won't transcribe it here because nothing we said was important. I bring it up only because it was the last time in a long time that Nate and I were in a room together, working together, as friends. Although it was a horrible day considering the circumstances, I can't help but look back with a small degree of nostalgia for that simple reason.

We ate lunch together, just the two of us. Later that evening Jonny and Kara visited, and we all sat around planning what to do: protests, letters to politicians, civil disobedience, capitalizing on some of our more powerful connections, the usual stuff. We spoke of Marie often but when we did, we said things like "*When* she comes back ..." and "She'll laugh when she hears about this." We all knew she was alive somewhere, thinking, feeling, but not knowing where she was or what she was feeling or thinking made her absence feel all the more conspicuous. Was she in pain? Was she hungry? Scared? Was she locked in a dark room somewhere not knowing where she was or why? Was she as ignorant about the details of her situation as we were? These and more questions raced through our heads despite our efforts to shake them out and remain focused on getting her back.

I later discovered that at this time when we were sitting in her flat planning her inevitable return, she was already on a plane with several other prisoners heading for a prison camp located on an island somewhere in Southeast Asia. She was aware of her situation. She was not in pain, but she'd have known what was happening to her and by whom and probably she knew the reasons why. She would've been scared, terrified in fact, the kind of fear that seems to squeeze the air out of your lungs. I don't know what effect that information would have had on our evening as we interspersed our conversation with occasional jokes, smiling at each other with ignorant, impotent hope, unable or unwilling to really entertain the possible reality of the situation.

The next day I was scheduled to fly to Berlin for a twofold trip. I was being sent there by the OP to meet with several dignitaries who were attending an international summit meeting, representing Overmen scientists. While I was there, I was also invited to give a talk to a group of activists who had convened to protest the international community's complacency regarding human rights abuses in one or several African countries, I can't remember the specifics. I thought it was perfect timing and used my opportunity to plead Marie's case to international leaders as well as already sympathetic activists. I was mostly politely ignored by the former but enthusiastically embraced by the latter. Unfortunately, the activists were small in number and smaller in influence meaning the entire trip produced little results.

I returned to Winnipeg the following Monday. I went to Nate's that evening. It would be the last time I saw him for many years.

I sent him a message to let him know I was stopping by but received no response. I thought it was odd but considering the circumstances I didn't expect him to behave like he normally would. I arrived at his apartment and knocked on the door. He answered. I found his features startling for they were void of expression; he looked lobotomized, yet behind his eyes, underneath his expressionless skin, I could detect something that frightened me. Thoughts began swirling round my head looking for an explanation for his appearance.

I didn't say anything. I didn't even greet him. I could only stare as he stared at me. I didn't attempt to enter either, so I remained standing in the doorway looking in.

"Was it you?" he said finally. But I didn't respond. "You're not the only one with connections. A colleague of Marie's ... Sam Keller. You know him?" I shook my head. "He's an editor at The Future. Apparently, he's been following you. Looking into things. I guess he has with every Immortal he knows. He doesn't trust any of you. When he told me this, I was livid. I thought, How could you not trust your friends? Do you really believe they'd betray us? And then you said we shouldn't trust anyone. Not even you. I began to think Sam was on to something. But I still thought, not you. Never you. That's impossible. Marie locked her study room door because you warned her. We didn't know it was you we were keeping out. We didn't know we were protecting ourselves from you. He saw you, Sam, he saw you meeting with someone and he heard you telling them about Marie and stories she was working on. He saw you give him things. Papers or envelopes containing what? Marie's work? Well, he did some digging and this person, he said there were two, and they're both Overmen. So, you've been meeting with, what, spies? You've been spying on me? On Marie? On Jonny? What have you been telling them?"

"Nate ..." I started, thinking I could simply turn in Reuben but couldn't finish my sentence because my mind immediately began spinning uncontrollably. "It's not like that. I can explain. I have to meet with them."

"What did you tell them?"

"I can explain," I repeated, and then my mouth froze as if it was refusing to relay the words my mind was sending it. "I can explain everything," was all my mouth was allowing to be said.

Was it me, I began to think in that moment while Nate stood waiting for me to explain myself as promised? How much did I tell the Tall Man? Did I tell him more than I realized? But no, I thought, it couldn't have been me. I was careful. I was foolish at the beginning with Larson, but thanks to nothing more than moral luck that didn't matter. Larson was on our side and wouldn't have told the OP anything that could put Marie in harm's way. But I couldn't remember. I just couldn't be sure. I still can't.

To this day, 400 or so years later, I'm still not convinced it was Reuben who was to blame. I just want it to be him, terribly so. Or if we are to share the blame, at the very least I wish him to have done the worst of it, the way a child who has broken a window might welcome a collapse of the entire house to hide the signs of his mischief.

"If it wasn't you then who was it? Can you tell me that?"

"I can't." I sputtered.

"You can't? So, it wasn't you? Or was it?"

"It wasn't," I said finally but added, "I don't think—"

"You don't think?" Nate screamed. "What does that mean? What is wrong with you? Why can't you tell me anything?"

"I ..." I couldn't speak. I could feel my mouth open, but the words were stuck in my throat.

"You don't think it was you?"

"I don't know."

"But it could've been you?"

"No. I can't ..."

"What can't you tell me?" Nate's voice had quieted. "Is Marie gone because of you?" The pain that was hiding beneath his visage suddenly broke to the surface, and his voice began to quaver. "Please tell me it wasn't you." He began to sob, and I wanted to sob too but remained impotent, completely silent, with a mouth that was still frozen half-open. "If it wasn't you then tell me. If it was you then lie to me. I won't be able to handle this if it was you. Why are you so fucking silent?" he shouted in frustration.

"I'm so sorry, Nate," I finally managed. "I'm doing everything in my power to get her back."

"Don't tell me that." His body was by this time shaking with emotion and he looked unlike anything I had ever seen. "There's nothing you can do now. It doesn't matter what you will do or want to do, it only matters what you did or didn't do. What are you sorry for?"

"For so much." I stopped myself realizing I couldn't say anything. I couldn't defend myself. I couldn't even place the blame on Reuben. And I couldn't lie to him, either. Silence was all I was capable of.

"For what?" he asked again, his voice sounding defeated. But I didn't answer.

A look of reservation came over him, his shoulders dropped, and he began to breathe in deliberate, controlled breaths. All that emotion that was bursting uninhibited a moment ago had withdrawn. I could see that he had given up trying to get an answer from me. Without an answer, there was only one thing he could do. He looked down, then closed the door.

I stood staring at the closed door, not wanting to leave, not wanting this moment to pass. For as agonizing as this moment was, I knew that when it passed my connection to Nate would be severed completely. But now, while this detestable moment lingered, while only a door stood between us, I still had a reason to be there, to be so close knowing he was just on the other side. But to leave that door, I could think of no reason, no circumstance which would bring me back to it.

I continued to linger in that moment. I don't know what I thought might happen. I suppose I maintained some faint hope that he might open the door again, take pity on me. Maybe he would look through his peephole, see me still standing there and let me in. But I was also terrified of listening to him say another word, ask another question which I couldn't answer. I have no idea how long I remained there. Of course, eventually, I had to leave. It took all my strength of will, but I managed to push myself away and walk down the hall, feeling all the while the door pulling me back.

As I made my way home, the reality of my folly began to take shape in my head. I had been, all this time, like an unskilled trapeze swinger, barely managing nearly impossible maneuvers, but my luck had run out and I was now falling without a net to catch me. Nate, Marie, Jonny, Kara, they were, I now realized, my only friends, my only family. The Overman Project, the community of Immortals, they didn't love me, they wouldn't fight for me, they offered me nothing. They demanded my complete loyalty and in exchange I was granted the privilege of being loyal to them. I never asked to be created by them. I never asked to be an Immortal and so they never gave me anything I asked for. I asked to be loved, however, and Nate gave me that. Marie, despite our differences, gave me that. And they never asked for anything in return.

Nate wouldn't forgive me, I was sure of that, unless, perhaps, I somehow got Marie back. Although, he still believed it might have been me who sent her to that camp in the first place, and maybe it was. I don't remember. I'd prefer to die without remembering. The truth of my involvement in Marie's disappearance is buried somewhere amongst every other wrong I committed in that great haunting of mine. The truth is buried somewhere amongst these words, amongst the lies I've been telling. Somewhere the truth exists. But I'm too old now, I'm too tired. I don't care to find it.

Chapter 24 ~ Never

No one ever saw Marie again. She died in the camp, apparently of an infection. I don't know much of the details. Records from that time are available and I'm sure if I looked, I could find her and learn exactly what happened but in all my years I have never managed to bring myself to do such a thing. I have, however, spent many nights imagining her life from her abduction to her death. I've done this so many times now that I have constructed a narrative in my mind built from stories I read about other prisoners, which is entirely consistent with the history as if it were a story I had studied as opposed to created. Here it is.

Marie arrives at the camp only a few days after her abduction. She is still shaken, unaware of why, exactly, she is there, who, exactly, took her and when, if ever, she'll see Nate again. She spends her first day being processed: fingerprinted, strip-searched, head shaved, dressed in orange, and shoved in a small room with twenty to thirty others. Her first night she crawls onto her bed, the top bunk, and cries for the first time since her abduction. She stifles the noise she's making by burying her face in her pillow to avoid disturbing those trying to sleep but it doesn't matter since she can hear the muffled sobs of others around her. Eventually she's able to stop crying but can't sleep, not yet, not in this bed in this room, without Nate lying next to her.

The next day is orientation. She's shown where she'll do her morning exercises, report for work duty, eat breakfast, lunch, and dinner, where she'll get her hair cut, and where she'll shower. She is shown in one day what every other day of the rest of her life will look like. The corollary to this knowledge is the revelation that every detail of her previous life she will never experience again. She's shown that she'll never again be surrounded by close friends at one of her and Nate's famous parties; she will never eat her favorite Hong Kong style noodles, taste good wine. She will never ride her bicycle, never go to the cinema, never eat at a restaurant, and never catch a taxi, never, never, never again. And she'll also never get to do the things she always wanted to do. She will never ride a horse, read Middlemarch, or visit Tibet. But most of all, she'll never again sleep next to her husband, never feel his warm body breathing heavily next to hers, never kiss his lips, never laugh at his jokes, never march in protest side by side, never experience another moment to add to the colossal-but-somehow-never-big-enough collection of moments she has amassed with him. Everything she has done and experienced so far is all she will ever experience. She will experience no more. She will memorize her daily routine in the camp and perform it perfectly and exactly every day until the day she dies.

She died of an infection of some sort which would have been easily remedied if she had received the proper care. There are so many ways this could happen to Mortals that it could've been from nothing more than an untreated cut on her hand, a simple slip, a quick brush against a sharp piece of tin. She ignores it until it begins to swell and turn colors. She seeks medical help but is ignored. When she protests, she's thrown in solitary confinement. A hunger strike leads to force feeding, a tube shoved down the throat and liquid nutrients poured down like topping up a car with oil. This keeps her alive but does nothing to stop the spread of infection that's festering in her hand. When guards bring her food or take her out to force her to bathe, she shoves her infected hand in their face and demands a doctor. They react as if being threatened or assaulted and she's punished more, usually by being beaten with rubber truncheons. She becomes too weak to stand and is dragged out of her cell. The burning that was unbearable in her hand has now travelled up her arm. She's delirious, unable to think clearly. In their eyes she's deranged. Being mortal, she's too weak to handle a little bit of day to day work or a bit of "quiet time" as the guards had been known to call solitary. They finally find her unresponsive, lying on the cold concrete floor of her cell. She's still alive, but the infection has reached her heart. Her blood is poison throughout her entire body. There's no transfusion for these prisoners. They were not meant to leave. She's placed on a gurney and is finally fed antibiotics intravenously. The doctors know it's futile, but something must be done. They have to convince themselves that they tried, that they aren't monsters after all.

That's likely how it was. That's the vision that keeps me up at night in complete clarity as if it's not a fabricated memory at all but that I am transported there like Ebenezer Scrooge by a Christmas ghost. I see her face straining against the pain before losing all expression as she drifts off to oblivion.

But there are other details I see because I like to think that she did more than just follow the routine laid out for her. I like to think she still had moments. I like to think, or I believe, that hidden beneath the dirt covered face her mind continued. Her mind, which was furnished with so much lovely poetry, remained her own. And while those beautiful words she had memorized repeated in her head and slipped out quietly from her lips, I believe they brought with them memories of Nate, and Jonny, and Kara, and little James, and all our friends and all our parties. Those memories, still so fresh in her young mind, she would replay them, visit them like she was popping in for a quick visit, a cup of coffee, a cigarette, and talk and laugh and raise her cup and toast the past. I believe she had times, maybe few and fleeting in which a smile would break through to the surface so anyone present, anyone also suffering as she was suffering would see it and smile also and think of their own friends, their own family, their own memories. Then they'd go back to their routine and perform it like always but with that smile fresh off their lips and those lovely remembrances still dancing just behind their tired eyes. I'd like to think that she did more, that she met people there with whom she built friendships that, if she and they were Immortals, would outlast their long lives. She, I believe, remembered and smiled until her last day.

Marie's disappearance was such a significant moment in my life I'm still, to this day, sometimes convinced I can remember everything in perfect detail. But I know this is not the case. They say that every time one recollects a memory, they remember it less accurately. So that would make Marie's disappearance and the surrounding events one of the least accurate of all my memories. Not that I believe I can remember anything in much detail from so long ago anyway

Chapter 25 ~ The Fear Spreads

When Nate was taken for that brief period, the overall social climate was such that people still felt they had power enough to conduct the sort of protest that led to his release. This proved to be a bit of a shock to the Overmen who realized what needed to be done was to change that very climate if they wanted to ever attempt something like that again. So that's what they did through campaigns of fear. By the time Marie vanished from our lives, the fear had grown to such a degree that most people had begun to feel paralyzed by it. This is why so few gathered to demand her release like they did her husband's. Of course, they were horribly afraid of being taken away themselves, but in addition, they were also afraid that the OP was right all along and that these extreme measures, vanishing people, were necessary to save the world from the horrors of overpopulation and other evils attributed to Mortals. I'm sure many, if not most, wished there was some other way, but they were too scared to think of another way. So, they just huddled around the Overman Project, trembling with their heads bowed, and agreed that it knew best.

When people like Marie were taken, which continued to happen in greater frequency, they didn't just become memories, they vanished from the past as well as the present. They suddenly didn't exist at all, not now, not ever, and certainly not ever again. The camps reputations grew to become legends and then myths so that they eliminated people's ability to think or feel about what actually happened to their lost brothers, sisters, mothers, fathers, friends in any rational sense. No one knew if they were alive or dead, they just knew they were gone. And not knowing what happened to them seemed to eliminate their ability to process what happened to them, so they just accepted that they were gone, and nothing more. Gone where? No one knows. Like some twisted superposition they were dead, alive, both, and neither.

During this time the OP also began recruiting Mortals in greater numbers. Their movement to save the world, not only from the destructive nature imbedded in mortality, but death entirely, united the world in their fear and hatred of anyone who threatened to disrupt their goals. What goals exactly? Depends on whether one was a Mortal or Immortal. The OP's goal had evolved, if you ask me, into the complete domination of the human race while the Mortals' who signed on just wanted to feel they were a part of something greater, like a sort of immortality-by-association in which they could be included in the movement even if they weren't themselves Immortal. I'm not sure if their thinking was that being associated with the Overmen would grant their eventual death meaning or if they felt that they would somehow attain immortality through association. Not actual immortality of course but a sort of vicarious immortality. It's difficult to say exactly what they thought except that they thought very little about it. Whatever their reasoning, it was enough to give them incentive to betray their fellow Mortals in large numbers and their actions, although not completely coming to fruition until centuries later, would eventually lead to the complete annihilation of the Mortal race.

The ways in which the Mortals became such assets to the Immortals were in several ways. One was simply volunteering for low level jobs. Some managed to work their way up the ladder which paid decently enough. The OP fed them a steady flow of comforting propaganda so they could always be happy in the belief that their work would be forever remembered. These jobs ranged from simple office clerks to recruiters, even to camp guards. Although hopeful parents in most countries were still required to obtain offspring permits, those Mortals who joined the OP were contractually obligated to forgo any attempt to procreate.

The other way someone could swear fealty to the Overmen was to volunteer to carry Immortal children since the OP still depended on Mortal women to act as incubators for Immortal children. These women would not be allowed to care for the children after they were born since by this time Mortals and Immortals were almost completely segregated. Their only function was to allow themselves to carry the fetus to term. Many women did this multiple times even to the risk of their own health and the OP was more than happy to allow it. Many women would volunteer again for the procedure mere days after they had given birth. Again, I believe the reason so many were so willing was because they projected themselves onto the children. Immortals had dominated so much of the world as they knew it that they wanted to get as close to immortality as they could. This was one of the ways to do that.

While this was happening on one side of the conflict, those opposed to the Overman hegemony were growing angrier and more radical. The militants were growing in strength and causing more damage while everyone else, all the way down to the pacifistic activist, were being associated with them. The way this came about was twofold. Firstly, what one might call "evil" had in fact seeped its way into the sects of so-called militants which gave those who opposed them legitimate reason to refer to them as such. Their tactics grew to include bombings of shopping malls and government buildings full of innocent civilians. Secondly, the OP's propaganda campaign, which was now backed by thousands if not millions of Mortals willing to denounce their fellow

Mortals, as if doing so also denounced their mortality, was incredibly effective at convincing the terrified populace that those peaceful demonstrators were just as dangerous as those terrorists blowing people up. The irony was that the OP's propaganda campaign convinced thousands of people that the demonstrators were in fact the ones conducting propaganda. They were told that they were just terrorists attempting to recruit and fuel sympathy for murderers. And many believed them.

This tactic, of treating peaceful activists like terrorists, was one of the greatest recruiting tools of the actual terrorists. These people had no animosity to anyone but the Overman Project and the governments around the world were now filled with nothing but Overmen. When they were suddenly treated, not as peaceful activists but terrorists, many thought they might as well take the road everyone already believed they were on. It wasn't just activists who graduated to terrorism, many having skipped the grades of rioter and bomber altogether, but many who had nothing at all to do with any sort of resistance movements. These people, usually in less developed countries, were some of the most innocent of anyone during this time but were forced, or at least felt that they were forced, to take up arms against what they saw as oppressors. In the many civil conflicts that were raging all over the world, many innocents were indiscriminately killed. This resulted in many family members of the murdered taking up arms and joining one of these terrorist organisations as the only response they felt they were capable of. The irony of watching an army fight an enemy whose numbers were only growing because the fighting continues might have provided some degree of amusement if the results were not so horrific.

This was the beginning of the most tumultuous time of the revolution. There were many factions fighting against one another on the side of the Mortals for reasons already described. On the side of the Overmen, however, things were much more organized for the simple reason that loyalty to the OP meant questioning nothing. I admit that I was one of these loyal lackeys during this time. Nate and Marie had kept me connected to the Mortals' plight; they gave me reason to question the OP and to analyze their methods, motivations, and entire raison d'etre. They allowed me to witness firsthand their perspective, to feel as though I were one of them. When that connection was severed, I had nowhere left to go but back into the open arms of the Overmen.

Since this document is meant to be, for the most part, a detailed confession, I'll dedicate some time to describe the kind of person I was, the type of person I allowed myself to become. But first I must describe more the mindset that was required for me to be able to become such a person.

The Overman Project learnt early on that the best way to guarantee loyalty amongst their little creations was through isolation. This lesson had not yet manifested when I was a child which is why I was able to attend Tills Elementary and meet Nate. This delay in implementing such complete control over us is the reason older Immortals like myself and Larson were more sympathetic to the Mortals. Younger Immortals' lives, however, were dominated by the Overman Project to the point in which many had never met a Mortal in any context aside from a one-time handshake and a quick spatter of small talk. None had personal relationships with a Mortal, and few even had professional relationships with them. For them, the OP was the only source of information, education, friendship, family, and casual acquaintance. The Overman Project fed them, clothed them, comforted them, and of course, created them. They knew nothing outside of that which was exactly what the OP wanted. This allowed them to have an entire people group, numbered in the tens of millions, willing to do whatever they were asked.

Another important step the OP took was to either get a law passed or reinterpret already existing laws, depending on the country, which essentially stripped those who were considered a terrorist threat of their citizenship. The reason for this is very simple: the laws in place protecting people from abuses of power only applied to citizens. Without that designation, no law could protect them. This allowed them to send more and more undesirables to camps all over the world because they were not, technically, infringing on anyone's rights since rights, as they were understood then, were dependent on a person's status as a citizen of a sovereign state. It was a tactic used before in Mortal history. Immortals who felt a tinge of discomfort at the prospect of eliminating someone's basic human rights could still sleep at night by reminding themselves that they weren't doing anything to Mortals that they hadn't already done to themselves.

It should be obvious how devastatingly effective this tactic was. If you'll remember, the OP had already managed to convince a large portion of the population that an activist was basically the same as a terrorist. This opened the door for just about anyone who dared defy the will of the Overmen to be labeled a terrorist threat and, therefore, be stripped of their citizenship and their human rights.

Nate, thank God, was never considered such a threat. After he lost Marie, he abandoned his activism, at least overtly, and remained out of the spotlight for years. This saved him, I believe, for the OP already had him under careful watch. Any act which could have been interpreted as subversive would have surely led to a similar fate as Marie. He did later resume his activism in the form of pamphlet writing but I'll get to that later.

I continued my work as an ambassador, although by this time there was nothing distinguishing my job from a run-of-the-mill propaganda minister and, in fact, propaganda minister is what I and my coworkers jokingly called me. Instead of travelling from country to country to explain the many benefits of immortality to their leaders, I was now working directly with country's leaders, most of whom were now Immortals, to turn public opinion against any criticism of our immaculate movement. I was now convincing the populations of countries that the Overmen were benevolent leaders and the Overman Project had only their best interests in mind. They were the only people evolved enough to properly lead a country to some sort of utopian society in which every person would live like kings, queens, princes and princesses and anyone who dared to stand in the way of this migration from societal atrophy to complete enlightenment was an enemy of progress. In fact, an enemy of every living breathing thing, and must be resisted at all costs. I didn't believe this nonsense when I had Nate and Marie to ground me in reality and I doubt I believed it when I was so obsequiously promoting it, although I may have somehow managed to convince myself of it. It seemed many of us then managed to convince ourselves by twisting truth into lies and then calling truth lies and lies truth. It was like we were making animals out of balloons and then pretending we had created life.

My first permanent posting was in Ukraine. I lived in Kiev where I worked with their government to unite all Eastern Europe in the goal of immortalization. Although it sounds like I had a large role to play in that movement, my job consisted mostly of working alongside former advertisers, artists, writers and the like to create various propaganda campaigns which were spread, if I may say, recklessly. I was one of many whose job was to oversee a small group who would come up with ideas. I'd review each pitch from my team and the ones I approved would be sent to someone higher up the hierarchy. If those higher-ups would approve of it, then we'd be given a budget with which to materialize our idea. Not exactly the job for a trained scientist. I found it very boring, but it kept me a member of the only family I had and so gave me an identity, even if it was an identity I despised.

What surprises me most about this time, even to this day, is how my actual thinking changed. Although, as I mentioned, I probably didn't really believe what I was pretending to believe, I still found myself feeling disgust when forced to think about any Mortal. They ceased to be people to me as if I bought the very propaganda I was selling. Mortals were suddenly conjuring up thoughts of long dirty fingernails, greasy hair, and flaking scalps, diseased skin, rotting teeth. I imagined their barbarous treatment of their own women and minority groups. Those minority groups conjured equal or greater feelings of disgust. I pictured their backwards ideas, their terrible history of wars and ignorance. It became an impulsive, involuntary reaction whenever I saw them or heard them or even heard someone talking about them. I was certain I could smell them when they were near me, a mortal stink which would stain my nostrils for hours after I had managed to escape their presence. I must have known that it was only in my head, but I forced myself to be convinced of it until it was impossible for me to behave in any manner that reflected what I knew as opposed to what I felt. I became capable only of acting on the lies I told myself. They became my reality and the driver of my actions. It was the price I had to pay to be a part of them: The Overmen. It was what I had to do to once again find euphoria in those words spoken by Professor Mesnick. We could be God, I thought, as long as we kept finding ways of convincing ourselves.

I have more to say about this period but nothing regarding myself. My daily routine had become so uniform, so monotonous that there is nothing much I could say, at least for now.

Chapter 26 ~ Crow's Feet

The Karski brothers both avoided activism during this time. As already mentioned, Nate was still recovering from the shock of losing Marie and Jonny thought it best to focus on his wife and son, who was almost a preteen by this time. This couldn't last forever, though. In that world it was becoming quite difficult to keep out of trouble. In fact, trouble had a knack for finding unsuspecting people who wanted nothing to do with it.

Jonny and Kara's flat was located in a small apartment block in the Wolseley neighborhood. Although it was far from ostentatious, it was an impressive size with a view of the Assiniboine River. Their ability to afford such a place was due to Nate's generosity and his generosity was fueled by his feelings for his nephew and his desire for him to have a decent living space since his illegal status forced him to spend much of his time indoors. His education took various forms including his parents' friends, who often offered their services as tutors, and a small make-shift classroom which was made up of a handful of other illegal children. When those weren't available, his parents, uncle and aunt, before she disappeared, often took the role of teacher. Looking back on those years James would say his only real complaint was the desire for normalcy, to experience the freedom as he would have if he were born legally.

It was on a Monday morning when all this changed. Jonny was preparing breakfast for his family in the kitchen. James was sitting at the table listening to his father natter away like he often did about something or other, and Kara was in the washroom getting ready for work.

"The trick with scrambled eggs," Jonny said to his son, "is making sure you whisk them up so they're frothy in the bowl before dumping them into the pan. See?" He turned and showed his son his whisking technique which to the boy appeared vigorous to the point of frenzy.

"You're going to make a mess, Dad."

"No, I'm not. Just watch. See that?" he stopped and displayed his work. "Looks like a yellow milkshake. That's what you want." He turned back towards the stove. "People say you have to put milk or cream in there to get them fluffy, but you don't. You just have to put some effort into it."

"What flavor do you suppose a yellow milkshake would be?" James asked pensively.

"What? I don't know. I don't think there is such a thing."

"Lemon?"

"Could be lemon. But lemon and milk don't really seem to go together do they. Banana."

"Yeah but bananas aren't really yellow. I mean, the outside is but you wouldn't toss the peal in."

"Very true, my son." Jonny began breaking up the egg in the pan.

James thought for a bit longer before noting, "I don't think what you said makes much sense, Dad."

Jonny turned around and leaned on the counter. "Excuse me?"

"Well, you said the eggs looked like a yellow milkshake."

"So?"

"If there's no such thing as a yellow milkshake, then they can't possibly look like one, right? Like, they just look like eggs. You can't say they look just like something that doesn't exist."

Before Jonny could respond, Kara walked in the room, face made up in a minimalist way—just a bit of mascara and some cover-up. She was dressed for the day in a black skirt, white blouse, and heels.

"Eggs are ready, my dear," Jonny said and prepared three dishes on the counter. Kara took her seat.

"What do you two have planned for the day?" Kara asked, and then grabbed a slice of toast from a plate in the middle of the table.

"Do we have plans?" James asked his father.

"We have plans to make plans," Jonny reassured.

"Do any of those plans involve changing out of your pajamas?" Kara asked with a subtle playfulness.

"I don't want to make any promises we can't keep. But if the time comes when it seems our pajamas might get in the way of our plans then a change of clothes will of course be integrated into the plan."

"And what plan is that?"

Before Jonny could answer the doorbell sounded. The sound it made wasn't the usual sound doorbells make but instead a sort of, "eeeeeehaaaaaaaaa," which James likened to an electronic donkey. Because of the horrible sound, no one who knew the Karskis ever rang it, electing to knock loudly instead, so the few times it did ring they knew it was someone unfamiliar with the usual proceedings of the place.

"Oh for Christ's sake," Jonny turned his attention to the door. "Who …?"

Kara sat up from the table and stood staring at the door. "James," she said quietly, and James knew immediately he should step outside the room.

"It could be anything," Jonny said in an attempt at reassurance, but he, too, felt a sting of apprehension. He approached the door and looked through the peephole. The bell rang again followed by loud knocking.

Jonny quietly walked away from the door and towards his wife. "Get James out of here." The knocking was growing louder now, more impatient.

"Who is it?" she asked, also whispering.

"Don't know, but they look—"

"This is the police! Open up. We know you're there," a voice shouted.

"Get out," Jonny yelled and ran back towards the door. The knocking stopped suddenly. Jonny put his eye to the viewer just as the door flung violently open knocking him to the ground. The apartment was suddenly filled with police. Jonny was swiftly turned on his stomach and handcuffed. He tried but couldn't see his wife or son. They would have taken the fire escape, he thought. They may have gotten away. But his optimistic hopes were quickly dashed when he heard Kara scream.

"Get your hands off my mum," James' small voice was barely audible amidst the sounds of grown men's voices shouting back.

"If you fight, we will hurt you," an officer yelled.

"Don't touch them," Jonny screamed, still searching what little of his apartment he could see from his compromised position. "Don't you fucking touch them."

"Dad!"

"I'm in here, son."

"Shut the fuck up. No talking."

"What's going on? What's happening?"

"Don't touch my son. You—"

"Shut the fuck up."

"Jonny?"

"I can't see you."

"Dad!"

"It's going to be all right"

"I said shut the ..." Jonny didn't hear the rest. He instead felt a heavy blow on the temple. The room began to spin with small sparks of light flickering round him. He was pulled up from the floor and forced to sit in a chair. In his daze he saw his wife and son being marched past him and out the door. He could see that they were both yelling and struggling but all sound seemed to be muffled. They both briefly looked at him and shouted something before they disappeared out the door.

Sitting in the chair, Jonny's senses returned. A woman with dark hair pulled back in a tight bun and wearing civilian clothes stood in front of him. She introduced herself as Detective Gagnon and explained that his and Kara's crimes were what she described as procreation without a permit and housing an unregistered person.

"What happens to my family?" Jonny said coolly, having collected himself.

"Prison, likely. I don't really know. That's not my job. My job is to track you, which I did, and take you in, which I'm about to do." She grabbed Jonny by the arm and helped him stand. "Let's go."

They began walking out of the apartment, down the lift, out the front to an unmarked police car parked amongst other unmarked vehicles along the street. All the while Jonny was looking for any sign of Kara and James. Would he ever see them again? He thought. Would he be sent to a camp now like Marie? Would Kara? What would become of James?

At the police station he was placed in an interrogation room in which Detective Gagnon sat across from him.

She began describing how they discovered James and the evidence against him. He was shown photographs, reports, a plethora of evidence the point of which was to convince him he had no case. "You'll be convicted," she said emphatically. "There's not much anyone can do for you."

"Can I call someone?" he asked with a defeated tone.

"No. Not now. Once we're done here you are free to call whomever you like but right now—"

"What about my lawyer?"

"Yes, of course. Don't worry, you're entitled to legal counsel. But before we get to that, I want you to understand the gravity of the situation."

"What was I supposed to do?" Jonny smiled ironically.

"I suppose you should have reported to the authorities when you found out your wife—"

"Do you know how much the fines are for having a child without a permit?"

"Then you shouldn't have had the child. Look, like I said, that is not my job."

"You're a Mortal," James said, studying her face. "Your crow's feet," he smiled again, and circled a finger around the corner of his eye. "It's a give-away."

"Yes, I am a Mortal."

"Why do you do it?"

"This? It's my job."

"But you're helping them. If people like you, with authority, with influence, if you stopped helping them there'd be nothing they could do."

"If I'm honest Mr. Karski, I'm not a very political person."

"Will we be sent to a camp?"

"A camp?" Detective Gagnon tilted her head to the side.

"You know what I'm talking about. Don't pretend like you don't."

"I have no idea what you're referring to," she said so convincingly Jonny almost believed her. "You'll likely serve some time, of course, but I wouldn't worry about anything beyond that," she spoke with a reassuring tone as if attempting to convey more knowledge of what Jonny was talking about than she was willing to admit.

"Can I have your word?"

"My word? On what?" She feigned confusion.

"That nothing more than prison will happen to us?"

She took a moment, possibly thinking of what to say without acknowledging what couldn't be acknowledged, and with what Jonny thought was an air of compassion said, "I'm sorry, but I can't. But I can tell you what is likely. This isn't … this is the sort of thing that usually gets resolved with some years in prison and possibly a fine. I've never heard of a case like yours leading to anything more than that, if that's any consolation."

Jonny laughed as a feeling of relief filled him from head to toe. "As a matter of fact, it is."

Jonny and Kara weren't sent to the camps, which made sense to them in hindsight. Those were for political dissidents, ones who didn't break any laws but couldn't be left free to stir up trouble. They were fined though, an astronomical amount, and sentenced to two years each in a federal penitentiary. The Overman-infected government justified the fines by claiming they simply calculated how much of a burden an illegal child is on taxpayers. To Jonny and Kara, however, it seemed to be designed for no other purpose than to cripple them financially and hopefully make an example. They couldn't pay it and the penalty for not was more time served, so Nate gave them the necessary funds. Although it didn't cripple him financially, Nate did have to downsize significantly afterwards. He sold his apartment and took James to Gerald, a small fishing town 80 kilometres north of the city where housing was cheaper, and the Overmen maintained only a minimal presence. He purchased a small cottage just outside of town on the shore of Lake Winnipeg.

Chapter 27 ~ Time Served

Kara and Jonny were sent to different prisons to serve their time, Jonny to Stony Mountain Penitentiary and Kara to Pebble Creek Institution for Women. Although both served their time by keeping themselves mostly out of trouble and were both released inside of their two-year sentence, Kara's experience was most noteworthy and so I'll make her my focus for this chapter.

Upon arrival she was processed and shown her new living quarters—a typical cell room for those days: 2 meters by 2.5 meters, steel toilet/sink combination, bunk bed, small desk—all of which she shared with another woman.

Every prisoner in the facility was given a daily job to do. Kara's was laundry. A typical day for her was waking up at 5:00 a.m. at which time she, along with the other prisoners, would be counted by the guards. She then went to breakfast in the cafeteria and then to her job in the laundry room. She'd perform this duty until lunch. After lunch some prisoners would have a couple hours of free time. During this time Kara would often read in the library, write emails, or walk about the prison yard. After this it was back to work if there was any, which there usually wasn't, or back to her cell until dinner. After dinner there was another couple hours of free time until 8 p.m. when all prisoners were sent back to their cell. In total, most prisoners spent about twelve-fourteen hours a day in their cell. While there they were allowed to do whatever they'd like which was obviously limited to whatever they had available. For Kara this meant more reading or writing, which she'd do on a typewriter which she was only able to obtain thanks to a generous donation by Nate and James. At 11:00 it was lights out, although she usually went to bed before this since, as she said, sleeping was a way of escape and so she would do as much of it as she could.

Her time was, like her husband's, mostly uneventful but for one specific event which led her to becoming acquainted with one specific person. This person's name was Abby Dalisay. They worked together in the laundry room but didn't form any sort of close bond until the protest.

The run-up to the protest began years before Kara even entered the penitentiary. Complaints about the living conditions in the prison went mostly unanswered for years. Prisoners, especially those who were considered a nuisance to the government, would find when they applied for parole that their hearings lasted an average of six minutes and were almost always rejected before the applicant could even make her case. This, amongst other issues such as rampant sexual abuse by the mostly male staff, led to the inevitable breaking point that took the form of a massive sit-in in the prison yard. Thirty prisoners entered the yard during their free time and refused to leave. Kara was not amongst them, but Abby was. They made a list of demands including less time confined to their cells and an avenue in which to file grievances and hold the guards accountable for misconduct. Once it began all other prisoners who were not in the yard, including Kara, were sent to their cells. After only ten hours the guards surrounded the protesters and began forcibly removing them from the area, using brutal force. Many women were beaten and were hauled off, some with severe injuries. One pregnant woman miscarried later that night. Those considered the greatest instigators were sent to solitary confinement while the rest were held in their cells twenty-four hours a day for weeks as punishment. There wasn't really anything that distinguished one protester from another. The reason they weren't all sent to solitary is because they simply didn't have enough rooms. They created the story that only the worst offenders were put in solitary, I guess, to try and convince future would-be protesters that taking part in a protest would lead to punishment but helping organize one would lead to more severe punishment. Abby was one of the ones sent to solitary.

After three weeks she was released. Kara saw her walk slowly into the laundry room, her arms wrapped around herself tightly as if she were afraid she'd unravel if she let go. She was already a small, young woman, thin, short, with fine, delicate looking features, but now she looked unhealthy. She walked to the long table on which a pile of freshly washed sheets lay and began folding. Kara stood across from her and was in the middle of performing this same task.

"Hey," Kara said quietly, as if afraid that speaking any louder would cause her to spook and run out the room.

Abby nodded and it seemed to Kara that she was trying to hold back tears.

"Are you all right?" Kara asked with the same softness.

"Mmhmm."

Kara began folding another sheet, while thinking of something to say. "I, um, I think what you did was really brave."

"Thank you," Abby whispered and cracked a slight smile. She cleared her throat and said a bit louder, "Nothing seems to have come of it, though. Looks like it was a waste of time and effort. And that poor woman lost her ..." a crack in her voice prevented her from finishing her sentence.

"You never know what comes of these things," Kara tried to reassure.

Abby smiled again and wiped away a tear.

Kara never intended to make friends while in prison. Her responsibility was with her son and she made up her mind at the beginning that she'd keep her head down, do her time, and get out as soon as possible. For this reason, she refrained from interacting with other inmates in any intimate way. She'd give them friendly smiles and greetings and would engage in the most basic small talk, but she never wanted to get involved with any of them personally. Such close relationships, she reasoned, lead people to do things they otherwise wouldn't and the last thing she wanted was to have more time added onto her sentence because she participated in some nonsensical protest in solidarity with her friends. But seeing young Abby, looking now like a brittle leaf that could be blown away by a drafty window, stirred up maternal or possibly just sympathetic feelings in her and she couldn't keep herself from reaching out.

The weeks that followed saw the two women get to know each other far more intimately than Kara had intended. Kara, being well over a decade older, was looked on by Abby as a sort of mentor—her soft seriousness was both calming and reassuring to the young woman—which naturally led Kara to view Abby as a sort of protégé.

"So, what brings you to this place?" Kara asked finally after Abby began to resemble her old self.

Abby grinned and lowered her head. "Drugs," she said sheepishly, and ran a hand over her black hair which she kept short and combed back. "I ah …"

"You don't have to tell me. It's not any of my business anyway. I shouldn't have asked."

"No, it's kind of a funny story, actually."

"A funny story? I find that hard to believe."

"Well, I'll let you decide. See," Abby dropped her unfolded sheet on the table, "I was a student at the U of W—"

"What were you studying?"

"Theater and Film."

"Sounds fun."

"I loved it. Only finished my second year, though, before I ended up here. Anyway, I live with my aunt and uncle in the North End. They don't have a lot of money. I don't have a lot of money, either, but wanted to get a place closer to the University. So, I remembered a cousin of mine used to deal a little weed here and there, or a lot of weed here and there, and ended up making a lot of extra cash. I thought I could do the same thing. Turns out some people have a knack for that sort of thing. I didn't."

"What happened, if you don't mind me asking?"

"Not at all. Well," she smiled, and it seemed to Kara that her telling her story was distracting her from the trauma she so recently experienced, "I asked my cousin to kind of point me in the proper direction which he adamantly refused to do. So, I, um, so I stole a bag of weed, like a big bag," Abby indicted with her hands a size of about twenty centimetres, "from him and took the whole thing to university with me in my backpack. I didn't really know what I was going to do with it. I didn't think I could sell it as it was, so I just kept it in my backpack for days. I forgot about it, really. Then one day at the mall some cops were there with some drug sniffing dogs and, well, that's about it. Because of the amount I had I was charged with possession with intent to distribute."

"I didn't laugh once during that story. It's not funny at all," Kara said before breaking into wide smile.

"Yes, I suppose funny wasn't the proper word."

"Unfortunate, perhaps."

"Yes, it was definitely unfortunate."

"It wasn't even amusing."

Abby tried to smile. "It's not a good story. But it's what happened."

"I think you owe me a laugh."

Over the next year Kara learnt that Abby's parents had both passed away, her mother when she was ten from a brain hemorrhage and her father when she was nineteen from heart failure. She then moved in with her aunt and uncle who were both first generation immigrants from the Philippines and had no children of their own.

"They've both been pretty active politically. They're good at organizing, stuff like that. I'm always afraid they're going to disappear one day but so far they've managed to stay off the government's radar."

"They must play it pretty safe."

"They do. But they have …." Abby stopped as if she were suddenly afraid she might not be able to trust Kara. "I probably shouldn't say anymore."

"Then don't, that's fine," Kara said with a tone of slight admonishment. "It's always best to err on the safe side."

"I can trust you though, right?"

"You can, yeah. I mean, *I* of course think you can, but you might not yet. But don't trust me or anyone until you are convinced you can."

It didn't take long before Abby did feel she could trust her. A few weeks later she told Kara that her aunt and uncle hosted secret meetings in the basement of the restaurant they ran in the North End of the city.

"People have dubbed it The Speakeasy because it's set up like a little tavern. They even have a bar which my uncle likes to man."

"Who visits this Speakeasy?"

"Lots of people. All concerned citizens. If you're ever interested, you know, when we get out of here, you should come to a meeting."

"Oh, I don't know," Kara said, shaking her head slightly. "I'm sure my husband would be more than happy to, but I have a son to raise."

"Doesn't your husband have a son to raise, too?"

Kara laughed, "Yes, of course. I just mean, he's more involved in that sort of thing than I am.

"Well, you're both welcome. And my aunt and uncle are a lot of fun."

"Do you go? Or, did you before you came here?"

"I didn't really. I mean I lived with them and often worked at the restaurant, but I was never really interested, you know. But, when I get out of here … well, I think I might make it a more regular thing."

Chapter 28 ~ Life Resumes

Kara was released two months earlier than Jonny, during which time she moved to Gerald and lived in the cottage with Nate and James. She didn't intend to stay there indefinitely but wanted to wait for her husband to be released so they could find a place together. Returning to life after her time in prison required some adjustment. The freedom to go anywhere she liked was at first breathtaking almost to the point of intimidation. She spent her first week eating and drinking everything she missed and spending a great deal of time walking into town buying a coffee and drinking it on the beach while looking across the murky waters of Lake Winnipeg. It was late summer and although autumn was still a month away, there was already a slight chill in the air. She woke up early for these excursions, usually around 6:00 am and was back before her son and brother-in-law woke up, which they usually did between 10:30 and 11:00. She'd often buy breakfast for them from the local shops and restaurants or else she would buy groceries with which to make breakfast. When she wasn't needed inside, she'd spend every moment available out of doors, even if that meant just sitting on the patio with a book. She felt she had enough of confined spaces for now.

Nate and James wanted to throw a welcome home party for her, which they did, but she insisted it be small. She felt it inappropriate to celebrate too much while her husband was still behind bars. After his release two months later, they finally threw a proper celebratory get-together with many of their friends from the city. Abby had been released from prison six months before Kara and so Kara made sure to invite her. She came with her aunt and uncle.

The cottage was painted yellow, which had since become weather worn and chipped in places, and white trim around the windows and doors. The front had a short driveway and a small yard which, on this day, was used as a parking lot, and concrete steps leading up to the front door. At the back there was a covered deck facing a much larger yard, lined with trees on the sides with a small rocky beach at the end. Because of the smaller living space in the cottage compared to their old apartment, the partygoers were forced to spend most of their time either sitting on the deck or on one of the many lawn chairs scattered all round the back yard. On the deck there was a barbeque which was being used to cook an assortment of meats and vegetables, all of which were being prepared beforehand inside by a motley crew of guests. In order to feed everyone, the barbeque was in continuous use for over an hour during which time the creak of the screen door continually opening and closing to bring out trays of food supplemented the more dominant sound of the crowd's murmur.

"I don't suppose," Kara said to Abby, "that you could grab that pitcher there and follow me out to the deck." Kara already had a large tray of raw burger patties and was referring to a pitcher filled with some sort of rum and fruit juice-based cocktail.

"Of course," Abby said cheerfully grabbing the pitcher while Kara quickly disappeared out the screen door. Abby turned to her aunt and uncle who were also standing in the kitchen, her aunt looking rather bored while her uncle was quietly examining the furnishings and decorations. "Do you guys want to stay here or come out with us?"

"Will you be coming back in?" her uncle said, with one hand resting in the small of his back and the other holding his still folded reading glasses. He was, Abby explained earlier to Kara, always an investigator. Wherever he was he had to walk about and examine every object that might contain some originality. Family photos were always the first to be examined when he was in a new place and from there, he'd make his way to the art, then furniture, then everything else from the wallpaper to the carpet. At this moment his attention was being held by a small, framed painting of a sailboat in a storm.

"If you'd like," Abby was holding the pitcher with her back at the door.

"I'm fine," he said and turned his spectacles to a small wooden shelf with three wood carvings of giraffes, each one a different size.

"Aunt Danica?"

"If you're staying out there, I'm coming with you," Aunt Danica stated matter-of-factly. "No point staying in here watching him watch everything else." Danica Dalisay matched her niece in her small frame but unlike Abby, and unlike her husband, she was always bursting with things to say and people to meet. While her husband enjoyed examining inanimate objects, her passion was examining people in all their variations. She often told her niece that she got enough alone time with her husband and so took every opportunity to talk to someone who might talk back.

"Okay, Uncle Pat, if you need us, we'll be just out here. Do you want anything before we go?"

"Oh, he's not listening to you," Aunt Danica said having made her way to the door which was still blocked by Abby. "He's thrilled by boredom. Come on, let's see what's happening out here."

Outside Abby deposited the pitcher on a wooden table which acted as the de facto bar and scanned the yard. Kara, she could see, was making herself busy asking guests if there was anything they needed. Her being the only one she yet knew at the party, she turned to her aunt, but she had scurried off and was already engaged in a conversation with a woman who looked about her age. Abby sighed, sauntered to the bar where she mixed a cocktail, and then walked down the steps onto the yard and towards the beach. On her way she passed Jonny and James playing bocce ball in the yard.

Having not spent time with his son during his incarceration, Jonny appeared determined to make up for it. This was a marked change from his usual behavior at parties which usually saw him jumping from group to group keeping everyone entertained. It was understandable, though, all things considered, but it wasn't the only change that Nate and Kara noticed in him since his release. There seemed to be a bit of darkness that had developed amidst his usually jovial disposition. His wit was more biting, even hostile at times, and he was quicker to anger. It was subtle enough that James didn't seem to notice but it was there, keeping just barely out of sight, hinting that perhaps there was much more to this new feature than had yet been revealed.

Nate soon appeared with two drinks sitting one down in the cup holder on a nearby lawn chair and sipping the other. He stood out of the way watching the game.

"That for me?" Jonny said.

"Yeah, still drink Keith's?"

"I drink whatever is within reach these days."

Nate smiled and took a sip from his tumbler.

"Ooooooooooo, so close," Jonny called to his son whose ball rolled two meters passed the jack.

"Can't think of how to start a conversation with someone just released from prison," Nate said after a minute of silence. "What did people say to me when I was released?"

"All kinds of bullshit. Pardon me, son. A lot of people resorted to, 'Feel good to be back?' I think that was the silliest thing I remember people saying. 'Glad to have you back' was another one."

"Well, what would you recommend I say?"

"Ha, it's just as hard for me to think of anything." His tone seemed a bit harsh, like it was underlined with annoyance. "You know what it's like. Good shot, son!" Jonny walked to the line next to James. "I think you win this round." He turned his attention back to Nate while walking towards the balls. "How'd you get over it all?" he asked, collecting the scattered balls and tossing them into a group.

"Um, I don't know. I don't know that I have, really."

"It changed you, didn't it? Yeah, I know, it changed me, too. Not in the same way, though. Unlike you, I won't be sitting on my ass all day."

"Is that what you think I do?" Nate asked not yet sure if his brother was joking or accusing.

"Come on," Jonny abandoned the game and walked to his beer. "I don't know what you've been doing since that whole thing. Actually, I do know what you've been doing, and it isn't much. I don't know how you can just ignore everything now. I can't, frankly. I'm convinced now that doing nothing isn't an option. I can't ignore it anymore." He took a sip, wiped away some beer that had spilt on his chin and replaced the bottle on the holder. "After seeing what they lock people up for. How they treat people," Jonny marched back to the balls, picked one up and took a bowler's stance. Nate could see him unconsciously shaking his head before he tossed the ball which hit one of his own balls with a loud smack.

Feeling slightly attacked but not wanting to start something with his brother so soon after his release, Nate just bobbed his head, pretending not to be hurt, and said, "Well, I'll leave you two alone."

"Hey, no. I'm sorry. I shouldn't have said that," Jonny shouted quickly before Nate could walk away. "And Marie … I wasn't thinking about Marie. But things are different now. For me at least. That's all I'm saying, and I have trouble seeing how anyone else can think differently. Especially someone who's had the same experience, ya know."

"Yeah, people are different, though, Jon."

"Yeah, I know. And it is different for you. I don't know how I'd react if what happened to Marie happened to Kara. I'm just … I can't explain it. I just want to do something. I don't want to be here," he tossed his ball with more force than he appeared to intend and walked back to his beer.

"Does this mean we're done playing?" James asked, still holding his ball.

"Let me just talk to your uncle for a moment, son."

"Okay." James busied himself with bowling both colors.

"I can't sleep," Jonny confessed abruptly. "I can't sit still. I must do something. Someone has to, obviously. All I could think about while I was in there was what I would do when I got out and, now I'm out. But I don't know what to do." He lowered his voice. "Sometimes I think of doing something a bit more drastic."

"What do you mean?"

"I mean, things are getting worse and worse. We must do something. It's become a war, hasn't it?"

"War?" Nate said with some astonishment.

"You don't agree?"

"I might, I really might if I gave it some thought, but really, man, I just wanted to bring you a beer."

Jonny paused for a moment before laughing and slapping his brother's shoulder.

"I'm trying to be a good host and you start talking about fucking war? Jesus, man. Drink your beer. Let your son beat you at bocce ball. War can wait."

"I suppose there's a valid point in there somewhere." Jonny finished his beer and Nate took the empty bottle from him.

"I'm going to go get you another one of these. When I come back think of it as a take-two. This time, instead of bringing up war, let's start with the weather and your health." Nate turned and walked towards the deck. There he was met by a small energetic woman who appeared so suddenly Nate thought she must have been lying in wait.

"You're Nathaniel Karski," she exclaimed and tried to shake his hand but, noticing both were occupied with empty beverage containers, grabbed both his wrists and shook them instead.

"I am."

"My name is Danica, I'm the aunt of … where did she run off to? Anyway, my niece is a friend of your friend."

"I see." Nate's smile grew. "And which friend is that?"

"Kayla … Karen …."

"Kara?"

"Possibly."

"That's my sister-in-law."

"Probably her then." She finally let go of his wrists and clasped her hands to her chest. "It's a pleasure to meet you, anyway. That's all I wanted to say."

"And you."

"Say, if one were to start reading your work, which book would you recommend they start with?"

"Are you saying you haven't read any of my books?"

"I didn't say that, no. But I mean, that does happen to be the case."

Nate's smile had now grown into a bubbling chuckle. "It's just that you seemed like such a fan. I assumed you'd have at least read When the Wind Stops."

"What's that?"

"One of my books."

"Is that the one you'd recommend?" Danica was smiling broadly and seemed to be about to explode with excitement.

"Well, I suppose it's my most famous book."

"I can't wait. It's been great talking to you."

And just as quickly as she appeared Aunt Danica Dalisay disappeared into another crowd.

"I see you've met Aunt Danica," Kara, who happened by, said to inform him that his exchange with the animated woman had been witnessed.

"She's full of beans, eh."

"Yes, she is a bit of a firecracker. You should meet her husband."

"Is he anything like that?"

"They are yin and yang."

The two of them walked together up the stairs of the deck and to the bar where a queue had formed.

"Have you talked to your husband? He seems a bit on edge."

"Yeah, I was actually about to bring him a beer."

"That's what I'm supposed to be doing."

"You were taking too long I suppose."

After getting their drinks sorted Nate and Kara began making their way back where they had left Jonny and James but quickly noticed the bocce ball set had been abandoned. They made their way to the small rocky beach, surmising, rightfully, that there was nowhere else for them to have gone. Sure enough, father and son were found skipping rocks across the still water of the lake.

"Abby?" Kara said noticing her friend sitting on a large rock to the side with her knees pulled up to her chest.

"Hey," she responded with a friendly grin.

"What are you doing here by yourself?"

She nodded towards the lake, "It's a beautiful view."

"It is." Kara walked to her and sat on an adjacent rock. "Where're your aunt and uncle?"

"Uncle Patrick is inspecting the house, I'm guessing but it's an educated guess, and Aunt Danica is ... well, right there."

"Hullo."

Everyone turned to see the fiery woman hurriedly making her way to the group, kicking up stones and sand as she did so.

"So, this is where everyone is hiding." She had a bottle of something in her hand which she lifted to show everyone. "I brought some rum so we wouldn't have to run back and forth. Hope that's all right."

"Of course," Nate said, taking the bottle from her as she moved towards her niece. "Um, have you met my brother Jonny?"

"I haven't but it's a pleasure," she said and turned 180 degrees away from her niece and marched towards Jonny with an outstretched hand.

"Pleased to meet you," Jonny said with an amused expression and shook her hand.

"Are you a writer, too?"

"I am not."

"Ever wanted to be?"

Jonny shrugged, "Not really. Never been my thing, writing."

"Hm," and turning from him queried loudly, "Has anyone seen that bumbling old tortoise of mine?"

"You have a tortoise?" James broke from his rock throwing to inquire excitedly.

"I do yes, he's about this tall and answers to Patrick."

"Not a real tortoise then?" James seemed disappointed.

"When you see him, you'll understand."

"I last saw him inside the house," Abby informed.

"No use trying to get him. If he starts now, he won't make it here until sunrise tomorrow." Aunt Danica was shuffling about like a bee collecting pollen. She continued to keep everyone satisfactorily entertained for another half hour before her husband indeed appeared on the beach with them.

"Where have you been?" Aunt Danica asked upon seeing her husband saunter to where the grass met the sand.

"I've been keeping busy," he said slowly, placed is hands behind his back and began rocking contently on his heels.

"Keeping busy? A fish in a bowl could keep you busy. It's true."

"Well, I suppose that would depend on the type of fish,"

"Really, he's always interested even when there's nothing interesting around. Watching paint dry is on his list of things to do before he dies."

"It's getting cold out isn't it?" Uncle Patrick said, seemingly unaffected by Danica's criticism.

"Is it time to be heading in?" Nate asked. He had been looking out across the water in a sort of trance and hadn't noticed how dark it had become.

"I think so," said Kara, "can't forget we have a lot of other guests to entertain."

"Jonny?" Nate looked to his left and saw his brother sitting in much the same way he was and in a similar trance-like state. It was dark, however, which meant that Nate couldn't detect the bouncing knee. And the other voices from the party and the sound of the gentle, lapping, waves meant he couldn't hear the constant and deliberate sighs. For while Nate's quietude reflected his inward melancholy, Jonny's silence was an attempt to quell the barely manageable anxiety. At that moment it was so strong he felt if he let it out it could provide enough energy to swim straight across the lake before him.

"What's that?" Jonny said.

"Shall we go in?"

"Sure," Jonny jumped up and marched briskly past everyone before stopping and turning around to Patrick. "You're Patrick Dalisay, correct?"

"I am he."

"Can we have a chat?"

"Of course."

Everyone else continued to the cottage while Jonny and Patrick had their conversation where they stood. Or where Patrick stood. Jonny instead paced round him as he spoke, about what no one watching could tell, while Patrick listened intently and only turned in his spot to keep Jonny in his view.

Later that night Jonny explained his conversation with Mr. Dalisay to Kara when they were alone in their room.

"What was all that about with you and Mr. Dalisay?" Kara asked, sitting on the edge of her bed and rubbing lotion on her hands and arms. Jonny was pacing again as if he hadn't stopped and simply managed to pace his way into his bedroom. While Kara was already dressed for bed Jonny hadn't even taken off his shoes.

"I can't stay here," he said distractedly as if he were talking to himself.

Kara stopped rubbing her arms for a second, breathed in deeply and then continued. "And what does that mean?"

"It means, I can't do nothing."

"You have to go somewhere to do something? You can't do something here?" She was trying to remain as calm as possible, but her stomach was already in knots.

"I think so. I mean, what are we doing here? We're in the middle of nowhere now. There's nothing around us but trees and a giant lake. What can we possibly do here?"

"Well, darling, I had this idea that after you got out, we could find our own place." She placed her hands on her lap and sat straight. "I never expected you'd want to live here with your brother indefinitely. I think James would like us to have a place of our own, too. We could even move into Gerald if you'd like. James would be closer to the school, closer to his friends."

"It's not that. I mean, that's not enough. What would we do in Gerald? Same thing we're doing here. Nothing. We can't keep doing nothing. All everyone here does is nothing."

"Could you stop that, please, the pacing."

"We need to be out there," he motioned to the window with an open hand. "We need to be where it matters, where people are doing things."

"Please, honey, stop—"

"We should be fighting. What did we do tonight? We had a party. We invited friends over to drink and eat and talk about nonsense."

"Stop," Kara shouted finally. "Stop, please. Stop this pacing about and ranting. I don't need to hear you say anymore. I know what you're saying."

Jonny stopped and stood in the middle of the room. "I'll lose my mind if I stay here while the world round us crumbles."

"I wanted to get a place. For us, like we had before." Kara's voice began to crack, showing some deep emotion she was not used to showing.

"And then what?" Jonny walked to the bed and sat beside her. "I have to go. Patrick said he can put me I contact with people he knows, and they can get me involved in the resistance in Ottawa."

"Ottawa?"

"They're making real strides there. I could be of help. I have… we have a lot of experience with this sort of thing. Of organising and—"

"I'm not going to Ottawa. I'm not bringing James to Ottawa."

"No, of course not. I'm not asking you to come. In fact, I'd rather you didn't."

"So … how much time do we have with you before you go?"

"A few days." Jonny's voice softened.

"A few days," Kara repeated, her tone openly displaying her anger. "A few fucking days? You just got back and now, in a few fucking days, you're leaving us again?"

"When things quiet down … when all this gets sorted … when we start to see some real progress …" Jonny kept starting sentences like these, repeating them like a chant, but couldn't find any words that might finish them.

"I wanted a house with you and James," Kara stood up. She was furious but her face was strewn with tears.

"When things quiet down … when all this gets sorted …" he kept saying.

Chapter 29 ~ A Short Stint

Jonny left for Ottawa and after he did so, life in the cottage became quiet. There were few parties, if any, just evening drinks with the occasional friend popping in for a visit. Nate still wrote but less prolifically, preferring instead to spend his days building forts in his yard with his nephew, sitting in local coffee shops with quiet friends or his sister-in-law, and avoiding the topic of politics altogether. His demeanor was different; he smiled less, talked less, and when he did talk, he moved his hands less, often keeping them tucked close to his body as if to keep himself small and inconspicuous. His thoughts turned often to his wife, wherever she was, and when not to her then to his brother, wherever he was. He found himself spending hours a day with thoughts of them racing into and out of his head with no clear direction and himself feeling helpless to do anything for either of them. On top of these thoughts, I must add, he also thought of me. At least he told me so years later. He fretted often, he confessed, not knowing where I was or what I was doing but pretending to believe I was doing more good than harm. I don't really have anything more to add to that. Just that it still makes me feel good believing he thought of me during those horrible years.

The name of Jonny's organization was Yesterday's Forecast, often shortened to YesFore, and their modus operandi was originally dedicated to peaceful, nonviolent protest and civil disobedience. But, after several of their people disappeared, never to be seen again, they went underground and began to protest in other ways while maintaining their dedication to nonviolence. Some of these ways involved large displays of vandalism that would often take weeks to plan and many hours to execute. They would perform these daring feats under cover of darkness like elite military units but instead of guns they were armed with spray paint, plaster molds, papier-mâché, and other products with which to leave large, flashy, and conspicuous messages all around the city. Once a project was agreed upon, they'd prepare as much as possible and then rehearse to ensure everything went as smooth as possible. One such project included a miniature wall, complete with barbed wire and a couple proportionately small guard towers, erected in front of the Canadian Tribute to Human Rights. On the plaque that reads: "All human beings are born free and equal with dignity and rights," the word "all" was crudely crossed out with red spray-paint and "some" was written next to it. Another, one of their most provocative, was a large display featuring a ten foot tall Overman eating tiny Mortals from a cereal bowl with a spoon; this one was erected in the middle of Rideau Street and managed to block morning traffic for an hour until it could be removed. They had bolted it to the pavement.

Jonny often returned to visit his family in Gerald. He would be welcomed home like a soldier on leave from war. During these visits the little cottage in Gerald would be filled with laughter and loud conversations that stretched into the night and often into the morning. He left in Ottawa that anxiety and anger that had followed him out of prison and to everyone in Gerald was back to his old self. Fishing trips would be planned on water and ice, depending on the season, and parties would be held. Life in general returned to the Karskis even if it was for a fleeting moment. But when he left, he took the gaiety with him and left the feeling of gloom behind.

Then on one such visit which was meant to be only for the Christmas holiday, Jonny didn't go back. He arrived a couple days before Christmas intending to leave sometime after Boxing Day but couldn't seem to bring himself to do it. There always seemed to be something for which it was worth staying a little bit longer. At a Christmas party with old friends and family, he learnt of a New Year's Eve get-together which would feature a number of friends he hadn't seen in years. "It's only a couple extra days," Nate reasoned, and Jonny acquiesced. Then after the New Year's party he was told of a popular folk band playing at the local pub in Gerald in a fortnight. Again, he was easily convinced, this time by his wife who was a fan of the band, to extend his stay. And then another thing popped up and another and another. It soon became apparent that it wasn't the things popping up that were keeping Jonny in Gerald but something in Ottawa that was keeping him away. Sometime at the end of January Nate asked him if he wouldn't like to just stay permanently to which Jonny replied, "You know I can't. In fact, I'll have to be leaving as soon as possible." But a few more weeks passed, and he remained.

Finally, one night, when Jonny was alone with his wife getting ready for bed, he explained his reluctance to return.

"Are you afraid of being caught?" Kara asked. She was already in bed trying to read a book but couldn't maintain her focus.

"What's that?" Jonny replied, sitting on the edge of the bed pulling his trouser leg over his heel.

"I'm trying to figure out why you continue to avoid going back to Ottawa. Is it because you're afraid?"

"I'm always afraid. It's frightening work," he got his trousers off, stood up, and began unbuttoning his shirt.

"But that's not why you're still here?"

"Are you trying to get rid of me?" he laughed and climbed into bed. "Would you rather I was in Ottawa?"

"Of course not. But I'm curious," she said in her matter-of-fact way. "You seemed so desperate to leave, after what happened to Marie and after prison but now you seem almost uninterested."

"I've just been enjoying spending time with my family." Jonny snuggled up next to his wife. "For example, I thought tonight you and I might spend some time, you know, communicating our feelings." He began planting light kisses on her bare arm.

"You're avoiding the question. Why don't you want to go back?" Kara persisted.

Jonny halted the kisses. "I never said I didn't want to go back, did I?" Jonny was becoming annoyed. He pushed himself up and settled on his side of the twin bed. "Why must there be something the matter? Why can't I just be enjoying this time with you and James?"

"But I've noticed it's not just that you are staying here far longer than you intended, it's that you haven't even talked about what you're doing in Ottawa. You haven't told any stories or given any details about what you're doing."

"Haven't I?" his voice sounded tired now.

"Not at all. Usually whenever you come for a visit you regale us with stories of the people you work with, the projects you work on, and more. You used to make me jealous with your stories. This time you haven't said a word about it."

"Things are different now," Jonny admitted finally. "There aren't the stories there used to be. It's not the same."

"What do you mean?" Kara shuffled over, sensing a heaviness in her husband's words.

"I'm fucking tired. Could we talk about this in the morning?"

"Of course."

The next morning after breakfast Jonny and Kara hopped in the car with the intent to go to the supermarket. James was left in the care of his uncle, so they had time to themselves.

"Don't go straight there," Jonny said to his wife. "Let's drive round for a bit."

"Like we're teenagers?" Kara smiled.

"Just like that," Jonny smiled back and turned in his seat to face her.

"Are we going to find someplace to park and make out?" Kara asked, laughing.

"I just want to drive for a bit. It's beautiful here. The snow makes everything look like a fairy tale. Let's go south, through the cottages."

"Sure." Kara stopped and turned the car around at the first opportunity. As they drove past the heavily snow-covered evergreens and birch and into cottage communities, Jonny kept silent while his eyes absorbed the wintery scene.

It was obvious to Jonny that Kara wanted to bring up the conversation from the night before and although he now felt willing to discuss it, he first wanted to take a moment to collect his thoughts.

They passed through another collection of snow-covered properties, most of which had dark windows and un-shovelled walkways, but a few winterized cottages were clearly lived in. When they passed the last cottage and the scenery changed back to thick forest, Jonny suggested turning back around lest they end up driving all the way to Winnipeg. At the first opportunity Kara did just that.

Jonny sighed loudly to signal that he was ready to speak and then said, "I've been trying to think of a way to say this without it sounding insane but the more I try, and the more I fail, the more I realize that perhaps there is no sanity in what I have to say."

Keeping her eyes on her driving Kara nodded to encourage him to continue.

"Things are becoming more complicated," he said in one slow breath as if being deflated.

"Of course. The world has gone mad."

"Yes, mad, absolutely mad. You can see it from here, despite how far removed we are in this place. But in Ottawa, amid everything, madness doesn't quite suffice, I'm afraid. Horror might have been a sufficient word at one point in time, but that word's meaning has been eroded enough that it no longer qualifies." Jonny was speaking slowly as if taking time to weigh the effect of each word before he spoke it, something not normally characteristic of him. "There are possibly no words yet to describe it only because so few understand what it is. One usually has to suffer horribly to know what *unword* it is that I'm talking about. And those who know it are in no mood to ascribe to it a proper description."

"Have you suffered greatly over there?" Kara asked with a sudden air of concern.

"I've been lucky. But I know many who have." Then after a short pause corrected himself, "*knew* many who had. My friends there, many have disappeared—same as Marie. Once some friends of ours were raided, a couple with an adopted toddler, a little girl, sweetest thing. During the raid something went awry and all three of them, the little girl included, were shot dead. I could tell you more stories like that. They're trying to make us afraid."

"Is that why you haven't returned? You're afraid?"

"No, their plan isn't working. We aren't becoming afraid, at least not more so than we already were, we're becoming angry. No not angry;

it's not that either. The reason I haven't returned is because of what that suffering and anger and more, that *unword*, has done to so many of my friends. It makes them unrecognizable. Their loss of dignity, loss of identity, trauma, it makes them into something else. Something terrible. Something inhuman capable of inhumane things. They're no longer content with erecting statues or painting walls or holding meetings. They're only content with ... maybe only capable of, doing unspeakable things."

"What kinds of things," Kara's voice was barely above a whisper.

"Unspeakable," Jonny repeated.

"Do they want you to do these things for them?"

Jonny didn't answer at first as if the question surprised him even though he anticipated it. But he couldn't think of what to say or how to say it. "Well, our group, YesFore, it still stands for what it always has. It still condemns violence and promotes civil disobedience and all that. Those who embrace those other things don't have a place with them."

"So, what's the problem then?"

"Well, you see," Jonny turned to his wife who maintained her focus on the road, "the problem is that, when I'm there, *I* want to do those things. Those unspeakable things. I'm often unable to think of doing anything else. And, another thing, I've started ... I mean, I did something." He paused to let the confession sink in. "I did something," he repeated, "and I fear if I go back, I'll do more."

Jonny had no thing more he wanted to say and although Kara had much more she wanted to say, her mind couldn't detach itself from his all-too-brief confession long enough to construct a sentence. She instead drove to the supermarket in silence replaying her husband's words in her mind. What kind of thing did he do? The possibilities, the implications, they flashed through her head. Once they arrived and had parked, they sat in the car for a while, both knowing there was more that needed to be said but neither knowing how to say it, as if everything that needed to be said were more *unwords*.

"You'll stay?" Kara said finally. "You'll stay for good?"

Jonny smiled and raised an eyebrow. "It's beginning to look like it, isn't it?"

"I want you to say yes, you'll stay with us." Kara wasn't going to let the conversation die without at least a verbal contract.

Jonny smiled again and then slowly and unsurely nodded his head. "I think I will. For a bit longer at least."

Violent groups had begun popping up all over the world and in greater numbers. Bombings were becoming frequent occurrences, initially in underdeveloped nations but before long, it became unsurprising to hear about a building going up in flames in London or New York. In Kiev, where I was stationed, the café on the first floor of the office building I worked in was bombed. A few people were killed and over a dozen injured. It was believed that they somehow found out that the OP was renting office space on the upper floors and so we became a target. Why they decided to bomb the café instead of the office space we were using is still a mystery to me. It could have been because of the difficulty reaching our floor when the café was right there on the first. I think they were hoping some Overmen would be amongst the victims but that wasn't the case. The only victims were regular innocent Mortals.

When many of the bombers, even the most violent ones, decided that their tactics weren't having much of an effect, groups of militants began popping up in greater frequency until they eventually outnumbered the bombers, although bombings never seemed to go out of style. Many people quit bombing groups when they either got tired of senseless violence or hungry for *more* senseless violence. The tired ones went home or resumed regular non-violent activism while the hungry ones ran foaming at the mouths to the only place that could satisfy their bloodlust: the militants.

It might seem strange for me to separate the bombers from the militants since they both were responsible for many murders but there is a very specific difference which is why I insist on the separation. Bombers would plant their devices in a building, walk away, and set it off. They weren't present when people were killed. For the most part they didn't see the damage they did to people. They were, in a way, more cowardly but they also didn't take pleasure in the suffering of the individuals they killed or maimed. The militants, on the other hand, saw their victims' faces. Saw directly what they were doing to people. Now this makes no difference to the people being maimed or killed by either group, but it does draw a distinction between the people doing the maiming and killing.

Jonny kept his word and stayed. One evening, a couple of months after his conversation with Kara in the car, he finally elaborated on that brief confession. While both in the middle of undressing and sitting on opposite sides of the bed with their backs to each other, Jonny unexpectedly began to tell her the story. First, he explained his official job in Ottawa. He told her he was a planner and organizer for events or, as they often called them, operations. This position he was thankful for, he said, because it kept him away from the actual field work which obviously posed the greatest risk of being caught.

Shortly before he left, he took part in the most ambitious project YesFore had ever attempted; he was the chief planner. It involved a three-day long graffiti campaign throughout the city. The targets were carefully scouted out beforehand and for two weeks they practiced and refined the plan.

One of the artists was named Ron Hawke, a large, jovial man. Ron often used the moniker Ratattack for his work when he was younger and so many of his friends called him Rat or Ratty or RataRon or other variations. He was in his forties, married with a teenage son by the time Jonny met him. The two became quick and close friends upon meeting.

Ron was responsible for painting the biggest and most ambitious piece which was planned for the last day of the campaign to cap it all off with a bang. It depicted the classic Overman—square jaw, bald head, blue eyes, as often depicted in early OP propaganda—emerging from a cocoon made entirely of the bodies of Mortals. His idealized head was attached to the body of a grotesque butterfly with puny wings and his signature torch was slipping out of the grasp of his spindly insect legs. The slogan painted in red letters underneath was, *Humanity, a small price to pay for eternity.* For the weeks leading up to the event, Ron cut out many stencils to be used for his masterpiece and eventually a spot was chosen on a large building that would be visible from Parliament.

For three nights artists from YesFore ventured out into the city, accompanied by lookouts armed with two-way radios to leave their messages to be seen and interpreted the next morning. Every morning after these nightly excursions they'd wake up to find that most of their work had already been covered up or erased but a quick check online showed that the authorities were never quick enough to stop photos from being taken and displayed permanently on the internet for millions of people to see. By the third day, when it was time for Ron to make his mark, many people all round the country were talking about it and speculating if more paintings would appear. This also meant that the police and even the Public Protection Agency had begun an investigation into the sudden increase of subversive art around the city. It was obviously well organized which gave them their first clue that it was the product of a group like Yesterday's Forecast. Contacts that YesFore had in the police service let them know that the police were working with the PPA and that the risk was greater than it was before. Despite this warning, Ron chose to finish the campaign.

Jonny stayed up all night waiting for his friend to return in a safe house YesFore rented in the neighbourhood of Varnier. Finally, just before sunrise a soft but hurried knock sounded the apartment door. Jonny opened it quickly and Ron slipped inside, sweating and breathing heavily but alive and carrying a broad smile on his face. Jonny looked furtively up and down the hallway before quickly closing the door.

"I did it," Ron said through panting breath after the door had been shut. "Fuck, I'm a bit old for this but I still managed it." He peeled off his jacket and dropped into a tattered armchair, leaving his boots on.

"Why are you so out of breath?"

"Someone saw me just as I was finishing." He leaned forward and put his head in his hands.

"What? Who?"

"I don't know, but I managed to lose him."

"He chased you?"

"Yeah." Ron laughed a bit. "I don't know if it was an out-of-uniform cop or some over-zealous citizen but whoever it was there was only one of them and they're gone."

"Jesus, Ron."

"Don't worry about it. Can I get a glass of water? I'm fucking parched."

Jonny poured a glass from a water cooler and handed it to Ron. "Well," Jonny said, sitting on an ottoman, "how'd it look when you were done?"

"Gorgeous, man. Just gorgeous." Ron sat up excitedly. "Unfortunately, I didn't manage to snap a photo of it like I would have liked, you know—"

"Because of the man chasing you."

"Right, but I hope to all hell someone photographs it before they cover it up. Fuck me it was beautiful"

"Are you going home tonight?"

"Naw, my missus and the boy will be sleeping; I don't want to wake'em up."

Their conversation was then interrupted by the sudden sound of a man yelling in the hall. Jonny and Ron jumped up and ran to the door. Ron put his ear to the door while Jonny looked through the peephole.

"What's going on?" Ron asked his friend.

"I don't know. Some old fuck across the hall's yelling at someone. I can't see who it is though. Oh fuck!"

"What?"

"The old fucker's pointing at our door." They both ran to a window on the far end of the room that looked out onto a back alley. They had prepared for a situation like this a thousand times both in their mind and in conversation, so they knew what to do without speaking a word. But a level of panic still struck them, impairing their movements with a sudden clumsiness. Jonny fumbled with the window and held it while Ron squeezed his large frame through it. Once out he maneuvered his body until he was dangling from his fingers and then let go, dropping a single story onto the hard pavement, onto which he collapsed into a maladroit roll. He picked himself up and looked up to watch Jonny perform the same movement, although with a little more finesse. When they were both on the ground they ran further down the alley, further away from the growing commotion in their apparent safe house. When they were a safe distance they split up.

Jonny ran until his legs burned and he felt he might throw up. Feeling he was likely safe for the moment he stopped under the black shadow of a quiet overpass. He leaned over with his hands on his knees and tried to catch his breath. Despite the below freezing temperatures, he had developed a good sweat and he unzipped his winter coat to allow the cool air to fill it up. He walked towards his apartment, avoiding streetlights even though he knew that made him appear suspicious; he was too exhausted to think clearly. His mind was filled with thoughts of Ron. Ron, Jonny was well aware, was not a fit man. He couldn't have run far before being forced to stop to rest.

The next morning Jonny phoned Ron but there was no answer at the house. He asked his comrades if he had shown up at any other safe house or friend's apartment, but no one had heard anything from him. After hearing that, Jonny didn't have to go to his house to know what happened. He knew he was gone forever. He knew because it had happened so many times before and it was always the same way. Suddenly they can't get a hold of someone. And that someone is never seen again. But one thing he didn't expect to find when he went to Ron's was an empty house. His wife and teenage son were also missing. YesFore used what resources they had to try to find out what happened to the Hawke family, but all leads led nowhere which could only mean one thing.

Jonny tried for years, possibly for the rest of his life, to understand why the Overmen took Ron's family instead of just him. He envisioned a thousand scenarios in which his wife and son somehow get involved, somehow learn the identity of someone they shouldn't, somehow anger the wrong person, somehow do something that could possibly warrant such a reaction, but he never learnt the actual truth. His best guess, the one he thought most plausible, was that Ron returned home that night but was discovered, likely by being followed. When the OP went in to get him his wife and son protested, possibly violently, and were taken as well just to prevent more of a scene. And once you were taken, in those circumstances, you were never released.

Those in YesFore were furious over what had happened. The group was torn. Many wanted to do something more extreme to get back at them, to punish them. But the majority agreed that such action would be counter-productive, and any suggestion of violence was swiftly discarded. At least officially. People in the group were starting to get tired of their friends disappearing and so behind closed doors many members began to whisper about a desire to give them what they deserve. Some quietly left YesFore only to later be found to have joined a militant group and, for many, it was assumed that Ron and his family's disappearance was the catalyst. Jonny admitted he, too, was torn. Not long after the graffiti campaign was over, the reaction to their hard work died down and it seemed to Jonny that it was all forgotten, that they had achieved nothing.

Jonny was first approached by his friend and comrade Charlie King. Their first conversation never explicitly mentioned bombing a building, but the thought was hovering in the air round them as they spoke. During the conversation Charlie used words like "revenge" and "punishment" and admitted that he thought, This whole activist bullshit doesn't work now. Not in this day and age. He mentioned that if they hope to make any difference they're going to have to adapt to the times. At one point he asked Jonny if he would help, for what he didn't specify, but Jonny, without any consideration or enthusiasm, replied in the affirmative. The actual plan to build a bomb remained floating in the air throughout many more conversations between Charlie and Jonny, never being brought up directly but slowly revealing itself to be the obvious choice. When they were comfortable enough to admit to each other that that is exactly what they had been talking about all along, the plan was almost complete.

Jonny was, during the early planning stages, compliant to an almost submissive degree towards whatever Charlie asked of him as if Charlie were the foreman of the operation and Jonny his apprentice. In fact, I think Jonny preferred this since I believe he felt it removed him from some of the responsibility. In a way he felt more like a factory worker building munitions rather than a soldier. And when the bomb was being built and the target being discussed he allowed himself to be relegated to the sidelines and took the role as a secretary rather than take part in the planning process. So then once the explosive was put together Jonny sat down with Charlie and told him he had done all he could and wouldn't take part in the actual operation. To Jonny's surprise Charlie patted him on the shoulder and nodded, agreeing that that was for the best. Such a reaction surprised Jonny who was prepared for a long, impassioned speech about his duty to Ron's memory. But as he left the safe house, he thought that Charlie knew all along that he couldn't go through with it. Jonny couldn't help wondering, why was it so easy for Charlie?

The target Charlie had chosen was a police station since, as was common knowledge, the police had been essentially subsumed into the Public Protection Agency and were more than willing to help them find and capture members of YesFore and other groups like it. The plan was to plant the bomb in a garbage bin near the front entrance early in the morning during a shift change. On that day, Jonny woke up before Charlie, they were both staying in another safe house, and told him he was leaving.

"Now? And leaving for where?"

"Home. I can't do this, but I can't go back to painting pictures on the sides of buildings either."

"Let's talk about it tonight. After this is over."

"No, I'm leaving now. I feel like I need to leave before you ..."

Jonny got dressed, said goodbye, and left for the bus station. While sitting in the sparsely crowded waiting area the faint sound of a distant explosion rumbled through the building. Everyone stood up and ran to the windows, looking in all directions for any sign of smoke or commotion. Jonny remained in his seat and put his head in his hands.

Jonny later found out that the bomb Charlie detonated killed one officer and injured six more. Charlie himself was quickly identified and less than a week after the attack he was arrested. A short trial found him guilty and he was sent to prison where he spent the rest of his life. Jonny's involvement was never discovered.

When Jonny had finished telling his story, he and his wife sat in silence with their backs to each other. They listened to each other's breathing, the only indication that the other was still there. Kara finally turned her head and broke the silence by saying quietly, "I love you, Jon." She then leaned forwards, turned off the lamp, and crawled under the covers. A moment later Jonny did the same with a careful and diligent hand as if everything around him could be shattered with a single careless act. He held his breath until he was under the covers and staring at the blackness above him. He lay there close to the edge of the bed, unsure what reaction his wife was experiencing behind her reserved features. Before long, though, he heard movement and then felt his wife's warm arm wrap around his body and her head lay gently on his shoulder.

After his confession to Kara it was apparent that, at least for a while, Jonny would remain in the cottage with his wife, son, and brother. Although he was happy with the arrangement, he admitted there was still a lingering anxiety that he couldn't shake. Leaving again was out of the question. In order to continue to feel as though he was still doing something productive, he became very much involved with the goings-on at the Speakeasy. Although his role there involved little more than organizing meetings and making connections, it was sufficient to quell the rage that had been building over the years and it allowed his life to return to some sort of normalcy. He was around to play with his son and sleep next to his wife and for a while life seemed to be moving towards something like contentment.

Chapter 31 ~ Subject Blair

Ever since Marie vanished from his life Nate was unable to consider doing anything that felt like moving on. He unconsciously decided that he'd put his life in stasis so that if she ever unexpectedly reappeared in his life they could pick up where they left off. This included writing. But as the years passed something began to change inside him. He was finding it more and more difficult to carry on like Miss Havisham and thoughts of writing soon started to replace some of the hours he spent waiting for Marie to walk through the front door. He felt guilty, something like betrayal, but the more he sat waiting the more his thoughts began to turn towards action.

Over the course of many late nights talking with his brother and sister-in-law he became convinced that the best way to remember his wife was to be productive. "You know," Kara said one night, "that the last thing she'd have wanted is for your life to end with hers. You still have the option to live and she would, in my opinion, be annoyed if you willingly stopped living your life because she was forced to. That's playing right into the Overmen's hands, isn't it? Two writers with one stone. If I know Marie as well as I think I do, and I do, she'd be a little more than upset with you if you were to allow the OP to appear that efficient."

Nate agreed and throughout that winter and into the summer he began to write. He wrote, at first, counter-propaganda pamphlets which Jonny, through his connections at the speakeasy, managed to get distributed through the proper channels so they eventually found their way to all corners of the globe. They were all written anonymously with the innocuous title of A People's Chit to Our Oppressors' Chat. The Overmen eventually came to refer to them as the Chit-Chat pamphlets.

The contents of the pamphlets were mostly a collection of information about the OP's atrocities all over the world, details about our tactics and advice on how to resist effectively, as well as much criticism on harmful or ineffective forms of protest such as violence or appeasement. Nate's wasn't the only stream of information being spread across the world of course, but it quickly joined ranks amongst the most effective. In total, I believe there were only a few hundred writers whose anonymous profiles reached the height of Nate's.

In Kiev where I was stationed at this time the thought that Nate could be one of these dissident writers did enter my mind but I had been quite vigilant in keeping thoughts of him out of my head, so good in fact that doing so became a sort of reflex. However, on occasion I'd get a pamphlet from a writer we codenamed Subject Blair. The first time one was sent to me I had it analyzed to see if it in any way matched similar dissident literature that was already archived. If it was just the one, we tended to ignore it since we didn't have the resources to hunt down every angry person who tossed some strong words together. It came back that there were no matches, so I dismissed it. In fact, I didn't even read it, preferring instead to rely on our analysts and their conclusions. Not long after that first pamphlet, however, our analysts started to notice recurring patterns in the writer's style and before long I had an entire folder dedicated just to them and I made a recommendation to track this writer down. It didn't mean much since analysts had already deemed him unlikely to be in my jurisdiction, but it shows the impact that Blair's writing was having if he had become a concern for us on the other side of the world.

I admit I felt an immediate pull towards this mysterious dissident and found myself reading and rereading the collection of his pamphlets I had obtained. I often found myself doing so not for the sake of my job but because I found them legitimately enjoyable, although I never would've admitted such a thing and probably didn't quite believe it myself. It wasn't that they were better written than other pieces that I was tasked with examining, although they were quite well written, and it wasn't that what he or she was saying was entirely unique compared to others, although they were compelling. It was the familiarity that drew me to it. I felt as though I knew the voice on those pages. It felt like nostalgia, like a smell that reminds you of the house you grew up in.

After months of Blair's pamphlets piling up on my hard drive and consuming my thoughts, I began my own investigation. I grew to hate the writer because of how much he made me question what I was doing and think of things I had worked so hard to put out of my mind. I began to think of Nate again which made me angry. I thought of Marie again and felt shameful. But I couldn't stop reading these condemning messages even though I knew they'd bring me only discomfort and anxiety. I decided I must find the person responsible and make him stop.

My secretary, Daniel, looked at me with a dumbfounded expression when I told him to bring me every bit of information that was available on this anonymous dissident.

"Which one is that, sir?"

"Subject Blair."

"Okay, may I ask why?"

"I have reasons."

"I don't doubt that, sir, but as far as I know he's not an immediate concern in this part of the world."

"I think he happens to be of *significant* concern," I wouldn't look at him as he stood in the doorway with his head tilted to one side. I instead leaned over my desk pretending to examine a dossier on another anonymous person who was likely of no significant concern to us either. I looked up and tried my best to be authoritative. "That's all."

"Yes, sir." He disappeared.

I spent that entire night in my office looking over all the scraps of information that were available. It was sparse and not very informative but that didn't stop me from scouring every word written by him and about him, every expert opinion, every theory, every dead-end. I only stopped when I noticed the sun peaking between two buildings outside my window as if it were spying on me and asking why I had such a sudden interest in something that didn't concern me. I felt guilty and a fear of being caught overwhelmed me. But caught for what? I wasn't doing anything that could give grounds for suspicion. Had I become suspicious of myself? My cowardice suddenly took over and I began deleting everything my secretary had given me that day in a hurried panic leaving only those documents which were already on my computer. I looked out my window and saw the Sun had only gotten higher. A better vantage point. I ran to the window and closed the blinds in a flourish.

That afternoon I sat at my desk, having calmed myself with a cup of tea and a few desperate gulps from a bottle of scotch I kept on hand, unable to work, unable to even turn on my computer. I felt stupid. Why had I asked for Subject Blair's information? I have no reason to waste time on him. I had been foolish.

As the day continued and my thoughts began to focus, I clicked on my computer and, as if I was under a spell, selected Blair's folder while simultaneously trying to convince myself not to. I did so without moving anything more than my fingers as if I believed there were spies peeking through invisible holes in the walls. I opened a file containing an essay he had written entitled "The Overman and the Immortal." I had read it before, many times; it was one of my favorites. In it he writes about the difference between the two.

The Immortal is no different, except that detail explained in the name, than the Mortal. It is not with the Immortal that our struggle lies. It is not the Immortal who persecutes dissenters; it is not the Immortal who disappears undesirables; it is not the Immortal who denies the right to procreation; it is not the Immortal who perpetuates lies and buries truth. The Immortal is not an enemy. The Overman, however, does all the above. Although it is true that everyone who carries the name of Overman like a medal of honor is, by definition, an Immortal, every Immortal is not an Overman. Those of us who struggle can only hope to make real progress if we are able to make this distinction; for many of the necessary steps we must take to reach the end of this bitter revolution are not possible without those sympathetic Immortals who willingly hold our hands and steady us as we wobble towards our goal.

This made me think of Nate and reminded me of things he used to say so I closed the document and resumed my sitting and tea drinking. But soon my mind was racing again, and I clicked on the folder with the intention of deleting it but thought that might appear suspicious too since there was no reason for me to purge *every* trace of Blair. I instead made a different decision, one which made even less sense. I called my secretary in my office.

"Yes, sir."

"Could you get me those documents on Subject Blair again?"

"I'm sorry, sir. Again, sir?"

"That's right."

"There were no new files since yesterday."

"I'm sure of that. I want the same ones again."

"The exact same files?"

"Yes, that's right."

"Was there something wrong with the format?"

"Same format as yesterday, please and thank you."

"Was there a problem with the ones I sent yesterday? They weren't corrupted, were they?"

"Not at all."

"So, you have the documents but want them again? I can show you how to copy them if that's all you need."

"I don't have the documents," I exclaimed, exasperated.

"I see."

"So, just do the same thing you did yesterday. Same documents, same format, same everything, it's not too much trouble, is it?"

"Of course not." I could tell he was starting to get bored of the conversation. "I'll have them for you right away."

"Thanks."

When an attachment titled "Blair" appeared on my computer I ignored it and tried to distract myself with other work and made plans to delete them again later though I knew I wouldn't. That evening I found myself repeating the previous evening almost perfectly as I looked through everything I had available for some hint as to the writer's origins but found nothing. I was nearly ready to give up when something caught my attention. It was in a pamphlet titled "They Are Powerless, We Are Powerful!" Like all the pamphlets by Blair, I had already studied it exhaustively, but it suddenly became familiar in a way it wasn't before. It suddenly became personal, like hearing it from a friend as opposed to a distant stranger whose face I'd never seen. It was *his* voice, I thought with overwhelming excitement: Nate's. "Those who wish to rule over us, to subjugate us, are completely dependent on us for the very power they intend to use against us." His words. I'd heard him say similar things many times before. "We the people have the power to make those who intend to rule over us bend the knee, to make the richest beg, the strongest collapse." Could it really be him? Surely, many other dissidents have said the same or similar things. "By simply saying no, we deny them power and become ourselves the most powerful force on the planet. But by submitting we give them that power. We must never submit, comrades. Our goal then is not to eliminate those who seek to oppress us but to convince enough people in the world to deny the Overmen their power. As we unite, we take power from them."

I began to reread every pamphlet, essay, and article Blair had written and suddenly heard Nate's voice in every syllable. It had to be him. I hurried home with the documents and searched my apartment for Nate's books which I had kept tucked away in a cupboard. I compared the style from his novels to that in the pamphlets. His sentence structure. His vocabulary. His stylistic flourishes. It was him. It had to be. I was sure of it. His voice. He had somehow, in all improbability, found me.

Chapter 32 ~ Personal Revolution

What was I to do with this information? I sat on it for weeks, letting it eat me from the inside. I couldn't sleep, could barely eat, could think of nothing else even though my thoughts were so fragmented that I was only capable of something that would resemble thinking to an observer. But the knowledge I had obtained loomed in every corner of my mind making it nearly impossible to keep that knowledge from consuming me. The question, what to do now, was always dancing about, blocking any other thought from entering my mind. But trying to concentrate on an answer was, at this point, beyond my mental capacity.

"There's only one thing to do," I told myself many times, often while lying huddled in bed as if the knowledge that was tormenting me was lying in wait outside my bedroom door. "I must expose him. Why would I think of anything else? I am an Overman and we are God, are we not?! Who is he? A Mortal. He's not me. He's not us." But I didn't expose him. I lay in my bed, impotent.

I was an Overman, I thought, and nothing else. After my falling out with Nate, the OP formed my entire identity. I thought I'd die for them. I would do anything they asked me to do. If they told me to betray everyone I loved and then kill myself, I'd have done it just as long as I could still be a part of their magnificent group. I thought this way at least, but as I lay in that bed hiding under the covers like a frightened child, I was struck with the realization that I was not as devoted to the OP as I had thought. If I were, there wouldn't be any question about what to do. A true Overman would perform his duty to the movement without hesitation. This thought frightened me. Because if I wasn't a true Overman, if I wasn't "God" with the rest of them, then what was I?

Work was difficult during this time. I'd arrive at the office and shuffle past everyone I knew without saying a word. I didn't have the energy to even flash a fake smile. Then I sat at my desk and tried not to read Blair's writings, a task which I always failed within the first hour of arriving. And once I started, I got lost in that deep, dark well until the late evening when paranoia would force me to quit.

Sometime, during one of these mental excursions into Blair's writing, I was struck with a sudden thought. It so struck me in fact that I physically pushed myself away from my desk and grabbed my head as if to rip it off. How stupid I am, I thought. Of course he'd still be writing. Why wouldn't he? He'd never stop. After Marie ... his resolve was probably only strengthened. I didn't need these papers to show up on my desk to tell me what Nate's been up to; I've always known what he's been up to. I simply chose not to do anything about it. I chose not to think of it, not to believe what was certain. I was never a true Overman.

I stood up from my desk, closed the blinds, locked the door—even though it was dark and most of the staff had already gone home—and began pacing. I had taken up smoking around this time and remember pulling on each cigarette like the smoke was oxygen and I was drowning. Did the Overmen already know about Nate? He's surely on their watch list. They must be keeping a close eye on him. If they know about him, do they know that I know? Are they waiting for me to turn him in? Waiting to see if I'm truly devoted, truly an Overman?

I sat down and immediately began typing out a report to be delivered the next morning detailing my findings. But after only two paragraphs, I frantically deleted everything I had written, stood up, and began pacing again. I repeated this sequence many times that night, sitting down, writing, erasing, standing up, pacing, sitting down, writing, erasing, standing up ….

I was still in my office, blinds closed, door locked, when the morning staff began to roll in. Shortly after 6:00 a.m. my doorknob rattled followed by a knock.

"Yes?" I yelled. I was in my chair, leaning over my computer with my head in my hands staring down at the keyboard.

"Sir? You're door's locked."

"Yes," I yelled again. "Give me a moment."

"Yes, sir."

I leaned back, wanting to pull out my hair. I lit another cigarette and put it out after one drag. I got up and unlocked the door. Daniel was standing outside with a folder under his arm.

"I was just going to deliver this to you, sir." He handed it to me then surveyed the room with mild astonishment. "Have you been here all night?" Although I avoided eye contact, I could feel him scanning my person and making notes of my appearance: same clothes as yesterday but dishevelled, red eyes, messed hair, tired voice.

"There's a lot of work to do," I said dryly and took the report from him. "It's been a long night so could we keep the interruptions to a minimum today?"

"Of course, sir."

I locked the door behind him and dragged my feet back to my desk.

I slept in my chair for several twenty-minute intervals, always waking with a start. In between such intervals I would again try to write a report on Nate, but I never got past those first few paragraphs. After the fourth or fifth time I became adequately convinced that I would never actually be able to go through with it and should stop wasting my time trying. Of course, once I reached that conclusion I was faced with the obvious corollary: if I wouldn't do my duty to the movement, I wasn't part of it.

The word "revolution" is originally an astronomical term which refers to the movement of the heavenly bodies, specifically their cyclical movement around one another—to revolve around something so as to eventually end up in the same place from which it started. When the word was first used to refer to political change it was this original usage that was intended to describe a return to a previous system of government, namely, a return to monarchical rule after the overthrow of the Rump Parliament in England. In this sense "revolution" used to be synonymous with restoration.

It wasn't until after the American and French revolutions that its meaning changed to refer to a sort of dramatic transformation. I always thought both meanings worked rather well to describe the change that occurred in my life at this time. Mine was a great change but it was also a return to a previous identity. And the force that propelled me throughout this revolution was that irresistible pull towards something like an identity. I've mentioned it before but it's worth wasting a bit more time on the subject just for the sake of understanding the power of such a force. I had to belong to something to feel any sense of self-worth. A group, a clique, a family, really anything would probably do. Just something that I could belong to. Something that meant something to me to which I could point to and say boldly and proudly, "I am one of them." Friends and family, in my opinion, are the ultimate example of this because they are the most natural and appear to be the healthiest for the individual. But movements are powerful things and the Overman Project was a movement of terrifying magnitude and members felt as though the power in the movement had infected them. An identity is one thing but to identify with a world-shattering power such as the Overman Project is more addictive than the most powerful of drugs. It is also the most life altering of drugs since its effects on the mind are devastating and often irreversible. Once admitted into the movement and once addicted to the association, it can become impossible to quit without outside force. And if one doesn't have an alternative identity to attach themselves to, then even outside forces cannot break them of their addiction.

Chapter 33 ~ A Favor for an Old Friend

My motivation was, like most of my actions during this time, driven greatly by cowardice. I figured it was only a matter of time before Nate would be discovered and when he was, I'd be questioned as to why I left him alone to his own devices while knowing full well that he'd continue his dissident writing. Although I couldn't bring myself to turn him in, I also couldn't let him be caught so I intended to keep the Overmen off his scent in order to cover my own tracks.

For days after, I continued to lose sleep over what course of action I should take to protect myself. After a perusal of the contents on my computer, I decided the best course would be to once again delete all the files and pretend I knew nothing. I began to close all the open documents on my computer but before I hit delete, I thought it was probably best to spend a little more time considering my options. I couldn't bring myself to turn him in, but I couldn't just ignore it and let someone else track him down. I knew some more involved response was now unavoidable. He had, after all, been a public dissident with a rather high profile in the past and it was no doubt that the OP hadn't completely forgotten about him. Although it would be difficult for someone else to come to the same conclusion I did—I only discovered it because of a combination of my personal history with him and my serendipitous position in the Agency—it was still possible that once someone got on the right trail they might follow it to him. I instead decided to try something different.

The next day I called Daniel back into my office. "Is there any more information on this Blair person that's available? I need every last bit."

"No, sir. Like I said, I gave you everything …," he cleared his throat, "both times."

"Well," I managed to overcome my previous nervousness and took on a more authoritarian air. "If anything else, and I do mean anything else, pops up, you are to bring it to my attention without delay. Is that understood?"

"Of course, sir. May I ask—"

"Is it your job to ask?" I snapped with some annoyance.

"No, sir. But if you wouldn't mind obliging me, an investigation on Subject Blair is already ongoing, a number of them actually in a number of countries."

"Was that your question?" I said, imagining myself as a tyrannical king and he my lowly subject.

"Not quite. Why is it that you're suddenly so interested in a case that has only been handed to you for a, what one might say, a heads up? The current hypothesis on this Blair person's whereabouts does not place him anywhere near our jurisdiction. I just wouldn't want you to get sidetracked from your duties."

I leaned back in my chair and rested my arms on the armrests in what I thought must be an intimidating pose. "Might I ask why you have suddenly taken such an interest in the way in which I perform my duties to the Overman Project?"

"Forgive me, sir." His *sirs* were starting to get on my nerves. "I'm also just doing my duties to the best of my ability. As your secretary, I am obligated to help you perform your duties and if I see a distraction it is my duty to bring it to your attention. Our duties, you see—"

"Stop saying *duties*, man," I snapped. "I have reason to believe the popular hypothesis is wrong. Although I'm not yet convinced myself, I believe this Blair asshole might be hiding out somewhere … you know what, it's not really my *duty* to explain this to you. At least not until I have sorted out some more of these details."

"Of course, sir. Forgive me, sir."

"I'll call you when I need you."

"Yes, sir."

It was well over an hour after our little spat that I suddenly realized Daniel, my loyal secretary, was far more curious than a secretary ought to be. Although I assumed I'd be under closer scrutiny than others in my profession, since it was no secret I had past ties with prominent activists and dissidents, I never thought my own secretary would be tasked with keeping an eye on me. I realized I had to tread lightly.

I spent several weeks formulating my plan. During this time Daniel brought me two more essays believed to have been written by Subject Blair both of which supported my belief that Blair equals Nate. I decided I needed to find some evidence that Blair was hiding in Eastern Europe. I needed to be able to provide convincing evidence for this claim and explain what it was that convinced me in the first place. I began looking through similar styled writings from dissidents believed to be hiding in my jurisdiction hoping to be able to link Nate's to them. I abandoned this idea when I realized that getting the dogs off Nate's trail by siccing them on someone else wouldn't be the most ethical thing to do—one of my few moments of ethical clarity at this time. I had to *create* someone who could be Blair, someone who sounded like him, someone who spoke like him, but someone who makes a mistake that Nate never would. Someone who somehow gives away his position in his writing—a plausible mistake, a subtle mistake. The only problem with this plan is that I, of course, had to be Blair. And as I have already explained in the very first chapter of this narrative, I was never much of a writer.

Chapter 34 ~ Anna

While I was busy orchestrating my redemption in Europe, another change was taking place in Nate's life. It happened at the Speakeasy. Her name was Annabelle, but they shortened it to Anna. She had long, fiery red hair that spiraled out in all directions. Her white porcelain skin was spotted with freckles from head to, I assume, toe. She was tall and somewhat gangly with slouched shoulders which I surmised was a habit developed during her insecure teenage years to compensate for her towering height; she was quite a few centimeters taller than Nate, although Nate wasn't exactly known for his stature. One thing that was obvious upon meeting her was that whatever insecurities she may have had that resulted in those slouched shoulders had been successfully excised as an adult.

Her personality matched the colors and wildness of her hair and one might think her a caricature if she wasn't so natural in the way she conducted herself. When she smiled, she seemed to do so with her entire body. When she laughed, which was often, she'd throw her head backwards which caused her abundance of hair to fan about in waves like a stone making ripples in a pool. As a spectacle she was mesmerizing. She was also completely infectious. No one could resist laughing with her even if they weren't sure at what they were laughing. When she tilted her head as a sign of sympathy, everyone took notice and sympathized with whatever was at issue. She controlled the room like a maestro whose orchestra was everyone who was near enough to hear or see her.

Nate rarely attended meetings, only doing so on this occasion because of Jonny's persistence. He found himself incapable of paying any amount of attention throughout the gathering but after, when the meeting was over and the socializing was in session, he was introduced to Anna. Afterwards, he swore he had never found a political event quite so exhilarating and would surely attend another.

The Speakeasy was in the rather spacious basement of the Dalisay's restaurant. It had concrete walls which were bare and concrete floors which were covered in a number of cheap rugs to keep their guests' feet warm during the winter months. On the wall near the staircase was a table on which Mr. Dalisay set up as his make-shift bar—the Speakeasy looked and functioned much like its namesake—and which he manned as soon as the meeting was over, never leaving his station until the last guest had gone. His introspective demeanor didn't afford much in the way of conversation skills so tending the bar was a way for him to be present while avoiding conversation. During meetings foldable chairs were arranged in rows facing a projector screen, which they used to show documentaries. Between the screen and the front row of chairs stood a small, round, bar table on which speakers could keep their notes and bottles of water. After the meetings were over the chairs were usually rearranged round the room as people moved them to accommodate whatever conversation they were having.

Nate and Anna were first introduced to each other after the meeting was over when Nate found himself sitting with a small group who were discussing something of interest to everyone but Nate. The conversation stopped when she entered the fray and she became the sudden focus. Nate, being the only new attendant that evening, was immediately introduced. She shook his hand and smiled and told him she liked his books and then, just when Nate thought he should use his renown to evolve the handshake into a conversation which itself, he hoped, might evolve into a great number of things, her attention had been commandeered by the insufferable group. He didn't even get her name.

"Jonny," Nate whispered loudly when he found his brother seated around a wooden table with another noisily chatty group.

"Nate," Jonny mimicked his brother. "Nate, this is Terry, Bill, and Nick. They all work with ChangeNow. Gentlemen, this is Nate, whom I'm sure you are aware is *the* Nathaniel Karski." Terry, Bill, and Nick all feigned a perfunctory act of obeisance.

Nate waved quickly, "It's a pleasure," then patted his brother on the shoulder. "Jon, may I have a word?"

"Is it important?" Jonny tried to talk low enough to not be heard by Terry, Bill, and Nick, but having paused their conversation to accommodate Nate's intrusion they couldn't help but hear. "We were just getting down to business. You see, ChangeNow is a community—"

"I know what ChangeNow is," Nate blurted out, and then smiled apologetically at Terry, Bill, and Nick who all nodded in unison.

"Good. Then you know that they need our support. We're working out a way to get a permanent flow of funds from one of my contacts in America—"

"I just have a question and I don't want to ask it here. It'll take a second of your time. Sorry about this," Nate smiled politely, and all three men lifted their glasses.

"One question?" Jonny asked, holding up a finger.

"What if I have more? I'm not going to commit to only one."

"You said one."

"Just come with me."

"I'll be right back, gentlemen." Jonny followed Nate to a corner of the room.

"Who's that?" He nodded in the direction of Anna.

"Anna."

"Anna." Nate worked the syllables round in his mouth.

"Okay. Glad I could help." Jonny turned and began to make his way back to his seat.

"Get back here." Nate reached out and grabbed Jonny by the back of his shirt and pulled him back to him, causing Jonny to spill a few drops of his drink onto the floor.

"Twat. What's wrong with you?"

"You think I just wanted her name? Tell me some details."

"You pulled me over here, out of a rather important conversation I might add, to talk about a girl? You know the entire world is in the middle of a revolution, right?"

"Just some details. These are *your* comrades."

"Her name's Anna."

"Yes, yes. You said that. Something more. Something I can use to talk to her."

"You're a famous writer, man. Use that."

"She didn't seem too impressed."

"Well, I don't know. She's a bit into politics."

Nate looked incredulous. "She's *here*, chucklefuck. At a po-li-ti-cal meeting. I know she's a bit into politics. Next you'll tell me she's not fond of the OP."

"Okay. What else." Jonny looked at his brother and smiled slyly. "Wait. Hold the phone. I haven't seen you like this … ever. Are you going to ask her to be your girlfriend?" Jonny mocked.

"Piss off."

"I'm sorry, man. It's just a bit surprising. And amusing."

"So, what are you going to tell me?"

"Okay. She likes fast cars."

"Shit."

"What?"

"I hate fast cars."

"Right. But you could pretend."

"No."

"Okay. She likes books."

"You should have led with that. Why say she likes fast cars when you know I don't and not say she likes books when you know I do?"

"Relax. She also plays piano and guitar and I think bass maybe, or drums."

"I don't play anything."

"But you like music."

"I do."

"There ya go. She likes books but doesn't write them, you like music but don't play an instrument. Done. Now I'm going to abandon this silly conversation and continue my serious one over there." Jonny took off leaving Nate sipping his drink in the corner by himself and keeping an eye on the red spirals floating round the room.

And that's how Nate spent the rest of the evening, standing in a corner trying to think of a natural way to tell the dazzling redhead that he likes music. Jonny twice paid him a visit, first to ask if he needed anything and second if he wanted him to do anything, like pass her a note I suppose, but Nate responded with a shaking head both times. At the end of the evening when the guests were leaving, Nate made his move. He was putting on his coat when Anna appeared next to him with her coat in hand. He said without thinking, "Productive evening?" It came out all right he thought. Not too deliberate. Not too panicked, quite casually in fact. He credited this casualness to the liberal amount of cocktails he consumed in his agitation.

"I don't know if I'd say that," she responded. "I enjoyed myself. Not sure if anything got accomplished though, if I'm honest." Then she leaned in close to Nate and whispered, "But don't tell those two." She giggled and pointed to two young men covering themselves in toques and scarves while carrying on a heated debate which Nate assumed had been ongoing for quite some time.

"They're a passionate couple aren't they," Nate said, trying to maintain his casualness. Sounded a bit too eager this time, he thought. Slow it down.

"They've been yelling at each other for over an hour. I tried to get involved but between the screaming and the unintentional spitting I had to retreat."

Nate threw his head back and laughed. Did he laugh too hard? He'd rein it in next time. Just a smile and a single syllable *ha*.

"I'm not even kidding. It was like they both had tiny men hiding behind their teeth shooting at each other with water pistols."

Nate threw his head back and released another loud laugh to his immediate dismay. He recovered quickly though. "I'm sorry you had to witness that. Sounds rather gruesome."

"It was a massacre. All was not quiet on the Western Front."

Nate thought about trying to use her literary reference as a springboard for a conversation about books, but he came up blank. He instead smiled and panicked as nothing came out of his mouth.

"Well," he began and was going to say something about helping her deal with the trauma of surviving such a conflict but before he could say another word she said, "Will you be here next time?" seeming to not notice his false start.

"Yeah, of course. You?"

"Of course. I'm Anna by the way." She extended a hand.

Nate's initial reaction to her introduction was to say "I know" but quickly stopped himself. "Nate," he said and shook her hand.

"I know," she laughed again. "Everyone here knows who you are. I'll see ya next time."

"Yeah."

Nate did see her next time, and the time after that, and after that. He found himself attending these meetings less to help organize a revolution and more to learn about her. Throughout the course of the next few months he learnt that she owned and managed an antique shop, that she not only liked fast cars but often raced fast cars at various tracks round the country. And despite thinking she lacked interest in his own novels, he discovered that she had in fact read three of them.

Chapter 35 ~ I Become Blair

Writing did not come easy for me, especially writing in such a way as to imitate an internationally renowned writer. Luckily, I had spent enough time around Nate to be able to at least imagine what he might say and how he might say it. I became a method actor, in a sense, getting into character as Nathaniel Kaski. I adopted his mannerisms, leaning in my chair like he did, moving my hands about like he did, and talking like he did, although I had no one to talk to so I talked to photos and mirrors. I began to drink rye whisky and give speeches to imaginary dinner guests and throw my head back when I laughed. After doing my best to become Nathaniel Karski I sat down to try and write like Nathaniel Karski.

The first few things I put down were nonsense, things I imagined he might say in a conversation. I remembered him telling me that he'd write like he spoke and then edit it later to sound "more literary". I wrote down imaginary conversations, things I might say and write responses as Nate. I wrote pages and pages of these fictional conversations. I then studied the topics about which he'd write and attempted to write my own versions of them as Nate and then compare my work with his. I'd mark the differences between the two and try another topic and another until I could no longer write as myself. I had become, as much as is possible, Nate Karski. Or at least Nate as how I remembered him.

Writing like past Nate was one thing but writing like current Nate was a different challenge altogether. This required a much different mindset than just behaving like him. I had to think the way Nate was thinking at that time, as a revolutionary, not just how I remembered him, as a reluctant activist. He had no doubt changed much during the years since I last saw him. As Blair, his writing was, despite its familiarity, still different from his earlier writing which I attributed to his attempt to hide his world-famous voice. His voice seemed much fiercer than I remembered which made him sound less structured and even less articulate. I hypothesized that he was using his speaking voice on those pages. That he simply refrained from editing. This is why, I thought, I was able to recognize it when others couldn't. There weren't many recordings of him giving his speeches so the only comparisons one could make were between the two sets of writing which was, on examination, different enough to fool someone who hadn't the time to compare the two thoroughly. That was it then. I just had to write as though I were speaking like Nate.

The next hurdle was to come up with a topic on which current revolutionary Nate would write, preferably a recent event which I could be confident he'd not have had the time to write about yet. Luckily, I recently received a report on a riot that took place in a camp in northern Belarus. The prisoners revolted and many managed to escape, at least for a time. The escapees were all eventually caught, rounded up and promptly executed without ceremony while anyone who was found to have played a role in the revolt, however small, was punished in an assortment of ways. It was the perfect story to write about. One, it was a story Nate would report on, especially new revolutionary Nate/Blair; two, it was a recent story on the other side of the world from Nate meaning he couldn't possibly have known about it yet and so couldn't have already written about it. He also would likely never write about it since it was only a drop in the bucket of similar stories.

The next issue I faced was getting the piece, after I had written it, out to the proper channels. I couldn't have it traced back to me. I certainly didn't want to be misidentified as a revolutionary just because I happened to write particularly revolutionary piece of journalism. That would be the exact opposite of what I was intending. I knew I couldn't avoid such an outcome on my own and decided the best course of action would be to contact an actual revolutionary to get my article out there.

The Agency had a large roster of prominent revolutionaries kept under surveillance but I, of course, not being an agent of the Security Branch, did not have access to their servers and so couldn't simply browse through a list of potential candidates like I was searching for a date. Luckily, many leading members of various groups were either well known or well suspected throughout all branches our offices, but I didn't have access to their dossiers and so could not be certain which one could be trusted. After all, I had to contact someone without revealing my identity or leaving a trail for the Agency to follow. On top of that, I also had to get my article published while convincing whomever I used that the article was written by Blair. I was also, as mentioned earlier, becoming quite aware that I was being watched by my own secretary and had to do all of this without raising any suspicion on his part.

This is what I did. Once I had written the report, I saved it on a dozen separate unused memory sticks, making sure each one was a brand that was not available in North America. Then, all in one night, I walked through the city, taking only public transport and keeping my face hidden from the nosy CCTV cameras, and put one of these envelopes under the doors or into the mailboxes of each of the candidates I had chosen. My thinking was at least half of them will take the risk of reading what's on the memory stick and hopefully at least one of those might be willing to get it to where it needed to go. After I did this I had only to wait for my own article to appear on my desk.

Weeks went by, however, and my article wasn't published. Finally, I called Daniel into my office.

"Sir?"

"Have there been any new developments on that Blair character?"

"No sir. If there were, I would have—"

"Okay, okay." I held up a hand. "If there are—"

"Of course, sir. On your desk immediately."

"Thank you."

"May I ask, sir …"

I instinctively cringed but said nothing.

"… have there been any new developments on your side?"

"My side of what exactly?"

"Well, you seemed to indicate the last time we talked about it that you were following some leads on this Blair character."

"I was."

"And … did they lead anywhere?"

"It appears they didn't. At least not yet." I got up and began pacing the room authoritatively with my hands tucked behind my back. "If I'm right, then he has eluded our efforts. If I'm wrong, well, then I am simply wrong."

Daniel smiled and nodded. "If there is anything I can do to help, sir."

"Unfortunately, I don't think there is. But I'll keep you updated. I appreciate your continued support and discretion on this matter." I thought it best to butter him up. "I don't say this enough, and I know I can be hard on you sometimes, but I think you are a tremendous asset," and keep him well buttered. I smiled at him like a proud father. "I'll call you if I think of something."

"Of course, sir."

While waiting for some response from my article I wrote many more articles, always in Blair's voice. For instance, I wrote an essay criticizing the OP on their lack of a discernible goal. I questioned whether they intended to simply annihilate every Mortal on the planet in their pursuit of domination or if they ever intend to create a world where both Mortal and Immortal can live together. The one that made the difference, though, the one that changed everything, was the one in which I detailed the use and production of propaganda used by the very department of which I was currently head. I dropped all my articles in the same mailboxes and under the same doors as the first. After months of this, I finally received one on my desk.

"What's this?" I asked Daniel without looking at it or at him. I was typing casually and maintained a feigned concentration on my computer screen.

"It's another report from Subject Blair."

I stopped typing for a millisecond but quickly resumed, writing sentence after sentence of nonsense before rapidly hitting the delete key. I did this long enough to be confident in my composure. "Excellent," I said finally. I typed and erased a few more lines before looking at him. "Have you read it?"

"I have not. But I did read a summary prepared by the Security Department."

"And?" I leaned back in my chair and opened the folder. In it was the summary and a memory stick. I held up the stick. "They couldn't have just sent it to me electronically?"

"They didn't want to send it to you at all. I have some connections and was able to get it to you this way. But please understand that—"

"Wait. Why didn't they want me to see it?"

"It would appear, sir, that some of the information in that article could only have come from one of our propaganda departments."

"Is that so?" I felt like vomiting. "So why'd you go through the trouble—"

"You said you wanted any more information that came out on Blair. I heard about this through some colleagues and thought it might help. But what I was saying before is, I would, of course, appreciate *your* discretion. I wouldn't want anyone knowing I delivered this to you."

"Daniel." I held up a hand. "Do not worry about a thing. I really appreciate this. You've done well. This could help me a great deal. Thank you very much."

"No worries, sir."

"Were there any others?" I said before he scurried out the door.

"Not that I'm aware of, sir."

When I was alone, I scoured the report. It was indeed mine. I fooled the resistance. I fooled the Overmen. They all believed Blair wrote it. And that I was Blair. I began to feel dizzy and my stomach began to churn, and I thought, what have I done?

Chapter 36 ~ Anything for the Overman

My success with the article boosted my confidence and I began to write many more. I still did so under the conviction that I was doing this just to cover my tracks and that I was still a devoted servant of the Overman Project. I honestly did, after all, when I thought about Mortals, still think of them with a significant degree of disgust and superiority. At least Mortals as a people. Mortals as persons, as Nate and Jonny and Marie and Kara and young James, I felt nothing but adoration. This was the genius behind our propaganda—what I was doing. We managed to create in the minds of millions, possibly billions, of people a complete disconnect between their perception of the Mortal race and their perception of individual Mortals. When they considered their Mortal friends next to their Immortal ones, they pictured them as equals or at least not so low as vermin. But when they considered the Mortal race against the Immortal race the difference couldn't be greater. This is how we were able to disappear millions of people. Protests only arose for individuals, for loved ones, friends, even respected coworkers, not for the entire Mortal race.

There were, of course, multitudes who didn't buy our propaganda and those were the ones on whom we had to keep a close eye. Those also happened to be the people to whom I sent my work when I wanted it published. And it was those people to whom I continued to send my work even when my initial goal of protecting Nate was accomplished. The rather uncomfortable result was that Subject Blair had suddenly become far more prolific than ever before and I, being head of the department of propaganda, was tasked with countering his constant stream of dissident literature. It was at this time that I decided I had dug myself into a bit of a hole and must begin to look for a way out.

"This Blair character …" Daniel was in my office again asking more questions that annoyed me.

"Yes?" I was once again sitting at my desk preparing to dodge those questions.

"I heard through the grapevine that he's now thought to be hiding out in our little neck of the woods."

"Is that so?" I began tapping a pen against the corner of my keyboard.

"Is that what, if you don't mind me asking, what you were working on?"

I thought for a moment. "Between you and me?"

"Of course." He approached my desk as if he expected me to whisper something in his ear. I leaned back in my chair.

"Yes. To a degree."

"Really? What tipped you off?"

"I don't know." I stretched and used my pen to scratch behind my ear. "Certain things in those articles made me think he may not have been in North America."

"But what specifically?"

"A bridge, for example."

"Did you say a bridge?"

"That's right. He mentioned crossing a bridge in one of his articles and his description didn't sound like a North American bridge. Or Western European bridge for that matter. I think it was the Charles Bridge in Prague."

"Yeah, but that was recently. You seemed to be on to him before he wrote that one." He was right. I had in fact included a description of the Charles Bridge in one of the articles I had written. "It couldn't have been that." And he was far too informed for my comfort.

"You seem to know more about these articles than I do." I laughed and tried to sound jovial. "You could be right. I looked over so many, you know."

"Well, whatever the case, however you stumbled upon such a valuable piece of information, you appear to have been correct. Well done, sir."

"Anything for the Overman," I said casually.

"Anything for the future," he said, gave me a meditative smile and exited my office.

I wasn't sure how long I could keep satisfying his voracious appetite for inconvenient conversation so decided I had to come up with a second part of my plan. Now that I could be satisfied Nate was safe, which meant I was also, I had to begin insulating myself from any sort of inquiry. To do this I would have to find a way to plug Daniel's incessantly sniffing nose.

Chapter 37 ~ A Raid

Meanwhile, Nate was officially courting Anna, and Jonny was still in Manitoba working with local groups. He still talked about leaving again to go "fight on the front line, or maybe the second from front, or at least third from front depending on where one would place the front". His jokes about it never managed to quell Nate's fear that he may leave again for the last time. But he kept himself busy organizing with ChangeNow, an organization that mobilized groups of people into protests and letter writing campaigns whose de facto headquarters had become the Speakeasy. He also helped Nate write his pamphlets and get them properly distributed. It was quieter in Gerald than what any were used to, but they were getting older, meaning, they were finding themselves with less vigor and so less of a drive to travel round the world to risk arrest, beatings, or internment. But things, no matter how badly they wanted, couldn't stay quiet forever.

Nate, Jonny, James, and Kara were sitting on the deck of their cottage that overlooked the lake. It was late, nearing 10:00 in the evening, but at this time of year, in late July, the Sun always agreed to stay up late to provide light for the chatty cottagers.

Nate noticed the grass needed to be mowed again; he would get James on it sometime this week. James was looking at the same overgrown lawn thinking his uncle would surely ask him to mow it sometime this week. At least he'd get some spending money out of it. He thought about getting a job for the summer but he quickly discovered that as long as he was willing to do some odd jobs around the house, he was able to make enough money to avoid the boredom of full-time work while still having enough to go to the local cinema with friends and drink coffee at the local shop.

"Dad?" James turned to his father who was sitting on the railing.

"Son?" Jonny replied.

James held up his empty wine glass. "One more?"

"How many have you had?" Jonny scrunched his face in a quizzical expression. He never had a problem with his teenage son having a couple glasses of wine in the evenings with the family, but he was never sure where the line between family bonding and irresponsible parent lay.

"That was just my second."

"In how long?"

"Like, two hours."

"How full were the glasses?" Jonny hopped down from the railing and pretended to examine the wine residue. "Was it all the way up there?" He pointed to a drop clinging near the top of the glass. "That's no way to fill a glass."

"No. I swear," James laughed. "I swoosh."

"You what?"

"You know. I swoosh." James demonstrated by moving his glass in small circles.

"You swirl?"

"I swoosh *and* I swirl."

"Is that a fact?"

"Yes. And all that swooshing and swirling causes the wine to climb up the side of the glass giving it the appearance of a once topped-up glass when in fact it was merely half. Less than half, really. More like a third."

"When'd you start talking like that?" Jonny backed away and leaned against the railing. "You sound like your uncle."

"When? Well, I guess after I heard my uncle explain why he should have another glass of wine. I thought, I could do that."

"Well, then let's hear your uncle, the great debater, explain why you shouldn't have more wine." Jonny turned to his brother. "Uncle Nate?"

"Well, this really is a matter to be resolved not by fancy speeches but by concerned mothers. Kara?"

"Well," Kara started, "the boy seems sober."

"That he does," Jonny agreed. "But it is that exact state that I wish to maintain. The question isn't, is the boy intoxicated, it's will he be if he has another full glass?"

"A third of a glass," James quickly corrected.

"Somewhere between a third and a full."

"Well," Kara continued, "there's almost exactly enough wine left in this bottle for each of the four of us to have … let's see … maybe about a third of a glass. Would it tarnish our yet untarnished reputation if the boy were to have one more glass if the glass was indeed only a third full?"

"Jesus," Jonny laughed, "You're all talking like Nate now." He put his finger to his chin in an exaggerated expression of thought. "Fine, let the boy enjoy one more glass … a third."

"A third." Kara popped the cork and poured the last into the four glasses.

The Sun had nearly set during their banter causing the automatic light above the screen door to flick on and illuminate the deck. They remained for another hour talking a little louder and sipping their wine with greater frequency. Another bottle was opened. James, however, was denied a fourth glass and the night felt to all as close to perfect as any night could have been. Or this is how I like to imagine this last evening.

***

The next morning Nate was awoken by a frantic Jonny. He stormed into the room, "Something happened."

Nate felt groggy and a little hungover, but he quickly jumped out of bed and followed his brother into the kitchen. Kara was sitting in her bathrobe with a cup of coffee and a far-off look on her face.

"What's going on?" Nate asked buttoning up his shirt and fixing the collar.

"There was a raid last night." Jonny talked in a loud, angry whisper trying not to wake James.

"A raid? Where?"

"The Speakeasy."

"Oh God."

"What do we do?" Jonny asked frantically.

"Well," Nate said with his arms held out in a helpless expression, "What can we do?"

"We have to do something."

"Who was taken?"

"The only people there were Danica and Patrick. Abby said they're gone."

"You talked to Abby?"

"Yeah, she's the one who told me. She's coming here right now?"

"She can't come here!" The words burst out of Nate's mouth before he could stop them.

"What do you mean? She needs a safe place."

"Are we a safe-house now?"

"Sit down, you two," Kara said momentarily breaking from her racing thoughts. "And keep your voices to a minimum. James is asleep."

The two men sat down, Jonny next to his wife and Nate across from them. Both folded their hands on the table and leaned towards each other.

In a still loud but calmer whisper Nate said, "I know she needs a safe place to stay and if we're all she has I'm more than willing to keep her here for a bit but we'll be putting everyone here at great risk if we do."

"She needs us. We need to help her."

"If her aunt and uncle are gone then the Overmen are likely looking for her. They know that your wife—"

"I'm right here," Kara said, showing slight annoyance.

"Yes, and you and Abby had a close relationship in prison which I'm sure Public Protection is aware of. We'll be monitored, likely, is what I'm saying."

Kara turned her head to face Nate, "I agree with you. We'll arrange something for her after tonight. But for now, she's already on her way."

A half hour later Abby arrived, having been driven from the city by another contact. When she entered the cottage, her arms were wrapped around herself reminding Kara of the first time she talked to her in prison after her stint in solitary. She was sat down at the kitchen table and offered a drink but refused.

Kara, Jonny, and Nate sat with her. None said a word; there was nothing to say.

That afternoon Jonny drove to the city to meet a contact to discuss what to do with Abby. At the cottage Kara spent the afternoon with Abby. They spent most of the time on the beach, sitting on a blanket. The cottage, Abby said, felt too claustrophobic. Kara agreed knowing these next few days may be the last the young woman had to spend outdoors.

"That's everyone," Abby said in a quiet voice as if she was far away. She was sitting with her knees pulled to her chest, like she was trying to make herself as small as possible.

"What's everyone, sweetie," Kara asked, rubbing her back.

"My parents are gone. My aunt and uncle were all I had left. They're gone now, too."

"We don't know that yet. It's too soon to tell."

"We know. It would be a pretty big shock if they were released. No, I know they're never coming back. We all do."

A moment passed before Kara said, "You have us now. We can help you. And not just us; the whole community that your aunt and uncle were a part of, they'll all do everything to help you. We're all kind of a big extended family."

Abby nodded and forced a smile. Her face was wet with tears that had streamed slowly but steadily ever since she arrived.

Kara stared at Abby's profile, studying her features. She was so young to have lost so much, she thought. She felt in that moment that she'd do anything to keep her safe, to keep anything more from happening to her. But she knew that she had little power to make that happen. If she were honest, she'd admit that she felt incredible anxiety just having the young woman in her home knowing that at any moment black vans might show up and take them all away. Every noise she heard, every bird's fluttering wing, every cricket, every snapped twig, she gave her full attention imagining it were someone sneaking up from the surrounding woods.

"Shall we go inside?" Kara asked finally.

As they stood up, they saw Nate approaching.

"Hey, everything's under the floorboards," he said as they met him on the lawn. He had spent the morning and afternoon gathering every piece of material he had written about the Overmen and anything else that might incriminate or elicit suspicion if the house were suddenly raided.

"They won't find them there?" Kara asked as they made their way back to the cottage.

"Well, it feels pretty solid when you walk on it so there shouldn't be any reason why they'd rip them up. Unless they decide to rip up the floorboards in every room, I don't think they'll find them. I would've liked to take everything and hide it thirty kilometers away but the longer we wait the more likely it is that they'll show up."

That evening Jonny returned with news that he had found a safe house for Abby and that they should leave immediately.

Chapter 38 ~ Expected Visitors

Shortly after midnight Jonny returned to the cottage. He had dropped Abby off with some contacts he knew from the Speakeasy who then took her to the safe house, the location of which was unknown even to Jonny in order to better ensure her safety. After returning, Nate and Kara stayed up with him, sipping tea around the kitchen table waiting to see if Public Protection agents might show up. Indeed, a few minutes past five o'clock in the morning headlights shone through the front windows of the cottage. The three sitting at the table passed glances at one another but didn't say a word as they waited for a knock on the door. Nate answered, feigning sleepiness as if he had been woken up.

"Yes?"

There was a crowd of agents standing on the front porch and on the lawn; the one in front flashed a badge.

"Agent Wexford," Nate read out loud.

"May we come in?" Wexford asked. He was a large man in every sense of the word. Tall with a round belly, square shoulders, a large goatee, thick grey hair, wide nose, and bellowing voice that made everything he said seem like a demand.

"May I ask why?"

The agent smiled, took a step closer and said, "No."

It was useless and possibly dangerous to resist so Nate opened the door for him. Wexford marched in followed by a cavalcade of agents of lower rank. Nate walked to the kitchen table, now vacant, followed by Wexford and both men sat down while the other agents began searching the cottage.

"What are they doing?" Nate called after two agents who were handling the furniture rather carelessly. "There's no need for that. Don't you need a warrant for this?"

Wexford smiled, "This will only take a moment. Sit tight." He began tapping his knuckles on the table and released a sigh.

"Hey, my nephew's in there," Nate yelled at an agent who had opened James' bedroom door.

"What's going on?" Jonny asked suddenly appearing from his room with Kara right behind him.

"These men are looking for something. For what they haven't told me."

Kara walked briskly to her son's room before the agent could turn on the light. "He's in his underwear," she yelled at the agent. "Let him put something on first."

The agent obliged and stepped out of the room while Kara could be heard inside explaining to James what was going on. She soon exited followed a moment later by her son who had put on a pair of jeans and a sweater.

"Maybe if you tell us what you want, we can help speed up the process," an annoyed Kara asked, wrapping her arms around herself. She and her son were standing behind Nate while Jonny had taken a seat at the table.

"It shouldn't take long," Wexford said again with another sigh and a couple swift taps on the table.

As they waited, they noticed flashlights floating round the back yard, illuminating the tree line and the still water and the rocky beach. The darkness kept the holders of the lights invisible. Inside, the occasional radio would crack, and an agent would mumble something followed by another crack. Their couch cushions were flipped up and gloved hands swept through the crevasses, pulling out loose change, a pencil, and some hard candies. Walls were tapped on with the ends of flashlights, the floor was tapped on with the soles of shoes, although Nate's hiding spot was luckily not discovered, the bookshelf was emptied of books, the toilet basin lid was removed, every drawer was opened and its contents spilt.

Finally, after over an hour in which no member of the Karski family was permitted to leave the kitchen, they were informed that the search was over.

"Thank God," Kara said shaking her head. "Can we go back to bed now?"

"*You* can, yes. But *you*," Wexford pointed a finger at Jonny, "will have to come with us."

"What? No," Kara yelled and leapt towards her husband as if she were about to push him out of the way of an incoming train.

"Please don't," James also yelled, following his mother. The two took positions on either side of Jonny. "Please don't take my dad. Please."

"Come on," Wexford said and motioned for Jonny to stand up. "I'm sure you know there's no way out of this." Jonny, for his part, lowered his head, took a deep breath and then obeyed. "All right, let's get on with it then."

"No! No, no, no," Kara kept saying as two agents grabbed Jonny by the arms and led him to the front door.

"Why?" Nate asked following his brother as he was taken outside. The sun had started rising illuminating the yard with a soft light. He could now see there were a total of four black SUV's in his front lawn. "What do you want with him? He hasn't done anything!"

Kara and James stood on the front steps watching in horror, their faces white.

"There's nothing to be worried about. We just want to talk to him," Wexford casually reassured. "He'll be back in no time." And then offered a morsel of hope by repeating, "Hey, I promise. He'll be back in no time."

Nate tried to continue to follow but another agent quickly put himself between him and his brother.

"Jon," Nate yelled. "Jon!"

Before Jonny could answer he was put in the back of an SUV and the doors were closed.

"I want your word," Nate yelled at Wexford who was walking to another vehicle. "I want you word that he comes back here."

Wexford turned around to face him, "Thanks for your cooperation," was all he said before climbing into the back of the SUV and closing the door.

Nate marched back inside the cottage while Kara and James stood and watched the black vehicles disappear round the bend on the heavily wooded road.

The weeks following Jonny's arrest were similar to the other times members of their family were taken. Calls were made, meetings arranged, protests organized. But nothing could really be done to get someone back who had disappeared. The only hope they had was the thought that Jonny hadn't been *disappeared* like the others, that is, he wasn't snagged in the middle of the night with a bag over his head without a warning. He was arrested in front of his family with the identity of the arresting officer known. It felt, they reassured themselves, like a "normal" arrest, something that might have happened years before to someone suspected of a robbery. This small, frayed, string of hope was all they had but they clung to it like a life raft after a shipwreck.

Chapter 39 ~ Anna and Marie

Anna arrived at the cottage shortly after midday. To park she had to squeeze her car between a press van and a thin birch tree which appeared to have already come in contact with some other vehicle whose driver was less adept at driving. It had been three months since Jonny was taken with still no word as to his whereabouts or wellbeing. Some contacts from the Speakeasy had put Nate and Kara in touch with a film crew who wanted to include them in a documentary they were filming about the existence of the internment camps. Because of this, their tiny cottage was overrun with people when Anna arrived. She had brought with her a tray of coffees from a shop in the city and balanced them precariously in one hand while the other carried a large bag filled with food items. Before she reached the front door of the cottage it swung open and a young man she didn't recognize and who was chatting on a mobile phone exited and lit a cigarette.

"I know, I know … I said I know," he kept saying into the phone. "Doesn't matter, we have dozens of people supporting this thing, I'm sure they'll all chip in …"

Anna slid past him and into the cottage. James greeted her first, very briefly and with only a nod since an apple in his mouth prevented him from speaking and a large milk crate of electronics kept his hands from removing the apple. The entire cottage was bustling with people, many of whom she recognized from the days of the Speakeasy.

She walked through the living room and into the kitchen where she put the coffees and food on the counter. She scanned the cottage for any sign of Nate or Kara and when she found none, she busied herself unpacking the groceries from the bag. Nate had called her before she left the city asking her to bring stuff to make lunch for fifteen people. The coffees she brought just for Nate, Kara, and herself.

"Ah, did you just get here?" Nate said after bouncing in through the screen door. He was talking quickly and seemed out of breath.

"Yeah, I hope sandwich meat is fine." She held up a loaf of bread in one hand and a bag of ham in the other.

"That's perfect. Just leave it there; anyone who's hungry can help themselves."

"So, what can I do?"

"Well, James is helping set up a sort of studio there," Nate said walking quickly through the kitchen towards the living room with his arm extended and finger pointing in James's direction. "That's where they're going to do the interviews. When it's done, they're going to put it up on a website that's being designed with the help of that guy outside." He pointed to the man on the phone Anna passed when she first arrived. "Those people out there …" he hurried back into the kitchen and pointed out the back door, "… are a film crew. That woman, also on the phone there—"

"In the grey skirt?"

"Yeah, she's going to do the interviews. She writes for The Future, the magazine my wife used to … ah, work for. Her name's Claire. She's going to interview all of us, Kara, James, and myself and a bunch of people from the Speakeasy. They're all outside. Everyone is going to say something about each person who disappeared from the Speakeasy. We're going to try and make it a thing, try and put some pressure on them."

Anna and Nate had never talked about his wife save for the occasional reference to her here and there, but they were usually in the form of a slip of the tongue like the one Nate just made. She thought of digging a bit deeper but decided it wasn't the time. "I see. So, what can I do?"

"Um, I don't know. I just kind of wanted you here. I hope that's all right."

"Yeah, of course."

"I didn't take you away from anything, did I?"

"Not at all. I'm happy to be here."

"Okay, well, come with me." Nate led the way out the back door.

Anna and Nate had been seeing each other for some time now. Although they had yet to discuss the actual status of their relationship, Anna was certain Nate considered them a couple. She was fine with this for the most part but having not yet talked about his absent wife in any informative way kept her from being as convinced of their relationship's status as he was. A lingering question she had was whether Nate believed her to still be alive and if she was, well, what sort of relationship would be in store for them if there was a chance Marie could show up at some point in the future. Because of this she proceeded with the relationship with much caution and was nearing the point in which she must refuse to go any further until her concerns were addressed.

"A lot of people, eh," Nate said looking across the yard from the top of the deck. "I guess most are friends from the Speakeasy here for support and to be interviewed but a lot of them, all those ones crowded there actually, they're part of the film crew."

"Are you making a whole documentary? Is that what this is going to be?"

"Yeah, they're doing a documentary on the disappearances, not just from the Speakeasy but in general, but they're using what happened at the Speakeasy as a kind of main example."

'You're going to put your face and name on this?" Anna asked unable to hide her concern.

"Well, they're hoping my name will give some needed attention to the film when it's released."

"But aren't you just guaranteeing that you be disappeared next?"

Nate tilted his head to the side and smiled uncomfortably but didn't answer.

***

That evening, after the filmmakers had finished for the day and everyone had gone, Anna and Nate were in the living room. It was dark, the only light coming from a small lamp on the adjacent wall. Kara and James had gone to bed already and Anna had agreed to spend the night instead of driving all the way back to the city at such an hour. It was a week into November and outside snow had begun to fall softly, creating a thin white blanket over the yard pierced sporadically with the blades of errant grass.

"How was the day?" Anna said standing with the door open a crack smoking a cigarette.

"Ah," Nate stretched his arms above his head and yawned. "I think it was all right. They got a lot of footage. Hopefully they can use some of it, most of it."

"You don't seem terribly optimistic." Anna flicked her cigarette out the door and took a seat beside Nate.

"It's hard to be anything but cynical at the moment," Nate turned to face her, studied her features, her radiant hair, her bright eyes. "But you're right, I should be more optimistic. They seem like a competent crew. I'm sure they'll make a great film." He smiled cheaply.

"You're not really selling it," Anna laughed. "I'd like to see that as a review." She took on the exaggerated voice of a television announcer, "The makers of the film seem competent."

"Sorry." Nate sat up straight and feigned enthusiasm. "Everything was *great*. The documentary will be a major success."

"Now rein it back a bit," Anna laughed.

"It's hard to be excited about anything, really," Nate said and leaned his head against the back of the couch.

"I can't imagine," Anna lay her head next to his.

"I can't stop thinking about him." Nate turned away from her and grabbed his tumbler off the end table.

"Not just him, though," Anna began to tease the black curls on the back of Nate's head. "You've lost a lot in this struggle."

"Everyone has," Nate closed his eyes as if to fall asleep.

"Maybe. But," Anna checked herself before continuing, "your wife—" her voice barely above a whisper.

"My wife?" Nate's eyes opened and he turned again to face Anna.

"You never talk about her."

"She's gone."

"Do you know anything about where she is or …" Anna trailed off. She wanted to continue talking about Marie but couldn't find the words for such a delicate topic.

"She's just gone. Like everyone who disappears, she's gone. The details don't matter much I suppose."

"Do you think she'll ever come back?"

Nate tried to imagine such a scenario but where any thoughts of his wife might have been there was only an empty space and his mind could only contemplate the emptiness of it. "She's just gone," he said after a prolonged silence. "She'll never come back. Sometimes I wonder if she was ever even here. My memories of her, they're starting to fade. I imagine soon she'll be erased from the past just like she has been from the future."

Anna suddenly felt overwhelmed. She rested her head on Nate's shoulder and began to cry. Nate wrapped an arm around her and kissed the top of her head. He didn't cry, though. He hadn't cried yet for her and he still couldn't cry now.

Chapter 40 ~ How Monsters are Made

Over a month later, about a week before Christmas, Kara received a phone call. It was a quarter to six in the morning. The sound of the vibrating device on her nightstand jolted her awake and before her eyes were fully opened, she had it to her ear.

"Yes?" she said into the receiver followed by a clearing of her throat.

At first there was only silence before a quavering voice cracked, "It's me."

Kara put her hand to her mouth and began to sob while her husband did the same on the other end.

Kara ran into the living room shouting, "It's him. It's him." She banged on her son's door before throwing it open. "It's him. He's all right. It's your dad."

She didn't wait to see her son's reaction; indeed, she hadn't even turned on the light in the room to see what it might have been before she ran out and began banging a fist on Nate's door. Nate, having been already woken by the shouting answered immediately.

"Jonny?"

Kara was holding her phone out to him. "He's here. We have to go get him."

"Mum," James said exiting his room and rubbing his eyes. "What's going on?"

"It's your dad," she said showing him the phone.

Jonny had been driven to the corner of Grosvenor and Stafford in the back of another black SUV and deposited without ceremony. It was there, seated on a bench, that Kara, James, and Nate found him. He was wearing the same clothes he had on when he was taken in addition to a grey hoody lined with white fleece, a grey toque, and thin grey mittens. The clothes seemed to hang off his alarmingly thin frame. When he saw them, he couldn't say a word, he could only cry and when they ran to hug him, he seemed to crumple in their embrace. He shook so violently that Kara and James feared he might collapse into a heap if they were to let go. Nate stood back, giving them some room to reunite. As he watched the now frail body of his brother shake in the arms of his family, Nate was hit with the impression that something far more than his physical appearance had changed.

Jonny later explained what happened to him. He was taken to a facility, the location of which he never knew, and questioned as to the whereabouts of Abby and the identities of any remaining members of the Speakeasy. When it became obvious he wasn't going to tell them anything, they changed their tactics. For the next few weeks he was kept in complete isolation, never seeing another face and not knowing what time of day it was. It was so quiet, he said, that he thought he could sometimes hear his blood pumping through his ears. When this sensory deprivation was interrupted it was with piercingly loud music, shouting, blinding lights. His disorientation was such that he began to question what was real and at times if he was in fact still alive. "It was horrible," he would say faintly when relating his experience to his family. "And I'm still honestly not sure if I told them anything. I can't be sure."

This trauma defined Jonny for months afterwards. He'd spend most of his time in bed, often waking with jolts, screaming, not knowing where he was. His dreams took him back to that cell, to the silence, to the noise, to the chaos. Most of his time in bed was spent awake, staring at the door, the bookshelf, the lamp, wondering if these objects around him were in fact a dream and his nightmares were reality. It was quickly agreed upon by Nate and Kara that he should never be left alone. When he did leave his bedroom, he would say and do little. He'd often spend his waking hours sitting and staring intently into some distant plane, like prey vigilantly watching a distant predator. Suggestions were often presented for a walk, or a drive, but he would invariably refuse to leave the cottage, only going so far as to have an occasional drink on the deck before hurriedly returning to the safety of the cottage walls. It seemed to Nate and Kara that he viewed the cottage as the only safe place, a sort of sanctuary and if he were to ever leave, he'd immediately be picked up again and brought back to that cell, dark, and isolated, and hopeless. But even in that sanctuary he didn't feel safe, only safer than outside of it. That oppressive cell was waiting for him to return, he was convinced of that, and the only thing keeping him from it was his insistence on never making himself vulnerable, never leaving the protective walls of the cottage. In this way he made the cottage another cell, one that was self-inflicted but a cell, nonetheless.

But, also like Nate, his old self slowly began to reappear in bits here and there. But both Kara and Nate noticed that his old self, as it returned, was accompanied by something new, something unnatural, and something angry, and vengeful. It bared an unnerving resemblance to the anxiety that had wormed its way into Jonny's life after his prison term but had now grown exponentially as if the anxiety before was only a monster in its larva state.

One evening, with the cottage to themselves, Kara and Jonny sat on the couch in the living room. Jonny was only marginally present. If Kara didn't maintain a conversation his mind would drift away, and she'd have to find some way to pull it back. Even with him sitting next to her she still felt like she still missed him, like he was still far away being held in some prison. There were good days, though, and they were becoming more frequent. This evening capped the end of one of those good days and because of this his sudden gloom was harder to take.

"Are you okay?" Kara asked, hoping he'd snap out of it so they could end the day on a happy note.

"Yeah." He smiled weakly. "Just tired."

"This was a good day," she said hoping a reminder of the fun they had might inspire some more.

"Yeah. It was."

Kara's frustration was beginning to grow. Not at Jonny, but at those who did this to him. She wanted to get her husband back not just for his own sake but also to spite the Overmen. She wanted him to get better and live a long healthy life in defiance.

With no other topic keeping his mind away from wherever it insisted on going, she said, "Do you want to talk about it?"

He turned to her with a look of incredulity, "Of what? There's nothing to say. What would I say?"

"I just ... I want to know ... I don't know what. I can't imagine what they did to you there."

"I told you what they did to me." Jonny spoke harshly.

"I mean ... I just want to help you. We all do and lately you've been ..."

Jonny sat up. He had finished a beer and crushed the can with a loud crunch while walking to the kitchen.

"Jonny," Kara called after him. She sat up and followed him to the kitchen where he was grabbing another beer from the fridge. She leaned against the door frame. "You don't have to talk about this if you don't want to, but I want you to know that we all want to help you."

"I know," Jonny said coarsely. He cracked open the can with a hiss and sipped the foam off the top. "I'm not angry at you. Or anyone in this goddamn place. I mean, how could I? None of you did anything wrong." He walked past Kara and sat back down on the couch. "It's them, out there," he motioned to the front door, the same out of which he had been hauled by Wexford months earlier, "they're the ones. They need to answer for what they did. For what they did to Abby's family, for what they did to me, for what they did to you—just trying to take care of your fucking son—for what they've done to everyone who's not one of them." He took a loud sip and wiped his mouth with his sleeve.

"I know they did horrible things to you," Kara said having remained standing in the doorway. "But you can't let them change you. You have to let us help you."

"It's not me. See, this is what you're not getting. It's them," he motioned outside the door again, "what's wrong with me, what you think is wrong with me, is them, it's all them."

"I know."

"But here we are in this shack a million miles away from what's out there. Goddamnit!" he stood up and began pacing the room. "I don't want to talk about this anymore." He marched to the fridge and grabbed another beer, despite not yet having finished the one in his hand. He grabbed his winter coat from the coat rack and marched out the back door onto the patio. Kara gave him a moment before following him.

"Darling," she said standing with the screen door open, clasping the collar of her sweater to keep out the cold winter air. Jonny had taken a seat and was staring out across the snow-covered lawn and towards the frozen lake. "It's freezing out here."

"You don't have to follow me out here; I won't be long."

Kara was about to say more but her attention was grabbed by headlights from an approaching vehicle lighting up the cottage behind her. "Nate and James are back," she said softly and to herself since Jonny didn't seem to hear.

Kara met her son and brother-in-law as they came in through the front door while Jonny remained seated on the deck. After inquiring about their evening out—they had gone to watch a movie at the local cinema and presumably gone out for something to eat afterwards—James was promptly ordered to wash up and go to bed.

"How's the night?" Nate asked her after James was in the washroom. He had suspected that Kara would try to talk to Jonny about his recent behavior and wanted to know what he should expect.

"So far not very productive. He's outside right now. He's angry."

"Is there anything I can do?" Nate asked, feeling helpless.

"I don't think so. He just needs time. He's been hitting it pretty hard and not really in a mood for talking."

"I understand. I'll leave him be then," Nate said and retreated to his bedroom.

"Honey?" Kara poked her head out the screen door again.

"Yes?"

"Everyone's gone to bed and I think I'll do the same. Are you going to join me?"

"No, not yet. I'm going to stay up for a bit."

"All right. I'll see you in the morning."

The next morning Nate woke about 9:30, which was early for him, but thoughts of his brother's state of mind consumed him and resulted in a restless night. He wandered through the cottage for a moment before he noticed something scattered in the snow across the back yard.

He slipped a pair of leather boots over his bare feet with the intention to investigate but before he made it to the door, he heard a groan. To his right he saw his brother curled up on the couch, wrapped in a throw blanket, and waking from a presumably drunken sleep.

"You spent the night out here?" Nate asked incredulously.

Jonny looked round the room, squinting his eyes before sitting up and saying, "I suppose I did."

"What's that in the yard?" Nate pointed to the scene which looked to him like splintered wood.

"Oh," Jonny said, and Nate detected a hint of embarrassment in his tone. "We need to deal with that before Kara wakes up and sees it."

What needed cleaning up were the remains of a wooden patio chair Jonny had confessed to smashing with a croquet mallet.

"Do you remember why?" Nate inquired while loading up a bundle of splinters in his arms.

"I was angry."

"I gathered that."

Jonny took a moment before confessing, "I'm always angry these days."

"Do you want to—"

"Talk about it? No. I'm not in the mood to talk about this or anything related. Not now, anyway. Not when it's this cold. It's fucking bitter out here isn't it." Jonny looked up at the bright morning sky. "I think it's colder when the Sun's shining bright than when it's hiding behind clouds."

Nate and Jonny never talked about "it" again. Nobody did. Weeks passed with a heavy, silent tension permeating the cottage until Jonny finally broke it by announcing to his wife that he was leaving. He told her that he had no choice, that he couldn't stand cowering in some isolated cottage while good people were fighting and dying "out there."

"I thought you didn't want to do that anymore," Kara said, seated at the table with her hands wrapped around a hot cup of coffee.

"Do what?"

"Do what your friends over there were doing. You told me—"

"I remember what I told you. I'm not saying I'm going to do that. I'm not planning on blowing anything up. But there are other ways to resist."

During this exchange, while Jonny paced about the room, Kara's face was drained of all emotion, as if the events of the past couple of years had left her with nothing left to express. Her answers and questions to her perturbed husband were delivered in monotones and her eyes maintained a stoic gaze, not at him, but out the window, across the snow-covered yard, and far out over the frozen lake.

"Besides," Jonny continued, "at this point killing Overmen doesn't seem like such a bad thing does it. How many of us have they killed?"

"You are going to—"

"I didn't say what I'm going to do," he snapped.

"Is this YesFore you're in contact with?"

"Of course. They're always looking for more help. I can probably go back and do what I did before."

"Are they still doing what they did before?"

"Yeah, I mean, I don't know. I'm sure. I know they've got their fingers in other things now, too, but peaceful protests, that was always they're cup of tea."

Nate walked through the front door, holding a pair of skis and poles, and saw the two of them in the kitchen. When Jonny saw him, he stopped pacing and sat down across from Kara. Kara kept her eyes fixed on the nothingness across the lake.

As Nate brushed himself clean of snow the door opened again, and James walked through carrying his own ski equipment. "Hi," he said and waved a mitted hand.

"Hi, Son," Jonny said, his voice still carrying the sound of his agitation.

When Nate had removed his outerwear, he joined them at the table and all three sat in silence.

"What's going on?" James said when he had made his way into the kitchen. His hair was wet from melted snow and his cheeks were still rosy from the cold.

"Ah, we're just chatting," Jonny said and stood up. "How were the trails?"

"Good. We saw a deer." James took the last remaining seat at the table. "Besides that, it was basically the same as every ski day."

"Sounds fun. Hungry?

"Yeah, starving."

"Me, too. I'm going to run into town to get some stuff for dinner. You want to come?"

"I just took off all my winter clothes."

Jonny stood up. "Well put them back on again. It only takes a moment."

"Fine." James stood up and followed his dad to the front door leaving his uncle and mother alone at the table. "Can I buy something from the store?"

"*Buy* implies having money."

"Well, can you buy me something from the store?"

"I am, I'm buying you food to eat tonight for supper."

They continued to banter as they pulled on their warm clothes and walked out to the car.

Alone with Kara in the kitchen, Nate felt he knew without being told what kind of conversation they had while he was out with James. "We can't stop him, can we," he said. "I wish there was something I could say, or do, that could convince him to stay."

Kara sipped her coffee catatonically and stared out the screen door. Softly she said, "But you know, and I know, nothing we can say or do can keep him from what he's going to do."

Nate heard her sniff before she took another sip, but she never shed a tear and her voice remained rigid. She had been preparing for this, Nate thought, for some time now.

Chapter 41 ~ The Lost Boy

Jonny had maintained contact with his old comrades while he lived with Nate and soon had made arrangements with them to leave once more. Everyone pleaded with him to stay but he had made up his mind.

"Don't you want to change what's happening?" Jonny said to his wife as she pleaded with him one last time not to go. "Aren't you sick? Aren't you tired? Don't you want to do something about it all?"

"Of course I do. I hate them for what they've done. I dream of killing them. I dream of killing every one of them."

"So, you understand."

"I do. But I also understand that this is not the way. My dreams have no place in the real world, in this world."

"But what else can we do? You say this isn't the way. But then what is the way? Writing pamphlets like Nate? Inconveniencing them by chaining myself to a statue until they cut me down and arrest me? Annoying them by waving a sign outside a building? Things have only gotten worse. They've taken away my friends. You know what happened to Marie."

"I know." She already knew nothing she could say could keep him from going and so her voice became quiet in defeat. "But your family is still here. Still alive. James is here. I'm here."

"Are you suggesting I wait until you're taken away? If James disappeared into a black bag tomorrow would you still try to stop me from going? Am I to wait until it's appropriate to react? Am I to wait until you disappear? I'm leaving to fight now because things have escalated and are escalating faster and faster. I know you're still here, and I want to be here with you, but I can't wait for you or James to disappear before I do something."

"There are other avenues."

"I assure you there aren't. It's not a protest anymore. It's not a group of people challenging bills being passed in parliament. It's war. It's us against them. I'm not going with the intention of dying. I'm going with the intention of fighting for a better future. For you and James. You two are my life and it's my job to protect you, to ensure a better future, or any future."

After this conversation she abandoned any more attempts at stopping him, deciding to spend the last days together trying to be as happy as possible. Instead of discussing where he was going and what he was doing they talked about fishing. They drank more wine together, went out to eat expensive food together, went for drives, hosted parties.

Every moment they dedicated to making the best possible memories, for James and Kara to keep and for Jonny to take with him.

The day he was leaving—a car was scheduled to pick him up sometime after dinner— Nate and Jonny drove into town to pick up some things for dinner. Nate drove while Jonny sat quietly staring out the window. Nate could tell he was nervous; he could hear it in his quavering voice when he spoke and the constant deep sighs.

"Are you ready to go?" Nate asked.

"I am," Jonny replied and sucked in air slowly.

"Do you know what you'll be doing when you get there?"

I have some ideas." Jonny had always been quite vague as to what he was expecting to do or where he was expecting to go. The family had learnt it was no use trying to get him to explain.

"Is there anything I can do, either now or in the future?"

"Just keep writing. That helps."

"I can do that. Once you're there, can you come back whenever you want?"

"I don't know."

Nate wanted to press him, but he knew he could never get more out of him.

"Here we are." They pulled up to the supermarket which was crowded with people. Small towns like Gerald were slower to adopt segregation laws like the cities because of their small or often nonexistent Immortal populations at the time. Because of this, more and more Mortals from the cities were moving to rural communities to escape the discriminatory laws and maintain their dignity. Populations in many small towns began to swell but without the necessary government funds for infrastructure to expand, these towns quickly became overcrowded micro-cities.

They parked half a kilometer away and walked, grabbing a discarded shopping cart on the way. They made their way to the entrance without saying a word to each other. The walk was slow, having to stop whenever a vehicle attempted to pull in or out of a parking spot and dodge the multitudes of people pushing shopping carts in seemingly all directions. Once they finally made their way inside, they agreed to split up to make the best use of their time. Nate was left with the cart.

After about forty-five minutes Nate had managed to collect all the items he was tasked with but hadn't seen Jonny since they split. He thought it best to park his cart near the entrance where they first separated and wait instead of trying to maneuver through the sea of others. Time continued to tick by with no sign of Jonny and Nate had begun to grow impatient. He looked in all directions for any sign of him but saw instead one anonymous shopper after the next scurrying by, holding lists in front of their expressionless faces, looking for signs indicating the contents of isles, waving other shoppers past with polite grins, none of whom were Jonny.

Nate's impatience grew to annoyance before turning finally to concern. Where could he be, he thought. And what could possibly be taking him so long.

He began to push his cart through the crowd, excusing himself often and constantly yelling above the noise for one person to move and another to stay right where they were. He didn't understand why he was overcome with such concern; Jonny was a capable adult, after all, in a place that posed no distinguishable threat, but his worry slowly grew into a panic. As it did, he was suddenly transported back to his childhood. He is six years old; Jonny is three and has just tripped over that protruding root that ran from the base of the big oak in their backyard. He's crying, holding his knee and Nate is running to him. He puts an arm around him and helps brush out the dirt that's imbedded in his palms and knees. Nate's twelve now; Jonny's nine. Nate has friends over; I'm there. We watch a horror movie and let Jonny stay up with us. That night when Jonny is crying in his bed unable to sleep for fear of the monsters in his closet, Nate leaves his friends camped out in the living room and comforts his brother until he falls asleep. Nate's seventeen; Jonny's fourteen and trying to establish himself amongst his peers. Older kids, Nate's age, pelt him with snowballs calling him a faggot. Nate hears about it and confronts the boys and gets beaten bloody. The two of them walk home from school that day each with matching tissues in their noses saturated in blood. Now they're both adults. Jonny's lost. Where's he going? What is he doing? What can Nate do now?

"Hey." Nate spun around to find the source of the familiar voice. His brother jogged through the crowd towards him trying not to drop the bundle of condiments, vegetables, and wooden skewers he had in his arms. "This place is a madhouse." When he reached the cart, he leaned over and dropped everything he was carrying. "Is that everything?"

"Yeah," Nate said solemnly. He pushed the cart to the checkout and Jonny followed.

***

Despite the attempts to lessen the blow, when Jonny left, Kara was devastated. Her calm demeanor that she had become known for collapsed and she fell into a deep depression for days. James, on the other hand, wasn't sure how to feel. He was confused and terrified and angry. He locked himself in his room when he was home and spent the time staring at the walls or ceiling trying to find some way to process everything that had just happened and what may happen in the future. Not even a year had passed since his father had come home from his last long absence but between then and now, they had built a relationship that they simply didn't have before. He refused to eat with his mother or uncle, not sure if they were to blame and not wanting to know if they were. He spent most of the rest of the summer out with friends, finding comfort in other distractions. Nate didn't know how to take it either. He felt like he understood his brother's intentions but hated his methods. Luckily, he now had Anna who provided some comfort. And of course, he had his writing into which he poured himself fully.

Chapter 42 ~ Time to Leave

In Kiev, it would have been about six months after the events of the previous chapter, I was informed by my secretary that a documentary had been released which included footage of my "old acquaintance" Nathaniel Karski.

"What kind of footage?" I asked trying not to appear too interested.

"He, his sister-in-law," Daniel spoke slowly, studying my face for a reaction, "and his nephew all gave interviews. These interviews were conducted in a cottage which is situated outside of the community of Gerald about seventy kilometers north of Winnipeg."

"And you're telling me because of my past ties with him?"

"It's information I thought you'd like to know."

"Thank you."

"There should be a copy of the documentary on your hard drive already if you'd like to give it a look."

"I will. Later. But I will. Thanks again."

"You should also know that there is talk of doing something about the documentary. Something about your friends who were involved in it, possibly all of them." As he said this, I thought I saw a barely subdued expression of glee pass over his features. "Again, I just thought you'd like to know."

I sighed, trying to appear indifferent, then said, "It must be pretty inflammatory, what they said in the documentary," I leaned towards my computer and opened the file containing the documentary.

"I wouldn't say that. But they're considering your friend's previous disruptive behavior. He seemed to have learnt his lesson after his wife …" he paused again and I could feel him studying my reaction, "… got into some trouble a few years ago. But this might be a sign that he's falling back into his old ways."

"Well," I said looking up at him and sighing, "if anything else comes up I'll give it a look. Although I'd be surprised if what's on this video is enough to warrant any major intervention."

"Did you know his brother is suspected of aiding and abetting a wanted fugitive?"

"I didn't."

"Did you know, according to our sources, that he has recently vanished?"

My heart sunk for a moment as I misinterpreted what he was telling me. "Vanished? Was that our doing?" I know I failed in hiding my concern because Daniel seemed to catch it and a barely perceptible grin appeared in his face.

"No. I mean he ran off on his own accord, presumably to do something stupid. Either way, that family seems to be incapable of keeping their heads down if you understand my meaning."

"Of course."

"And because of that, some have considered it an option to just—"

"I think I understand," I said holding up a hand. "You've been more than helpful bringing this to my attention." I suddenly recognized his tone as one not entirely appropriate for a secretary and thought I better reset the order of things. After all, he hadn't said "sir" once. "Is there anything else?"

My sudden commandeering of the conversation seemed to have ruined his gleeful mood and he frowned as he said, "No, that's all for now," and left me alone.

Alone with my thoughts I found myself once again weighing my options. Should I try and help Nate again? Daniel was growing more suspicious by the hour it seemed and any involvement on my part might put him over the edge. But could I leave my old friend to fate after going to such great, albeit rather clumsy, lengths to protect him? I thought I should do something, even if it was something small, if for no other reason than to keep anything else from cluttering up my conscience. The first thing I would do, though, is request a transfer and if I got it, and only if, then I would step in and try to convince those in charge of the decision to leave Nate and his family alone.

I, unfortunately, didn't have the option to request a specific location to which to be transferred—the OP didn't want anyone to have too much control over their own lives—but I could make a formal request for transfer. To where I might be transferred was entirely up to those on top of the hierarchical ladder. When asked the reason for my desire to transfer I gave the usual, "I think I would be more effective somewhere else. I believe I have learnt all I can at this particular location and I'm eager to learn more to be a better Overman. I think it's time for someone else to have the opportunity to advance to my position," and I gave a number of recommendations.

To my surprise my request was accepted. The reasons for this were many. One, the Overman Project's obsession with keeping tabs on every aspect of everyone's life meant there was simply too much information to sort through. Whatever suspicious behavior Daniel reported about me turned out to be insufficient to conduct an official investigation and so I was kept relatively off their radar. This is even more surprising when one considers my previous relationships with revolutionary Mortals in my past. But I think the reason their knowledge of those relationships didn't lead to any further investigation was because all Overmen from my generation had relationships with Mortals; it was just the way things were back then. If they were going to investigate me, they'd have to investigate any and every Immortal with a similar history. They were also aware that I indeed betrayed those friends. That seems to have convinced them that I wasn't much of a threat. After all, what kind of person betrays someone only to turn around and offer a helping hand?

Once I was set to leave, I submitted a suggestion to those who were likely to be involved in the case being considered against Nate. In the paper I argued that silencing Nate would bring more attention to him than if they leave him alone. After all, I wrote, his participation in the documentary seems to have been in response to his brother's arrest but since his brother has been released, he would have little reason to continue with any dissident behavior. Aside from his participation in the documentary, there is little indication that he has been doing anything subversive or will do anything in the future.

I have no idea if my intervention had any significance in their decision, but Nate was indeed left alone. In fact, I have no idea if they were ever considering silencing him or if what Daniel told me was just something he'd made up to provoke me. None of the possibilities would have surprised me. And either way, whatever Daniel was trying to do he had apparently failed. I was leaving and he wasn't coming with me.

***

Daniel seemed unenthusiastic about my departure. I knew he suspected much more about me than the OP was willing to believe and probably felt close to exposing me. In fact, it's possible he was, which is why I was so adamant about getting as far away from him as possible. Once he learnt about my eventual departure, he began dropping hints that he knew more than he was letting on in the form of snarky comments and obscure questions.

"You seem less interested in Subject Blair lately," he asked while dropping off some folder on my desk.

"Do I? Well, there are other things to worry about, aren't there."

"I thought you'd be more interested in him now that it appears he's closer to your jurisdiction than previously thought."

"Question for ya," I said fingering through the folder, "since you're sharing your thoughts: do you think people don't care what you think because you're a secretary or are you a secretary because people don't care what you think?" I looked up from my folder to see his face fuming. We stared at one another for a small but awkward moment before I released a boisterous laugh. "I'm kidding. You're a great secretary, Daniel. You know I'm joking right?"

"Of course, sir." He forced a smiled, but his face was still bright red. "Is there anything else?"

These small interactions continued up until the day I left. On my last day he entered my office with a small black gift bag closed at the top by a red ribbon. I thanked him and opened it to see a small marble sculpture of a Neanderthal rubbing two sticks together.

"What's this?" I asked, holding it up for examination.

"It's the past," he said stoically. I noticed he omitted his usual "sir".

"Thanks," I placed it on my desk and pretended to sort through some files.

"You know," he, for the first time since I met him, sat down in the chair across from me, "Neanderthals, contrary to popular belief, are thought to have been quite intelligent."

"Yeah?" I leaned back realizing I wasn't getting out of this.

"Yeah, they used tools just like that one using sticks to make fire." He nodded towards my new figurine. "They even buried their dead which shows a very sophisticated level of intelligence and, what we could call, human emotion. In fact, it's possible that Homo sapiens and Neanderthals even interbred."

"Fascinating." I lathered the word with sarcasm.

"But they weren't Homo sapiens," he continued. "Their interbreeding probably didn't result in many, if any, offspring. Although they shared many similarities there were obvious and incompatible differences between them and Homo sapiens. Because of this incompatibility one had to go. We still don't know how the Neanderthals became extinct. There are many theories: climate change, malnutrition, or, possibly, extermination by Homo sapiens." He let this last suggestion sink in for a moment. "Whatever the case, it can be surmised that there simply wasn't enough room on the planet for two dominate species. Although similar, one was superior and that one, the more evolved one, the more enlightened one, had to snuff out the other so that it could flourish. It sounds cruel and, in some way, it had to have been cruel. But what were the alternatives? Should Homo sapiens have allowed themselves to vanish into the dark annals of prehistory? If they were the superior species, didn't they have the right, even the obligation to ensure that they were the ones who came out on top?"

He left me enough room to say a word, so I took advantage of it. "Is this your vision of the future? Are Mortals Neanderthals; aren't we all Homo sapiens?"

"We are more than Homo sapiens, aren't we?" He adjusted in his seat as if this topic excited him. "We have eternity before us. We have eternity to perfect ourselves. To become gods. And we'll do it. It's inevitable. But it's a long journey and our goal is far in the distance. Before we can get there, we have to take the first few steps regardless of how unpleasant they may be." He paused as if to leave me time to say something more, but I said nothing. "They may be our Parents but, like all children in relation to their parents, we've outgrown them and now we can see how poorly they compare to us. Like all of our evolutionary ancestors we far surpass them and like all our ancestors they must step aside to make room before we can reach our full potential."

"Are you talking about extermination?" I said, my voice weak like a mouse as if I were asking my executioner if I'll suffer before I die.

"They are pathetic, retched creatures, aren't they? I know you feel it, too. You can't help but feel it. It's the natural reaction a superior species has in the presence of an inferior one. We share common ancestors with apes, rats, cockroaches even. All these foul creatures are our family, just like Mortals are, but are we expected to treat them as equals? Would you not stomp the life out of a cockroach if you saw it? Or a rat? You may not feel any animosity towards a chimp, but would you share your food with one? Would you want to share your home with one, your bed, your dinner table? They, Mortals, have a rather disgusting quality do they not? And the chimpanzee is disgusting to *them*. And just like they have dominion over the chimp so do we have dominion over them."

"Mortals aren't chimps, or Neanderthals."

"But we aren't Mortals. We are above them just as they are above the others. We may appear similar now, but we are young, infants really, with an eternal path towards perfection. We may see similarities now, but in a thousand years we will look back at our Parents and wonder how we ever shared a planet with such primitives."

I smiled awkwardly and studied the figurine. I found myself wanting to believe him, but …

"I know you struggle with your sympathies. I know your history with them. We all do. You made the right decision coming here. Serving your fellow Overmen. It can't have been easy having been so close to so many of them. They can appear on the surface like enlightened beings, especially since we are still just infants. I said it already, but we really are infants, aren't we? If infancy is the first one percent of a being's life, then we are new-borns. But in their maturity, they barely match us in our infancy. We must look to the future, to what we will become, not what we are now. I don't know why you've decided to leave. I just hope it's not because of them."

I looked up at him and placed the figurine on my desk.

"It's not," I said emphatically.

"Good." He clapped his hands together. "Think. Just think. In a million years, how will you remember them? How will any of us? And how can we possibly care?" He grabbed the figurine and held it up as if to show it to me. "They'll mean as much to us as the Neanderthal does to them."

He stood up and placed the figurine on the desk with a thud. "Good luck, sir," he said reverting to his usual secretarial manner. He extended a hand.

"Thank you." I stood up and we shook. "I'm sure we'll meet again."

"Of course." He smiled, bowed slightly and left my office.

A moment after he left, I grabbed the figurine and examined it closely. Gently, I swaddled it in paper, and placed it back in its gift bag.

Chapter 43 ~ The Hounds of Humanity

I was transferred to a small office in Hanoi, Vietnam. It proved to be a very different experience from what I was used to. I essentially had the same job as I did in Kiev but now, I was working within a country whose Mortal population had already been diminishing rapidly for a much longer period. Having managed to get full control of the Vietnamese government rather early on and successfully isolating them from the rest of the world, the Overmen had near total cooperation of the remaining Mortal's in the country.

Because of the state of the country, my job as propaganda minister was relegated to creating posters and pamphlets to make sure the already devoted populace remained devoted. This involved fabricating reports on the ongoing fight against our would-be oppressors and continually legitimizing our dear leaders by describing the great efforts, which only they could accomplish, to keep the people safe and free. It was a simple job and far less prestigious than my position in Kiev, but I believe the reasons I was sent there was as a sort of punishment for requesting a transfer. It didn't bother me at that point. I was so torn between my disdain for the Overmen and my love for them and my disdain for Mortals and my love of Nate that I was happier having a job in which I had time to try and organize my growing pile of dilemmas.

It was here, in Hanoi, that I lived for over a decade. I went to my job every day and reviewed and approved proposals from my small group of employees. I went home after work and drank beer and watched films and television shows. I stopped writing, as Nate, or Blair, or myself, and just glided from one day to the next.

While my world remained relatively stagnant during this time, the world in which my friends lived only grew more chaotic. In many countries, Canada included, Mortals were suddenly being rounded up and sent to communities around which walls were built and check-stops installed. The purpose of these open-air prisons was to control dissidents or potential dissidents who had not yet done enough to warrant the hassle of disappearing. Inhabitants of these ghettos were required to carry identification cards on their person at all times and if they wanted or needed to leave, they were required to get special permits which were only issued on rare occasions. The streets were often patrolled, and a random stop and search policy was implemented to check for contraband. This didn't stop many Mortals from finding ways to sneak contraband in and out and soon black markets were developed throughout the country. Gerald was turned into one of these ghettos which exacerbated the already crowded conditions. Lake Winnipeg, whose shores ran along the east of town, was patrolled by boats armed with spotlights and infrared monitors. Guard towers were also constructed to monitor any unusual activity which turned out to be any activity at all since the beaches were completely off limits to Mortals. This didn't last long, however, because eventually the Overmen built a wall cutting off all access to the beach.

To keep everyone in one easy-to-monitor area, anyone who lived beyond the limits of the perimeter were forced to move inside the town proper. This included Nate, Kara, and James whose cottage was a good ten-minute drive from town. It was no doubt that the reason they were chosen to live in the open-air prison was because of Nate's writing and their connection to Jonny. Sending them to an internment camp would have been more hassle than just walling them in.

Nate continued to stay away from any direct action aside from his writing, knowing that he was still likely being watched closely. James, on the other hand, after he had graduated high school, found himself almost immediately working for a clandestine business which specialized in smuggling anything there was a market for including books, alcohol, cigarettes, red meat, and clothing. Nate disapproved but James was an adult now and there was little he could do to stop him. Besides, it was James who smuggled Nate's writing outside the perimeter, a role he took over after his father left.

On most occasions, James was tasked with bringing in a load of assorted supplies through a tunnel which had been dug under a part of the perimeter on which a wall had been built. This was a common practice for smugglers. It was too risky to dig tunnels under areas without a wall since the lack of wall usually meant a live patrol that might hear or see something. The walled off areas, however, were usually left completely unguarded. It wasn't that the OP had absolute faith in their walls, but they knew that most people would be unable to climb over them and since manpower was still quite limited, they had to rely on walls where guards were unavailable.

Amongst the items he was to retrieve was a stack of the weekly newsletter which was written by members of the resistance still functioning somewhere out there. The resistance had become the stuff of legends, or perhaps more appropriately, myths. No one heard much about them from any source but their own. Most people were unsure what they were doing, where they were "resisting" or if there was any sort of eventual goal they hoped to achieve and what new developments were happening towards that goal. There was also little central organization due to the successful isolation and fragmentation of resistance groups by the Overmen. Because of this, their legend was supported almost entirely by rumor and speculation. Their newsletters contained a great deal of information but since it was written by them, and few knew who "them" were, it was never certain what they were leaving out or what they were making up. Everyone assumed they weren't including all their activities in their newsletter and everyone filled in the missing pieces with their own theories. Those who maligned them assumed they had committed more atrocities than they were reporting while those who idolized them assumed they had achieved even greater accomplishments than they were reporting. No one could give much evidence to support either assumption.

In addition to the resistance newsletter was the official and almost constant Overmen broadcasts. These, everyone also assumed, could not be trusted but the people became quite efficient at deciphering which parts held some truth and which should be completely disregarded. If they reported on a bombing in Toronto most people believed there was indeed a bombing in Toronto. When they said it was the result of infighting between different factions in the resistance, everyone assumed the Overmen were involved somehow. And when the Overmen released a report saying they killed fifty-armed resistance fighters, everyone believed that they indeed killed one hundred people but were positive not all, if any, were combatants. The Overmen had a long history of declaring anyone killed in any conflict a combatant unless proven otherwise.

Meanwhile, Jonny was living in Ottawa working with a small group who called themselves the Hounds of Humanity, a radicalized branch of the resistance. A great many of the members were, like Jonny, former members of YesFore. He was unregistered since he'd been smuggled into the city through underground networks and so spent his days indoors in a safe house with others in similar situations to avoid being seen and carded in the daylight. During this time, they would pick targets, create plans, and build bombs. They had already successfully bombed over a dozen locations killing many in the process. Some innocent civilians were also killed—mostly innocent Immortals whom the more radicalized members of the Hounds of Humanity began to consider less than human—but they justified this as collateral damage and an unfortunate but expected result of necessary actions. If an innocent Mortal was killed they justified it by shaking their heads at any Mortal who would betray their people by associating with Immortals, or if such a justification was not possible, they'd say that they were in a war now and war always produces innocent casualties.

This radicalization was common amongst the resistance at this point. The anger and trauma felt by the constant abuse for so many years had led many, Jonny included, to go to these extreme lengths.

Other more moderate groups often condemned their tactics but rarely enough to cause a rift between them since they all believed they were still fighting for a common goal. And they did have a goal, however desperate it might appear. They believed that by continuing their bombing campaign they could put enough pressure on the government that they would listen to their demands for equal rights for all citizens, Mortal and Immortal. What happened instead, to a great degree, was that they provided the OP with free propaganda. The Overmen would say that the Hounds' actions justified their own actions. They proved that Mortals were barbarous and must be controlled by the more civilized, the more enlightened. It was for this reason that the Overmen never stopped antagonizing them. When the Hounds blew up a government building the OP would raid another house, sometimes killing the inhabitants, sometimes disappearing them, all under the pretext that they were arming and abetting terrorists and so were terrorists themselves. This would result in a violent response which would result in another raid and so on. Every act of terrorism led to more subjugation. Every act of subjugation led to more terrorism. If there was an end which might justify these means, no one could articulate what it was. Because the point of it all, you see, wasn't an end, the point was just to keep going even if it meant burning the whole world to the ground.

Chapter 44 ~ A Day in the Life of James Karski

Anna's antique shop was still open for business although it could hardly be described as an antique shop now. As the walls were erected around the town and her clientele shrunk to only those within, who no longer had much need for antiques, she was forced to diversify her stock. There were still plenty of antiques in the store, left over from when that was her primary business, but she had given much away to those who needed them and what remained she repurposed for more practical use. The Edwardian mahogany cylinder desk was now used to display yarn and knitting accessories since there was a new market for making and mending one's own clothing. The walnut bureau was used to store and organize her paperwork and the rosewood bookshelf displayed any literature she could get her hands on that had not yet been banned—the banned literature she got her hands on she kept in a hollowed out vertical strung piano. On this piano she kept her coffee maker and a collection of homemade pastries. Selling baked goods had become one of her newest ventures although she was forced to keep the prices so low that she made little profit. This was due in part to the limited economy in the walled town and in part to her lack of skill with an oven. Her pastries were edible but were admittedly bland and often over or under cooked. Despite her inexperience with edible products, she slowly introduced more and more variety until before long she was considered to have one of the best assortments of mediocre baked goods in town. People would come into her shop and sit in one of the many ladder-back oak chairs around the Spanish-style refectory table and sip cheap coffee, nibble on pastries, talk, read, or sit in contemplative silence. Even with the changes she made, the community continued to refer to the shop as Anna's Antiques or even more commonly Anna's.

James, in his new vocation as a smuggler of contraband, was one of Anna's many suppliers of products both legal and illegal. For the most part, the Overmen were content having Mortals locked away and paid little attention to what they were doing as long as no one appeared to be planning an uprising. This didn't stop them from arbitrarily raiding shops and homes and harassing random people on the street, but these tactics were rarely used for anything other than cruel amusement or to "confiscate suspicious material" which was a euphemism for "steal someone's possessions."

James entered Anna's Antiques with his hands in his pockets and his cap pushed high on his head and sauntered to the table where Anna was sitting enjoying a cigarette and coffee. Across from her was a gentleman with white hair which had receded to the complete opposite side of his head from which it originated—a tell-tale sign of an aged Mortal. James stood just behind Anna, who appeared to find the old gentleman amusing, and waited for him to finish speaking.

"I never wanted to leave this town," he was saying, his voice sounded hoarse like he had spent the better part of the day screaming at the incoming death that was barrelling towards him. "Now that I can't, the last thing I want to do is stay."

Anna smiled and crushed her cigarette in a half-eaten muffin. "Where would you go if you could leave tomorrow?"

"Go? I wouldn't go anywhere." The gentleman barked as if the words were loaded in a quick-draw pistol. "Where would I go? I wouldn't leave if I could." He sipped his coffee. "But as long as I can't I feel I must."

"Excuse me," James interrupted.

"Gene, you know James." Anna motioned to him.

"Yup. Hullo, young man."

"Gene." James put his hands on the back of a chair and smiled a roguish smile, something he had adopted after a few years successfully dodging the authorities.

"You look older since the last time I saw you. How old are you now?"

"Twenty."

"Well you're not old yet but you're getting old. I'm old. I'm really fucking old. You'll get here though."

"Old is somewhat relative in this day and age is it not?"

"Not for you or me. Old is old for you and me. It just is what it is. For them out there keeping us in here." He motioned outside the dirty window and added, "Old is nothing."

"That seems to be the reality, doesn't it," James nodded.

"They can make us like them ya know. They have the technology. They just don't want us living forever, too. They want to keep it all for themselves, those goddamn bastards."

James pondered for a moment then said, "But if they made us like them, wouldn't that make us one of them?"

Gene did some pondering of his own. "Well, we would still be us. But we would live forever like them, is what I'm saying. They couldn't have that."

"But the only difference between them and us is that they live forever," James continued. "So, if we also lived forever, we'd be them. They'd be us."

"Yes," Gene said enthusiastically, "But we've always been us. So, all I'm saying is, they couldn't have people like them who have memories like us." Gene seemed quite satisfied with this answer and smiled broadly. "That's it, see. We would be us *and* them and they couldn't have that."

"But would you want to be an Immortal, Gene?" Anna interjected.

"Yes! Of course I fucking would. I'd give anything to be like them. Who wouldn't?"

"You'd want to live forever?" James asked.

"No, of course not. Who would? I plan on dying within the next decade; being immortal wouldn't change that." With that Gene turned to the dusty window and sipped his coffee.

"Your logic is astounding, Gene, as always," James said. "Anna, you have a minute?"

"Of course." Anna got up and the two walked to the cramped office in the back. "Did you get my flour?" she asked when they were safe from peering eyes of listening ears.

"I did. No wholegrain but lots of white. I also got your baking soda."

"Great."

"Aside from that I have two boxes of stationary shit for you. I got the paper you asked for, white mostly but some yellow and blue if you feel you're in need of come color in your files. And I got you that day planner. Aside from that, I also have some pens, a few rulers, some metal pencil cups, and a package of fridge magnets that look like wooden buttons." James delivered his goods to several shops in the ghetto but because of Anna's relationship with his uncle he always gave her first pick.

"Just the white paper is fine. And I'll take a pencil cup. I've never had a pencil cup before."

"That can't be true." James looked incredulous.

"Well, I've had cups I put pencils in, but I've never had one in which the sole purpose was keeping pencils."

"There's nothing quite like it," James said and laughed.

"Are the magnets actually wood?"

"No, they're plastic but they look like wood. They're quite nice actually."

"Sure, I'll take a couple."

"A couple as in two?"

"A couple as in … uh, five, I guess."

"So not a couple." James smiled playfully.

"Not a couple. Five." She held up five affirming fingers. "Is that all?"

"That's it for today. I do have a few boxes of pencils but unfortunately, they're going to the school. I was told students must share both pencils and erasers. I guess while one kid erases another writes, and then they switch."

"So, I'll have a pencil cup but no pencils?"

"Sorry 'bout that. Do you have any requests for next week?"

"Glacier water, if you can find any." This was code for vodka. Although there was no official law against alcohol in Gerald, the Overmen would often raid places suspected of having it. Their reasoning was that liquid courage may lead to riots. The real reason everyone suspected was to sell it back in the black market since the patrolmen weren't allowed to consume any alcohol or narcotics while stationed. This theory was apparently confirmed by James himself who had somehow marked a few bottles which were then confiscated only for James to buy them back from some other source. It was also probably a way for the bored patrolmen to pass some time.

James left Anna's Antiques and headed towards Hardy's, a hardware store east of Center Street. On his way he saw two patrolmen walking towards him. He was certain he'd be searched since they rarely missed an opportunity to search the son of a known resistance fighter and the nephew of a former dissident. He stopped when he was about two meters away and waited for them to approach. Keeping his head lowered to the sidewalk he raised his arms. He couldn't see their faces, but he could hear them laughing as they approached.

"Okay," one said. "Do you want to search him or should I?"

"He's yours. Anyone that eager to be searched won't have anything."

"I don't know. What if that's exactly what he wants us to think?" James felt the man's hands pat his sides and reach into his coat pockets. "See, he's got something." The man had found James' notepad and pencil he used to keep track of his orders.

"What's that?"

"I have no idea." James heard the flutter of pages as the man explored the notepad. "Drawings. And fucking lousy drawings, too."

"Drawings? Are you an artist?"

"No sir. Just like to doodle," James said, keeping his voice low and respectful. The drawings were James' way to avoid being caught with damning information. A cat holding a bottle meant Anna wanted vodka and a single X on the bottle meant she wanted just one. Scattered around the cat was a stack of paper, a cup, and five small circles that didn't look much like button magnets, but James knew what they were. Every one of his customers was a different cartoon animal, the school, for example, was an owl. James wasn't an artist by any stretch of the imagination, but he could scribble rough pictures quickly enough that he soon developed a sophisticated system.

"These look like shit."

"I know, sir. Like I said, I'm not an artist."

"But can you even call yourself a doodler? Did you draw these with your teeth?" With his head still lowered James could hear the other patrolman laugh. "When does a bunch of ugly fucking scribbles become a doodle? Can you really just draw anything and then call it a doodle?"

"I don't know, sir."

"I wasn't talking to you, young man; I was talking to my partner here. You obviously don't have a fucking clue." He laughed boisterously. "This here in my hand is proof enough of that?"

"I see, sir."

"Well, regardless of how godawful this is, I'm afraid I'm going to have to confiscate it, young man."

"Why, may I ask?"

"Well, you don't really have the right to ask but I'll tell you anyways. The reason, you see, is because no one at the barracks will believe me when I tell them just how bad, terrible really, these stupid fucking drawings are. Morale is low and I think a good laugh will help that. So, in a way, you're helping the Overmen with your work. Keep it up."

"I can't, sir."

"What do you mean? Why can't you?"

"That's the only notepad I have. If you take that I can't draw anymore."

"Well, we wouldn't want that." James could hear him ripping out pages. "Here, you can keep your notepad but I'm taking these. For morale. It's for the greater good. You understand?"

"Yes, sir."

"Good lad. Enjoy the rest of your day."

The guards sauntered away, and James continued to the hardware store.

"James," the shop owner greeted him as he entered. His name wasn't Hardy, it was Raj, but he adopted the name for his store because he liked how Hardy's Hardware sounded.

"Raj. How're things?"

"Slow. You're the first person I've seen today."

"Aw, it's still early."

"No need for such optimism," Raj smiled. He was a large man with a square jaw like a hero in a comic, and a figure so rotund no superhero costume could possibly contain it. "It is what it is." Without saying another word, he began making his way to the back of the shop.

Once in the storeroom, Raj sat at his desk and pulled out a clipboard. "Ah," he leaned back in his chair and tapped his pen against the clipboard, "so what do you have for me?"

"What do you need?"

Raj told James what he needed; James told Raj what he had. They discussed prices, quantities, and how different products might be substituted for others. For example, Raj needed 3-inch nails, but James could only get his hands on 3-inch coils used in air nailers. So, Raj agreed that he could remove each nail from the coil and sell them separately. They discussed business for a few more minutes until James had three pages of sketches depicting a bear surrounded by an assortment of unusual looking items.

"How is the business?" Raj asked as they were making their way back to the front of the store.

"It's all right, I guess."

"What kind of things are you able to get exactly?"

"It depends on what's available."

"Anything you wouldn't normally offer a hardware store?"

"What are you asking me, Raj?" James said having a good idea what he was asking.

"I'm not asking anything because I *can't* ask anything, can I." At the front of the shop Raj walked behind the checkout counter and began writing on a notepad.

"Well, I can get what I can get."

"I understand," Raj said then ripped off a page and handed it to James. James glanced quickly at the note before handing it back. All it said was *guns*.

James stared at Raj for a moment contemplating. "What are you intending to build with those?"

Raj crumpled the paper in a ball and, much to James' amusement, popped it in his mouth and tongued it into his cheek like it was a hard candy. "I was thinking about organizing a community project. Everyone will be invited to participate. We could make this place something else. And I think the project would be a great community builder, you know, a kind of morale booster, a coming together sort of thing."

"Of course, I can't promise anything," James said, flashing his smile. "I'm limited to what's available and if the materials aren't, well, it's just a matter of getting what is and what isn't available. But if anything comes up, I'll let you know."

Raj appeared to swallow the piece of paper. "Sounds good, little man." He extended a thick hand which James shook.

"See you next week if not sooner."

James could've gotten his hands on some guns if he wanted to, but he knew it would never be enough. The number of weapons needed to smuggle under the wall to organize a proper uprising would take months to accumulate and the risk of keeping such a large stockpile sitting around hidden throughout the town was far too risky. Random checks and raids would undoubtedly unearth something which would lead to a massive raid and horrifying repercussions to those suspected of being involved, and quite possibly everyone who wasn't. This didn't keep him from fantasizing, however. As he left Raj's shop and walked towards his next client, he allowed his mind to fill with images of him and his friends gunning down every Immortal in the vicinity. He'd first lead a group to silently assassinate every Overman patrolling the streets. This would be carried out under the cover of night. Once the last patrolman's throat was slit, they'd storm the main gate, throwing homemade explosives into the guard shacks which would alarm the nearby guard towers that something was up. But no need to fear, James' group of revolutionaries previously wired those same towers with explosives. The guards in them only had enough time to notice their friend's bodies smoldering on the ground below before they were turned into bloody fragments. They would march survivors through town and hold court—

"Hey James," a voice called out to him from across the street. He broke from his fantasy and looked and saw an old classmate waving.

"Hey Cole." James waved back.

"Coming to the show tonight?"

"Of course. You?"

"Of course."

"Great. See ya there."

James shook the violent images from his head. It was no use, he thought. "Might as well imagine myself growing wings and flying out of here."

It was nearing 6:00 by the time James had visited his last client. He had no more run-ins with patrolmen. When he arrived home Nate and Anna were in the kitchen making dinner with Priyanka and Anil Kapoor, the parents of the family they shared their flat with. Both husband and wife emigrated from India almost two decades earlier, shortly after they were married and shortly before they gave birth to their daughter Shreya who was at this time somewhere in her mid-twenties. Much to the delight of the Karski's, they had brought much of their culture's culinary tradition with them, so their apartment was often filled with the smell of cumin, star anise, cardamom, saffron, and many others. Tonight, was no different.

James sat at the table with Anil who was casually browsing the pages of a book. Shreya was on a ratty couch on the other side of the room reading something on her phone. When James sat down, she put her phone away and joined them at the table.

"What's it like out there now?" Anil asked, nodding towards the window.

"It's pretty calm," James said as he began folding a serviette into an airplane. "I think most of the patrolmen are getting ready for the show tonight. So, there aren't that many about. I just had one encounter after I saw you, Anna, but aside from that I hardly saw any."

"Did they harass you much?" Anna asked, visibly concerned.

"Not really. Just the usual." James ran a finger down the bottom of his airplane to complete the last fold. When it was done, he tossed it aside and looked up at Anil. "How are you guys doing? Need anything?"

"Need? No. Want? Plenty. What do we want again?" Anil leaned back and craned his neck towards his wife who was standing next to Nate chopping vegetables.

"Anything you can get your hands on," Priyanka laughed. "Really, we can always make do. But of course, better ingredients are something we always need."

"Want," Anil corrected.

"We *need* them to make what we *want*," returned Priyanka.

Anil looked up from his book at James and Shreya and flashed a smile.

"When's the show?" Shreya asked.

"Nine, isn't it?" Anil said licking a finger and turning a page.

"Nine." James confirmed.

After dinner both families walked to the stage in the nearby park where a jazz concert was to be held by a handful of musicians. These concerts were, for many, the only source of entertainment. The Overmen allowed them because they really couldn't find any reason not to and they felt it helped keep them content and their minds on something besides revolt. Although this night was a jazz concert, it wasn't always the same. Every weekend different bands played different music from all over the world to reflect the various cultures that had amalgamated, albeit forcefully, into the community. This week was piano, bass, trumpets, and drums from New Orleans; last week was talking drums and polyphonic singing from the Ivory Coast, and the next week was a solo performance by a sitarist from India. Often multiple groups would play together to form an eclectic sound: er hus mixed with electric guitars mixed with didgeridoos mixed with violins. But tonight, was jazz.

When Nate and his group arrived at the park the band was already playing, and the crowd was already immense. They were forced to stand at the back of the large crowd, so the musicians looked like small figurines, but the music was still heard perfectly. Through it all James kept his eyes closed, bobbing his head to the sounds, forgetting the patrolmen who searched him, forgetting the dangers of sneaking under the wall, forgetting even where he was. Instead he found himself in the city, not Winnipeg, perhaps Paris, in a dimly lit but lively club. A haze of smoke hangs in the air. The steady murmur of patrons conversing in French is punctuated by bursts of laughter and jovial shouts. He's sitting at a table. Across from him is a young man, his age, smoking a cigarette and smiling flirtatiously at him. Under the table the young man's foot touches James'. James smiles back and bobs his head to the music. The music. The music. In a sudden puff of cigarette smoke the young man disappears, the club disappears, the laughter and pleasant murmur of the crowd disappears. Only the music remains.

James was so lost in himself that he didn't immediately notice someone pulling on his sleeve and calling his name. When he opened his eyes, he saw his uncle who had hold of his arm and was gently trying to pull him away. A woman he knew well was with him. He shook his head free from his thoughts and followed Nate and the woman until the three of them were far enough away from the music to hear each other.

"What's this about?" James said, annoyed at having to abandon his jazz fueled reverie.

"Jane just gave me this," Nate said, referring to the woman next to him, and handed James the most recent issue of the resistance's newsletter which was opened to the obituaries.

"I'm so sorry," Jane said, "I'll leave you two alone."

James didn't look at the newsletter. He was certain what it said. He just stared at his uncle whose eyes were already brimming with tears. Then James' knees buckled, and he collapsed onto the grass. His uncle ducked down to help him up.

"I'm okay. I'm okay. We should get rid of that," he said, motioning to the newsletter which had fallen onto the grass. "There are too many patrolmen round here."

"It's okay." Nate grabbed the newsletter and shoved it into the front of his trousers.

Nate sat with his nephew for the rest of the concert, on the grass, both with tears streaming down their faces. Neither said a word to the other until the concert was over.

Chapter 45 ~ The Fall

Kara took the news of Jonny's death much like she took the news of his leaving. She fell into a nearly catatonic state for days, not eating, not even leaving her room. James would often go in to check on her, but she'd remain in bed, silent, lost in some dark and distant thought. She didn't cry, though; she didn't show much emotion. When she saw James, she would sometimes smile but James could tell it took incredible effort and it would vanish almost immediately after it appeared.

James learnt, about a week after the initial news of his father's death, how he died. They said he was building a bomb with some of his fellow comrades in their apartment. Something went wrong and the device exploded killing everyone in the room and injuring many in and outside the building. They said he didn't feel a thing, probably never even knew what happened.

Despite knowing that his father was gone forever, the realization that he would never see him again took a while to fully absorb. He still found himself imagining the day he would burst through the door, filling the room with his enormous personality. Just as soon as this whole stupid conflict is over, James thought. When the realization finally hit him a day or two later, he was sitting in the living room of their apartment reading. He often found his thoughts wandered while he read especially when something in his book recalled something in his life. In this instance he was reading some classic novel depicting a distant future totalitarian state which ends with the main character being forcibly lobotomized and betraying his friends. This led him to picture his father and the great changes he'd seen in him throughout their all too short and fragmented relationship. He remembered him always jovial, always armed with a witty comment. He remembered him self-aware, able to self-deprecate without appearing insecure.

The year before he left, when their relationship became more tangible than it had ever been, he also remembered him deeply empathetic, aware of what everyone else in the room seemed to be feeling. He remembered him thoughtful without being too serious. How was he after he left, he thought? James was very much aware of the horrible acts of violence some of the branches of the resistance had committed. The fact that his father died building a bomb troubled him, although what else would he be doing? He remembered him not as someone who could be capable of the acts of which he was supposedly guilty. Was he also lobotomized? Not by some futuristic machine but by his environment? By the deaths of his friends and family? By the continued stripping away of his dignity and the dignity of those he cherished? How else can he explain the opposing natures? The Jonny he knew, the father he knew, couldn't blow up a café filled with innocent victims. The man who killed innocent people couldn't laugh with him the way he did or listen to him when he asked for his paternal support. Jonny chose to leave, everyone knew that, but it wasn't the same Jonny. He had been changed and he didn't choose to be changed into the version of Jonny that left. Someone or something else was to blame for the change that drove him to leave, to build bombs, to kill. But how, now, would his father be remembered? Did he die a martyr or a monster? If he's only remembered as a monster is that what he was? These questions haunted James for the rest of his life.

***

Time continued to pass in Gerald. The first year after Jonny's death was the hardest. Celebrating holidays and birthdays without him had already been a difficult task but they always had the hope that his absence wasn't permanent. They always kept alive the possibility that one day Jonny would throw open the door and things would return to how they were before. But now when they decorated the Christmas tree or welcomed the New Year, they knew that they had celebrated the last with him years ago. But the first year passed. During the second year after Jonny's death an uprising erupted but was quickly and violently supressed. To prevent another, the Overmen outlawed any congregation of more than ten people which meant the concerts in the park were suddenly no more. Then three years had passed and then four. The fifth year after Jonny's death saw the tunnels James used for smuggling discovered and demolished. James now had nothing to do. Stronger security was installed, and random searches became more frequent. James continued to smuggle but doing so required much more ingenuity and the flow of contraband into Gerald slowed significantly. While this was happening inside their walls the revolution, which had by this time evolved into the Mortal War, continued to rage outside their walls.

***

Finally, more than five years after Jonny died, Overman power in Germany crumbled after the Reichstag Handover. I don't have anything to add to this event that hasn't been said already except to note that I believe it was inevitable. It didn't have to happen in Germany. It could have and would have happened anywhere else in the world eventually.

People will permit tyranny for a while but only for a while. As long as it is easier to do nothing rather than something, the powerful may have their way but over time that apathy dissolves until, like a starving man hunting for food, action becomes the natural, easier decision. This is essentially what happened in Germany. The people took to the streets. The government sent men to beat them, humiliate them, imprison them, and kill them. But the people's resolve only grew stronger because they had already been beaten, humiliated, imprisoned, and killed. What was more of the same to them? Did the Overmen think they didn't know before marching in the streets what they were facing? Then the men sent to do the beating and shooting and imprisoning also found it easier to turn their weapons away from the unarmed people and towards the oppressors. This turn of events was also just a matter of time, for soldiers, being human, can only take so much. And when that happened, it was all over. Suddenly, those who had all the power had none and those who were powerless had it all. When word of what was happening in Germany spread other countries soon followed suit. Eventually, most of Western Europe had, to varying degrees, freed themselves of Overmen control. Then two years after freedom appeared in Germany it made its way to Canada.

What seemed to be a chain reaction didn't reach every corner of the globe. In fact, most of the world, including many European states, remained under the OP's control, although they stopped calling themselves the Overman Project at this time. But it was enough to create quite a few pockets of freedom for Mortals who were lucky enough to live in these places or capable enough to escape to them.

For the people in Gerald, this meant that one day everyone woke up to discover that the patrolmen were gone with no ceremony whatsoever. The day the Overmen left, the people walked the streets cheering, some produced hammers and began chipping away at the wall to the neglected beach and, by the end of the first day, holes big enough for grown men to squeeze through were created. The stage in the park was filled once again with people for a celebration unlike anything it had seen before, and every musician of every genre had a chance to express their delight with their own instruments. Shops opened their doors and placed all manner of contraband on the shelves for all to see. The act had no entrepreneurial value since no one had much money to purchase illegal magazines—it was an act of defiance. Others seemed unable to believe it was true and practiced caution as they stood outside their doors but refused to join the festivities; they couldn't shake the feeling that the Overmen were waiting just beyond view only to storm back in for a show of force. But that never happened.

The great conflict, at least in this part of the world, had truly come to an end.

The Karskis and the Kapoors walked together to the main gate and, seeing that it was indeed abandoned, walked through to the outside world. Anil wept with his wife and daughter each holding an arm. James stood, with his mother on his arm, in awed silence as he surveyed the highway before him that stretched out into the distance, into the world. Nate and Anna walked hand-in-hand, gaping at their surroundings. Anna couldn't hide her bright smile which seemed to express the emotion that Nate wasn't able to. They all spent the day exploring the abandoned barracks, guard towers, and offices that, for all these years, housed their oppressors. They ended the day in a guard tower from which they could see the town, the great lake and its beaches, and the road leading away from it all.

Chapter 46 ~ I Become ...

Despite the major reforms across the globe, Hanoi, where I was still stationed, experienced none of them. The Overmen's grip on the country remained as tight as ever. However, when I heard what had happened in Canada, I volunteered to offer my services and was quickly taken up on my offer. The Overmen were attempting to undertake a massive campaign to save face amongst the Canadian people without having to relinquish all control and because of my connections to Mortal dissidents and popular figures, they hoped I'd make a valuable asset. I was given a job similar to the one I had in Asia and Eastern Europe but instead of espousing lies to vilify Mortals, my primary objective was to spin the Immortals' side of the story in such a way as to convince the people that their actions were somehow justifiable. It was obvious it would be a short-lived position since no amount of spinning could convince the people that forcing them into large prisons and killing them indiscriminately were for the greater good. But I took it despite knowing this just to get back to someplace I could identify as home.

I was stationed in Ottawa near the parliament building, in front of which was a near constant sea of protestors. The anger was still palpable. Despite the immediate efforts like abandoning the open-air prisons and closing many of the internment camps in the country, most people weren't about to stop fighting until every last demand was met. Obviously, this never happened since Immortals were still predominately the ones in power but there were some reforms that happened immediately after the Overmen's dissolution of power. For example, the government passed a law allowing couples to have a maximum of two children if approved for a permit and the process for obtaining a permit was made much easier.

The Overman Project was also technically removed from power, but all this really meant was that they no longer referred to themselves as the Overmen Project. Only the worst offenders of human rights, those directly responsible for the open-air prisons, local internment camps and assassinations, were forced to resign. And most of them were simply sent to other countries like the one I had just left never to have to face prosecution or even a strongly worded rebuke. It was for issues like this that drove people to continue to protest.

After only a few months with my new job I found myself becoming anxious, about which I couldn't understand. I felt every waking hour—which was most hours since I seemed to have misplaced my knack for sleep—on the very margins of panic, like the slightest nudge could knock me into madness. With the collapse of the Overmen I felt directionless and homeless, no where to go and no where to stay. The propaganda I was making suddenly seemed to be for a movement that was terminally ill and my association with it made me ill as well. Instead of going home after work I instead found myself walking endlessly and aimlessly through the capital as if I was looking for a runaway housecat whose name I could no longer remember.

The first time I visited the site of Jonny's death I did so by accident. I had been made aware of his death and the details surrounding it shortly after it happened but managed, quite successfully, to avoid thinking about it. I was, after all, an Overman and had eternity to think about things like that … or something like that. After moving to Ottawa, I was immediately hit with a dreadful premonition that the closer I got to that ghastly place the closer I would come to some horrible event, what exactly I didn't know nor dared to imagine. I think I half expected to find him there, waiting for me, surrounded by smoke and debris and wagging a finger. I imagined him saying, "You turned me into this. You and your lot." So, when I happened upon the spot while walking the city in a fugue it felt like something had drawn me there, some sort of force of attraction like gravity. I stood and stared in front of the building, which had been completely repaired, and so my vision of Jonny standing in rubble was immediately dispelled. If gravity was what brought me there, the singularity was somewhere inside for, I felt a powerful drive pulling me towards it. I resisted after much hesitation but returned the next day by the same relentless force.

The building was a rectangular, ugly thing made of brown bricks with windows that opened vertically. There were grey concrete steps leading to the entrance with black metal railing which had come loose at the base. I stood like before staring at it until the front door opened and a young woman walked out with a backpack slung over one shoulder.

"Excuse me, miss," I said before she could walk away.

'Yes," she approached me, adjusting the strap on her shoulder.

"I'm sorry to bother you. I was wondering if you could answer a question for me."

"I can try."

"Years ago, there was an explosion in this building."

"Yeah, some guys were making a bomb and it went off."

"Would you happen to know in which apartment it happened?"

"Ah, I know it was on the third floor. But I'm not sure which one exactly, sorry. I live in the basement," she laughed. "And I didn't live here at the time."

"No worries. Thank you for your time."

She smiled and went on her way. I jogged up the steps and tried the door, but it was locked. I considered buzzing one of the names on the wall but couldn't bring myself to do it, thinking the less attention I drew to myself the less culpable I was. Jonny would have, I remember thinking. He always did what he thought necessary. I walked back down the stairs and waited until someone else came out. Then, without much thinking, I casually climbed the steps again and grabbed the door before it could close and walked inside. I suddenly felt incredibly nervous as if this was not just an apartment block, but a government facility or military complex and I would be shot if discovered.

I climbed the steps to the third floor and walked the hall in search of anything that might indicate in what room Jonny had spent his last moments. It was impossible to tell. Every door looked the same. I made it to the end of the hall where another glass door exited into a small parkade. Then behind me I heard a door open and close. I turned back around to see a young man locking his door before turning and walking in my direction. He smiled politely as he passed.

"Um, excuse me," I said before he could disappear into the parkade. He turned around and made an expression as if to ask if I was talking to him. His hand was on the door handle.

"Ah, yeah?"

"Sorry to bother you," I said and approached him. "I live in the basement."

"Okay," he shrugged.

"Someone told me that there was some sort of explosion here a few years back."

"Oh yeah, room, ah, 306 I believe." He nodded in the direction of the room.

"Oh, excellent. I was just curious and wanted to see it for myself."

"Yeah?" he said again and began opening the door. "You'd never know it. They obviously had to completely redo everything. I live in 308 and apparently my apartment was blown to pieces."

"Really? You didn't live there then, did you?"

"No," he laughed and began to sway the open door back and forth. "But the guy that did died in the explosion. Kinda weird living in a room where a guy was basically murdered."

"I can't imagine."

"Ah, need anything else?"

"No, you've been a great help. Thank you."

"Sure."

"Ah, just one more thing," I yelled after him before the door could close behind him

"Yeah?" he quickly grabbed and opened the door again and leaned in.

"Is there anyone living there now?"

"Yeah, Snorri, ah, something. An old crotchety fuck. Icelandic, I think."

"Okay, thanks."

When the young man had gone, I went to 306 and knocked on the door. I heard some movement on the other side. "Who is it?" a voice growled through the door.

"Are you Snorri?"

"Yes, what is it?"

"Ah, you don't know me, sir, but I was hoping to talk to you if you have time."

"What about?" Even through the door I could detect an accent.

"Could you open the door please?"

"I could do a lot of things. But I don't have to, do I?"

"No, I suppose not," I was beginning to think this was pointless. "The thing is, I knew someone who used to live in your flat."

"Is it me?"

"No sir."

"Does he live here now?"

"Well, no, he does not."

"Then why are you bothering me instead of this other person."

"Well he's dead, you see?"

"I don't see. What does him being dead mean to me?"

"I was just hoping to have a look at the room that he used to live in. That's all."

"This room looks just like the others. Why must you see this one?"

"Because, this is the one he lived in. He didn't live in any of the others."

"All the rooms look the same, you know. They do them alike."

"Yes, you mentioned that."

"So, bother someone else, look at their room and you will see what this room looks like."

"It will only take a moment."

"I don't have moments. I'm going now."

"But sir …" I clenched my teeth and fists and thought for a moment of breaking down the door. I stood there thinking of what to do next when I heard him again.

"You're still there. I can see you, you know."

"I know. Is there nothing I could do to get you to let me have a look inside?"

"Do you have money?"

After a quick negotiation I was in the apartment with Snorri. He wore a knit sweater and walked with a cane. He clearly lived alone and had little furniture and only a few pictures framed on the wall.

"Okay," he said. "You gave me fifty dollars. Fifty dollars buys you ten minutes."

"That's fine," I said and walked through the living room waiting for an emotion or a thought or something that I was sure I would find in there. Snorri followed close behind.

"Do you know anything about the explosion that happened here?"

"I know nothing about no explosion. You have nine minutes."

"But you do know about the explosion that occurred here a few years ago?"

"Yes, I know. But I had nothing to do with it. And I know nothing about it aside from that it happened."

The flat was small, just a living room, a washroom and a small bedroom. Another door stood next to the washroom, but Snorri assured me that it was a closet and that I had no need to look inside. Indeed, from the layout of the place I deduced it could only be a closet. The walls were painted white and there was a single window looking out onto the street below. Any evidence of an explosion had been properly erased.

"Was it like this when you moved in?" I wanted to keep asking questions, to find out every minute detail Snorri knew but it was obvious he knew less than me. Still, there had to be something, I thought, some reason I was there. One of my dearest friends blew himself up in this room. Where exactly? Was I standing in the spot? Was he there, in the corner? Or was it in the washroom? Or the bedroom? No, it was most likely here in the living room but where exactly? Was he sitting or standing? Did he realize he had made a mistake before it happened?

"Five minutes. Is there anything else you must see?"

I sighed, took one more glance round the room and said, "No. I think I've seen everything. Sorry to waste your time."

"Of course. Like I said, there's nothing to see."

Snorri escorted me out and closed the door behind me without saying a word.

I walked away from the building, going through what I saw in my mind, trying to retroactively find whatever it was I was hoping to find. But it was just a room.

That night I dreamt of Jonny. I saw him working diligently on his bomb. Who is it for? What are he and his comrades planning to blow up? Who is meant to die from it? He's seated at a foldable table on a worn lawn chair. His face is grizzled, a three-day beard grows thickly over his once child-like features. I see him manipulating a screwdriver and a soldering iron. His comrades pace behind him, smoking cigarettes nervously. Sweat beads off his forehead and rolls down to his chin. Then, without the slightest warning, everything erupts in flame. The wall next to the washroom blows apart in thick chunks. The couple sleeping in the adjacent apartment are covered in debris and are soon surrounded in thick smoke; one of them, the male, eventually succumbs to his injuries. Cars parked along the once quiet street are blaring their sirens. Screams echo through the halls and down the street. Smoke billows out of the shattered window. When the smoke begins to clear, three mangled corpses lay unrecognizable amongst pieces of furniture, pieces of bomb material, pieces of their own bodies. What was once Jonny, no longer bears any resemblance. The scorched body lying in a pool of blood and gore is just that, a body. Matter arranged in a smoldering form. Nothing more. It had been transformed and lost all discernable parts.

When I woke from the dream, I felt paralyzed. Not with fear or any apprehension, for the dream didn't terrify me, but by a feeling that I no longer could control my body just like Jonny could no longer control the charred remains left lying on the floor of apartment 306. I could've moved if I had tried but the task seemed so impossible, I didn't even try. I instead remained staring at the ceiling for the better part of the day. My phone rang often which I correctly assumed was the office calling to inform me I wasn't there, but I didn't answer it. I didn't believe I could.

When I finally decided to test whether my mobility had truly abandoned me, I felt something like a pang of disappointment when the test proved negative. I rolled out of bed and got dressed even though the workday was almost over, and I had nowhere to be. Once dressed I climbed back into bed and decided that even if I could function like an able-bodied person, I could think of no reason why I ought to. I didn't climb out again until early the next morning.

I avoided work again the next day, ignoring the constant calls, and was eventually visited by a colleague who stopped by to check up on me. I told him I simply wasn't going to go back to the office. He told me that I must. I told him that I was training to be a scientist before this whole mess had started and had decided that I was going to do nothing more for the Overmen not related to my chosen fields. He reminded me, with a pastoral tone, that I was an Overman, too, and had eternity to pursue my passion but that we all must put our own desires aside for a much greater and eventually much more rewarding cause. I said I didn't find the cause especially great or rewarding. He said, now with an instructive tone, that abandoning my duties might greatly impede my opportunities as a scientist. I told him I was tired and would consider what he said. He patted me on the shoulder, paternally, and said he was confident I'd make the right decision. I opened the door for him. He said not to worry about missing a couple days work but that he would be so accommodating as to explain to everyone that my absence was due to the utmost understandable circumstances and that I should not be reprimanded in any way. I put a hand on his shoulder and politely ushered him out the door. We exchanged goodbyes. He gave me a tender smile and I closed the door.

After that encounter I decided to move back to Winnipeg. After all, that was where I was from. That's where I spent my formative years, where I went to school and then university. Although I tried not to think of Nate and the others it was their memory that was pulling me there, or at least the memory of how I felt when I was near them. I didn't tell anyone that I was leaving. I just left.

Chapter 47 ~ Returning Home

When I arrived in Winnipeg I had nowhere to stay so I rented a room at a cheap motel. I wasn't sure how long it would be before I had a steady income again and decided to be frugal with my savings. The first week I explored old areas I used to frequent but everything had changed so much. Buildings had been torn down and new ones built in their place, streets had been renamed, and the people seemed to be all a different variety than the ones I remembered. I didn't try to contact anyone for that first week but had already made up my mind that I had to reconnect with Nate, or at the very least see him even if he didn't see me. I wasn't naïve; I was certain he'd still want nothing to do with me, so I decided to organize a collection of my writing as Blair to show him that I had gone to great and dangerous lengths to protect him.

A quick search told me that he had been living in Gerald during the revolution but had returned to the city only a couple months before I arrived and lived with a woman named Anna. James had also moved to Winnipeg with his mother and they rented an old house not far from Nate and Anna.

Having found my old friends and now being in such proximity to them, I began to formulate a plan to contact them. While doing so I allowed myself to imagine their lives now. Although it was certain to be different from what life was like when Jonny and Marie were alive, I still placed them all in relatively the same looking apartment and with the same lifestyle. They, in my mind, would likely be throwing large parties again at which people would discuss politics and literature and philosophy. I imagined them eating ethnic cuisine and drinking from cups that never emptied of wine or whisky. The first blow to this fantasy of mine came when I rode a taxi past Nate and Anna's apartment and saw a rundown little building made of the same ugly brick as the apartment block in which Jonny had perished. James and his mother's house, I learnt after another drive by, was also quite dilapidated and I later learnt that they only rented the second floor while another family of four rented the first.

My plan to contact them took various forms before I settled on sending Nate a letter. I figured doing so would give him time to consider meeting me before making a final decision and remove some of the stronger emotions that might manifest themselves upon seeing me in person without warning. After a week of deliberation, I finalized the letter and included a telephone number so he could contact me. A couple days later I received a call.

Once I was sure it was him and I was sure he knew it was me I began to blabber rapidly, like I believed he would hang up on me if I stopped talking.

"I'm sure you don't want to see me since we ended things so, ah, poorly last time but things are starting to calm down, at least on my end, and, um, I would like to see you again, even if it's just the one time, just to explain some things to you, and after that you don't have to see me again but I think it would be … um … I think I at least need to see you to, ah, to talk about things and … well … really I want to see how you're doing considering all that's happened since we last talked … are you still there?"

"Yeah."

"Okay, because I know I've not been a good friend, or a good person, or …" I could hear my own voice shaking as I spoke as if I were outside on a January night despite being inside on a July day. "We can talk about all that though when we see each other … if you want to see me, that is." I took a breath and tried to slow and steady my speech. "Is that something you'd like to do?"

"Yes, I'm sorry, this is quite unexpected," he spoke as if he hadn't noticed me rambling. "I hoped to hear from you again but with all the chaos, you know, the last decade or so had been just so fucking—"

"I know," I said wanting to cry but unsure why. "I know."

"Yeah, let's not talk more about this over the phone. I see this is a local number. So, you're in the city?"

"Yeah, Sherbrook."

"Okay. Well, what time works for you?"

"Literally anytime."

"Okay, then tomorrow? Lunch?"

"Yes. That sounds lovely." My voice began to shake again.

"Tomorrow then."

We made plans to meet at half past noon at a café on Portage Avenue. After hanging up I sat at my small kitchen table and allowed my shaking to continue into the evening. I couldn't help agonizing over the phone call or the impending lunch the next day, so I poured a drink and another and another to try to give me something to occupy my time and my mind. I passed out shortly before midnight and woke at 6:00 the next morning. The anxiety for my reunion immediately returned upon waking and I spent the morning neglecting food and beginning but not finishing various projects. I read the first half a chapter in a novel, I watched the opening credits of a television show, and I walked half a block from my house before returning. I finally decided to walk to the meeting place which took only twenty minutes and arrived forty-five minutes early.

I sat with my leg bouncing under the table and my neck constantly twisted one way or the other trying to see him approach through the shop windows. Every time the door opened, I looked that way and every time someone walked past the window, I looked that way. I thought I might go mad with anxiety.

Then he entered. It was undoubtedly him, although the changes in his features since the last time I saw him were startling. The first thing I noticed was his hair. The curls that still covered his head were no longer black but an equal mix of black and grey. I stood up when I saw him enter and he saw me immediately. He smiled and the corners of his eyes wrinkled into crow's feet. He waved broadly before jogging over to my table. I could now see crevasses had appeared on either side of his mouth which were covered slightly by patches of dark grey and black whiskers.

We hugged. Or rather he threw his arms around me. I stood still for a moment with arms to my side, unable to reconcile this aging man with the friend I had left so many years ago. I finally wrapped my arms around him and began to cry. I didn't quite know why. But I couldn't stop. I sobbed into his shoulder and the nape of his neck, snorting and wailing while he held me, seemingly unashamed of my display. I don't know how long we stood embracing in that café but when I finally caught my breath and pulled myself away from him, I felt embarrassed immediately. I couldn't look at him but kept my eyes glued to the front of his shirt as if I were looking for a box of tissues in his breast pocket. He kept a hand on my shoulder as I collected myself. When I finally looked up at him, I felt I might break down again and so asked if we might leave the peering eyes of the other patrons. He agreed and we walked outside.

The sun was so warm, I remember.

"Where should we go?" Nate asked. His voice sounded different to me, deeper and a bit raspier.

"Anywhere," I said with my face towards the sun and my eyes closed tightly.

"And how shall we get there?"

"Walk?" I turned to him and again felt a lump climb up my throat.

"Sounds perfect," he smiled compassionately. "Lead the way."

We walked down Portage Avenue not saying much. The traffic was loud, the sidewalk was busy. To escape it all we turned off the street and ventured south towards Wolseley. Even when on the quieter street we didn't say much. Or I didn't. Nate spoke with some regularity, but I couldn't shake the feeling I was in a dream. After a few minutes of walking we happened upon a small bakery with a few patio tables outside. Inside it was small with only a few tables, all empty. There were, however, two people in line under a sign that said *Order Here* so we took our places behind them.

"So," Nate said obviously searching for something to say. "How have you been?"

"It's hard to say," I said after clearing my throat and swallowing. I still felt it difficult to speak.

"Well, it has been a wild few years."

"It certainly has," I managed to crack an ironic smile. "How is James?"

"He's well. He's living with his mum."

"How is she?"

"She's all right I suppose. She's working with Anna, ah, my girlfriend."

"Ah, and how's that?"

"How's what?"

"The girlfriend—Anna I mean. How are ... what's she like?" I struggled to get the words out in a coherent sentence.

"Oh, great. Well, good. Yeah, she recently opened a little clothing store on Academy ... um, I guess you need to meet her."

"I'd love to. I really would."

It was our turn to order. We ordered two coffees and two butter tarts. I insisted on paying. Once armed with food and beverage we sat at a table on the patio.

We ate our tarts and sipped our coffees slowly. There was a tension, a desire to say everything, to ask every question but neither of us could find the words. We both knew that there were thousands of things to say but couldn't sort through them all to find one that could take precedent. So, we continued to flounder through small talk. That was until Nate said, "So ..." and I felt my stomach knot. "Where have you been all this time?"

I sighed deeply before opening my mouth to answer but before I could say a word ...

"It's okay. You don't have to say anything if you don't want to." He popped the last bit of tart in his mouth.

"I have a lot to say to you," I said. "I didn't think this would be so hard but I still want to say ... I've ..." I could feel emotion bubbling up inside again and stopped to take control of my breathing.

"You're here now, right? You're living in the city?"

"Yes," I nodded, thankful he had stepped in. "I actually live near here, just—"

"Right, Sherbrook," Nate motioned with a thumb behind him. "I live here, too. So does James and Kara. We have lots of time. We haven't seen each other in over a decade. We don't have to jump right in to talking about what happened then."

"Okay, I think I'd prefer that."

"Okay, good. So, what should we do now?"

"Do you think James would see me?"

"Yes, I told him I was seeing you today."

"And Kara?"

"Of course. I regret how things …"

I held up a hand and, for the first time since the day began, felt like my speech had returned to normal. "Let's not talk about that now. Like you said, we have time."

"Of course."

We made plans to have a party at Nate's the coming weekend. Because his place was so much smaller, he warned that it wouldn't be like the old days. "Just us. You, James, Kara, and Anna." Part of me wished there would be more to take attention away from me, but I agreed. The night of the party I showed up with flowers, a bottle of wine, and a box of chocolates.

"Oh wow?" Nate said as he received my packages. "Does this mean I have to spread my legs for you later? Come in." He motioned with his head and I followed him inside. Anna introduced herself immediately. I smiled and gave a timid wave.

"This way," Nate said walking down the short hallway to the living room. "Everyone else is in here."

The apartment was very small. Exiting the hallway, I found a living room on my left and the kitchen on my right. In the living room there was a couch and armchair around a grey ottoman which once had wheels but now sat immobile. The top of a TV tray sat on top of the ottoman to give it a flat surface on which drinks could be placed without worry of spillage. Two windows, one behind the couch and another over the sink in the kitchen both faced the same way which was towards the colorless brick wall of the adjacent building. When I entered Kara and James stood up from their seats, James from the armchair and Kara from the couch, and greeted me.

"Hello," I said and waved again. James I could tell was an adult now, looking like a mature Immortal—like me. Kara looked old. Older than Nate even though she was indeed younger. She, too, had grey in her hair and wrinkles on her face but unlike Nate she seemed to have been drained of all life. She smiled at me but not with her eyes and she seemed horrifyingly frail.

I was offered a seat on a piano bench although I saw no piano. I smiled politely and sat down.

"Would you like me to take your coat?" James asked, eyeing me ambiguously. I hadn't realized I was still wearing it and quickly removed it and handed it to him. He took it and walked to a door in the hallway I had just walked through and tossed it inside. I later learnt that that was the bedroom, the only one in the place.

"Here." I turned towards the voice and saw Nate handing me a tumbler. "Gin and tonic? Still?"

"Yes, that's perfect," I said receiving the cold beverage. I took a sip immediately.

"Is it to your liking?"

"Yes. Thank you."

When everyone else had settled, the conversation began. I remained quite removed from the interactions, still feeling somewhat embarrassed for my display of emotion a few days earlier. I sipped my drink until it was gone and then pretended to keep drinking just to give myself something to do. Nate at some point noticed and got up and made me another. It was another three or four before I felt comfortable enough to try to engage in the conversation but every time the revolution or the war was brought up, I'd withdraw and simply observe.

James, I saw, was much like his father, jovial, sharp witted, and full of spirit. Anna was a delight and seemed to bring Nate much happiness. I wondered how often he still thought of Marie. Kara, however, was as disengaged as I knew I appeared to be, so the entire conversation was carried by the other three.

After a few hours James and his mother decided it was time to call it a night. Kara, James explained, was rather tired and he had to be up for work in the morning. I asked him what he was doing for work and he said he was a carpenter's apprentice. After they had left, I asked for my coat.

"No, no, no," Nate said. I could see he was mixing another drink for me. "Stay. You don't have to be up for anything tomorrow."

"I suppose you're right."

"You may as well spend the night. Just like old times, eh?"

"We have extra blankets. And this couch pulls out into a bed," Anna said patting the armrest.

"I don't want to inconvenience—"

"Fuck that," Nate said walking from the kitchen with two tumblers in hand. He handed me one and then licked some spillage off the side of his hand. "I haven't seen you in an age." He plopped himself down next to Anna. When he sat slouched his belly pressed against his t-shirt. "Was that all right? Seeing them again?" Nate asked, motioning with his drink to the door through which Kara and James had just disappeared.

"Yes, it was wonderful to see them again."

"You hardly said a word."

I noted Nate was more direct when he talked. Like the last decade eroded his once soft manner.

"Sorry. This is all just … it's … it's hard to explain I guess."

"No worries. We're all adjusting to this new life, this new world."

"I haven't … I should confess," I shifted in my seat. "I haven't had any contact with … um …"

"Mortals?" Nate asked with both eyebrows raised.

"… in a long time."

I could tell the confession had made Anna uncomfortable and I felt I had revealed too much.

"None at all?" Nate asked.

"No. Well, a few words here and there but nothing like this."

"Well, we're not so different from your lot, you know."

"Of course. It's just that, I haven't been happy, really … um …" I looked down at my hands. They were smooth, hairless, with not a single callus. Nate's I could tell, even from where I was sitting, were rough and hairy with deep creases over the knuckles. "Wow," I said and laughed at myself. "I really don't know where to start. And even if I knew where, I doubt I'd know how." Nate and Anna both smiled. "How're James and Kara?" I queried perfunctorily. "He's a carpenter's apprentice you said?"

"That's right," Nate nodded. "He likes it. He said the other day that he can see him doing that for a while but would rather find something else eventually. He always wanted to go to university but that's just not in the cards for him now, unfortunately. Not enough money or time I'm afraid."

"And Kara?"

"She's coping. When Jonny passed away it … well, not much to say about that. I'm sure you can tell by looking at her that she's not the same woman she was."

I shook my head and dropped my eyes to my hands.

"It was awful," Nate added quietly and retrospectively as if to himself.

"Of course," I said raising my eyes to him again.

"But one day at a time, right? James would like to get his own place, living with his mum isn't exactly how he'd have planned it, but he doesn't like the idea of leaving her on her own."

"I understand that."

"Another drink?" Nate was already up and walking towards me with his hand out. I handed him my glass. "But now that we're all back in the city," he yelled from the kitchen accompanied by the sound of ice hitting glass, "away from all that mess up north. We all have more opportunity to work out what we want to do and what we can do."

"And what are you doing now?" I said and received my fresh cocktail. "Thank you," I held up my glass and tapped it against Nate's before he sat back down. "Are you still writing?"

"I am."

"He's a playwright now," Anna said feigning a pompous air. She lit a cigarette and blew the smoke out the side of her mouth.

"A playwright?"

Nate opened his arms and bowed facetiously.

"Well, well, Bill Shakespeare. No more novels?"

"There's not much of a market for my novels these days."

"Theater," Anna interjected, "allows him to write, produce, and get in front of an audience before the censors can really step in."

"Well," Nate said, "it's not that they care much for a play that will only be seen by a hundred or so people. A novel that is sold a hundred thousand times will obviously be of more interest to them."

"Wow, so is there anything you're working on now? Anything that I could see?"

"Yeah, I'm always writing."

"I have to see one."

"I don't see why you wouldn't, now that you're back."

"Are you still writing essays or anything like that?"

At this question Nate and Anna appeared to grow uncomfortable. "Well, that's the thing. The revolution might be over, but the Overmen's eyes and ears are still ever present. I haven't written an essay in a long time. There's no money in it for one," he said laughing, "and there's a great risk involved. At least in the articles I'd want to write."

"Of course," I said, moving my empty glass in small circles so the melting ice clinked together. "But you *were* writing essays were you not?"

"I did, for a while, yes. But that was back then and ... well, let's not talk about back then, not yet anyway."

"Right," I said and felt comfortable enough to smile at our constantly referenced agreement.

"So, what do you plan on doing here? And what brought you here if you don't mind me asking."

"Not at all," this time I stood up and motioned to his empty glass.

"Yeah sure," he handed me his glass.

"Anna?"

She lifted her beer bottle and shook it, "Please. Seems I'm about empty."

I walked to the kitchen.

"Beer's in the fridge and gin should be right there."

"I see it."

As I mixed our drinks I began to talk. "The thing is, I'm not doing anything here. I um ... kind of abandoned my job in ... it doesn't matter where. But I quit, I guess."

"You guess?" Anna asked.

"Yeah, I just left so I'm sure the message was clear enough. And I came here. I just wanted to come home, I guess."

"You guess?" this time it was Nate repeating my words to me. I handed them their drinks and resumed my seat.

"It's all ... well, like you said, it's the past and we don't need to talk about the past. At least not yet." I smiled again.

"Hear, hear," Anna raised her drink and Nate and I did the same.

The next morning, I woke up on a strange couch in a strange room. After a moment of inspection, the memory of the previous night began to surface. I heard hushed voices somewhere in the room and when I managed to lift my head to investigate, I saw Nate and Anna sitting drinking coffee at the kitchen table. They seemed to be in the middle of some lighthearted conversation.

I sat up and rubbed my head.

"Good afternoon, my darling," I heard Nate shout.

"Is it afternoon already?" I inquired and stumbled towards the light of the kitchen.

"I'm afraid it is. No need for concern. We've only been up for about forty-five. There's coffee in the pot, my friend."

"Coffee would be much appreciated," I growled and poured myself a cup. I sat down with the happy couple and sipped. We sat in silence although Nate kept passing sunny glances between Anna and me.

"What?" Anna said, breaking into a curious grin.

"This is just surreal. Having you here," he nudged my knee with his, "just feels ... I don't know. I don't want to say like old times because it doesn't quite feel that way but ... it bears a similarity to old times, I guess. And having breakfast after a night of drinks, well, that is like—"

"Like old times?" I said.

"Yes. Quite like it."

"Where's this breakfast you speak of?" Anna looked round the near empty table in an exaggerated motion.

"And judging by the time of day it would be more like lunch, no?"

"Well, breakfast is just, as the name implies, the breaking of a fast. So, whenever this break takes place doesn't matter as long as a fast is being broken. And since it's unlikely any of us ate in our sleep I'd say the next meal we have will fulfil the criteria. And as to where this elusive meal is, I say we venture out of doors to find it?" Nate passed a few enthusiastic looks at us and when he found no objections said, "All right then. Finish your coffees."

And so, I was back in Nate's life. We mostly avoided talking about the past and when it did come up, we handled it delicately. James acted dubiously around me for the first few months, watching me closely and treating any potential friendship with caution. I understood, though. He was very young when I left and so wouldn't have known what went on. I inferred from his behavior that he suspected me of something, but he didn't know what. I think having his uncle embrace me as he did, though, allowed him to eventually find me certifiably safe. I admit that I was always suspecting a turn in our friendship. I knew Nate was never sure what I did or didn't do and how much of my actions led to Marie's disappearance and so I thought the uncertainty would eventually lead to his rejection of me. But it never did. Part of me thinks he deliberately chose to believe my role was minimal. That he polished his memories of that dark time in order to create a situation in which I could be welcomed in his life without conflict. You see, I think I reminded him of the past and connected him to it. Marie was gone, Jonny was gone, Kara had been transformed. I was all he had left from that time. Because of this I think he arranged his memories in a way to keep any contradictory feelings towards me hidden, like arranging one's furniture to hide a hole in the wall. Of course, that's only speculation. We simply never really talked about it.

The years following our reunion were like the years preceding our falling-out. There are thousands of stories which I could and would like to relate here but they don't serve the purpose of this narrative and so unfortunately, I must exclude them. The highlights I will include but they would be more fitting in a chapter of their own.

Chapter 48 ~ Like Old Times

These years passed quickly, far too quickly, yet are furnished with so many wonderful memories. James finished his apprenticeship and started a business building houses. He built one for his mother less than a block away from the one he built for himself. He continued to take care of her until she passed away. He also built a cottage, with the help of Nate, Anna and me, just outside of Kenora, a small city east of Winnipeg on the Canadian Shield. We would spend as much time there as we could, fishing, canoeing, and conversing long into the night. Nate continued to write plays and had them produced in venues across the city. He became a bit of a local folk legend with his tales of overcoming adversity and the possibilities of a new and better world. His work became popular which frequently attracted the attention of the FDIS—Federal Domestic Intelligence Service, essentially the rebranded Public Protection Agency—but the days of black bags, and disappearances had thankfully passed and there was little they could do or wanted to do since persecuting a playwright was bound to bring them more criticism than they were willing to bear. Anna's shop did well. Although she preferred her antiques there was no longer a market for them since most people were still trying to recover from the revolution and had little money to spend on novelties, but she managed to find satisfaction in selling clothes. She eventually branched out to sell other items like she used to in Gerald and began referring to her shop as a general store and gave it a rustic décor.

During this time, I also met a great many of Nate and Anna's friends whose relationships were formed during the revolution. The most significant one I met was Abby Dalisay who, after being successfully smuggled first to British Columbia and then to the United States, was given a new identity and spent the years leading up to the Overmen's collapse working at a farm in Northern California. Once it was safe to return to Canada, she did so with a husband with whom she eventually took advantage of the new two child policy.

About a decade after I returned to Winnipeg Kara passed away. She was diagnosed with stomach cancer and died only two months later. She never regained her old demeanor that disappeared after Jonny died. It was like the two of them, once they found each other, quickly developed a symbiotic relationship. They were so dissimilar but only because they were different parts of a greater whole. To participate in humanity, one must first feel human and I think Jonny and Kara both felt most human together. When he left for Ottawa, he left that part of him that connected him to the rest of humanity. Likewise, when he died, there was a part of her humanity that was suddenly gone and without it she could never reconnect to the rest of us. She was not quite sixty years old when she passed.

***

Sometime later I had Nate and Anna over for dinner. After we had eaten, we moved into the living room. I can't remember how the conversation got to this. We were talking about the last few decades and the changes we had seen and experienced. This somehow led to us talking about the time before I returned, not anything personal, just the state of the world then. Anna made mention of Nate's writing and I was reminded of Subject Blair.

"You did a lot of writing back then, eh?" I said. The alcohol had been doing its job and we were all quite loose with our conversation. The kind of drunk when one begins to believe that nothing could be said that would be deemed inappropriate.

"I did some, yes. It was always tricky since I had to have it all smuggled out and I had to take precautions not to leave a trail the Overmen could follow. It was horrible actually when I think of it."

I sipped my drink and smiled to myself while weighing out in my head the pros and cons of revealing my intervention from across the globe.

"Why are you smiling?" Nate asked, smiling himself.

"I was just thinking of something. Something that happened when I was away."

"Oh?" Anna leaned forward. "Is it something you'd like to share?" I didn't talk much about my time away so whenever I made mention of it, they always showed unusual interest.

"You don't have to of course. We never have to talk about that."

"I know. I know." I stood up and placed my glass on the coffee table and stood next to the fireplace gazing into the glowing coals of a fire that had recently gone out. "I just … don't know."

"I have an idea." Anna sat up straight as if she was mimicking the exclamation point at the end of her sentence. "We're all blotto right now and so our inhibitions are obviously compromised."

"Compromised, eh?" Nate laughed.

"Yes. Compromised. So, let's leave talk of the past, whatever you were considering telling us," she motioned to me with two open hands, "till tomorrow when we will be thinking clearer."

Nate suddenly looked incredulous. "Tomorrow? We'll be hungover is what we will be. I don't know if thinking through a fog will make things much clearer."

"Well tomorrow evening then. When we have sufficiently recuperated, you can decide if you'd like to share with us what you're thinking of sharing now."

I nodded my approval and returned to my seat. The next day, as Nate prophesied, we were all much too hungover to remember the previous night's plan much less put it into action but after an afternoon of coffee, water, and a hearty meal of eggs and bacon the thought returned to me. I didn't do anything with said thought until the evening was upon us and we were sitting again in my living room drinking coffee and watching television.

Without saying a word, I stood up and walked to my bedroom where I had in a cardboard box every article I had written as Blair as well as a large collection of the articles Blair had written. I sat on the bed and opened the box and leafed through the stack of papers inside remembering those days as a devote Overman, unable to reconcile who I was then with who I was now. These papers, I thought, represent who I really was; they represent my refusal to allow myself to be completely subsumed into their silly movement. But I did, didn't I? Don't I have clear memories of hating all Mortals? Didn't I actively try to further the movement? Aren't there still many countries in which I enthusiastically preached the Overman message who are still in their iron grip?

"What's going on?"

I looked up from the open box at Nate standing in the doorway.

"What have you got there?" He came and sat on the bed with the box of papers between us. "What's all this?"

"This is what I wanted to tell you about last night."

"Oh?" He pulled a few out of the box and looked through them. Some were mine and others were Blair's. I held my breath, waiting for him to recognize them.

"Who wrote these?" he asked without looking up from an essay on free speech.

"Do you not recognize them?" I asked. "Some of them are mine, in fact."

"You wrote these?" He held up the papers and made a congratulatory face.

"I did. Some of them. Some of them were written by … well, by you."

"Me?" Nate looked down at the papers in his hands and then began to shuffle through those still in the box.

"I recognized your writing when I was in Kiev."

"Kiev?"

"I was the minister of propaganda," I confessed and dropped my eyes to the floor. "So, my job was to paint truth as lies and lies as truth and that's what I did."

Nate put the papers down on the bed. "So that's what you were doing all those years ago."

"But," I said as if the next word out of my mouth would justify everything I had done. "Then I was given these." I pulled out the rest of the papers in the box. "This isn't all of them, but I brought many with me. We called you Subject Blair."

"Subject Blair?" I could see Nate was becoming confused.

"Yeah, your writing was appearing in Eastern Europe and I was tasked with countering the things you were saying. I was supposed to write propaganda to make you look like a liar or a saboteur or anything that would discredit you. While I was supposed to be working on that, others were working to track you down and put an end to what you were saying. The thing is, I knew it was you while no one else yet did. But I believe they would've found you eventually. They were narrowing your location down. So, I decided to step in and keep them from finding you. I protected you."

"Yeah?" Nate picked up some more papers and began skimming their contents.

"Yeah. What I did was, I began writing as you, as Blair, but leaving clues in my writing that you were writing from somewhere in Europe. That way they would be too busy looking for you there to follow the real leads they had."

"I see." He continued to skim through article after article.

"That one I wrote, see, here, I describe the Charles Bridge in Prague."

Nate began to laugh. Although, it wasn't the response I was expecting I was happy he hadn't condemned me for what I did for the Overmen. "Is this one Blair's?" He held up an essay.

"Yeah, yours."

"I ... I'm sorry," he said and laughed again. "I didn't write this."

My heart seemed to stop, and I forgot to breathe.

"I didn't write any of these." He picked up article after article from the box and shook his head while looking at each one. "No, none of them."

"But ... look," I grabbed one that I knew well and opened to a well-worn page. "See, here. *They Are Powerless, We Are Powerful.*" I began to read quickly and then slowed when I got to the part that said, "Those who wish to rule over us, to subjugate us, are completely dependent on us for the very power they intend to use against us." I looked up at him as if to beg him to agree that these were his words, but he just shrugged. "Those are your words. I heard you say them before at many meetings."

"I do remember saying something similar, and I'm positive I've written something similar, but many people did. That was a common belief amongst us. I wasn't the first to say it or write it. In fact, I likely got it from someone else."

I dropped the papers on the bed; some slipped off and fell to the floor.

"Hey," Nate put a hand on my shoulder. "You still protected whoever this Blair person was. It doesn't matter that it wasn't me. And I appreciate that you tried so hard to protect me when you thought it was me." He then began to laugh again. And then I laughed. We laughed until our bellies hurt.

Chapter 49 ~ What Happened, Happened

Anna had never been able to put out of her mind the fate of Marie. It became somewhat of an obsession of hers to find the truth or at the very least find some information with which to paint a picture. Sometime after the fall of the Overmen in Canada a freedom of information act was passed that allowed many people to access documents that were previously classified. Anna scoured through dozens until she managed to find a few brief mentions of Marie, her kidnapping, her imprisonment, and her death. She made copies and showed them to Nate one evening when they were alone together. Upon reading the highlighted portions, which were in fact few and rather vague, although they did paint a clear enough picture to leave no doubt, Nate broke down in a sea of tears. Anna held him as he convulsed in a crumpled heap on the chesterfield.

For Nate, this moment was monumental. After her disappearance he couldn't even think about what happened to her because he couldn't be sure. She was, as he described to Anna, just gone. There was no *where* for him. There was no alive or dead, no future. She was, in a way, frozen in the same state she was the last time he saw her and because of that he had given up any hope of moving on properly. He had concluded long ago that he'd never see her again but besides that, he didn't have anything else to believe about her. With the information now before him, he felt he could finally mourn his wife's death and celebrate the life she lived.

I saw him the next day. I arrived early in the morning and even then, a good twelve or thirteen hours after he had been given the report by Anna, his eyes still carried the tell-tale signs of tears having been shed. I wasn't aware of anything that had happened, and Anna, to my knowledge, never knew that there was a possibility that I was involved in Marie's death, so when I saw Nate in the state he was in, I was immediately concerned. "What have we done now?" was my initial thought. He took me into the living room where the papers Anna had brought him were scattered across the top of the ottoman.

"What's all this?" I asked, taking a seat on the chesterfield and picking up a loose sheet.

"She's dead—Marie," Nate said, his objective tone juxtaposed by his red, teary eyes. "She died in an internment camp in Southeast Asia."

"Oh my god," I said and began searching more closely. I suddenly felt a sense of dread. Was there anything in here to incriminate me? If there is what does it say? After all, what role *did* I play?

Nate sat down next to me; he released a deep sigh which made him appear more relieved than mournful.

"How did she ..." I started, still scanning page after page, but didn't finish what was surely an obvious question.

"It doesn't say. She died in hospital, though." Nate released another long sigh. Then for a moment he didn't move as if that sigh was his last breath but then he said, "I miss her so much, even still." This confession made me look up from the pages and check the apartment for any sign of Anna, unaware that she was the one who had produced the documents. "It's been almost twenty years I guess, hasn't it?"

"About that, yeah," I said.

"I wish things had been different, so different. I wish so much of what happened didn't and what didn't, did and just that everything was different. I often think, why couldn't I have been born earlier, at a time when none of this would have been possible. Or what if I were born in a different place, from a different family, or even as an Immortal. But what happened happened the way it did, and I can't change any of it. I can't change what is the truth of the matter."

"I wish things had been different, too," I tried to sound comforting.

"You know, I can't choose to believe something that I know is not true." This statement caused a slight pang in my chest. "I know Marie is gone and I know what happened to her now," he said motioning to the documents before us. "But there is still so much I don't know. And as long as I don't, I can believe what I choose." I didn't respond; I couldn't. "Of course, ignorance is bliss and all that but choosing to believe something knowing there are large gaps in your story and the gaps might reveal something monstrous is not blissful, it's sufferable. But sufferable is the best some people can ask for. Marie was a journalist. Her job was to try to pull back every blinder on every eye, pull out every piece of cotton in every ear. The truth, the raw, real, objective truth was what she would chase after and I championed her along. I still would. But I think, sometimes, blinders on our eyes and cotton in our ears serve a purpose. They allow us, sometimes, to keep living when we otherwise might not be able to go on. They may even lead to illusions but maybe not all illusions are quite so detrimental. Maybe we don't all have the strength to deal with what's behind those illusions, or those blinders." I couldn't bear to look at him while he said these things, figuring I knew what he was referring to. I instead stared at a corner of the room and held that gaze. "There's much I don't know and will never know and that's becoming a fine thing as I get older."

I stayed with him for the rest of the day. We talked a lot about Marie, about the old days before the revolution, about our time in University, about our days as schoolboys all the way back to Tills Elementary where we first met. "We looked the same age then," he joked. "You're frozen in your twenties. I guess you'll always be frozen." His voice became more serious as he went on. "What's in store for you then?"

"Well, I'm hoping to get a job at the University. I've already been in contact with an old colleague that happens to still be there."

"But I mean after that?"

"After I find work?"

"Forever, I mean. What will you do forever?"

"I suppose I haven't a clue," I said after a thought.

Chapter 50 ~ Without Warning

Ever since my reappearance in Nate's life I felt like his acceptance of me was undeserved, like I was living off his charity and had no way to pay him back. This feeling was somewhat supressed when I believed I had done him a service in Kiev but after discovering who Blair was, or more accurately who he wasn't, I felt my debt to him was still greater than it ever had been. The thought of owing such a debt weighed heavily on me so I made up my mind to try to pay him back any way I could. The problem I found, now that the threat of the Overmen had passed, was that Nate's life no longer needed protecting and so my options as to what I could do for him to make up for my monstrous past were limited to things that could hardly be considered significant.

One of the first things I did, which I thought would help my friends, was I hired James to build me a house and paid him as well as I could maintain without going bankrupt. I had previously purchased a large plot of land outside the city. This was the same land on which my current house stands, although the house James built has been repaired and altered and added to so much there is essentially nothing now that I can point to and claim that it is from the original. But it is where I still live and in fact from where I am currently writing these words. I think my hiring him did help him financially, but it did little to help my conscience. Likewise, I helped Anna in her shop, bought everything I could from it. I loaned her what money I could afford when she needed it and developed elaborate advertising campaigns using my expertise as former propaganda minister. For Nate, I similarly worked tirelessly to promote his plays and tried to use what little influence I still had to keep away the FDIS. But it wasn't enough and as I watched them all show more and more signs of aging, I knew I had to do more if I were to make up for my transgressions before they were no longer round to accept my penance.

That is when I began the work that led me to become what I am now, although I could never have imagined at the time it would lead to this. I had James build me a separate building adjacent to the house he had already built. It looked from the outside like a large garage but inside I installed a quite sophisticated laboratory, given my limited funds. I was a scientist after all, and I was determined to use my skills to do what the OP said was impossible.

Years passed with little to no progress. I was underfunded and was working in secret since any wind of what I was doing could put a sudden and irreversible stop on my entire project. The government, even though not technically run by the OP, was still authoritarian. While I worked, my friends continued to show symptoms of mortality. Whether I cursed it or pleaded with it, Death insisted on making me watch as my friends slowly succumbed to its will. Soon, even young James had grey speckled hair and deep lines distorting his features. Eventually a feeling of helpless rage engulfed every second of my life as I watched Death careening towards them, and I was powerless to stop it. What I needed was more Time but Time, it soon became apparent, was in cahoots with Death, working together towards a mutual aim.

These are some of the many indications I received that the end was getting closer and closer for my friends. Anna, after she had turned sixty-five, retired. Unwilling to see her shop close its doors for good, I bought it from her and hired others to manage it for me since I was already too preoccupied between my covert research and my position at the university. I kept the shop exactly like she had it for as long as I could; even managed eventually to make a decent profit from it.

Nate continued to write despite also passing that sixty-five-year mark. I don't think he saw his writing career as a job. It was more like a way of life for him. Just another part of his day like eating or sleeping. Also, his profession, unlike Anna's or James', didn't require him to perform any strenuous physical tasks, although the mental task of writing at an advanced age is, as I can now attest, still quite a challenge.

It wasn't just jobs, though, that my dear friends retired from as they grew closer to natural death. They retired from simple activities that they could no longer perform, like Nate who stopped going for afternoon walks after the cartilage in his left knee dissolved leading to doctors replacing the joint with a stainless-steel imposter. Eventually, Nate retired from drinking alcohol as his innards no longer knew what to do with the stuff. And, after his hearing began to fail, he retired from prolonged conversations that lasted into the early mornings. His hearing loss exacerbated our already far too brief conversations since they were now stippled with the frequently repeated phrase, "What was that?"

Despite this or because of this, I kept working on my secret project. As I felt time getting away from me, I reduced the number of classes I taught to a minimum in order to immerse myself as much as possible into my personal research. James would frequently come by the house from the city to visit and take me to see his aunt and uncle. I'd often refuse but he'd respond by reminding me that they won't be around forever. I'd usually throw something in frustration or curse Death and Time and my feeble attempts at stalling either before acquiescing to his request. "What I am doing," I would yell as I followed him to his car, "is trying to give us more time. Infinite time in fact." He'd smile and nod and tell me I was a good friend.

I arranged for the best care for Nate and Anna when they had retired. I had hoped they would move in with me at my house outside of the city, but they said they preferred to stay where they were. They liked all the conveniences a city can offer, and I understood that. The place I occupied was far enough away that a trip to the supermarket required a vehicle and time, while in the city they could have their groceries delivered. They also had all their fellow retirees nearby with whom they would often visit or have over. The house I purchased for them was a single story with a garden in the backyard. Anna, who was still perfectly mobile unlike her husband, liked to spend her afternoons tending to it and enjoyed experimenting with various plants and herbs not native to the province. When I would stop by, I'd often see her bent over pulling weeds, harvesting vegetables of dubious quality. Although she enjoyed gardening, she was about as good at it as she was baking. She usually wore a straw sunhat with her now silvery-white hair pulled back into a ponytail. On these days Nate would often be seated on a lawn chair on their deck, built by James and myself, computer on lap, cup of weak tea on table, and eyes glued to his wife as she labored away. This was the scene which I interrupted one afternoon after James had successfully pulled me away from my work.

We pulled up in James' truck which he parked on the street and walked around to the back of the house where we knew we'd find them.

"Hullo," James shouted as we rounded the corner. Anna stood up with something green hanging from her left hand and her right blocking the sun from her eyes. When she saw who it was, she waved broadly, dropped the green, and walked out of the garden to greet us. Nate remained in his seat but when we came into view, he placed his computer on the table and stood up on wobbly legs. His back was slightly bent forward, having lost its ability to straighten years ago.

"Hullo there," Nate said still on the deck. We shook hands.

"Hey boys," Anna said and gave us each a hug and a kiss on the cheek.

James climbed the couple steps to the deck and sat down in the seat his uncle had just vacated.

"I'll grab you something to drink," Nate said and began hobbling to the door of the house.

"Sit," I said, hating to see him so feeble. "I know where everything is."

"I'll give ya a hand," James said and gave his uncle his seat back.

We sat around the table with the hot summer sun glaring down on us and were refreshed by cold beers and, in the case of Nate the teetotaller, a soda water and lemon.

"So, what have you been up to over there?" Anna said, cooling her neck with the cold beer bottle. "You hardly ever come visit us."

"I was here last week," I said defensively.

"You used to be here every day," Nate pointed out.

"Well, once a week isn't so bad, is it?" I said. "Man, it's hot."

"Listen to him changing the topic," Anna said, smiling and waving a hand as if to shoo my attempt away.

"He's working," James said, making a failed attempt at my defense.

"Wasn't he also working when he used to come visit us every day? What's so important now that's forced such a change in his schedule?"

"I don't know," James said, seeming to have now realized his mistake but not knowing what else to say and not enjoying the attention being now on him said to me, "What are you working on again?"

"It's nothing, it's just a bit time consuming, that's all. I know it's eating up a lot of time, I'm sorry." I began to ramble. "I'll try harder," I said meaning I'll try harder to finish my work, but Nate and Anna took it to mean I'd try harder to come see them. I then realized the role I had grown into. I grew up with Nate, and Anna was younger than I was but here we were, they, an elderly couple nearing the end of their lives and me, their pseudo-grandson.

"Your garden looks great, Aunt Anna," James said leaning over the railing.

"Yeah, it's all coming in nicely."

While they talked, I began passing glances between their faces. They all looked so different than they once did. So weathered, so ravaged by time. Nate looked the most weathered. The wrinkles had so completely changed his face that I remember thinking I would never have recognized him if I hadn't watched it happen. The hair he had left on his head was solid grey. His beard, which helped cover some of the changes when he let it grow long, was itself grey and in parts white. Anna, too, was noticeably changed by the years. She still kept her hair long, unlike many of her geriatric friends, but her radiant red hair had slowly faded over the years until it lost all of its beautiful color and her bright blue eyes, which combined with her hair used to make me think of a watercolor painting, had also faded to a greyish blue. But they still sparkled, especially when she smiled. James had changed the least but still looked so different from how he used to. His hair was speckled with grey and his perpetually tanned skin was becoming rough like leather. He still maintained a bit of his youthful demeanor, his mischievous nature which he inherited from his late father, and his quick wit, also a gift from Jonny. And here I was, having not changed since my third decade of life, sitting with my peers, some of whom were younger than me. One of whom I often babysat as an infant. The whole thing suddenly appeared like a horrible farce.

Despite my own terror at watching my friends retire their lives, I refused to allow myself to believe that their deaths were inevitable. As long as I could continue my work, I believed I could find a way to keep them here which made every moment away from my laboratory almost unbearable. Because of this my limbs were often bouncing with anxiety without my being aware of it.

After a couple drinks James fired up the barbeque and began cooking chicken kebobs and hamburgers. I offered to help, doing so I thought would keep my mind in the same place as my body, but he refused, leaving me sitting with a knee bouncing rapidly. I found it difficult to look at Nate when he talked; the lines on his face and rasp in his voice just reminded me of my failure.

With the food prepared we went inside and sat around the dining room table. The interior of the Karski's house had their usual cosmopolitan influence with art and furnishings from all over the world. There were also many antiques scattered about the place, a sign of Anna's influence.

After dinner we moved to the living room and listened to music and talked about the past, a topic that slowly became a favorite. We also talked briefly, of course, about politics and world events but the conversation always returned to the adventures of their younger days, the great parties they threw, and the fascinating people they met. Current events seemed to them to have lost relevance. Nate was still spry enough to stay up just past midnight which we did before he clapped his hands together and announced it was time for him to go to bed. Anna soon followed, leaving James and I alone. Not ready to retire ourselves we poured more drinks and carried on the night with hushed voices so as not to wake the sleeping elderly.

"How's your work?" James asked, not knowing what exactly my work was but knowing that I believed it to be of the utmost importance.

"I'd rather not talk about it," I admitted. Talking about it, even as drunk as I was, had the immediate effect of causing my thoughts to get trapped in my lab with no obvious means of escape. "Let's talk about something else. How's your work?"

"It's fine," he said and then proceeded to relate a story in which his workers, while he was away from the worksite for a couple days, had somehow managed to install the roof of a three-story house backwards so the north side was facing south. When he returned and saw the mistake, he was forced to rent a crane to lift the roof, swing it around and put it on correctly before the homeowners came around to see it. He and I laughed throughout his tale but my knee, which had started bouncing when he asked me about my work, appeared ignorant of the humor in the story and kept right on bouncing.

As we talked, and as my knee carried on, I found my eyes drifting to and from various items that filled the room. All these things, I thought, would be left behind after they are gone. Those photos on the wall and the moments they caught will remain for James and me to look at and remember. The various figurines, the globe, the books and marble bookends in the shape of medieval knights. Everything I saw was a bit of them, chosen by them because of something inside them, an experience or memory or genetic trait or something else that made them want to buy *that* lamp and hang *that* picture. The lay-out of the furniture then caught my attention. Why put the chesterfield there? Why the bookshelf there? The arrangement became as interesting to me as the pieces of modern art that I found just as impossible to interpret. The whole room, the whole house, felt to me even then while they were still alive and sleeping in the next room like a shrine to their memory. But one that they made and one that could be studied and interpreted as a way to know who they were while alive.

The interaction I just described was common during this time. I'd be pulled from my work, usually by James but sometimes Anna and fewer times by Nate. I'd go to their place for dinner and drinks and spend the night sleeping on their couch, the entire time trying to keep my thoughts away from my laboratory and my knee from bouncing. Every time I paid one of these visits, I saw a new wrinkle, a new liver spot or patch of dry skin or blue or varicose vein and my knee would bounce once or twice to remind me where I should be and how I was failing them. Time began to speed up exponentially, so a week felt like a day and my friends' deaths were barrelling towards us at ever increasing speeds. Time eventually lost meaning as it flew past me in a chaotic blur. Yesterday Nate was seventy, today he's seventy-five, tomorrow he'll be eighty-three. And while time ravaged their bodies, I made only slow progress towards my goal which I began to realize was too far out of reach.

My last memory of Nate, he and I were eighty-nine years old. I visited him more often than the once a week schedule I had before, but I never spent the night anymore. I just came and sat with him at the kitchen table and talked. He sat slouched over a cooling cup of weak tea. Biscuits were laid out on a plate in the middle and he'd take a small bite and use his forefinger to brush all the crumbs from his creased lips into his mouth. His eyes were grey, his skin was grey, his hair was grey; all color had been sucked out of him. His mind had slowed only slightly but his hearing was poor, and I found myself having to simplify my language and speak loudly for him to hear and understand. He had stopped writing a couple of years earlier and now spent most of his time reading and being driven round by James. Some of his fans, he told me, who still read his work, would make arrangements to come to his house and talk and he said he even had an interview with an independent journalist who published the transcript in some literary magazine.

"I think I have the magazine somewhere in that stack by the couch," he said. With both hands wrapped around his mug he lifted it to his mouth and drank the last cold sip. He then leaned back and placed both hands on the table and began tapping his gnarled fingers. "Not a bad read. Although the girl described me as frail." He laughed. "I suppose I am, but she didn't have to mention it did she?"

"I suppose not."

"She was nice, though. Young, probably only twenty-three or somewhere round there. It's hard to tell now. When I was in my twenties, I thought I could tell the difference between a twenty-four-year-old and a twenty-seven-year-old. Now I don't think I could tell the difference between a twenty-year old and a forty-year old," he chuckled and lifted his cup to his mouth again before remembering it was empty. "But then again, now I'm sure I could tell the difference between a ninety-year old and ah, say, an eighty-five-year-old. I bet I could. I guess you have to be in the age group to be able to tell those sorts of things."

"Perhaps. Do you need anything?"

"I would like another cup of tea, actually. I keep trying to sip from this damn thing, but it insists on remaining empty."

I got up and grabbed his cup and walked to the kitchen counter where I turned on the kettle.

"It must be different for you," he said, still looking at the seat I had just vacated. "You look, what, twenty-five? Can you tell the difference between a couple years amongst the twenty to thirty demographic? I doubt you have the acuteness to distinguish between us octogenarians like Anna and I can ... well, I guess you're an octogenarian, too. She's better at it than I am, Anna. Whenever she guesses someone's age, she's spot fucking on. It's remarkable, really." He went on like this until I returned with his fresh cup of tea. "Ah, cheers," he wrapped his hands around the cup again.

"How is Anna?" She was out at a friend's house for lunch.

"Oh, she's excellent. Lively. She'll outlive me by a decade, I swear. Can't garden for shit, but she tries and enjoys it. You weren't around then but when we were up north in that prison, she had a bakery." Laughter burst from him. "It was awful stuff she made. The croissants were so hard you could kill a man with them. Maybe that was her plan.

Since they didn't allow us to have weapons, she'd bake some." When he finished his story, he had tears in his eyes from laughing. He wiped his eyes and then something seemed to catch his gaze. I followed his line of sight from the kitchen through the living room out the bay window that looked out onto the street into some infinite distance I was incapable of perceiving.

"There are so many memories to choose from," he said. "So many people who are gone to think about." He turned his grey eyes to me, still full of tears from his previous laughter. "With time running out I sometimes worry I won't be able to give everyone who deserves it enough of my thoughts. Who to think about now, is often the question that troubles me. Who to remember … and how. How do I remember my brother?" His eyes returned to the bay window and this time when I followed them, I saw he was looking at his wife who was being dropped off by some friends. I could see her getting out of the vehicle and waving to the passengers inside before walking towards the house.

"It's quite the thing, thinking of how things could have been." Nate continued as if he hadn't noticed our conversation was about to be interrupted.

"It is," I said pathetically, trying to understand what he was referring to.

"I love her, and I'm so happy with her. Our life together has been better than I could've ever hoped for," he said without breaking his gaze. "But we've spent our life together only because …"

The front door opened, and Anna walked in carrying a couple of shopping bags. Nate turned his attention to his cup of tea signalling an end to whatever he was about to say. I got up and helped Anna with her bags.

***

I wish I had more time to write about Nate. I wish I didn't have to stop here. I wish I could go on and write another thousand pages about him, stories of the things he did, things he said, the person he was. But I'm running out of time. I can't fill all these pages just with stories of him, as much as I'd love to do so. I must move one. Why did I wait so long to write this? Now this is all that will be left of him—my memories of him, my interpretation, my perspective written down. Such a limited perspective, too. I wish everyone could've known him. Not just from his writings which don't give a full picture of who he was but only a glimpse. Only a small peek into only what he was willing to reveal. I suppose everyone has known someone like him. Someone we wish everyone could have known, at least in some way. Perhaps if more people who had known him had written about him, we'd have a clearer picture of who he was. The kind of person he was. I don't possess the capacity to fully capture everything about him. Others who had known him might disagree with my depiction of him. I might be wrong about a great many things. But who I remember him to have been, the man I believe he was, is all I can describe here in this far too brief and far too inadequate account. I wish I had more time.

I was at home not a week later when I received a call from James telling me Nate had a heart attack and was in hospital in critical condition. I rushed to St. Boniface as fast as was possible. When I arrived, I was told to wait, which I did for two hours before James found me. He embraced me and cried without saying a word. When he took me to see his body, I found Anna sitting next to him holding his lifeless hand. His body, I remember, looked different; it looked empty.

Chapter 51 ~ Goodbyes

I helped plan the funeral with Anna and James. We went casket shopping together, a bizarre experience, we all thought.

"He wouldn't care what we do with that thing," James said, containing his laughter as he gawked at the price of a particularly expensive casket. "He wouldn't even want one of these. Can we just toss him in the hole sans-casket?"

"I don't think we can do that?" Anna said smiling.

"Or wrap him in a sheet. Or one of those vacuum-sealed bags you use for storing old clothes."

After the casket was chosen, a tasteful and inexpensive box that everyone agreed suited him best, our next task was picking out a headstone. I remember I couldn't help thinking that all the planning we were doing would never be appreciated by Nate. He was, after all, nowhere to be found. It was like throwing a birthday party for a friend who's out of country. We eventually settled on a basic tablet style made of granite. It was grey and the epitaph said, "Still are thy pleasant voices, thy nightingales, awake; For Death, he taketh all away but them he cannot take," from one of Nate's favorite poems.

His funeral had a large turnout. Nate still had a large following and many people from all over the country appeared to pay their respects. Passages were read from his books and other writers wrote poems in his honor which were recited. Songs were sung, good food was served and enjoyed, drinks were drunk, and tears were shed.

After the funeral I went straight home. I just wanted to be alone. I remember how quiet and colorless the world seemed after I had said goodbye to James and Anna and dropped them off at their respective houses. In my house I sat in that silence and greyness for an immeasurable amount of time, or so it seemed. Soon there'll be nothing, I remember thinking, nothing left to do, nothing left to look forward to. Soon they will all be gone. And then there will be nothing. There will be nothing forever.

***

After Nate's death, I put a hold on my work. It suddenly felt pointless. I failed in saving Nate. I was never going to be able to save anyone from that inevitable, fatal disease called death. I fell into a deep depression and refused to leave my house. James and Anna would visit frequently, but I was a terrible host. Despite my persistently morose demeanor, they continued to come, always seeming so cheerful. I could never understand why they didn't share my anguish. They laughed when they talked, told jokes, even about him. They continued with their lives as if nothing had changed but to me everything had changed, and it would never be the same again. Weren't their hearts broken, too? Didn't Nate mean as much or more to them as he did me? But from their conversations I did begin to understand. You see, for a Mortal, death is just a part of the whole game they play. Like the end of a good book or a well-staged play, it is the great finale, and no play or novel would be complete without it. His was a good life, a good story. And, they knew, every story needs an ending.

I didn't resume my work for years after Nate's death. Not because my grief over his absence debilitated my efforts but because I knew I was making no headway and that the amount of time I needed meant that all my beloved friends, the ones who still remained, would be dead before I completed my work. And that is assuming I could complete it in the conditions I was forced to accept.

Of course, James and Anna died, too, eventually, like every Mortal. I'll tell you about that now; no point delaying it I suppose. Anna died before James, since it was she who was older. But she lived over a decade after Nate had passed away. I remember her shoulders dropping over the years and her back becoming hunched as if death was already pulling her down into the grave. When she was too old to take care of herself, I arranged for a full-time staff to care for her in the house she lived in with Nate. I visited every other day, always wishing I had done so when Nate was still alive. She became wheelchair bound. Her skin became translucent, so blue veins in her hands and arms could be seen so prominently that one might have thought they could see currents of blood flowing through them if they examined them close enough. Her voice cracked when she talked. She was always cold and was never seen without a blanket spread over her lap. She died in her sleep just shy of a centenarian.

When James was too old to care for himself, he agreed to move into my house outside the city. I installed a chair that could carry him all the way up the stairs and wheelchair ramps over every step, much like I have now for myself. I remember one of our last conversations. It could've been the last but there's no way of knowing. He had just woken up from a nap in a recliner which had been designated as his chair. I walked into the room with a cup of weak tea, the same as his uncle drank during the few years before he died. He thanked me and asked that I put the television on to watch curling, his favorite sport. I did so and then sat on the couch next to him.

The characters on the screen were barking commands as the rocks slid down the pebbled ice. When he was younger James would sometimes join in on the yelling, loudly telling the people in the television what they should or shouldn't do. Now he just sat quietly so I was never sure if he watched because he still enjoyed it or if he was just continuing a lifelong habit. He would often fall asleep while watching, waking up after the game was over and asking me to fill him in on what happened. I was never much of a sports fan, but I learnt about the game for his sake.

"What will you do when I'm gone?" James asked out of the blue. He had been so quiet and still in his recliner I thought he had fallen asleep so was surprised both by him being awake and the nature of his question.

"What do you mean?"

"Well, just, what do you think your life is going to look like without me? What will you do with your time? I know you wouldn't be watching curling if you had a choice so that'll change. What will you watch instead?"

"I haven't given it much thought," I said allowing myself a laugh. "There are plenty of other shows I can watch to fill the time."

"Of course, I'm not just talking about TV programs. What will you do with your day? Who will you eat meals with? Who will you talk to?"

"I don't know. I'll figure something out."

"I worry about you, you know. I won't be around much longer. You need people. People other than me. You don't have any friends to talk to and people need someone to talk to. You should go out and meet people. Take a pottery class or something," he smiled ironically. "I'm serious. You will need someone when I'm gone."

"I just haven't given it much thought. I'll worry about it when the time comes. Now I'd rather not talk about it though."

"I want to talk about it." He sat up and placed his hands on his knees and adopted a serious air. "I want to make sure you're taken care of when I'm gone. I know you have money and a job but there's more to life than that. You need people. And you don't have any people aside from me. Even I have friends outside this house that I see from time to time, at least the ones that are still alive. But you have no one. That's not healthy."

"Don't spend any of your time worrying about me," I said, maintaining a crooked grin to counteract his serious tone.

He leaned back in his chair and sighed. "Just promise me you won't just stay holed up in this place for eternity. You can break your promise after I'm gone, I suppose. I can't stop you. But for now, while I'm here worrying about you, please promise me."

"I promise," I said, with exaggerated emphasis. "Now, can I get you anything?"

"No, I'm fine. I reckon it's time I called her a night, anyway. Can you give me a hand?"

I helped him out of his chair, and he hobbled off to bed. And I remember then I sobbed quietly, whimpering to myself like a child alone in the woods and afraid of what might lurk in the darkness. James was all I had left. After he died, I'd have no one, no where to go. I'd be lost again but with no direction. And this time I couldn't just return home and reconcile old relationships in order to have a place in the world. I would have no one, nothing, nowhere to go.

It happened a short while later. James first fell and cracked a rib, then was hospitalized. Given his age and frailty he never fully recovered and ended up spending the remaining year of his life in hospital. There he caught pneumonia and was too weak to fight it.

And just like that, they were all gone. I was alone.

Chapter 52 ~ The Window in My Cave

After James died, I reverted to a routine similar to the one I developed while living in Asia. I went to work, I came home, I watched television, I ate instant meals. My job at the university kept me physically moving but my mind became stuck in place, unable to deviate from routine and able only to experience the world passively. When I think of these years, decades actually, only one image comes to mind: me sitting in a dark living room completely alone with only the shifting light of the television to indicate a presence. I see myself sitting there, not moving, becoming a part of the furniture, looking not at the screen in front of me but through it. When I see myself there the screen is a window looking out of a cave in which I had retreated. The flashing lights, the advertisements, the laugh tracks, they worked to remove me from my own thoughts, allowing me to sink into the comfortable darkness of the room. They gave me not peace but emptiness. A mind devoid of thought, filled only with what was delivered through that flickering window. I'd crawl into this cave every evening. I wouldn't go to my bedroom, I'd curl up on the couch, surrounded by the ever-changing images, the ever-changing sounds, and sleep right there in the cave. I would emerge for work, but I'll admit I was a terrible professor. I taught three classes a week, went directly to the University, and came directly home when I was done. I was never in my office to meet with students. I avoided almost all interaction with anyone else in the faculty. I just wanted to get back to my cave and stare out my window. Of course, once there were no more students, I didn't have to keep any office hours. I became primarily a researcher so, aside from the occasional trip for conferences or meetings, I was able to do almost all my work from home. Little was expected of me since by this time little was expected of anyone.

Although my life was stagnant, the world continued to change, and I would learn about these changes from the window in my cave. So much happened in the world around me during this time that I felt like a tree lodged in the middle of a rushing river. From the security of my cave I saw the Overmen slowly regain control, although they stopped referring to themselves as Overmen and any reference to the Overman Project was avoided, it was still the same basic idea that drove the Overmen before. Of course, this was only until all the Mortals were gone. After that, terms like Overmen and the Overman Project were revived, mostly as references to a glorious past.

News reports kept me updated on the dwindling Mortal population. Although Mortals in Canada now enjoyed much freedom, other countries were still under brutal authoritarian regimes established by the Overmen. There were rumors already by the time James passed away that in some countries the Mortal population had been completely eradicated. In fact, this was not true at the time but became true not four decades later.

Eventually, I saw from my cave, and on the campus of my university, the sudden and shocking revival of authoritarian rule in Canada. After decades of relative quiet, these neo-Overmen made a comeback within mere days. They reinstated mandatory contraceptives and birth permits and once again police patrolled the streets. The difference this time was how immediate it all happened. No one had time to prepare or react. Yet, during this tumult I remained in my cave.

I watched the radical generations die out and be replaced by ones brought up solely on Overman propaganda. I watched as all reference to the Mortal revolution was carefully doctored to give the impression that those opposing the Overmen were backwards thinking extremists who were against progress. News reports told of heroic Mortals—some or most of which were completely fabricated—who fought against their own people for truth and progress and enlightenment and any other positive word they could shoehorn into their narrative. I watched as the entire country, like every other country, became completely isolated from each other. The OP themselves, of course, had full access to the outside world since by then they had control of the entire planet in some form or another. They were like helicopter pilots able to fly from island to island while the Mortals, and most Immortals for that matter, were the island's primitive inhabitants waiting for news and eagerly believing whatever they were told. I knew what was happening, but I stayed in the comfort of my cave.

Of course, peering out the window of my cave, I saw the last remaining Mortal and learnt of his death. Peter Howell, as we all know from history class, lived to be eighty-two years old and died a, one might say, radical devotee of the Overman Project believing he had been somehow chosen by the collective God, the Overmen, to, "pass the torch of humanity's past to humanity's future." His last and most famous speech he gave from Washington was watched by the entire world, including me, and although I could never be bothered to remember much of it, I can still remember him going on about "a new era" and "the end of the dark past".

Then, with all the Mortals gone, with the Overmen's goal seemingly reached, they turned their attention to new goals and new enemies. The fact that these new enemies were now all fellow Immortals didn't matter; they weren't the Immortals the Overmen wanted them to be. I saw more things from my window, but as time continued, the things I saw started to seem uncannily familiar, as if each event was a slightly different variation of another before it. Like all of society had become lost in the woods and was now walking in circles. I saw a war being fought in one part of the world and then another, almost identical, being fought in a different part of the world. I saw one leader come to power only to be replaced by another identical leader and the new enemies were barely decipherable from the old ones. Events were repeating themselves. Nothing was new, nothing was revolutionary.

After what felt like ages, an anxiety began to build up inside me, the cause of which I wasn't yet aware, and pulled me out of my cave to see the world without the filter of my window. I walked the streets, visited restaurants, talked to people, watched people. And I saw that these people had become small reflections of the world I had seen from my window, suffering from the same circular momentum. People all round me spoke and acted in a memorized fashion, conversations were perfectly rehearsed, everything was routine, even adventures. A whole world filled with old dogs unable to learn new tricks. And I realized I was just like them.

I retreated to my cave, and there I remained until I was contacted by an old friend, an old sympathizer of Mortals, Larson. I hope my readers remember him. After our reunion he'd visit me often and was my only friend for the better part of a century. His is a remarkable story I've related only slightly in these pages and wish I could elaborate on more. But again, time is against me. How odd it must be to my readers that I am concerned about time. It is a concern I'm sure most have never and will never face, at least not for now.

Chapter 53 ~ Who Knows

Whenever he'd visit, Larson and I would inevitably venture outside and walk through the yard around my house; this evening was no different. We walked to the edge of my property where we could see the city skyline. It was autumn and dusk so we both wore large coats, toques, scarves. As we stood side by side the sky slowly dimmed, and the city began to glow.

"I've not been there for ages," I said staring at the city I had once known so well but that now seemed like a distant and exotic locale. "I really haven't left my property in … I don't know how long. A decade maybe."

Larson sighed and ran his fingers over his short hair. "I'd say you're not missing much."

"You're probably right. I've seen it all before. And, besides, I can never think of a reason to go. I have everything I need here."

"Well, except for people," Larson said turning to me. "You're all alone here."

"You're here. You're enough."

"I'm here now. But these visits are rather fleeting. And really, I don't provide much in the way of variety. Wouldn't you like to have a conversation with at least one other individual?"

"Not particularly. At least not anyone alive today. Why? Who do you talk to besides me?"

"I have friends besides you."

"And who would they be?"

"You don't know them," he chuckled.

We began walking back to the house. With the Sun now set the lighted windows which littered the side of the dark house appeared like bright beacons guiding us back. The temperature continued to drop so that even in the twilight the fog from our breath could be seen with every exhale or syllable spoken.

"So, what's your plan then?" Larson continued as we walked. "Mope about, waiting for the world to slowly end? Live long enough to see the Sun expand and consume the planet?"

"Is that not your plan, too?"

"I suppose it is. I mean, I just do what I think everyone else does, try not to think of it. I have my routines which keep me occupied. And when I get bored of one routine, I replace it with another."

"Ever fear you'll run out of routines?"

"Nah," Larson said with a mix of honesty and facetiousness. "I eventually forget old routines so I'm able to redo them without getting too bored. I'm like a goldfish, once I make my way around the fishbowl, I've forgotten what I saw when I started. Although I must admit, by now every moment has a tinge of déjà vu."

Once inside the house we removed our outerwear and then mixed a couple rye and sodas.

"Cheers," we both said and clinked our tumblers together. Larson sipped greedily while studying my living room wall which was covered from floor to ceiling in framed photographs.

"Do you ever get bored of looking at the same photos?" he said, motioning to the wall with his drink.

"I often switch them out for others. I have boxes full of them in the attic."

Larson moved closer looking at one then another. "How old are these?"

I sighed while calculating in my head. "Off the top of my head, I'd say not one is less than four hundred years old. Ancient, all of them."

"I don't think I've ever seen this one before," he said, bending down and looking at a photo of Jonny and Nate sitting beside each other on the hood of a car.

"You must have. That one's been there for ages," I said. "It's been decades since I put that up."

"Really? I can't remember ever seeing it. You have so many I guess I've always missed it."

We began to walk down the halls of my house which were also adorned with framed photographs. Nate, Jonny, Marie, Kara, Anna, James, captured in various stages of age. Photos of their youth, their middle age, and their twilight years. As we walked, I could feel their eyes watching us from behind their panes of glass, like they were the manifestation of spirits keeping vigil over us.

"Do you ever wish you were a Mortal?" I said as we continued to move slowly through the house.

"Very often, yes," Larson replied contemplatively. "But I don't exactly wish to be dead, either. I suppose I wish they were still here, in charge of changing the world while we drift through the centuries of change they provide. We needed them; I think we still do."

"You're right, I think. But what are we to do now that we don't have them?"

To this question Larson simply shrugged and sipped his drink. I suppose because there was no answer and he knew that I was already aware of that.

"It is rather odd," he said after we had made it to the end of the hallway and had turned down another. "After all, they were the ones who made us. They were the ones who started the Overman Project. And because of that, they're now extinct. If only they could've foreseen what they were creating and the repercussions it would have on them."

"There was no way they could have predicted what happened. Perhaps immortality was always inevitable. Perhaps this world that it created was also inevitable. Perhaps all of it is the result of human nature and nothing could've ever stopped it. Moving forwards, changing the world, seeking out the next big leap forwards, it's innate in us. We're drawn to that forward momentum like we're drawn to food. Once the next leap, the next revolution is foreseeable it's only a matter of time before we realize it."

"But what now? What's the next great step forwards? The Immortal Revolution appears to have been the last."

We walked down another hall and then another until we were back in the kitchen where we fixed more drinks and situated ourselves around my breakfast bar.

"I tried, for a long time, to find a way to make them like us," I confessed. "I was certain I could find a way to give everyone the same gift we were given. Imagine if I had succeeded. They would all be with us here now."

"Do you think they'd want that?"

I thought for a moment. "I don't know. I suppose I never thought too much about what they wanted. I just knew it's what I wanted."

"Besides," Larson continued, "I'm positive the OP could have done it," he said with surprisingly emphatic certainty. "They had all the resources to do it. They must have been able to. My theory is that once there was a divide between us and them the OP didn't want to close it."

"You really think that?" I said incredulously. "You think they could have made the whole world immortal?"

"Sure. I mean, I don't think they figured it all out and then decided to keep it under the rug. I think they just never bothered to try. I think that once the Overman Project was run entirely by Immortals the thought of sharing the philosophers stone with everyone just never crossed their minds. But they could have. I'm certain of it.

"But enough about the past," he said raising his glass. "We're here now. Might as well make the best of it."

His theory had caused my head to spin and it took me a moment before I could fabricate a smile and clink my glass against his. What if he was right, I thought? What if the OP could have, the entire time, made them all like us?

"What are you working on now, old boy?" he asked, leaning on his elbows and smiling warmly. It appeared as though he regretted sharing his theory with me and was now trying to change the subject to something less depressing.

"Um, good question. Many things, I suppose." I tried to think of a proper answer, but my mind refused to leave the thought he had planted. "What if they would have done that?" I said after a pause.

"Done what? Made everyone immortal?" he said, seeming hesitant to return to the idea. "I don't know."

"There would have been no revolution. No war."

"I suppose, yes. But then, wouldn't we still be here? Wouldn't we still be slowly dying without any new people? Would it, in the long run, have changed anything at all?"

"It could have changed everything," I shouted. "Who knows what the Mortals could have done. Maybe it wasn't that new people aren't being born, maybe it's that those of us still here now can't fathom change because we were born and raised in the Overman Project. They would have at least had a different perspective."

"But that's just it, who knows. There's no use entertaining hypotheticals is there. It's also just as likely that after a few centuries even Nate and Marie would have grown tired and lost interest in the world just like everyone else."

"But we don't know that. The fact that the OP could have—"

"You have to drop it, old boy. It'll only consume you. If they could have, they should have. At least they should have made it an option. Maybe most of them would have opted out, an option we weren't afforded. But who knows?"

I couldn't let the thought go and for the rest of the evening my mind seldom drifted from that lost possibility. I couldn't help imagining all those people I had spent the last four hundred years thinking about every day being there with me, surrounding my breakfast bar, in that moment, discussing the next revolution.

We spent the evening drinking and reminiscing about the distant past. After we were both quite drunk Larson stumbled to my couch underneath a wall covered in photos and fell swiftly to sleep. I couldn't let the night end quite so abruptly and, after mixing what I swore was my last drink of the evening, began walking down the halls again, before eventually making my way upstairs to my attic. Along the way I tried to remember James building those hallways and those rooms and that staircase but, due to both the alcohol clouding my mind and the centuries that separated that time from the present, I couldn't conjure a single lasting memory. What I conjured instead was more fantasy than reality. I imagined him measuring the length of the wall from floor to ceiling before cutting pieces of wood on a table-saw. I imagined him removing tools from his stuffed tool-belt, putting them to use before exchanging them for others. I imagined him with a carpenter's pencil in his mouth as he poured over floor plans. But not one of these images were a memory.

My attic was bursting with objects from the last five hundred years. Old furniture with torn upholstery and missing legs purchased from Anna's antique shop; closets full of old moth-ravaged clothes; books, magazines, newspapers, stacked floor to ceiling. A path was maintained through it all, creating a simulacrum of a valley cut through a mountain range, and I a sauntering giant making my way through. At the end of the path, against a wall with a window which had long since been covered by my collection of mementos, lay several boxes stacked neatly. Next to the pile lay a small figurine of a Neanderthal making fire with sticks. I picked up the figurine and wiped off any dust it had collected, although, there was little on it since I had performed the same action only days before. I returned it to its place, and then began opening boxes. Some contained photos encased in plastic to protect them from the relentless effects of time, in others were hard drives filled with videos, others still were filled with printed articles also encased in plastic. I pulled out a photo of Nate and Marie sitting on a park bench and studied it, trying to replace my lost memories with its image. Trying to conjure more details surrounding the event for which the photo was taken. Why were we in a park? Was I the one who took it, is that why I am not in it? I imagined a scenario behind it. We were going to the park for a picnic, we stopped to rest on our way there. I played it out in my head, adding more details, pretending it was a real memory and not a manufactured fantasy. Satisfied with my invented memory, I set the photo aside and grabbed another one and repeated the procedure. I don't know how long I continued in this way, pretending that I was recalling legitimate memories while barricading my mind from the pestering reality that I, in fact, remembered nothing or very little.

I lost track of time completely until I noticed a few thin rays of sunlight sneaking through gaps between the boxes, betraying the existence of the attic window behind them. I remembered Larson asleep downstairs on my couch and gently returned the pieces of memorabilia that I had scattered around me.

When I awoke late the next afternoon, I found the couch already vacated and the bedding I gave Larson neatly folded. I sauntered drowsily through my kitchen where I noticed a recently rinsed plate and cutlery in the sink and surmised Larson had been awake for some time and had helped himself to the offerings of my kitchen. I made myself a slice of toast with butter and strawberry jam and a large black coffee.

Noticing the bright sunshine and blue skies from my window, I grabbed my breakfast and walked to where I was sure Larson would be. I found him sitting on my patio with a cup of coffee of his own and took a seat next to him. Neither of us said much except for "good morning," but contented ourselves by gazing at my lawn and watching the fallen leaves of red, yellow, and orange gently dance across the grass in the light breeze. After I had finished my small breakfast and drank enough of the hot, black liquid to feel a bit more like myself again I closed my eyes and lifted my head towards the autumn sun. Light and warmth drifted over my face and I felt a small bead of sweat run from my hairline down across my cheek. In that moment I remember I felt something like contentment, or would I have even described it as happiness? But how many more times will even the Sun provide such a feeling, I wondered. Can even the Sun eventually become meaningless, become stale?

I heard Larson sip his coffee and opened my eyes. "Beautiful day isn't it?" he said, his rough voice revealing exhaustion from the boozy night before.

"It still is," I replied. I became filled with a feeling of dread, like I had suddenly become aware of an unavoidable catastrophe barrelling towards us. Something like the feeling of dread Mortals must have felt knowing oblivion was unavoidable and would meet them inevitably. But what was coming towards me wasn't death, or at least not death in any traditional sense. It was something else. It was the death of my ability to feel, to appreciate, to live life in some meaningful way. I decided then and there that I must die before that happens. How? I hadn't the faintest idea. But I had time to figure that out.

Chapter 54 ~ The Beginning

I'm an old man now, my body slowly succumbing to the ravages of mortality; everyone knows this by now. But most don't know how I became so. I'm nearly out of time, but I still have some left, however small. Enough, I hope, to leave you dear reader with an explanation, in my own words, as to what I have done.

After much contemplation regarding the state of the world, the state of my life, and the likely possibility that both would carry on indefinitely, I arrived at the conclusion that I ought to die. So, I restored my laboratory and returned to my clandestine work. Once again, I had to work in secret which wasn't a problem for reasons I already explained in the beginning of this whole long-winded confession. I used my research from the days of trying to make my friends immortal to do the exact opposite, to rediscover natural death. The work with its illegal nature meant that I couldn't trust anyone to know what I was up to. I even kept it from Larson who was rather sore that I didn't trust him, but I couldn't be sure. This also meant no lab assistant and very limited resources. Because of these hurdles the project took over a century.

But finally, I found what I was looking for: the forbidden fruit, the formula to bring me that end I so desired. But like many dreams that at first appear too far to reach, once it was at arm's length I hesitated. I couldn't bring myself to use it. I realized I needed a reason, a legacy to leave behind. To forfeit my immortality, to experience the slow progression to old age and then death the way the Mortals did seemed incomplete without a reason to do so. So, I sat on my discovery for another half century, wondering what to do with it.

Then the world began to die. Not only had changed stopped, but the way things were going, how they had been going for centuries, began to slow down. Things stopped happening, worse than the stop mentioned in the previous chapter. In fact, the great change was that all significant change ceased. For me every day had already been the exact same for ages, but I began to notice that the entire world had begun to copy my example. Everyone was a bit in a computer program performing the same functions every second of every day. At two o'clock everyone in the world did the same thing they did the day before at two o'clock. At three it was the same. And at four and every other period of time. Everything and everyone were the same. This, it seemed, was the end of civilization, just an eternal, unsatisfactorily death rattle. I started to hear of reports of growing number of suicides throughout the planet. I had a vision that everyone on the planet was cursed with the same fate. To repeat every day exactly like the last until they do the one thing they can think of to create a change in their lives and end it all for no other reason than to have an end.

Years went by with death's blueprint sitting and waiting in my laboratory. I continued to stall, waiting for that final detail that perfects a masterpiece. But the longer I waited, the more entropic the world became and the more anxiety I felt towards my own future. Eventually, it was too much to tolerate. Reluctantly, I made the decision to perform the procedure on myself. This resulted in me being bedridden and dependent on medications I luckily had the foresight to prepare beforehand.

As I lay in bed feeling my body change, I was reminded of the horror I felt while I watched Nate and James and Anna grow old and die. I remembered feeling so terribly powerless to stop what was happening. A fear crept into my chest when I thought of my own body succumbing to these manifestations of old age. It is a disease, age. Once infected the symptoms manifest almost immediately and the body is never the same afterwards.

Years went by with not a soul knowing about my beautiful work and I soon became frustrated with the secret. By this time, I was very much aware of the brevity that was my existence, so I let word slip about the procedure in the form of a vague rumor about an anonymous scientist. It didn't take long before people were asking me if I'd heard the rumor and what I thought of it and, in some cases, what I was doing to prepare for such a future. There was a certain fear in their voices when they spoke of it that I didn't expect, as if it meant something terrible that they couldn't quite understand. The unknown, it seems, is more frightening than all the evil in the world. But there was also a trembling excitement which accompanied the fear, and together these two sensations rippled through the masses. It created energy that propelled people towards some answer that jogged them from their monotonous routines.

It didn't take long for me to notice my features begin to change, and not much longer for Larson to notice. My hairline began to recede and grey and white hairs began to appear sporadically about my temples and beard. For a few years he didn't say anything, but I could see him studying my features, unable to comprehend what he was seeing. Perhaps by this time he had forgotten what aging looked like and was unable to put two and two together. Finally, he asked, and I told him what I had done.

"It's you?" he said. His face turned white. "You're the source of all those rumors. What have you done, old boy?"

It took a while, but Larson eventually came around. Although he never requested he be given the same treatment I had given myself, he admitted that he understood. He had a harder time understanding why others began coming to me. "Immortality is a bore and a curse," Larson told me, "but death doesn't seem entirely pleasant, either. Think I'll stay a while and see if anything else comes up."

The next bit I'm about to relate must be vague and rather summary for two reasons. Firstly, I need to protect the identity of all those who came to me. And secondly, I've run almost completely out of time and must rap this story up as soon as possible if I'm to finish it before I'm taken away and put in a cell to live out the last few days I have in me.

The event that's about to take place, my being removed from the home in which I've lived for centuries and put on trial and then inevitably placed in a quiet and lonesome prison cell, will happen tomorrow. It is 11:00 in the evening as I write this and the guards monitoring me, keeping me from escaping—the odds of a person in my fragile condition making a run for it is an absurd concept—have been ordered to load me up in a prison van shortly after midday. So, my dear readers, my comrades, you'll have to understand my rush.

Yes, the rumors are true. Many people came to me looking for the same thing I gave to myself. And I obliged them. I will say no more about that. However, although I must keep a lid on most of the details there are some I must share. Months before I performed the procedure on myself, I happened upon another incredible discovery. I discovered that if I were to reverse the immortal code in a subject, I could also reverse his or her infertility. I tossed this discovery out of my mind at the time but after a large enough community of Mortals had been created, there was what some might call an inevitable miracle. I will reveal nothing about her. I will not be as clumsy with her anonymity as I was with my own, but I will write this: for the first time in centuries a child will be born.

Currently, this discovery is unknown to anyone but me and those who are directly involved: the mother and father. I reveal it now only because tomorrow I will be taken away and my voice may never be heard again, and I want the world to know that what I did was deliberate. Soon, her body will begin to change as the new life grows inside her. It is only one child, so small and so fragile. After so many years I have only a small legacy to leave behind—and it is hardly mine—but it is, if nothing else, a little hope.

So that's it. I think I've said and confessed all I intended to. And now, here I am at the end of my long and arduous journey. I don't know what will happen after I'm gone. Maybe all I've done won't change the world. I don't know what will happen and I don't know what world I'm leaving behind. I only know what I've done and what it means for me.

Now, for my final confession. For the last 150 years or so, I've dedicated my life to the pursuit of death. It was all I could think about for a very long time—all I wanted. But time changes people and ideas. I'm going to die very soon. Finally. And although the path that brought me here was orchestrated by my own hand, I also have this feeling that has been keeping my eyes open when they should be closed and my mind racing when it should be at rest. A feeling that maybe, I love this life. Maybe, if things were different, I might want to stay a while.

About the Author

Jordan Mund was born and raised on the Canadian Prairies. After high school, he worked numerous jobs (a substitute kindergarten teacher, steel worker for the Canadian National Railway, factory worker, coffee barista, telemarketer, and more) while writing in his spare time. At the University of Manitoba, he received a bachelor's degree in English and philosophy. He also travels extensively and currently lives in Asia with his wife and daughter, providing him inspiration for his stories and characters.